AXILLON99

A LITRPG ADVENTURE

MATTHEW S. COX

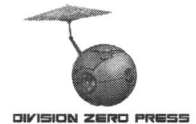
DIVISION ZERO PRESS

AXILLON99

———— A LITRPG ADVENTURE ————

© 2017 – Matthew S. Cox

Interior art by Ricky Gunawan

ISBN (Paperback): 9781980537632

CONTENTS

This book is dedicated to anyone who has ever stayed up late to complete just
one
more
quest.

STEALTH MECHANICS

Q uirky music nibbled at the edges of consciousness, a constant loop lurking in the non-space beneath the din of civilization, holding reality at arm's length. Fawkes kept herself as out of sight as possible, her back to the silvery wall of a ninety-story office tower in downtown Xiānjìng City, observing the steady blur of hovercars whizzing by. Alternating breaths flooded her mouth with the flavor of cheap ramen or the metallic, coppery taste of ionized air from the traffic.

She didn't feel like suffering the expense of a portal or the time drain of buying passage on a commuter ship, which left her stranded on Caelin IV for the time being, muttering curses under her breath at whoever decided interplanetary teleportation should cost fifty thousand credits. The mission she decided to solo while the rest of her crew weren't around only paid twenty grand, about mid-range for the sort of jobs she ran: something not too difficult, but also not boring.

Fawkes hated boring jobs—their experience rewards sucked.

She found her foot tapping in time with the pervasive background music. It, more than anything else, served to remind her that the glittering chrome-and-neon cityscape stretching out before her existed only in a slice of virtual reality beamed into her brain courtesy of a Neurona 3 interface helmet. Everything from the cold seeping into her shoulders through her shirt to the fragrance of noodle soup on the breeze had become incredibly believable compared to even three years ago when the game first launched.

If she concentrated on trying to feel it, the soft presence of her bed teased at the fringes of her awareness. The input from the helmet overpowered the rest of her senses and even inhibited physical motion. Jump scares could shock a person into moving for real and, depending on how a player set up before login, sometimes caused injuries.

Rumors circulated about a handful of players who had lost their grip on reality after the latest immersion patch. The idea of someone mistaking the humdrum physical world for the simulation, but believing a universe of space-craft, aliens, magic, and laser pistols as reality made Fawkes laugh.

Reality didn't have constant music.

At least, not without a mental disorder. In Axillon99, she became Fawkes, intrepid interplanetary infiltrator and thief. Outside this place, she had a much lamer avatar: Dakota Marx, a twenty-two-year-old nobody making coffee for a few bucks an hour over minimum wage.

Arms folded across her chest, she bowed her head and sighed at the metal sidewalk beneath her padded boots. Hot pink hair hung into her field of vision, almost painfully bright compared to her black form-fitting shirt. Wild hair color, one aspect of her nonconformist nature, followed her into the virtual world. In reality, she wore a stark shade of neon blue.

Team missions offered more experience and better loot, but they also required something she didn't have—other people. She *had* a team, but none of them happened to be online at the moment, hence the solo mission.

It made no difference how long she cased the target. As real as everything looked, smelled, and tasted, only other players would care if she tried to 'act casual.' The non-player characters, essentially computer programs, would react purely based on her character's skill values. They had no capacity to process her 'loitering around suspiciously.'

At a change in the holographic traffic signal dots, Fawkes pushed away from the wall and scurried across a street of polished dark-grey metal. Nimbuses of violet, blue, and yellow shimmered within the surface, reflected light from hovercar engines and floating advertisements. She kept her eyes focused on her target, the headquarters building of the Jīngquè Manufacturing Corporation, another ninety-story-plus towering monolith of mirror-chrome. Six Chinese characters, each ten feet tall, floated against the street-facing side of the building, from the second through seventh stories. When she looked at them, the English translation 'Precision Manufacturing Corporation' appeared in small text next to the huge red symbols.

On one level, she figured the little electronics prototype she needed to steal hadn't existed up until twenty minutes ago when she hit the 'job board' for a random quest. The mission text didn't mention what the prototype was for or who wanted it stolen; it never did for the throwaway side missions. The game had created a fictional 'prototype' object of unknown function, merely a token representing what she had to obtain for her mission.

Still, anything that let her feel like she got one over on a corporation made her happy, even if that corporation didn't really exist. These non-story missions rarely had static objectives or tied into any overarching plot threads. The game generated them based on simple randomness. However, she liked to open herself up to the immersion and enjoy the escape from reality. In her imagination, this little prototype represented the difference between a mega-corporation making more money and a planet's worth of low-tech colonists having affordable drinking water.

Her boots made no sound on the metal sidewalk as she approached the building, one benefit of taking the rogue/spy character class. A reduced detection range kept NPCs and 'creatures' from noticing her until she got close, and the almost nonexistent sound of her steps helped her avoid other players if need be.

The Jīngquè lobby took 'purple' and transcended it from a simple color to a mission statement. Violet-tinted marble covered the floor. Everything else from the potted plants to the hair of the man and woman behind the front counter existed in some variant shade of violet from retina-scalding intensity to almost black. A bank of elevators occupied the left side of the room, devouring and disgorging a stream of randomly generated men and women of varying age and appearance. The NPC workers came and went at the rate of a handful every few minutes. A huge glass-stepped staircase at the back of the lobby led up to a second floor.

Fawkes strolled over to the stairs and went up. Fortunately, the purple-crazy designer hadn't afflicted the rest of the building. The second story had all the look of a super-modern office. Frosted glass walls ran around the outside perimeter with regularly spaced doors, also of frosted glass. Small silver nameplates adorned each one.

A man in gleaming white armor jogged up the stairs and went past her. Based on the pair of energy swords across his back and the rifle in his hands, she figured him for another PC. Someone walking into a corporate office armed with enough firepower to sustain an insurrection in a third-world nation was a dead giveaway of a human player. He approached a man in a lab coat sitting on a bench in the center of the room.

"Can I help you?" asked the older man.

"Hey, doc. I dropped those medical supplies off at the street clinic."

The lab coat man stared at him for a silent, expressionless moment before his demeanor shifted as if he and this man had been good friends for years. "Oh, yes. Miss Leah told me you gave her the supplies." He pulled a small glowing plastic tab out of his pocket and handed it over. "Here's your payment."

Fawkes ignored them. Well, that at least explained the open second floor. Some of the NPCs in here had quests. She noted the 'doctor' for later. A few extra thousand experience couldn't hurt. Dropping 'medical supplies' off at a street clinic full of orphans would either be way easy or have an inexplicable random ambush along the way. Granted, the developers tended to put high experience rewards on 'good guy' type missions like that, while the darker missions gave more money or better loot.

She spent a while roaming the outside, checking out the names on the offices. A few of the doors opened easily while most were locked. Nothing looked interesting in any of them, save for a couple of silver wall vent covers, conveniently placed at ground level and perfectly sized for a person to crawl into.

Hmm. The prototype is going to be in the R&D lab probably.

Fawkes grabbed at nothing in front of her, and a game menu appeared. She tapped on the icon for 'mission notes,' which opened her mission journal, then poked a line reading *Eye in the Sky,* the title of her current mission. According to the text, a Dr. Parsons was the lead researcher on it, and she should look for a way into the lab.

Again, she made a circuit around the offices, eyeing nameplates. She passed by I. Bairnson, R. Cottle, and D. Mackay, before finding one marked A. Parsons – Research Engineering. Naturally, the door's lock showed red. Since none of the NPCs roaming around had a field of view on her, she activated stealth mode. Her body faded semitransparent indicating she had successfully concealed herself. Swaths of red appeared on the floor, denoting 'vision cones' for the various workers. Pale red indicated elevated risk of detection, while a narrower dark red cone inside showed where she would definitely get spotted. Security officers in dark violet armor had larger, longer detection cones compared to the workers, but none of them pathed anywhere near this office.

There's probably going to be a vent in the wall.

She plucked a small black box from her belt—her override kit—extended a wire from the side, and plugged it into a socket on the door panel. A 'hacking' mini-game popped up in a small holographic screen. In order to defeat the lock (or whatever object she targeted) she had to tap icons representing various nodes within the computer system, advancing a path from her starting location to the 'CPU node,' and do it before the red security line touched her blue line or beat her to the CPU node.

A grin spread across her face at the relative ease of it. Hacking skills didn't come cheap in terms of character points, so most lone wolves tended to suck at it since they refused to give up combat ability. Most of the time she played, she ran with a group of friends so the 'heavy lifting' in combat didn't fall on her shoulders. The developers wanted to keep players happy, so the average difficulty on hacking had been tweaked down to make up for so few players investing in those skills. This, of course, made her character a network goddess.

With a pleasant *chirp,* the door to Doctor Parsons' office slid open.

Fawkes put her interface tool away and stepped into a large, rectangular office permeated with soft cyan light filtering in from the frosted glass. The desk held a large amount of clutter, plus a super-thin display, keyboard, phone terminal, and a stack of optical discs. Unable to help herself, she ran around checking every openable drawer and cabinet, pocketing two energy bars and a fob with a 500-credit balance on it before locating an ID passcard carelessly left behind under the keyboard. A data pad next to the computer displayed the title page for a fiction novel, *Tales of Mystery and Imagination*. Oddly enough, by A. Parsons.

Programmers and their Easter eggs. She had no idea why they'd embed a novel into a video game, but didn't feel like sticking around long enough to read it.

Each item she picked up disappeared into her hip satchel.

She plopped down in the chair and tapped the keyboard. Another hacking mini-game got her past the password prompt and into Doctor Parsons' terminal. After skimming a few emails about his dog, complaints about the café food, emails to his wife Eve, and a suspiciously long diatribe about a malfunctioning air conditioning unit near the lab, she found an email from network security telling Doctor Parsons that they had to reset his password to Bubbles_1234.

Dakota broke character and let out a groan. Having a bit of skill at actual hacking made the idiocy of the supposed security people sending a password in open email painful. *This is a game. The password is here for me to find to do the quest. People aren't really this stupid.* She stared straight ahead with flat eyebrows, having caught herself. *Yes they are.* With a sigh, she forced herself to ignore the conflict between reality and fiction, and let herself become Fawkes again.

It took her a moment to find the vent she expected, blocked from view by a convenient potted fern. She moved the fake plant aside, opened the hatch, and crawled into a nice, clean silver-walled shaft. Cool air brushed at her cheeks, laced with the smell of food. A few sniffs got her debating between chicken parmesan or pizza, and also made her hungry.

"That's the best part of this game," she whispered to no one in particular. "I can eat as much as I want here and it won't make me fat." That got her thinking about in-game booze and recreational chemicals. "They phoned in the drugs though."

Getting 'high' in game consisted mostly of blurred vision, slowed motion, and penalties or bonuses to stats. Either the developers had no idea what it really felt like to get high, or they hadn't been allowed to include realistic effects for legal reasons. She grumbled at the developers for allowing kids to play the game. Maybe if it had an eighteen-plus rating, they'd do a better job simulating the effect of drugs. Of course, that got her wondering if virtual narcotics affecting the brain via a Neurona helmet could cause real-world addiction.

Huh. Maybe that's why they didn't do it.

Fawkes closed the vent cover behind herself, not that she had to—the security guards never reacted to open or closed vents—but it made her feel safer. She crawled into a T-junction and peered right then left. Nothing in Parsons' office had given any indication of what floor held the lab or which way to go in the vents.

"Hmm."

She summoned the ID card out of her inventory and read it. Doctor Parsons appeared to be in his later forties with shoulder-length brown hair and a beak of a nose. A small blue square at the bottom right corner contained the text 7C.

"Seventh floor..." She put the card back in her pocket and headed to the right at random.

Office after office passed, some with workers at their terminals, some dark. After rounding the corner at the end of the shaft, another hatch led into a larger vertical shaft with a ladder.

"Bingo."

Despite being an avatar in a hyper-realistic immersive online game, by the time she finished climbing five stories of steel ladder, her arms had become tired. While resting a few feet inside a horizontal duct on the seventh floor, she tried to figure out if the game forced her to experience the sensation of muscle fatigue or if the helmet had fooled her brain into thinking she should be tired.

In a few minutes, she caught her virtual breath and continued crawling. Metal clonked and creaked around her, the flimsy ductwork bending under her meager weight. Soon, the distant rattle of an overly loud fan caught her attention.

Aha! Busted air unit.

The mechanical grinding led her to a darker section of shaft on the other side of a right turn. Sparks flew every few seconds from the wall up ahead by a grille. A short distance beyond it, a square of light cut into slats appeared on the left side of the duct, indicating a brightly lit room outside. Fawkes hurried forward, her pink hair hanging down almost to the floor as she crawled. Each breath tasted like metal tinged with smoke. She scurried past the faltering air handler and leaned up to the vent cover.

Walls, floor, and ceiling of immaculate whiteness framed a huge rectangular room full of scientific equipment and giant computer cabinets. She didn't have the first clue what any of the machinery did, but they all looked fancy and expensive.

One man in a white coat milled around, standing over a table with a pink-purple glass cover. He poked and prodded at various controls, but whatever he did defied any attempt to understand. She watched him until his actions looped. As soon as she had a good feel for his pathing around the lab, she waited for him to be at the farthest point of his route and slipped out of the vent in stealth mode.

Fawkes pulled a small stunner off her belt while sneaking up behind the lab worker. He continued fiddling with dials and buttons on the fictional scientific machine, causing it to beep, whir, and emit bursts of bright light. When she got within grabbing distance, she held the stunner to the back of his neck, and the man collapsed to the floor, unconscious.

A small 'silent kill?' placard appeared above him. If she tapped it and selected yes, the NPC would change status to 'dead.' In the grand scheme of things, it meant little, since she'd long ago blown the 'pacifist' achievement.

Getting to level sixty without ever killing anything took a degree of patience and dedication that would qualify someone to be a Shaolin monk. This 'man,' even if she killed him, would reappear in twenty minutes as if nothing had happened.

Still, being *in* the game with the Neurona helmet, smelling, feeling, and tasting everything made murder a little too real for Dakota Marx. Fawkes might not bat an eyelash at it, but her player did. Of course, the game didn't show *too* much gore. If she silent-killed him, the body would twitch and stop breathing. With kids able to play, they couldn't exactly render a disembowelment.

Of course, modders had added that as an option, but only someone using the plugin would see it.

She'd passed on that.

With the technician out cold, she rushed around the lab looking for a tell-tale object with a glowing yellow aura around it, indicating a quest item. The sixth glass lid she opened revealed a bizarre electronic component that couldn't seem to decide if it was a handheld remote control or a circuit board meant to be plugged into something. Evidently, the game used a 'random electronic object' graphic for the quest objective.

The instant she grabbed it, the door flew open and a pair of security guards ran in, pointed guns at her, and shouted, "Stop right there!"

Fawkes scowled. "What's the goddamned point of stealth quests if they *force* a combat?"

Both guards fired at her, filling the lab with bright orange laser flashes. She flung herself sideways into a somersault. One of the incoming blasts hit her in the arm despite her acrobatic dive, but it hurt only about as much as being slapped with a wiffle bat by an annoying little brother. In contrast to the hyperrealism of everything else, injuries only provided enough of a sensation to announce a hit, milder than taking a paintball to the chest.

Her life bar appeared at the bottom of her vision, showing her down to ninety-one percent, denoted by a little red encroaching into the green at the far right end. Another innate attribute of her class reduced incoming damage by half if she got hit while attempting to evade.

Before the security men could correct their aim, she invoked a special ability, *Flicker*, which let her jump into stealth in an instant, even in the middle of combat. Her body went semitransparent and she scurried around the end of a big cabinet of research equipment, getting out of the middle of the lab.

"That's odd," said Guard One, as though he hadn't shot her a second ago. "I thought I heard something in here."

"Let's check it out." Guard Two walked around the cabinets.

Fawkes edged to the side, trying to avoid them.

Guard One's boot struck the unconscious man's leg, almost tripping him. "Damn. Who left this lying on the floor? We need to get maintenance in here to clean up."

"Lazy," said Guard Two.

Fawkes giggled, while the Dakota part of her brain rolled her eyes at the bad programming. Security guards would react to a corpse, but they evidently considered an unconscious lab worker as a misplaced bit of debris.

While the guards meandered around searching the room, she tiptoed past the edges of their vision cones to the vent shaft, but the hatch cover wouldn't open. She bonked her forehead on the wall, and growled.

"Dammit. Of course, I *have* to kill them. The developers wouldn't force the combat if they were going to let me sneak away."

Irritated, she drew her sidearm, a smallish black laser pistol. 'Equipped – PL144' appeared for a few seconds at the bottom of her vision. She'd carried that sidearm for the last six levels, and its low damage had started to get in the way. Of course, it had an enchantment on it that boosted her agility and dexterity, so she'd kept it more as a 'stat token' than a weapon. Ambushing made up for a lot of shortcomings in overt damage output. Then again, if she had a decent weapon, ambush would go from passable to obscene.

Still. Should be enough for these idiots.

Guard Two stumbled over the unconscious lab worker. "Damn. Who left this here? We need to get maintenance in here to clean up."

"Pff. Lazy," said Guard One.

Fawkes scooted behind a desk, aimed over it at Guard Two, and squeezed the trigger.

A brilliant blue beam appeared, connecting her gun to the security guard's helmet for a second. White light burst from the point of contact; he lurched forward with a loud groan. Fawkes' body remained semitransparent, which meant she hadn't lost stealth. Grinning, she scurried to the left and ducked behind a refrigerator-sized computer cabinet. At some point a few levels ago, stealth had gone from useless (everything always saw her right away) to godlike.

Guard Two swiveled around to face the direction she fired from, a one-inch-wide hole straight through his head. A health bar had appeared floating in space above him, showing him at twenty-nine percent health remaining.

"Did you hear that?" asked Guard Two, virtual blood rolling down his face. "I thought I heard something over there."

Guard One spun around, aiming his sidearm at where she fired from. "I don't see anything."

"I know I heard something." Guard Two—still with a laser tunnel in his head—looked around. "There's someone here. I know it." He paused before yelling, "I will find you."

"Only cowards hide," said Guard One.

Fawkes rolled her eyes. Every single NPC said that when they got within a certain distance of a stealthed player.

She waited a few seconds for them to drift apart before popping out of hiding to shoot Guard Two in the head again. The second shot dropped him like a sack of dirt, his laser pistol clattering to the floor and sliding a short distance from his lifeless hand. Fawkes ducked and crept around the other side of the tall cabinet.

"What was that?" Guard One hurried over to where his fallen companion lay. "I hear you. I'm sure there's someone here!" He turned and bumped the corpse of Guard Two. "Who left this here? I should call maintenance to have them clean it up."

Pff, lazy.

Fawkes stepped out into the aisle between two rows of scientific equipment. She intended to fire twice and put him down, but her first shot caused a bright red flash indicating an ambush critical hit for 548 damage. Guard One's head popped like a water balloon, spraying red everywhere. He fell to his knees, teetered for a second, and collapsed forward. Cartoony blood geysers without fragments of gore evidently didn't bother the ratings board.

She flinched at two men and a woman walking by the lab outside in the corridor, but the workers showed no reaction whatsoever to the gunfight that happened moments before, or the quite-obvious dead bodies of two security guards. The inanity of it made her laugh.

"I wonder if they do that on purpose so we know we're in a game?" She shrugged and crouched to check the two guards for loot.

After liberating 824 credits, a pair of crappy particle-beam handguns that did significantly less damage then her piece-of-shit, and two security officer ID badges (never know when a future quest might need them), she dragged the bodies into the vent to hide them, and pulled the hatch closed.

"Okay, that wasn't too hard." In the dim confines of a duct, Fawkes held up the little prototype object and smiled at the soft amber glow it gave off. "Hello twenty-grand experience. Come to mama."

2

EXTRA SHOT

Hazy green and brown faded in and out of view. The opposite wall of the coffee shop blurred, the faux stone merging with the emerald trim and separating again in an endless, mesmerizing cycle. Dakota caught herself before sleep sent her tumbling to the floor, and took a deep breath of caffeine-laden air.

She trudged over to the espresso machine and made herself a shot, grinning at thin stream of awesomeness gurgling out from the spigot. Steam fogged over her reflection on the metal face above the knob, making her appear less bleary-eyed than she probably looked. She leaned closer, checking her eyes for dark spots. Satisfied she didn't rock too much of the 'zombie' style, she slugged the espresso down and tossed the paper cup in the bin.

"You okay?" asked Trini, a short girl with long, straight black hair. The seventeen-year-old had been working there for a few months, and once mentioned she'd come from Morocco or Tobago or something exotic. Some people mistook her for Indian by appearance.

"Yeah." Dakota resisted the urge to wipe her eyes. "Stayed up a bit late. This swing shift is killing me."

Trini shivered. "Yeah, I know right. Here late last night and opening today? That's gotta suck."

While she *did* suffer a close-to-open day in her schedule, it hadn't been last night. No, last night went to the game.

Just one more quest and I'll go to sleep.

Dakota smoothed her hands down the green apron, managing a passably-alert smile at the small room full of round tables, tall chairs, and shelves bearing mugs, snacks, and other kitsch. Prior to the buyout in 2027 (the year of her high school graduation), it had been a Starbucks. She'd started working as a barista while a junior, and remained here at twenty-two. Of course, she now worked for the Amazon Café. About a third of the coffee went to walk ins, a bit to the drive-up lane, and perhaps half to drone pickups. As luck would have it, her store's downtown location, surrounded by office high-rises, made it a prime node for online ordering. The constant whirr of small drone fans as they flew in and out could drive a girl crazy.

Sometimes, people preferred to pay $9 for their coffee instead of $11 per cup, and actually came in the door or used the drive up. It never ceased to amaze her how many people would rather spend $2 on drone service than walk two blocks.

One such intrepid soul, unaffected by the dread of person-to-person inter-action, tromped in the door. He appeared to be in his late forties with a frumpy grey coat, ugly green scarf, and a surly set to his features. The instant she made eye contact, she knew he'd give her a hard time.

"Morning," said Dakota. "What can I get started for you?"

Her soul died a little more each time she asked someone that. Alas, this would be her home for the foreseeable future. Despite it being legit, a degree in computer programming hadn't done much for her. Then again, working here did cover her rent and probably entailed a lower amount of stress than a 'real' job might.

The man shuffled over to the counter and glanced up at the bank of moni-tors simulating slate boards. She pursed her lips at the jackass ignoring her like some android worker without a soul, but managed to keep the plastic smile on. Trini hurried off to the drive-up window, chatting via her headset with a customer outside.

Blake, the assistant manager, a twenty-one year old with even less drive to advance in life than Dakota, rushed out of the back room. His khakis strained to contain his legs; the man had an unusual build. From the waist up, he appeared reasonably average. Below the belt, he carried quite a bit of extra weight. A scruffy goatee of light brown ringed his mouth, something he thought made him more 'dignified.' Other than being a little too proud of his title as assistant manager, he didn't bug her too much. Being a year older than him helped though, as he could be a tad overbearing when interacting with the high schoolers.

While Frumpy-Coat-Man continued staring at the menu, Blake attacked the machines, whipping up a handful of lattes destined for drone delivery. Dakota watched him out of the corner of her eye. He usually hummed when working, but had the serious expression of a neurosurgeon.

"Something wrong, Blake?" asked Dakota.

"Huh?" he looked over his shoulder at her. "Why?"

"You look so serious."

"Oh, this is for Kauffman Stein." He snapped his fingers. "Has to be perfect."

"Right..." She turned back to watch Frumpy. A law firm that ordered a thousand bucks of java a week needed to be kept happy.

Frumpy lowered his gaze to Dakota and smirked.

She braced for a snide comment about her neon blue hair. It seemed anyone over thirty felt the need to give her crap about it. "Can I get anything started for you?"

"One of those"—he flapped his hand at the signs overhead—"caramel latte things. With an extra shot. I need to wake up."

She punched in the order on the flat panel. Before she could quote the price, he already had his smartphone up to pay. The system beeped, accepting the barcode on the screen. "Thank you. Your drink will be ready in a moment."

He made a noise part grunt, part grumble, and shuffled to the left.

Dakota grabbed a cup and went through the motions of making a caramel macchiato.

"Aren't you supposed to ask for my name?" Frumpy leaned close, peering over the counter.

She held back the sarcasm that wanted so desperately to erupt. "Usually when we're busy, we do, but you're the only one in here and I'm making your drink right away."

He grumbled to himself, leaning back and casting a frown at the display case full of breakfast food and pastries.

After finishing the drink, she set it up on the counter and smiled at him. "Here you are. Thank you and have a great day."

Frumpy took the cup and wandered with it over to the cream and sugar station. She cringed inwardly at the thought of someone adding even *more* sugar to an already overbearingly sweet coffee, but the man simply opened the lid, sniffed the foam, and replaced it without further modification. He started for the door while taking a sip, but abruptly stopped and stared at the cup. After a second sip, he spun around and walked back over.

She forced herself to keep smiling.

"You forgot the extra shot." Frumpy set the cup back on the counter, hard enough to make a little foam burp out the hole in the lid.

"I'm sure it's in there, sir."

He peered at the door into the back room. "You charged me an extra $1.75 for it, but it doesn't taste any different than normal."

Blake nudged her in the back with an elbow and muttered, "Just drop another shot in there."

"Sorry for the confusion." She stuck a small steel cup under the espresso machine and hit the button. Her forced smile must've flattened, as the man's eyes narrowed.

"Where's the manager?" asked Frumpy.

Blake emitted a strangled groan. His pride at being the assistant manager collided headlong into his need to get the law firm order perfect. "One moment, sir. I'll be right with you."

"Here you go." Dakota opened the latte, poured in a shot's worth of espresso, and covered it again. "One extra shot."

The plastic doors to the back room flapped open, revealing Hal Brown, the manager. His receding afro left the front middle of his head smooth and shiny. He wasn't the tallest guy in the world, (far from it) but had the muscles of a professional wrestler and a stubby neck as wide as his head. Whenever anyone mentioned shirts, he'd always bemoan having to order his custom since no 'standard' size had collars large enough for him to button. Despite his imposing physicality, he had a relatively soft voice, which sometimes caused constipated chuckles, since people wound up afraid to laugh at him.

"Can I help you?" asked Hal.

"I ordered a drink with an extra shot and your associate forgot to put it in. When I mentioned it, she had a bad attitude about it."

Blake gave Hal the 'this guy's an asshole' look over his right shoulder.

While the manager walked the customer off out of earshot, Dakota busied herself cleaning milk foam off the nozzle. "It's 2031. You'd think they'd be able to invent a machine that doesn't need to be wiped down after every cup."

Blake chuckled.

A few minutes later, Hal returned to the space behind the counter. "So... what form did the alleged attitude take?"

"A half-inflated smile I guess. I put the shot in, but he complained anyway. Guy came in here looking for an argument. Probably hoping to scam us for a free drink."

Blake arranged fourteen cups in an insulated box for drone pickup. "Worst thing she said was she did put the extra shot in. Guy was itching for a problem."

Hal nodded and smiled. "You look half awake. He probably thought he could get one over on you because you seem ready to pass out."

"Sorry." She leaned her head back, rubbing her neck. "Couldn't sleep."

"Maybe you should lay off that game of yours a little... before it microwaves your brain."

Dakota felt like a teenager all over again, eye rolling at her father. "The helmets are safe, Hal. They don't fry brain tissue."

"Hope so." He winked. "You're way too smart to nuke your brain cells."

She managed the first genuine smile of the day. "Thanks."

Blake pushed the tray out through the hatch to the pickup pad. Seconds later, a green and white drone dropped out from its holder on the roof, clamped onto the carrier, and hurtled off into the city.

A steady but slow trickle of customers walked in over the next twenty minutes, most winding up plopping down at the tables to relax and enjoy their coffee. The lull came to a sudden end when seven people entered almost back to back. One woman had a trio of tween girls with her who laughed and chatted amongst each other much to the annoyance of the other customers. Dakota smiled to herself while mixing up coffees, hot cocoas, and a few custom teas. She much preferred it busy. It made the day go by fast.

Once the rush abated, she leaned against the counter and sipped at a cup of black regular brew. The TV over the seating area showed a headline 'Steyr wins governor in surprise upset.' Dakota almost sprayed coffee over Blake. Instead of blasting him with java, she tried to hold back and wound up choking on it.

The people at the tables all looked up from their smartphones or tablets to gawk at the TV. Total strangers began conversing with each other about how obviously rigged the election had to be.

Blake caught her arm before she threw her drink all over the floor, eased the cup to the counter, and clapped her on the back until she started breathing again. "Whoa, don't try to breathe the coffee."

She laughed, which got her coughing all over again. Tears streamed out of her eyes, but she kept on giggling. "Coffee breathing isn't one of my superpowers."

"What are you choking for?"

Dakota pointed at the TV. "That Steyr creep won the election... what the hell is wrong with people?"

"Huh? Who?" Blake glanced at the TV in passing before swiping a rag from the counter and offering it to her. "Got some on your chin."

She took the cloth and dabbed at her face. "Thanks. And that's exactly what's wrong with people."

"Huh?" Blake blinked.

"Exactly. You have no clue who he is or why his winning is so fucked up."

"Language!" yelled Hal from the back room.

She sighed to herself before raising her voice to shout, "Sorry."

Blake shrugged. "I don't follow politics."

"Steyr's got so much baggage he had to run as an independent. Neither party would take him." Dakota started ticking points off on her fingers. "Three divorces and one dead wife under suspicious circumstances. He's been involved in two fatal car accidents while drunk and walked away without any charges. Bribery, corruption... everyone knows he's basically a paid employee of the medical insurance industry. And there's been like sixteen men who've accused him of sexual misconduct with them when they were underage. The worst is a report he'd been found in a hotel room with a minor boy."

Blake's mouth hung open. "That can't all be true. He'd never have won the election if there's any evidence."

"No shit," muttered Dakota.

The back door popped open enough for Hal to stick his head out. "Language." His serious stare turned into a smile. "Please. At least while you're on the clock."

"Wow, Hal. You've got good ears." Dakota raised both eyebrows.

A disheveled man in an olive-drab coat stumbled in and approached the counter. Long, scraggly black hair with streaks of grey hung well past his shoulders, and an air of mildew awfulness surrounded him.

Dakota took a deep breath before stepping closer, trying to hold her good air as much as possible. "Morning. What can I get started for you?"

The man began to smile at her, but his expression shifted to distress. A second later, he let out a long, sonorous belch that fluttered her hair. Whiskey fumes bleached her cheeks.

She barely managed to suppress the urge to gag. *Shoot me now.* Alas, *Flicker* didn't exist in real life to make her vanish out of this guy's sight and go hide somewhere. Still, she flexed her brain the same way she did to trigger the ability in the game.

Nothing happened.

"Uhh." The man wiped his face on his sleeve. "Real sorry about that. Snuck up on me. Lemme get a large coffee and one of them egg sandwiches." He set a twenty-dollar-bill on the counter.

"No problem." She smiled at him.

"That 'lection's so damn rigged," muttered the odorous man. "No way that guy should've even gotten six percent of the vote."

Dakota filled a cup with dark roast from the samovar. "Yeah, seriously. See, Blake, everyone knows what a b... awful person Steyr is."

"Thank you," said Hal from the back room.

She tossed a simple egg-on-a-muffin in the convection oven and hit the button. While it heated, she rang the guy up and gave him a ten-dollar-bill back as change. At a *ping*, she ran to the oven, boxed the sandwich, and dropped it in a bag along with three ham sandwiches from yesterday, too old to sell anymore but still perfectly safe to eat.

"Here you are. Have a nice day."

The man noticed the charity and saluted her with the bag. "You too, thanks."

Dakota melted into a lean on the counter and yawned. *Yeah. I'll have a nice day as soon as I get home.*

3

THE PRIZE

A few minutes past noon, the soft *ping* of the door chime snapped Dakota out of a standing nap. Before panic at being caught sleeping by a customer could stop her heart, the blurry form of an approaching dark-skinned man resolved into her more-or-less boyfriend, Eric Frost. He often joined her at the café for lunch since it only cost him a few blocks' walk. Today, he sported a particularly large grin.

Although he worked as a rank-and-file tech support phone agent for Ulticomm (a mobile provider), he usually wore a shirt and tie. She didn't mind his 'dress for the job you want' mentality, since it didn't involve her ass suffering uncomfortable dress clothes. Plus, she couldn't argue that he cleaned up rather well. The fragrance of fast food followed him, likely from the white bag in his hand.

"Hey you." She leaned over the counter and hooked a finger amid the buttons of his shirt, pulling him close enough for a quick kiss. "Lunch time already?"

"Already? The day is dragging. Feels like been stuck there for eight hours and it's only twelve. CSI just dropped a nuclear warhead."

Blake twisted away from the drive-through window to gawk at him. "Say what? A nuke? The hell is CSI?"

"Software company," deadpanned Dakota. "Cognition Studios."

"How did they get their hands on a nuke?" asked Blake.

I'm losing my ability to differentiate between naïve and stupid. Dakota rubbed the bridge of her nose.

"Damn, man. You need to drink some o' this coffee y'all's sellin'. Metaphorical nuke." Eric winked at Dakota before pulling out of his lean and standing straight. "They sent out a major announcement this morning. Surprised you aren't going crazy."

"Didn't even look at the computer when I woke up." She scratched at the side of her head. "You know exactly why I had a rough morning. And how are you so awake?"

"Yeah, but keepin' on going was your idea," said Eric.

Blake's eyebrows shot up.

"Video game, Blake. I stayed up too late." She sighed. "Peach tea?"

Eric nodded, practically bouncing like an over-excited boy while she rang him up for a large iced peach tea, then mixed it from the boxed concentrate. Hal didn't usually let his employees do transactions for friends and family, but that rule tended to apply more to the teenage staff than Dakota.

"Takin' my lunch, 'kay?" She glanced back at Blake, who nodded. After using the register terminal to clock out, she grabbed a turkey wrap from the cooler and joined Eric at a table. "So, what's this big news?"

He set his food down, but didn't move to open it. "CSI released the Neurona 4 helmets early. Already ordered you one."

She stirred a straw around her tea, smiling. "Awesome. That's really sweet of you, but I wouldn't call it apocalyptic news."

Eric pulled open his bag and took out a carton bearing a chicken sandwich. "Nah, the helmet's not the big news. To celebrate the release of the Neurona 4, they're doing a promotion type contest with a big ass prize."

Dakota paused, millimeters from sinking her teeth into the turkey wrap. "What, like a million bucks?" She bit down.

"Ten," said Eric.

She gasped in a flake of lettuce and started choking. Eric froze, poised to leap out of the chair for a few seconds until it became clear she had herself under control. Dakota buried her face in a napkin and coughed. Eyes watering, she peered at him. "Ten million dollars?"

Blake dropped something metal behind the counter.

"Yeah. You okay, babe?" He picked up his sandwich.

"Fine. Just wasn't ready for that. I'm zero for two in alternative breathing today."

Eric hastily chewed his first mouthful. "Alternative breathing?"

She smirked. "Yeah. Tried to breathe coffee earlier. Worked about as well as this."

"So, yeah... CSI put a mission chain in the game. First person or crew to complete it wins," said Eric.

"Shit. For ten million bucks, maybe I ought to try playing video games," said Blake.

"Language, please!" yelled Hal from the back room.

Blake ducked.

Dakota mulled the idea over a few bites of her lunch. "It's just a BS marketing gimmick you know. Either they've already picked who the 'winner' will be, and it's like an actor or something, or the missions will be so damn hard no one will ever win the prize."

"Yeah. I figure it's gonna be a pain in the ass." A huge grin spread across Eric's face. "But we have an advantage other crews don't."

Her right eyebrow inched upward.

Eric winked. "You."

Dakota rolled her eyes. "Fawkes isn't *that* über you know. Most of my gear is blue, and my weapon's a POS. So I put more points in the data infiltration tree than like eighty-five percent of the players, but that's not going to make a difference."

"Nah, girl. I mean *you*."

She hunched down over the table, leaning closer while whispering, "I am not going to hack into CSI. I'm pretty sure if they've made this quest impossible, if anyone completes it, they're going to triple check every log. Not sure about you, but *I* am allergic to prison."

"Yeah, you and me both." Eric shook his head. "That ain't what I'm sayin'. I mean you see things like no one else I ever met sees things."

"That's because my body is permeated with high octane caffeine from being in here all day. I'm starting to extend my consciousness into parallel dimensions."

He laughed. "Well, still. The others wanna try."

"You talked to them already?" She tilted her head.

"Yeah. Group chat this morning at like 8:05 once the email went out. CSI sent a notice to every player, even to cancelled accounts." Eric wiped his hands off on a paper napkin, which he tossed in the sandwich carton before closing it. "Tryin' ta get people to come back."

"Sixty bucks a month is still more expensive than a lottery ticket." She frowned.

"Yeah, but the odds are much better. Besides..." He grasped her hand, tracing his thumb back and forth across her knuckles. "Even if we don't come close to winning any money, we're going to be playing the game anyway."

"True enough." She stared deep into the chocolate brown of his eyes. Losing a night or two of gaming to spend some real world time with him didn't strike her as a bad idea.

She liked him quite a bit for a guy she met through the game a little more than a year ago. They'd progressed from 'grouping for a mission' to crewmates to real life friends—when he mentioned he lived in Manhattan too, she insisted on meeting him—and wound up somewhere between friends with benefits and a 'thing.' Boyfriend/girlfriend implied hopes of a future more concrete than either of them planned on, but she wasn't sure anymore.

"I'm thinkin' about you and me wearing those new Neurona 4 helmets."

She grinned.

"And nothing else." Eric winked.

Blake, again, dropped something.

She cracked up laughing. "I dunno. That's a little *too* vulnerable. Bad enough we can't move."

"The 'Four has a proximity sensor. You can set it to let go of your brain if something gets too close."

"Huh... how 'bout that?" She shrugged. "Handy, but I'm still going to leave the door locked when we're off saving the galaxy."

"Which galaxy?"

She shrugged. "Pick one. Just not the one the Blix are from. Everything there is too damn small."

Eric chuckled. "Yeah. So, you ready to get started tonight or you gonna crash as soon as you get home?"

"Well, I was kinda thinking we might do something together, but I suppose I can't say no to that look on your face. You're like a little boy about to get a new expensive toy."

"Ten million." He crumpled up his bag. "Damn. Almost outta time."

She figured she'd give it a couple days, maybe a week. Once the realization seeped into his brain that they wouldn't log in and find the prize money in the first two hours—and once the larger realization among the player community that the prize sat out of reach hit home—she'd insist on some real life fun instead of gaming for a good long time.

Like, probably three days in a row.

4

DEAD ANARCHIST

The world boasted several great monuments to Chinese culture: the Great Wall, the Forbidden City, the Terracotta Army... and Dakota's computer desk. Towers of stacked take-out cartons flanked her thirty-two inch monitor, well on their way to touching the ceiling in another few orders. A two-inch thick layer of sauce packets coated the desk, as well as upwards of a hundred plastic forks she'd never used. Empty containers that once held wonton soup snaked like a serpent up from behind the monitor in a tower that verged on toppling.

Alas, tonight wound up on the cheap end: instant ramen. The Wednesday-to-Friday stretch every other week toward the end of a pay period always got lean. Wearing as close to Eric's suggestion as she felt comfortable with (a large T-shirt, fuzzy socks, and nothing else), she reclined in her computer chair, munching on freeze-dried noodles and shrimp-flavored salt.

The fatigue that had dogged her all day evaporated at 3:30 p.m., as soon as her shift ended and she had free time to throw at Axillon99. For a two-year-old game, it still monopolized her attention. It might've even had something to do with why she still worked as a barista instead of chasing down a real developer's job. Time spent hunting for employment meant time not in the game world.

Technology had its disadvantages though. The Neurona series helmets had been mainstream for about ten years. As a kid, she'd grown up playing standard video games using a monitor, and didn't get her hands on a helmet until she'd turned eighteen and bought one with her own money. Her parents *still* believed the helmets belonged to an elaborate scheme by the CIA or the NSA to read minds.

At least a third of the games on the market continued to favor monitors. Either to cater to the slow adopters/suspicious types, or because the game didn't lend itself to *full* immersion. No one would want to deep dive for something like solitaire or a real-time strategy sim. Using a Neurona helmet lifted the player out of the real world and hurled them bodily into another place. Some people couldn't handle it, too freaked out by the realism in being shot at or attacked by monsters, and still preferred having the detachment of a physical screen in the way.

Of course, liquid cavemen (as the screen-users had come to be known) couldn't coexist in the same virtual reality as helmet jocks. The differences in reaction time and control ability proved too vast a barrier. Early games that attempted to mix interfaces wound up being woefully imbalanced, like a boxing match between a blind couch potato and a Special Forces soldier.

So, rather than deal with the complaining, software developers went in two different directions, sandboxing the environments. Monitor people played in games with other monitor people, Neurona players with Neurona players.

It had been quite a while since Dakota used her screen to do anything more than read email or research bosses/strategies for Axillon99. However, the one advantage the screen people had—being able to eat and play at the same time—she missed. So, she shoveled ramen into her mouth while sitting cross-legged on her chair and reading as much about Cognition Systems International's promotion as she could find online.

The email Eric mentioned had been sitting in her inbox since earlier that morning. It contained the same information as she could find anywhere else. A contest existed in the form of a quest/mission, and it started from a random loot drop. No one mentioned if that random drop could come from *any* hostile creature, a quest reward, or if the developers had made it a pain in the ass and limited it to raid bosses or starship combat.

In a game as vast as Axillon99, merely *finding* the quest could take months.

The playable area comprised something like thirteen billion potential planets, most of which came courtesy of random generation. Perhaps ten thousand or so static worlds existed, created by the designers with specific ties to the game lore or missions. The rest of the star systems existed as nothing more than a speck on a map until someone went there, at which point, the game generated everything in more detail. Once a player had visited a system once, triggering the generation routine, it would remain constant. Some people theorized that eighty-seven percent of the explorable space on the star map had yet to be 'filled in.'

While the game offered a variety of alien races, Dakota had stuck with a 'plain' human when she made Fawkes. As luck would have it, her whole crew had the same idea. For her, the alien races were a little *too* alien in appearance. Especially the Blix. Who wanted to play as a fourteen-inch-tall little green man with a huge head? Most Blix that left their homeworld climbed into robotic mecha suits that brought them up to a little bigger than human sized, since the rest of the universe wasn't kind to tiny people. Short girl problems had nothing on being a Blix out of their suit.

Some players stayed solo, doing missions planetside for the whole time they played, hopping shuttles or teleportation portals to new worlds when they got bored. Other players opted to form crews, often of five people, and ran around space in a corvette-class ship. Options there included running cargo, hunting pirates, being a pirate, smuggling contraband, exploring, or taking random assignments from the 'job board.' Generally, the trader types tended to stay solo and work their way up to freighter class ships to make more money faster. The very idea of it bored Dakota to bits. A game this vast—not to mention explosive—and people spent their time being an interstellar FedEx driver?

Then again, some places started accepting in-game money for real world purchases. The currency even had a real world abbreviation on the Exchange: AX. So maybe suffering the brain-liquefying boredom of being a star trucker had some merit to it.

Dakota finished off her ramen and set the plastic bowl on the desk before tapping the controller button to load the Axillon99 client. While a progress bar crept across the screen, she relocated to her bed two steps away, stretched out, and snugged her Neurona 3 helmet on. A thin bundle of wires connected from the top of the helmet to the PlayStation 7 tower. She'd gotten an aftermarket cord lined with hot pink flexible LEDs that made it appear to be an energy cable. After snuggling into the comforter, she flipped the visor down and waited for the sync process to start.

"Welcome to Axillon99," said a pleasant female voice via speakers. "Neurona 3 interface initializing. Security option has been set to cortical imprint."

A faint tingle spread across her head as the system read her 'brain fingerprint.' Much easier than remembering a password—and impossible to fake.

"User DM01852 authenticated. Press start button to initialize."

She reached up to the small rubber button above the right temple, and pressed it.

"Synchronizing in three... two... one..."

Vertigo came and went. For a few seconds, she felt as though she fell in a void of infinite blackness. Pins and needles ran over her entire body. The next thing she knew, she—rather Fawkes—stood in the login lobby. A room with electric-blue walls surrounded her, holding ten alcoves, nine of which were empty. Another Fawkes stood in one, like a life-sized Barbie doll still in its box. The game let people have ten characters per account (with an additional monthly fee for more space). If she had bothered to make any other characters, all she'd need do is walk up to one, and her 'active' avatar would change. To make a new character, she'd have to step into one of the empty slots.

As she always did, she approached the giant, shimmering energy portal that would take her into the game—and stepped through.

Fawkes appeared seated in the cushioned bench of a small restaurant adjacent to the Xiānjìng City starport, the same spot she'd logged out from. The missions she'd run last night didn't involve leaving the surface, even though the whole group had been there for them.

Her friend list showed Nighthawk as online, the only other member of her five-person crew currently in the game. She couldn't remember ever logging in and not seeing him, so she figured he either had no job or worked at the best job in the world, one that let him log in and play Axillon99 from his office. Hell, maybe he worked *for* CSI.

‹Sup Fawkes,› said Nighthawk by way of in-game text.

‹Not much. Just got home. U?›

She picked up the half-eaten *monstrous* doughnut she'd ordered before logging out last night, and continued munching on it. It transcended doughnut into the realm of small cake, and had a heavy dose of dark chocolate frosting with an inner core like hot molten brownie. Despite the treat being virtual, it was *so* sweet she expected her blood to turn to jelly after three bites.

‹Up in North Rosewood doing some bounty quests. Wanna group?›

Nighthawk played a gunslinger class, and according to her friend tab, he'd hit level forty-two at some point today. She'd once heard him mention an alt, a side character he sometimes messed around with, and it annoyed her. Dakota had made Fawkes as her first (and so far only) character, and she'd made it only to level thirty-seven as a rogue/spy hybrid. The two classes were similar, though the spy side contributed more to stealth and infiltration while Cognitive Systems' opinion of a rogue made them mostly a sneaky sort of combat character. Since both classes came from the same 'scoundrel' branch, mixing levels between them didn't have an overall effect on her combat abilities. Not like someone who combined, say, technomancer levels with a soldier, the worst-case scenario. They'd wind up being able to do magic *and* physical combat, but pretty much stink at both compared to an equal-level character that focused all in one direction.

Still, she envied Nighthawk, mostly for his free time. Level forty-eight had a really nice ability in the rogue list that she desperately wanted: *Shadow Mastery*. With it, she could engage stealth and stay hidden for a full minute no matter what she did. In her head, it sounded like a cheat code, running around getting ambush criticals on everything when nothing could see her.

But... eleven levels away. And combat out in the open kinda sucked. At least, with her focusing so much on the hacking side, she almost *had* to hide and ambush to have a chance to defeat a same-level opponent. Not like Nighthawk's gunslinger. He could own five or six enemies in seconds assuming none were 'captains.'

Hmm. I'm not above riding some coattails for some easy experience. ‹Sure. Inv plz.›

He sent a group invite, which caused two things to happen: a small octagonal frame appeared high and left in her field of view with his portrait, name, and life-bar. Also, a blue holographic window scrolled open in front of her bearing the question: "Teleport to group?"

She poked the 'yes' button. The world around her vanished in a blue flash. She appeared standing in a grassy field with a ripple of red laser fire going by on the left, leaving a trail of smoking holes.

"Holy shit!" shouted Fawkes, while diving behind a giant rock.

Nighthawk, standing out in the open with a large laser pistol in each hand, stopped shooting at some black-armored soldiers to gawk at her.

Fawkes curled up as laser blasts shaved fragments of her boulder away. Shards of rock rained over her head, some of which remained stuck in her pink hair. She stared right back at him. "What?"

"Uhh, nothing."

Nighthawk returned his attention to the group of enemies and began a slow walk forward while firing his pistols rapidly, alternating left and right. As soon as the pelting of incoming fire stopped hitting her boulder, she attempted stealth, and it worked. That meant none of the computer-controlled bad guys paid her any attention. Hiding while in combat required she use a special ability.

She poked her head up and prepared to use *Shadowblink* to teleport the fifty or so feet she needed to travel in order to get behind the enemies, but the last of them had already collapsed to the ground with smoking laser holes in his chest.

"It's safe now. I got them all," said Nighthawk.

He twirled his guns around his fingers and stuffed them in hip holsters. Except for the white plasticized body armor under his duster coat, he resembled a twenty-something cowboy straight out of the Old West, only with the long hair and 'beautiful' face of a male hero from a Japanese anime.

"Gee, thanks. Little warning next time." Fawkes stood and brushed dust off her black leggings.

"Oh, sorry." He scratched at his hat "I didn't even think... those guys are only thirty-nine."

She walked over to stand next to him. "Is that why they couldn't hit you?"

"Nah, that was *Showdown*. New ability I got this afternoon." He struck a confident pose. "Gives me one minute of protection like I've got heavy cover while standing in the open. Like you know in those old movies, where the good guy just stands there and no one can hit him."

"Yeah..." She frowned at the dead men in armor. "What's up with these guys?"

"Oh, mercenaries. Kidnapped some woman I'm on my way to save."

Another holographic window appeared: "Nighthawk would like to share 'A Wayward Bride' (mission) with you. Accept?"

She hit yes.

"Correction. That *we* are on the way to save." Nighthawk smiled and tipped his hat.

"Are you sure this woman wants to be saved?"

He stared at her like she'd spoken Greek. "Huh? Of course. It's the quest. Why wouldn't she?"

Fawkes put on Dakota's coffee-shop smirk. "The quest is titled 'Wayward Bride.' I'm betting this woman ran away."

"Oh." He mulled this over for a moment before shrugging. "Okay. So, what do we do?"

"Let's go ask her." She winked.

DAKOTA WALKED UP TO A LOCKED DOOR WITH A SMALL BARRED WINDOW, from which the terrified face of a blonde girl of about eighteen stared at her with huge blue eyes. Her guess had been close, but not entirely correct. Her suspicion turned out on the right track, however. The bride *did* run away, and her father had hired mercenaries to drag her back home. Those mercenaries, in turn, demanded more money once they had her.

She couldn't figure out if the developers were riffing on Romeo and Juliet or trying to do a Helen of Troy thing... or maybe just a Hatfield and McCoy reference. Either way, she could've sworn she'd already let this young woman out of her cell and brought her home for the reward. And for that matter, where the hell did Nighthawk go?

And why had her hair turned blue again? Fawkes had pink hair.

"Hey, I'm supposed to get an extra shot in this," said the kidnapped teen through the bars while holding up a latte cup.

"What?" blurted Fawkes.

"My coffee. Duh..." The girl stared at her like a spoiled princess. "You didn't put an extra shot in it."

Fawkes sighed at the dingy metal ceiling. "Dead mercenaries are littered all over the place. You're locked in a cell, and you're giving me shit about coffee?"

"I paid for the extra shot," said the girl.

"Ugh." Dakota rubbed the bridge of her nose. "I'm dreaming, aren't I?"

"How should I know?" asked the girl. "If you're dreaming, I'm going to say whatever you want to believe."

"And that's exactly what I would say if someone asked me that." Dakota sighed. "I'm dreaming."

The room faded away to blurry nothingness.

"Kota! Holy shit!" shouted a male voice.

She peeled her eyes open to find a hologram of her younger brother, Nebraska, standing at the foot of the bed, cringing away from her nudity. Groaning in protest, she rolled to the side, grabbed the comforter, and pulled it over herself.

"That's what you get for barge calling me, Brass." She yawned, then forced her eyes to stay open and looked at him. "Let it ring next time."

Nebraska risked a peek, and, seeing her covered, un-cringed. He looked a bit worse for wear, too thin, in torn jeans and a puffy orange winter vest. The flannel shirt he had on under it looked so dirty she practically smelled homeless vagrant through a holographic projection. Scraggly dark brown hair hung around his face like a greasy theater curtain, but at least he'd shaved. Without facial hair, he looked closer to sixteen than his actual age of nineteen.

"Sorry. Don't have a lot of time."

"Huh?" She propped herself up on her elbows and squinted at him, still not fully awake. "Are you being chased or something?"

"Naw, using a public terminal. Only got fifteen minutes."

"You're going to get shot," she muttered.

He rolled his eyes. "You sound like Mom now."

"So, what's so urgent that you barge call me at"—she twisted to look at the alarm clock on the little stand by the bed—"five fucking thirty in the morning?"

"I thought you got up this early."

"I do," she muttered, and let her body flop back into the mattress. "On a work day. But I'm off today."

"Oh, then you can sleep more after I hang up." He grinned.

"What do you want?" She stared at the ceiling.

"Umm." He stuffed his hands in the pockets of his winter vest and glanced down. "Can you spare a couple bucks? I'm out of food."

"Turn around."

"Huh?" He looked up.

"Unless you want to see me naked again, turn around."

"Oh." He faced away.

Dakota slid across to sit on the edge of the bed and grabbed her giant T-shirt off the rug. After wriggling into it, she padded over to the computer desk and retrieved her Android Supernova smartphone. Nebraska's holographic ghost wandered up beside her.

"Wow, nice phone."

"It's four years old," she muttered. "Got it used."

"Oh." He shrugged. "Still looks cool."

"You still using the same PayZon ID?"

He nodded.

"You know, I'm not exactly rich either." Dakota tapped at the small screen, navigating her PayZon app to send him some cash. "I sent you $100. That leaves me with $100 until Friday at midnight."

"Thanks, Kota." He flashed that same sheepish grin that always came out whenever she let him get away with something.

The look on his face reminded her too much of him being little again, so she glanced away. The parents had cut him off, but she just couldn't bring herself to. "You know, they have these things called jobs that generate money, which you can turn into food."

"Yeah, yeah." He kicked at the rug. "You know how it is. It's all organized, legal slavery. The fuckers in power keep us busy all day doing whatever, reward us with hamster treats. All the people's effort makes those bastards tons of money while we barely get by. I'm not gonna be no one's slave."

"I'm not awake enough to pick on you for horrible grammar."

"So, don't?" He grinned.

"Brass..." She turned back and made eye contact, desperation radiating from her. "You're on the street."

He waved her off. "It's not like that. I'm with a group of similar mindset. We are the revolution... eventually."

"Yeah, well, revolution or not, I'd much rather you were a wage slave with food than a free dead guy in an alley somewhere."

Nebraska rolled his eyes like she'd asked a seven-year-old to clean up his room. "It's nowhere near as bad as you think. We don't do the gang war thing. It's not a 'street gang,' Kota, we're an organized group. Like a militia."

She tried to grab his hand, but the holo-phone ghost broke apart into static where her fingers disrupted it. "Mom and Dad fucked us up, Brass. It took me a while to see it, but they are mental. There's a little validity in what they say, but they take it *way* too far. I hate seeing you out there like that."

"If we weren't related, would you agree with our goals?"

Dakota fidgeted. She couldn't deny her strong anti-corporation mindset. While her parents had advanced to thinking the entire political system had become an illusion for corporate control, she'd backed off from fully believing that to thinking that billionaires and huge corporations simply had an over-abundance of influence in politics. The whole 'the life you think you know is a lie' *Matrix* style head game sounded like a conspiracy theorist's wet dream. Her brother and his friends, all of whom were well into their twenties or older, had this far-reaching goal of 'overthrowing' the corporations and even the puppet government ala some neo-American-Revolution. Fortunately, the most hostile action they'd yet taken against The Man thus far amounted to activist posts on social media and spray paint.

"In spirit, yes. Big companies and billionaires have too much influence on society, but Dad is cracked. Politicians aren't android replicants."

"That's Congress. Senators are lizards," said Nebraska.

She froze, staring at him. "Please tell me you're making fun of Mom."

He cracked up laughing. "Yeah. That android crap is way out there, but you know the whole system is rigged for the elite. As long as we keep jumping through hoops like trained monkeys, nothing will change. We have to take a stand and do something!"

"It's not going to start from a dingy alcove under an overpass." She folded her arms. "It's going to come from the thinkers and the artists. The true underground. We have to *reach* people."

He shrugged. "You just called the Brooklyn Bridge an 'overpass.'"

"Look, I am dead on my feet here." She trudged back to the bed and sat on the edge. "I'll swing by sometime. You guys still in the same spot?"

"Yeah."

"Hey, Brass?" She peered up past a neon-blue haze at him.

"Yo." Her brother's hologram froze, one arm reaching for a disconnect button out of view.

She bit her lip, hesitating to mention Eric to her brother. An isolated life trying to stay on the fringe of society hadn't done much for her social life, and her time in college didn't leave her any lingering circle of friends. The number of people she would even *think* about getting real with represented an extremely short list that had at one time been four names long. Her parents had fallen off it two years ago when she decided they'd gone headlong into 'totally nuts' territory. Not that any bad blood existed, but she didn't trust them in matters involving critical thought. That left two, and she couldn't exactly talk to Eric about her feelings for Eric.

"Something wrong?" asked Nebraska.

"Umm. So, there's this guy I'm seeing."

He folded his arms. "Need someone's legs broken?"

Dakota laughed. "No, no... He's cool. Nothing like that. The problem is that I've been seeing him for like a year now and I'm not sure what he is."

"Huh?" Nebraska tilted his head. "Think he might really be a chick?"

"No. Shit's sake!" She threw a pillow through the hologram, not sure if she should be angry or laugh more. "It's just that, I dunno. We were friends and now we're more than friends, but I'm not sure why I've been hesitating at it going past that."

"Do you love the dude?"

"Yeah, kinda. I can't tell if it's just that I'm really falling for him or if I'm resisting 'being the girlfriend' because that's what society expects. It's what normal people do, and I don't want to become another society drone doing what people are expected to do."

Nebraska shrugged. "If you like the dude, go for it. That 'day job' of yours is already making you a drone. Love won't."

She shot him a sour look, but he did have a point.

An overly generic *ding-dong* sound filled the room.

"I'm getting beeped at, anyway. Time's gonna run out. Stupid pay terminal."

"'Kay. Take care of yourself. I'll be by soon."

Nebraska pointed at her, winked, and disappeared. The room became darker for his absence.

She squinted up at the tiny whirring motor pulling the hologram emitter back into the ceiling. Her brain woke up enough to be embarrassed at his walking in on her while she slept, but she didn't trust turning off his emergency access. Their luck, as soon as she did, he'd have some serious life-or-death issue and wind up dead because she didn't get his call. At least he hadn't barged in when she was with Eric.

The doorbell rang again.

"Hang on," she yelled, stood, and hurried to her apartment door.

A thirty-something woman in a white polo shirt with a red logo in it stood outside holding a package. Since she hadn't made any enemies in places high enough to send her a courier-assassin, she opened the door.

"Dakota Marx?" asked the woman.

"Yeah."

"Got a package for you."

A sarcastic response fell stillborn out of her sleep-deprived brain. She mutely signed the electronic pad, accepted the box, and trudged back inside. It didn't hit her that she hadn't ordered anything until after she set the box on the desk and fell face-first back into her mattress.

The helmet? Already!?

Her eyes snapped open.

Dakota jumped out of bed and pounced on the box, shredding it open in a few seconds. Beneath a layer of drab brown cardboard sat the shiny box for a Neurona 4 cortical interface helmet. She skimmed the feature list on the side, which touted increased performance. The Model 4 had a secondary data channel for double the throughput, which they claimed would allow game designers to 'break new ground' in realism. Enhanced proximity detection could create a view window into reality direct from the helmet hardware, regardless of the game involved, and it supposedly 'learned' its user after twenty or so hours of use, making some tasks such as logging out of the game faster and more seamless while simultaneously offering a deeper connection. The last feature claimed to protect even more against UMIs (unintentional motion injuries) caused when players' real bodies moved during a game.

"Hmm. Awesome and creepy all at once."

She tore open the box. Her grin died when she found herself staring at a hot pink helmet, the ears of a white cat graphic visible past the foam that looked suspiciously like Hello Kitty. The blackout visor even had her name printed on it like a fighter pilot. "I'm going to kick his ass." Dakota tugged the helmet out of the packing material, revealing the cartoon cat to be a pirate skull and crossbones version of the ubiquitous feline. She grinned. "Okay, maybe I won't."

5

INVENTORY MANAGEMENT

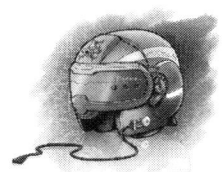

Dakota set her new Neurona 4 on the desk, and fell back in bed.

Waking up at work time on a day off violated the First Fundamental Law of the Universe. She flopped in bed again after a few minutes of touchy-feely with the new tech satisfied her urge for immediacy. It wasn't as if the game would drastically change due to a somewhat-improved interface. At least, not enough to warrant breaking the law.

Around nine, she woke up again, grabbed a quick shower, then walked naked to the kitchen and microwaved a breakfast burrito. Home alone, clothing had become something of a balancing act with the thermostat. If she could tolerate going without, she could do laundry less often and save a few bucks. Some months, a trip to the laundromat meant the difference between actual food and instant ramen. Amazing how well a girl could adapt to a chilly room—or tolerate wearing the same oversized T-shirt for two whole weeks.

With half of the egg-log sticking out of her mouth, she wandered across the apartment to the desk and picked up the helmet. For a brief moment, she debated sending Eric a picture of her wearing nothing other than the helmet, but changed her mind. An image like that *would* come back to haunt her eventually. She tended to avoid having her picture taken at all, much less something so compromising. The less of an info footprint she left, the harder a time The Man would have coming after her.

She held her breakfast with her lips to keep her hands free, taking small nibbles as she set about hooking up the new helmet to her cool custom wire. Once she got all the plugs connected, she flopped in the chair and ran the installation module. While that chugged away, she scoured the net for any information about the Neurona 4, focusing on a handful of deep net sites favored by the hacking community. Already, five known vulnerabilities made the rounds, but the most dangerous one looked like a way to forcibly log someone out of whatever game they were in. No one had posted anything truly scary. Still, the new helmets hadn't been officially released for a full day yet, so not finding anyone posting about serious glitches or dangerous properties only meant no one had discovered them yet.

Twenty minutes later by the time the installation finished, she hadn't come across any horror stories about roasted brains. With a grain of nervousness she hadn't felt since the first time she used an immersion rig, she carried the shiny pink helmet to the bed, arranged herself flat on her back, and got comfortable.

Dakota raised the helmet with both hands, giving it the evil eye. "Okay, you. Everything checks out, so I don't know why I've got a bad feeling right now. But I'll make you a deal. You don't mess with me, and I'll take good care of you."

The helmet, unsurprisingly, said nothing.

She gave it a curt nod as though it had accepted her terms and lowered it onto her head.

Soft whirring came from tiny motors that reconfigured the interior padding to the shape of her skull. The sensation of it moving caused her to grip the bedding and squirm. A few seconds after it went silent, she reached up and pulled the eye cover down. Neurona helmets had blackout visors since the first generation. Reducing sensory input to the eyes made it easier to send visual data directly to the brain and prevented conflicts or ghost images. A bright enough light to the eye could appear in the game world, creating a distraction.

"Welcome to Axillon99," said a pleasant female voice via speakers. "Neurona 4 interface initializing. Security option has been set to cortical imprint."

She waited for the familiar head tingle, but nothing happened.

"User DM01852 authenticated," said the voice. "Press start button to initialize."

Her breath echoed in her ears. "Okay. Here goes nothing." She reached up and pressed the login button by her right temple.

"Synchronizing to game server in three... two... one..."

The blackness of the helmet visor brightened to a field of pure white. In seconds, the constant thrumming and beeping of high technology broke the silence, along with the ever-present background music. The blank whiteness faded back to the login chamber. She stepped into the portal and appeared in the main room of her crew's starship, the *Stormbringer,* seated in the same chair she'd flopped in before logging out the previous night.

"Wow." Fawkes blinked and looked around at the weathered lockers, weapon cabinets, the giant round table, and the beat up chairs. "That was way smooth."

The air tasted like metal. Her boots and butt vibrated with a never-before-noticeable sensation, like an idling big rig. She touched the table, which also pulsed. Fawkes hopped to her feet and crouched, putting a hand on the floor.

Dusty grit met her palm—another new sensation—as well as the vibration, which she figured came from the ship's engines.

"Huh. Wow." She glanced down and brushed her fingers at her hand to clear dust. "Guess this is 'increased resolution.' New feels and smells." She glanced up at the metal grid ceiling and flickering LED light tubes. "I really hope the developers aren't going to start making us go to the bathroom." Those sensations still reached players' brains, but represented real world needs. Adding character 'bio functions' would probably cause many unfortunate accidents.

She headed to the right, down the ship's central passageway to the engine room. With each step, the vibration became somewhat stronger. Her workshop looked much the same as she remembered, a large room full of machinery, with a row of three huge components in the middle. Some of the tools on her rack looked more complex, as if they'd gone from having twenty moving parts to forty. A few changed color as well. The whole engineering bay smelled horrible, flooded with the caustic throat-scrape of the fictitious chemical 'Teslin,' essentially liquid electricity. The glowing-blue substance powered almost everything bigger than a backpack, from the ship's showers to its weapons to its jump drive. The game developers made no secret they'd named it as an homage to Tesla, but she doubted many players got the reference. Most people in Axillon99 possessed only the most rudimentary understanding of Teslin: if you shot a container of it, it blew up *big*.

Some areas even had randomly placed barrels of the stuff. She always forgot to shoot them when an enemy stood too close to one, but they never missed a chance to nail a barrel and catch her in the explosion.

She sighed and went to check over her station.

Characters in the game all had a 'class,' which represented their skill set and abilities. In Axillon99, player characters had two distinct classes. The 'primary' class such as rogue or gunslinger took most of a character's time, but players could also choose a secondary class that represented their role as part of a starship crew. A sneaky shoot-them-from-behind rogue compared to a knuckle-dragging heavy soldier wouldn't make a whole lot of difference in starship vs starship combat, so the designers created a split system. The game tried to balance ship action with character action, but a player could still choose to ignore one side entirely. Some pilot characters never left their ships for example. Few people truly understood the game's enormity in that one could play a single character on the surface of a planet and run missions for literal years without running out of things to do. Multiply that by a ridiculous number of planets... Though to be fair, the randomly generated missions didn't change all that much from planet to planet.

Fawkes' 'ship class' of techie gave her plenty to do, though it lacked the glory of being a pilot. If the *Stormbringer* suffered critical damage, she could fix

it during the combat. Otherwise, she sat at her console, shifting power allocations and providing temporary buffs. So far, they hadn't run into a space fight
difficult enough to really need that, so she sometimes planted her butt in a
turret for a little more fun.

While a full-immersion rig could be used to teach actual engineering skills,
Fawkes' proficiency in Axillon99 dealing with made-up spaceships with made-
up components didn't. It involved picking up a crazy tool and sticking it in a
socket somewhere. A bit like a wizard in a fantasy game mixing various
reagents to perform different spells, if she poked a particular component with
a particular tool, she'd do something to the ship. Same tool, different component would do something else.

"Well, this stuff looks more or less the same. Smells worse. Yay! $500
helmet and the best part is I can't stand to be in my workspace anymore." She
pursed her lips as that nagging feeling of dread came on. "Okay, gotta test
something."

She closed her eyes and triggered the log-off command.

"Logout request detected. Please confirm?" said the pleasant female voice.

"Confirm."

"Logging you out in three... two... one..."

The engineering deck flashed back to the bright white haze. A sense of
vertigo swirled around her brain for two seconds before the light dimmed to
black. She flicked the eye-shield up and stared at the ceiling of her bedroom.

For some reason, being able to log out surprised her.

"Ugh. I've been watching too much anime." She set the helmet on the
mattress. "Right. Good to go. Just need to prepare."

After a run to the bathroom and a quick snack, she flopped on the bed
again and logged back in.

The faster and less disorienting process might've been worth the cost of
the new helmet all on its own. Since none of the other players in her crew
showed as online, she walked back through the main room and into the
hallway leading toward the bridge at the nose end. About a third the way
down, the airlock let her out to a boarding tube that she followed into the
starport concourse.

A cool breeze laced with the fragrance of Chinese food brushed at her
cheeks. Gazing up at a lattice of amber-tinted metal beams, she suppressed a
shiver. The thin leggings her character wore hadn't felt thermally inadequate
before, but now her teeth almost chattered.

"Must be the helmet. Wow, it's cold in here."

Hundreds of people and creatures milled about, the vast majority
computer-controlled NPCs. Repetitive thudding drew her attention to a large
Draath male. He approached nine feet in height, the upper third of his body
gliding well above the rest of the crowd. They had the general shape of
humans, but their biology amounted to living rock, in this character's case, a
deep blue crystalline. Darker sapphire spots formed his eyes, and his fists

looked bigger than Fawkes' entire torso. The Draath had a reputation for being stubborn, pragmatic, and slow. They made excellent 'tanks,' especially for raiding groups, since their natural armor allowed them to take one hell of a beating.

She jogged to the right, passing a trio of brown-robed Simarin monks who all stared at her with their row of onyx eyes. Those aliens gave her the creeps, with their tall necks, heads shaped like upside-down raindrops, tiny mouths, and three perfectly round eyes. Their society revered the concept of three as a divine thing. The race got major bonuses to the 'aura' stat, which made them obnoxiously powerful with magic. That they somewhat resembled folkloric 'grey' aliens stretched tall and thin only made them creepier. A little kid player she'd randomly grouped with before joining the crew once called them 'buttmouths' since the tiny wrinkled opening beneath their nostrils bore an unfortunate resemblance to a particular orifice.

Still, Dakota tried as much as she could to avoid them, as well as magic in general, since she didn't think it belonged in a science fiction game.

Of course, fate's a sarcastic bitch.

Eric played a technomancer—a magic-user with spells based on affecting, enhancing, and in some cases creating, technological objects. She blamed her dad for that hatred of magic in games. Not so much the magic itself, but the need for purity in a genre. He'd played some old fantasy-based game way back before full-immersion caught on. That game had elves and magic and whatnot, but it also had gnomes with crazy machines and even guns. Her father *hated* that the developers put guns in a fantasy game. She had to have inherited that unconscious dislike for genre-bending from him.

Not wanting magic in a game about spaceships had even resulted in her friendship with Eric taking longer to start. For the first few months, she totally ignored him, reasoning that she could pretend magic didn't exist in the game if she simply refused to acknowledge it or interact with anyone using it. As time wore on, she'd acclimated to having a technomancer about and stopped acting as if he didn't exist.

She trotted over to a large wall of brushed steel with a billboard-sized display monitor. A handful of other player characters stood by it, each checking out posted quests in small mini-windows. Unlike the NPCs, whenever she looked directly at an avatar representing a real person, their character name would appear over their heads. Fawkes had taken a low-tier special ability that also let her see the exact character level of other players and hostile creatures. Much to her annoyance, all the people around her scanned as level forty or higher, except one: a blue-eyed, blonde Niath woman in a skimpy 'battle tunic' and sandals.

The Niath, another alien race, resembled angels: essentially ridiculously pretty humans with wings. Some even had pointed ears. She figured they represented this game's version of 'elves,' to appeal to players who usually went for 'the beautiful' race. In the game's lore, the Niath visited Earth thousands of years ago, mistakenly believing humans more advanced than they were at the time—and started religion by accident.

This particular one scanned as level six. Fawkes smirked at the revealing pink-coral colored tunic that exposed quite a bit of cleavage and leg, assuming the player was likely a man. Though, the game allowed *vast* customization when creating the character, and this Niath had relatively tiny breasts. Usually, guys playing female avatars did it to stare at themselves, so they made their female characters' proportions ridiculous.

She shook her head, dismissing those thoughts, and turned her attention to the job board.

The usual array of random quests scrolled out in front of her. One paying 15,000 credits leapt out at her, an oddly high amount for the random generator. She tapped it and read the description: the local law enforcement had run out of patience with a crime boss, and rather than lose even more officers, decided to post a bounty on him. The mission called for the assassination of an organized crime figure, who probably had bodyguards. She started to reach for the button to dismiss it, figuring it a combat quest meant for the kick-in-the-door types like Nighthawk, but hesitated.

Hmm. He might not start off in combat mode. Maybe I can ambush him and haul ass? Oh, why not. I can always abandon it if it's impossible. She tapped the button to accept the quest.

The edges of her vision flashed red the same instant a deep male voice said, "Pickpocket attempt failed."

Fawkes swiveled around, locking stares with the rather startled Niath woman who'd moved up behind her. Normally, some shithead trying to steal her stuff would get her fuming, but this 'girl' was only level six. No way in hell did she have even a tiny shred of chance at succeeding a pickpocket against a level thirty-seven rogue.

"Oops!" The girl spoke with a child's voice. She cringed back, covering her mouth with both hands, her white-feathered wings quivering as she trembled. "I'm sorry. I clicked the wrong button. I was only trying to look at your stats."

Fawkes relaxed. "Oh. It's okay. No worries." She returned her attention to the job board.

"I'm Rhiannon."

She twisted back to look at the winged woman. The nameplate over her head read, 'Angelgirl1344.'

"Hi. I'm Fawkes."

The Niath emitted a little girl's giggle. "Hi."

Fawkes started to glance again at the job board, but stopped when the woman flared out her wings to their full fourteen-foot span.

"I have wings!" cheered the woman with the child's voice. "Aren't they cool?"

Oh, shit. This is an actual kid. She cringed inwardly at the thought of a preteen showing so much skin. "Umm. Yeah, they're cool."

Rhiannon bounced on her toes, giggling. "Thank you. It's *so* fun to fly!"

Fawkes opened a private whisper channel. "Mind if I ask how old you are?"

"Ten. My birthday was last week. Got this game 'cause it had an angel on it. I love angel stuff! Your pink hair is kinda cool too."

"Your parents got you the game? Do they play?"

The Niath shook her head, her nearly butt-long hair swishing gracefully behind her as if underwater. "No. They don't have time for games. Both of them work a lot."

Fawkes glanced around to make sure no one was giving this girl the wrong sort of look. "Okay, there's something you should do for your own safety. Go into your options menu."

Rhiannon's eyes went wide. "Umm. Safety?"

"Creeps."

"Oh." She bit her lip. "But, I'm only ten."

"Your character doesn't look like it. Trust me. Go into options/social."

The Niath gazed into space for a second before a small holographic panel appeared in front of her. "Okay."

"Go to the voice option, and select 'character natural.'"

"It's on pass-through now," said the girl.

"Right."

"Okay, I did it," said the Niath with the voice of an adult woman. "Oh, wow. I sound like my mom now."

Fawkes smiled. "Correct. Now people won't know right away you're a kid and try to take advantage of you. And for heck's sake, you're still wearing the starter tunic. Have you been doing missions in that thing for six levels?"

"It looks angel-y," said Rhiannon. "No, I have quest armor in my pack. I just wear this in town because it's pretty."

"It's going to attract creeps."

"Eww. Okay." Rhiannon stood still for a few seconds. Thin armor bits appeared piece by piece, including a guard along the leading edge of her wings, all permeated with a neon pink glow. The highly stylized (and physically improbable) armor covered a little more than the tunic.

"Much better." Fawkes nodded.

"Hey, thanks. Did you just take a mission? Can I help? Wanna team up?" The Niath bounced on her toes.

"I would, but this is a level thirty-eight mission. You'd get smashed."

"Oh." The girl shrugged. She probably didn't care that much, but the Niath avatar's 'disappointed' face overstated sadness. "Okay. I'll find something lower. Can I whisp you if I get stuck or have questions?"

"Sure, why not." Fawkes accepted a friend invite.

"Bye!" Rhiannon waved with one hand and one wing before scooting back up to the giant mission-giving monitor.

Holy crap. Fawkes sighed out her nose. *Why do people let children play this game?*

On the way out of the starport, she stopped at a weapon store to check on upgrades for her 'getting old' handgun. A few laser pistols on display had slightly better stats, but nothing offered enough of a boost to be worth the steep price. She couldn't justify dropping 14,000 credits for another twenty points of top-end damage.

"Argh. Dammit!" said a man, one hand grasping a rifle sitting upon the store counter. He appeared to be trying to pick it up, but couldn't manage to lift it more than a few inches off the countertop.

Fawkes glanced to her left at the black-haired guy in soldier's armor. He held his arms slightly to the side, staring down at his chest as if someone had spilled something on him, but the white armor looked clean.

"Stupid useless crap." A box about the size of a loaf of bread appeared out of thin air and fell to the floor to the side. "Inventory is full my ass." With that, he picked up the rifle.

She glanced at the dropped item, which scanned as a ten-pack of limpet mines rated at 2500-4000 damage to all targets within a twenty-six meter radial area.

Holy shit! She gawked and stared up at the soldier, SgtBoone, who had a little '60' next to his name. *Wow, and I thought Nighthawk had no life.* Someone already at level cap had to have started playing the day the game launched (probably in open beta, too), and put in like full-time-job hours and then some. She entered stealth, crouched, and picked up the box of mines. SgtBoone didn't seem to notice or care. Hell, to him, they might've been worthless throwaway junk.

She scurried over to the counter and opened a trading interface. When the NPC merchant offered her zero credits for the box, she frowned. Hand grenades for sale within the same level/damage range were going for 40,000 a box. She about screamed until she noticed the description text on the mines. They came from a quest on some other planet, required to blow open an old mine tunnel, and could be replenished endlessly from a particular NPC. Obviously, they had no sale value to prevent people generating unlimited money by getting the free mines, selling them, getting more free mines, and so on.

Well shit. Guess I'll keep them.

Disappointed at not getting an easy ticket to a better gun, she trudged out of the store and headed into the city, staring at the minimap leading her to the lair of 'Bruno Black,' the crime boss she needed to eliminate. Naturally, the blinking quest indicator sat most of the way across the city.

"I guess having quests fifteen feet from the job board would be too easy."

She walked outside, opened her inventory control panel, and tapped the icon for her bike. Blue light flashed in front of her, forming the wireframe outline of a souped-up e-motorcycle. A second later, it filled in solid with gloss black body panels and glowing lime green accents. Fawkes hopped on and cranked the accelerator. The bike gripped the metal roadway like a magnet as she zoomed into the sparse randomly generated traffic.

A mixture of hovering vehicles, wheeled cars, and other bikes dotted the streets, reminding her a bit of those old screen-based games where the player ran around dragging people out through the windows and stealing the cars—not that she'd try that here. For one thing, being *in* such a realistic world made the idea of running up to a moving car terrifying. For another, she figured the developers of Axillon99 had heard of locks on car doors. Besides, evading or blowing up the police in this world wasn't 'expected.' The devs over-tuned the authorities. Security officers would sometimes spawn in out of thin air even if the 'crime' couldn't possibly have been witnessed by anyone. Also, on the 'static' planets hand-built by the development team, all the law-enforcement troops were level seventy, ten levels over the game's current level cap.

The game did a fairly reasonable job of simulating the real world physics of how it felt to ride a motorcycle. For most of her life, Dakota had regarded them as little more than two-wheeled suicide machines. Being unable to die in the virtual reality of Axillon99 gave her the courage to try one, not to mention the lack of a 'mount' made traveling planetside tedious as hell. Having gotten used to it in the game, she debated trying one out for real... but hadn't quite gotten over her fear of serious bodily injury.

Also, the pleasant wind whipping her hair around would probably be a lot less pleasant in the real world while doing 180 MPH. She ripped by other cars like they stood still, weaving in and out of lanes, cutting across sidewalks, and going over at least two grass fields to avoid blockages at intersections. She caught a little air off a small hill next to a picnicking family who didn't react at all to her shooting past them.

Heh. If I ever do this for real, I'll need to keep reminding myself to stay on the damn road.

Citizens showing zero reaction to some idiot on a bike cutting through a park broke immersion and reminded her she played a game. That brought her mind back to the quest at hand, a quest she probably shouldn't have taken.

Ugh. This guy is gonna be at least level forty, with friends. Oh well. I'm already out here, and it's not like I'll lose much if I die.

Quests that involved an instanced area (a separate section of the game world that only existed for the people doing the quest) or a raid would lock out if all the players inside died. Groups who attempted raid content (missions that required a full five-person team or in some cases multiple five-person teams banding together) hated wiping, because no one in that group could re-enter the instance until the weekly reset on Wednesday. One crappy player screwed up and caused everyone to die, the whole group would be unable to re-try that encounter until next week. This, of course, resulted in most of the 'pro raiders' being elitist douchebags.

Eric could fit in with them, not for his being a snobby dick, but he fit the mold for a 'hardcore' player. He'd think nothing of spending all Saturday in the same small area killing creatures over and over to farm up components for a device or spell he had that would help them out on a raid boss.

Fawkes sighed. That sounded *way* too much like work.

She drove into a bad part of the city where graffiti covered the walls of abandoned storefronts. Metal armor panels replaced glass here and there, some bearing phrases like 'Vos Dur go home.' Another alien race, the Vos Dur were a silicon-based life form the game described as 'androids with souls.' Few biological races trusted them thanks to decades of fiction about AIs going crazy and wiping out life. The game had tons of missions with themes of discrimination against the Vos Dur. Sadly, the 'difficult moral questions' the missions tried to ask usually boiled down to a simplistic choice between the player either deciding the Vos Dur lied and the evil AIs had to die, or the player saving the poor maligned machine people.

A group of four men loitering by a wall drew handguns and started firing lasers in her direction. Not wanting to deal with a random encounter, she gunned it and kept driving. The men chased her on foot for about a quarter mile before giving up and running back to where they started.

Following a waypoint arrow, Fawkes drove a few more blocks before she rolled to a halt. She stood in the road, straddling the bike, and observed the façade of a bar named The Wormhole. A pair of big-busted holographic women danced on either side of the door. One man in a shiny black coat, tight pants, and sunglasses stood next to the entrance.

She figured him for one of Bruno's thugs, but his lack of aggression gave her confidence. These guys wouldn't go straight to combat, so maybe she *could* be sneaky. The crime boss NPC might also be a quest giver for players going the 'evil' route, so players would need to be able to walk in without forcing an immediate combat.

At a mental impulse to put the bike away, her motorcycle degenerated back into a wireframe image and disappeared.

"I wish cars did that for real. Parking in the city sucks."

Fawkes tried to put Dakota out of her mind and get into character. Walking alone into a bar like this felt like exactly the wrong thing for a young woman to do alone. The realism of dark alleys, a breeze cutting through clothes, and shadows that seemed to watch her sometimes got overbearing. In fact, this isolated alley struck pretty damn close in overall color tone, arrangement, and mood to a spot back in the real world where first real boyfriend, Jimmy Tran, decided he didn't like hearing 'I'm not ready for that yet.' Only, they'd been parked by a crummy little diner instead of a dive bar-slash-organized crime front.

For a moment, Dakota became sixteen again, fighting to get out of the car and away from him. Fortunately, being young and stupid, he'd attacked her right in the car instead of making a move somewhere she couldn't have gotten away. She hit the horn and screamed, attracting the attention of a pair of biker dudes who came to her rescue. To this day, no one but her, Jimmy Tran, and those two guys with beards knew what happened. She hadn't even told Nebraska.

It had to be a coincidence that this particular alley came so damn close to that street in appearance. Obviously, the real world didn't have parked hover-cars or removable armored panels replacing shot-out windows, but things like an eerily familiar yellow air scrubber standing where she remembered a yellow newspaper vending machine, or the brick-red wall where the old ice-cream place stood across the street from the diner... too many things lined up too perfectly to be a coincidence.

And the smell.

Simmering grease. The same smell that lurked in the diner, that same cloying vegetable-oil-and-bacon foulness she spent an hour sucking in her nose while crying in the bathroom.

The line between Dakota and Fawkes blurred. Going in there felt like an awful idea. The mission could go fuck itself. She took a step back, but froze when her hand brushed the laser pistol on her hip.

What's wrong with me? I'm over that. Jimmy didn't even do anything but grab my tit. I got away. I won. He's nothing.

She scowled at the area. *Just a coincidence. A creepy ass coincidence.* That yellow box had to be random. Maybe she remembered wrong and there hadn't been a newspaper machine right at that exact spot. Shaking off her doubt, she concentrated on the idea of being in a game, being a badass character in a made up world on a planet other than Earth.

Fawkes rushed to the surface of her consciousness. She put on her 'I own the world' smile, walked past the thug by the door—who didn't even look at her—and stepped in to a room awash with the scent of beer and buffalo sauce. Plain round tables filled the middle of a fairly large area. A black-Formica bar stood at the left, a pair of pool tables all the way on the right. Random laser scorch marks decorated the walls around a bunch of nonfunctioning old neon signs. The only one that worked, a glaring pink 'restrooms' sign, flashed on and off over a hallway leading deeper into the building.

Four men who could've been brothers of the thug outside, wearing almost-identical outfits, stood around holding up the walls. Three NPC customers drank and munched on bright orange chicken nuggets. The older man behind the bar had a standard 'vendor' icon floating over his head, so she doubted he'd be a threat if a fight started. Another ridiculous truth: a place like this, players could usually kill all the NPCs in full view of the 'merchant,' then sell all the dead people's crap to a person who theoretically just watched them murder everyone. As long as the player didn't shoot the merchant, they'd remain calm. Though, if this vendor had a flag making him belong to the organized crime group, he'd probably go hostile. And of course, if a player killed him, all the stuff he had for sale would automagically disappear from his inventory.

Fawkes meandered among the tables, heading for the back hall. None of the men reacted to her until she came within a few steps of the one posted by the hallway.

"You'll wanna talk to the boss if you're willin' ta work," said the NPC.

She looked up at his face. *Hmm. Level 38 minion, no armor. Probably go down faster than those two security guards.* "Thanks. Boss in the back?"

"Yeah." He pointed at the alcove two feet to his left. "Down the hall here."

Past a pair of bathroom doors, a nicer metal door with laser burns led to a well-appointed office with a large, wooden desk like something out of a gangster noir film, anachronistic in a world of spacecraft and lasers. A white bearskin rug lay on the dark hardwood in front of a fireplace flanked by tall bookshelves.

The man sitting behind it all but glowed due to his coral orange blazer with tiger stripes. His puffy hair, fake tan, tank top, and thick gold chain amulet screamed 'fifty plus trying to be twenty again.' When she looked directly at him, the name Bruno Black appeared over his head, along with the number forty.

Ugh. This whole place is a reference to something, but I'm missing it. No one makes anything this tacky without there being an Easter egg. She squinted at the décor, trying to figure out what inside joke the developers were going for. Nothing this out of place happened at random.

Three more thugs stood around the room, but all four men ignored her. She explored the bookshelves on either side of a white-and-black tiger stripe sofa, searching around for anything out of the ordinary. A strange object on the left shelf caught her eye. She picked up a flat plastic square with a metal shroud on one end that slid back and forth. A label showed a cartoon middle-aged man with a balding spot and white suit on next to the title *Leisure Suit Larry*. The other side had a metal disc in the middle with two holes. Small text under the title read, '3.5 inch floppy version – disk 1 of 52.'

"What the heck is this thing?"

A faint *ping* echoed in her ears. She swiped her hand at the air and checked her update log, noticing that the game had awarded her the LSL achievement.

"Whatever. Since I'm not like, *old*, I don't get it." She huffed and dropped the strange object back on the shelf.

When she wandered closer to the desk, Bruno looked up at her. "Who the hell are you strollin' in here? I ain't never heard o' you. F'you wanna work for me, you gotta make a name for yourself first, kid. Now get gone before I change my mind about letting you walk outta here."

She wanted to tell him to eat a dick, but that might trigger combat. Plus, insulting computer code didn't really make her feel better. Instead, she backed away from the desk to stay out of his interaction range. Bruno obviously offered missions, but only to players with enough faction points in the underworld of this city—or maybe if they had universe-wide criminal records. The game tracked players on a hidden 'good vs evil' scale, and she clearly didn't have enough darkness to get any respect from this guy. She thought it pretty sad her video game persona had technically broken fewer laws than her real self.

Hmm. All three gunmen are level forty, too. I'm going to get shredded if I attack. She sighed. *Screw it. There's easier quests out there even if they don't pay as much.*

Fawkes took a few steps toward the door before stopping with a grin. She may as well pickpocket them. *These guys owe me gas money. Metaphorically speaking.*

She darted over to the back corner, careful to keep far enough away from the desk.

That spot didn't look like it would fall into any of the NPC's vision cones, so she tried to invoke stealth. Her body crouched ever so slightly and went semitransparent.

Awesome.

She crept a few steps to her left so she wound up right behind Bruno. Reaching for his belt with an open hand activated the pickpocketing interface. Since a pair of inventory screens appeared floating in front of her (her crap on the left, and a mostly empty one on the right for Bruno) she knew she passed the skill check. Though, if she tried to swipe anything too big, the system would test her skill again with a penalty based on the object. Taking a credit fob was easy. Swiping a character's pants that they're wearing at the time—not so much.

Bruno's inventory contained a combat knife, a pack of 'jelly candy fish,' and two Atomix pills. That told her Bruno would probably attack with melee, since the fictional drug Atomix provided a short-term massive boost to physical strength. More reason not to do the job. She'd never flatten a level forty with a single stealth attack using a piece-of-shit pistol she'd out-leveled. Combat would start, he'd eat a pill, then punch her into spaghetti sauce in a single hit.

Damn. Asshole doesn't even have the decency to carry anything worth stealing.

She sighed at the inventory screens and reached up to close them, but froze when she spotted the pack of mines.

Hang on a second... I wonder...

She closed the pickpocket window and backed up. Once free of risk, she accessed her inventory again and opened the container holding the mines, separating it out into ten individual items. When she 'used' one of the little black hockey-puck-sized devices, she got a mini menu that allowed her to set the charge timer.

The level sixty mine would incinerate Bruno three times over. She set the timer for five minutes and placed the puck on the floor behind the chair.

"You dropped something," said the thug by the right wall. He rushed over, picked up the mine, and handed it to her.

Without her doing anything, the hockey puck disappeared from the guy's hand and reappeared in her inventory. Its icon had a lit-up timer, marking it as still active and ticking down.

Shit! She looked around in a momentary panic, searching for a place to ditch the explosive before she killed herself.

Hold on a sec... it's in my inventory and the timer's still going down. She calmed and slipped back into stealth. *Pickpocketing works in two directions.*

Again, she crept up on Bruno and reached for his belt. She forgot to breathe, wound up with anxiety that she'd fail the pickpocket check and start a combat. Her bright-pink nails crept closer and closer to Bruno's side. *One more inch... Come on...*

The inventory screens popped open.

She slouched with a breath of relief. *Hmm. Maybe they let him be easy to pick-pocket since he's got nothing worth taking.* Grinning like a fool, she transferred the armed mine from her inventory to his, a reverse pickpocket.

He didn't react.

Just to be totally certain, she armed two more mines and set them to the same time remaining as the first one, now down to four minutes and three seconds, and put them in Bruno's inventory. After they transferred, she closed the interface, backed away from his detection distance, and dropped out of stealth. Casual, she walked out of the room and returned to the bar. *Hmm. Probably shouldn't leave the building so I get credit for the kill... assuming this works.* Time seemed to drag to a standstill as she paced around the bar tables.

The building shuddered with a powerful explosion that knocked most of the dead neon signs off the walls, caused the jukebox to turn on, and sent all the NPC patrons running around in random panic. All four thugs in the bar room drew handguns and went into a combat pose. Two of them said, "I think I heard something. Did you hear that?" at the same time, but they didn't open fire on anyone.

"Quest Update" appeared in gold-orange letters, lingered a moment, and faded away.

Fawkes stood still, the picture of total innocence. Thirty seconds later, the thugs put their weapons away. She hurried back down the hall. Everything in the office had become 'broken' versions of the former items. Books littered the floor, some on fire. The desk had ceased to exist, as had Bruno. Pieces of the three bodyguards lay scattered around among the books, and a circular red stain marred the ceiling above where Bruno had been sitting.

The gore had enough cartoonishness to it that she laughed.

"I can't believe that worked!"

Sure enough, when she checked the mission log, it showed the job as completed.

A glowing box appeared on the floor under the blood splat. She recognized a loot drop from an 'enemy with no lootable corpse left' right away and pounced on it. When a sleek black laser pistol with purple handgrips appeared floating inside a blue border, she let out a *squee* of delight.

The randomizer had given her a CL32 'heavy' laser pistol, a level forty 'blue quality' weapon, which put it roughly equivalent with a level forty-five 'common' one. The damage range of 142-213 more than doubled her current weapon (60-90). Then again, she had been using it since level thirty. She rushed the new one into her 'equipped item' slot, and the graphic on Fawkes' hip changed to the somewhat-longer—and much cooler looking—CL32.

"Yes!" She giggled.

Another object appeared, a standard data pad.

"Huh... what's this?" She grasped it and hit the button. The screen lit up with a text message:

We lost the signal trace out in the middle of nowhere by this trinary star system. The ship had taken so much damage, we had to turn back. I don't even remember where the heck we were... only that the middle star was blue. The debris field is still out there. As soon as I find a crew, I'm going back.

Below that, a line contained a string of random numbers and letters, which she figured as data corruption.

She scratched at her head. "Odd. Some kind of flavor text I guess, like the data corrupted."

"Quest update" faded in for a second or two and disappeared.

"Oh, it started a quest." She smirked and opened the log.

A new mission—*The Lost Dreadnaught*—appeared with the comments: "I found a datapad that looks like a couple of salvage operators got more than they bargained for. I wonder what's out there... or even where to start looking. I have a feeling it could be worth a lot of money... like ten million dollars."

Fawkes gasped. "Holy shit! This is the prize quest!" She squealed again and bounced on her toes. "Oh, shit. Oh, shit, Oh shit!" She started to hyperventilate with excitement, then froze, wondering if video game avatars could hyperventilate. *Holy crap, Eric and the others are going to shit their pants.* She bit her lip, dreading the idea she might not be able to share the quest with them, but when she saw that the share quest button hadn't been greyed-out, she cheered.

Her crew had a shot to chase down ten million real dollars!

"What the fuck?" asked a deep voice, scratchy and modulated with a semi-robotic twinge. A hulking form in black-paneled armor and a spacecraft pilot helmet had stopped one-step into the room, gazing around at the destruction. 'Reaper913,' another player, looked at her. A red tinge to his name identified him as either a frequent player-killer or someone who'd done enough 'bad stuff' that the in-game law had an open bounty on him. Any player to take him out would receive an email with a 'mission bounty'. Considering his level showed at forty-six, and his armor looked like what a soldier class would wear, she had no interest in combat. "You killed Bruno?"

"Uhh, I just got here." She pointed at the stain on the ceiling. "I think he had a bad meatball or something. You ever see a splat like this before?"

Reaper913 tromped over, heavy armored boots *thunking* across the floor. He halted beside her and gazed up at the ceiling in silence for a little while. "That's kinda messed up. Nope. Never saw a splat like that on the damn ceiling." He looked her over and emitted a grunt of contempt at her crummy gear, probably deciding it not worth it to kill and loot her. "Dammit. Spent an hour flying here to turn in a damn job."

"Yeah, I've been waiting for him to respawn, but... I think I'm gonna go do something else."

Leaving the other player to curse and kick debris around, Fawkes hurried back outside and activated her motorcycle.

6

INTERACTIVE

Fawkes ran solo missions around the city for a few hours, enough to hit level thirty-eight by the time the others in the group began to trickle online around seven that night. Nighthawk had logged in a little after three in the afternoon, but other than a 'hey what's up' text, didn't talk much. The social window showed him on a different planet, Galphaius, where all the missions started at level 44. He, too, had leveled up, hitting forty-three. It took all her self-control not to tell him that she'd gotten the drop for the contest mission. She wanted to wait until the whole group got together.

Axillon99 had a relatively severe leveling curve for online games. The first five levels went by fast. Someone who knew their way around MMOs in general could hit fifth level in about ten hours of play time. After that, the brakes screeched. The hardcore people could pull gaining a level a week up until around thirty, then closer to one per two weeks. She'd heard rumors that past level fifty, even the 'I have no life' players would only gain a level every three months or so.

It didn't matter *that* much. The developers tuned all of the 'endgame' raid content for level sixty. Once a player hit that point, they could only obtain more power by collecting 'epic' or purple quality items from participating in raids. Aside from a few super-rare cases of ability-granting items, they wouldn't gain any new skills or tricks until CSI came out with an expansion pack that raised the level cap and added more, higher level, content. Of course, since the game had been out for two years and only around thirty percent of the player base had reached level cap, no one expected an expansion pack any time soon. The game had launched with *so* much stuff to do, it didn't seem necessary yet. Not a day went by that someone didn't post about finding a new hidden instance on some planet or a never-before-seen world boss.

Fawkes zoomed across Xiānjìng City on her e-bike, heading for the starport. Her heart nearly leapt into her throat when she swerved around a cargo transport doing 175 MPH and almost hit the police car in front of it. Real world dread faded in a moment when the NPC cop ignored her.

"Oh, holy shit," she rasped, white-knuckling the handlebars. "Maybe I shouldn't get a real bike. I'd forget I'm not in a game and kill myself, or worse—lose a whole paycheck."

Her pulse still racing from the terror of a giant traffic ticket, possibly arrest, she slowed to a more modest 100 MPH for a few blocks. The game's police usually reacted only to players shooting civilian NPCs, causing property damage, or attacking other player characters in certain designated 'safe zones' designed to give new players a chance to get going before griefer killers made them quit.

It didn't take long for the thrill of her good news to chase away the spike of adrenaline. Fawkes drove her bike straight up the giant escalator into the starport, but it disappeared out from under her a short distance past the entrance. Some areas restricted vehicles in a less realistic manner than having doors too small to allow them to pass.

Thin borders around dark silicon-blue floor tiles lit up wherever anyone stepped on them, creating an endless wash of moving light along the ground. Every time she went into a starport, there would always be at least one or two first-time players walking around, mesmerized by the light-up floor.

She rushed past a group of player characters who'd set up 'merchant stations,' trying to sell in-game wares and a few who tried to sell real-world products. Next to a large, square installation where holographic fish glided around an arrangement of alien plant life, one female character in a barely-existent garment of thin metal struts and gossamer fabric danced for tips.

A forlorn-looking boy of about seven walked by, calling out "Sprocket, here Sprocket" over and over. She'd done that quest the first night the crew had spent on this planet. The boy's missing dog had fallen down a maintenance shaft out on the starship landing area, and couldn't get out. She, and thousands of other players, had saved him, only for the mission to reset and the poor virtual golden retriever to wind up stuck in the hole again.

Damn the realism. She forced herself to look away from the crying boy before she got upset. If the game would let her repeat the quest, she would, just to feel better.

She headed down the tunnel to the docking node, and from there went into the boarding tube where *Stormbringer* perched.

"Welcome back, Fawkes," said Galileo, the ship's AI personality, as the outer hull door opened.

"Thanks."

She hurried to the central room, where Nighthawk sat at the huge round table, playing combat chess with the pilot, Kavan Das. His avatar appeared to be in its late forties, with neat black hair, a deep tan, and a healthy amount of muscle under his armor. The character struck her as a chimera of a hot Mediterranean super spy and a pro MMA fighter. Fawkes (and Dakota) at twenty-two could've been his daughter by age, but a girl could have fantasies. The new Neurona 4's vastly improved throughput allowed the game to add a hint of an intoxicating cologne to his presence.

He still showed as level thirty-four, suggesting he hadn't had the time for solo missions in a while. No one in the crew, except maybe Eric, was in any rush to start hitting endgame raids, so there hadn't been any bitching about his slow leveling. She recalled his real name as William, and vaguely remembered him mentioning he worked as a software developer—though not for CSI. He did something boring, like accounting applications or some such.

Axillon99 offered two ways for a player to get their own starship. The cheaper method involved taking 'pilot' as one's alternate class and then working through an exhaustive set of missions that took the dedicated players three or four months to finish. That gave them a tiny Cobra-class ship, basically a flying wedge, that they could use to run solo missions. From there, it became an economics game, trying to earn enough money either by cargo runs, asteroid mining, or bounty hunting to buy the next biggest ship, and so on.

The other method, the one Kavan used, involved buying the 'extreme collector's edition' of the game for a staggering $900. Of course, that also included a lifetime subscription without monthly fees, so... perhaps it hadn't been as stupid as it sounded to her at first. He'd started with a ship about half the size of the *Stormbringer*, but had already upgraded to it by the time Fawkes ran into them. Kavan and Nighthawk had been stuck on a 'go here and kill these bad guys' mission, despite their both being soldier classes. Granted, Kavan had specialized in defense as a 'tank,' which was awesome in groups, but the lower damage output made some quests a pain to solo.

Fawkes had skipped that quest, being a rogue, since it appeared to involve heavy up-front combat. However, when Kavan asked her to help them out (and shared the quest) she decided to pitch in. As it turned out, the enemy had an auramancer way in the back, healing the enemies faster than Kavan or Nighthawk could take them out. While the guys kept the pirates busy at the front, Fawkes snuck in and around and attacked the healer from behind. With the NPC woman struggling to keep herself alive, the pirates out front fell fast, and they rescued the kidnapped settlers.

After that, Kavan invited her to join the crew since they were still missing one person and didn't have a rogue yet.

"Hey," said Fawkes on the way over to a seat. "What's up?"

"Privateer mission tonight." Kavan rubbed his chin, eyeing the holographic chess pieces.

She glanced at the half-consumed beer in front of Kavan and the choco-coffee by Nighthawk. That started her wondering if drinking coffee inside the game world would trick her brain into waking up for real. "You guys ever wonder if virtual coffee would wake us up?"

"No effect," said Kavan. "About the only thing it does is taste right."

"Think I'll grab a beer," said Nighthawk.

Kavan shifted his gaze up from the game board to him. "You sure you wanna do that? Gonna need you sharp in a few minutes."

"Oh." Nighthawk shrugged. "I got those punks by four levels. Shouldn't matter, but okay."

Whenever the *Stormbringer* got into a combat encounter, Nighthawk went out in a Gremlin fighter craft. It matched his personality: all guns, no defense. It had the overall shape of a broad head arrow with curved sides, and two giant particle cannons at the wingtips. To Fawkes, the design looked ridiculous. The gun tubes on either side should snap off as soon as the fighter pulled a hard turn, but being a video game, logic took a back seat to 'looks cool.'

A little pink ogre about two inches tall shambled forward two squares on the game board, roared, and smashed a blue goblin flat with one punch.

"Check," said Nighthawk.

Kavan leaned over the board, appraising the lay of holographic pieces.

Soft boot clanks came down the hallway. Angel813 glided in, the crew's medic. Despite her character name, she hadn't made a Niath. Long, ghostly white hair trailed after her like a gossamer mass of spidersilk. She had Chinese features with bright blue eyes, and a mild accent. In her mid-to-late thirties, she settled into a 'big sister' niche to Fawkes, and tended to 'mother' the whole crew, except for Kavan. Fawkes suspected her of being sweet on him, though as far as she'd seen, he had never returned any of her subtle glances.

Her green uniform had silvery armor panels over the vital spots, along with the standard medic insignia of a white field with a red cross on each shoulder. Seams in the armor emitted a faint violet glow. Rumor had it that in player-versus-player fights, sometimes healers would be spared if they didn't attack, but computer-controlled enemies didn't care. Fawkes thought otherwise: the healer usually wound up as the primary target.

Dakota had no small amount of jealousy for their medic—most of her gear was blue quality, with about half (including that armor) being purple. Despite her character having only reached level forty-one, Angel813 had the gear to stand a reasonable chance against enemies many levels over her. Again, Dakota opened an 'inspect' window and drooled at the armor and its 500-point damage force-field ability—an extremely rare bonus.

Some of the advanced armors could project a stealth field. She daydreamed about finding one of those. Players widely regarded the rogue class as weak for most of the level spread, but after level forty-eight, they verged on overpowered. Their best attacks only worked from stealth, but once gear or other special abilities allowed them to hide at will (or even use 'stealth only' abilities out in the open) they became obnoxious. Most of the strategy sites regarded the rogue class as the best one-on-one class, capable of melting down any opponent other than a tank. In group missions, they had some of the better damage output ratings—provided the terrain allowed them to get behind the bosses. Nighthawk and his gunslinger could keep up, but he didn't need to worry about positioning at all. A well-played rogue could pull a little ahead, doing three times the work for about a ten percent gain in DPS. The same way players tended to think of rogues as king of one-on-one, they regarded gunslingers as an 'easy' class for lazy players.

According to Nighthawk, 'that was only what the jealous people said.'

"Hey everyone," said Angel813. "Sorry I'm late. The ER was nuts. We had an influx of injuries tonight. Bad accident on I-91."

"Ouch," said Kavan. "Hope it wasn't *too* bad."

She sighed while lowering herself to sit. "One man died on the scene. Semi-truck nailed his subcompact, but it set off like a forty car pileup. Most of the other injuries were on the minor side at least, but *so many*." In reality, Angel813 worked as a nurse in Hartford, Connecticut. Though they had exchanged emails and she knew the woman's real name was Christina, they'd never met.

Nighthawk and Kavan both cringed.

Fawkes got up and went to the food printer, dialing up a choco-coffee. "Damn. That sucks. Makes me glad I don't drive."

"You don't?" asked Nighthawk with a look of surprise. "Why not?"

"I live in the city. No need."

"Which city?" asked Nighthawk.

"Damn New Yorkers," said Kavan, chuckling. "Manhattan isn't *the* city."

Fawkes stuck her tongue out.

"Oh, that's not too far. What are the odds?" Angel813 smiled. "I wonder if the game does that on purpose?"

"Does what?" asked Nighthawk.

"Where are you from, for real?" Fawkes slid back into her seat and sipped at chocolate-coffee-foam-awesome.

"Philly," said Nighthawk.

"Oh, like Kavan." Rallek, Eric's technomancer, strolled in, grinning. Faint cyan highlights glowed here and there on his matte-black armor. The fabric parts trailed after him like a hybrid between a wizard's robe and an anarchist's trench coat. Small devices on his forearms and belt blinked and moved about, charged with magic. A splash of bright violet broke up the solid black of his hair over his left temple. The character shared Eric's darker skin tone, though his facial structure appeared 'prettier.' He wound up looking like the evil prince from an anime movie, which made him seem like Nighthawk's nemesis.

"Hey!" Fawkes perked up in her seat, smiling at him.

"Uhh, yeah." Nighthawk leaned back in his seat, eyeing the game board. "We live near each other. Come on, old man. Your move."

"Old man is it now?" Kavan whistled, shaking his head—while smiling. "All right." He tapped a blue creature that somewhat resembled the Simarin, tall, thin, and robed. The three-inch alien stepped two squares diagonally left before shooting a tri-fork lightning bolt that incinerated three of Nighthawk's pieces. "I think if you analyze all probable outcomes of the game from this point forward, you'll realize your best result is a draw with an eighty percent chance of loss."

"Dammit!" Nighthawk scowled. "I hate this game."

"You're playing a strategy game against a strategist, and you're not a strategist," said Rallek.

Nighthawk glanced over at him. "What do you mean I'm not a strategist?"

"It's obvious. You went gunslinger. It's not a thinker's class." Rallek summoned a small techno-orb, which proceeded to weave around his fingers.

"Ha. Ha." Nighthawk rolled his eyes.

"Okay," said Kavan. "Since we're all here, we can take on that privateer mission tonight."

"Wait." Fawkes summoned the data pad from her inventory. "I got some awesome news first."

Everyone looked at her.

She jumped to her feet, bouncing on her toes. Small compartments on her armor full of random 'rogue tools' jangled and clattered. "I got the drop for the contest mission!"

"Nice!" Angel813's eyes widened.

Nighthawk didn't appear impressed.

"What?" Fawkes deflated a bit, glancing over the table at him. "It's a chance at a buttload of money."

"I got that drop two days ago." A similar data pad appeared in Nighthawk's hand. "It's not a rare drop... it's got like a fifteen percent chance to drop on any kill. Getting *on* the quest isn't the hard part. The mission itself is a total bitch."

Kavan shot Nighthawk a dark look.

"Oh." Fawkes sank into her seat.

Rallek patted her on the shoulder. "You can share the quest with me. I still haven't gotten the drop. Nice find."

She brightened. "Okay."

"I don't have it either. Been too busy," said Angel813.

"He does have a point though." Kavan shut off the chess game with a short, sharp wave. "That contest is supposed to be impossible. There's sixteen million players, it's a damn certainty someone with nothing better to do with their life is gonna beat us to it."

"Nineteen," muttered Nighthawk.

"What?" Rallek glanced at him.

"There's nineteen million players now. People are checking out the new helmet. They even have fart mods." Nighthawk grinned.

"Hard pass," said Fawkes. "I gotta deal with Trent already."

"Huh?" asked Kavan.

"One of the guys at the café I work with... I'm amazed the food doesn't rot in the cooler with him around. Dude destroys the atmosphere at least twice an hour. At least he's still in high school and only part time."

"He might have a condition," said Angel813. "If he's breaking wind that often, he should go get checked out."

Fawkes laughed. "I'm exaggerating a bit. But I'm not going to install a mod just so I can gag on ass gas in virtual reality."

Nighthawk laughed.

The mission log screen appeared as a floating hologram in front of her. She tapped on the contest quest and hit the share button. Similar ephemeral display panels scrolled open in front of Rallek and Angel813.

"Right, so we've been sitting on this mission for a while. Now that we're all here, I'd like to get it done. Big experience payout on it." Kavan grinned.

Fawkes looked at her mission log. '*The Scarlet Saber* [Group/SHIP 5]' showed an XP reward of 75,000 and a gold icon for loot rating, the best possible shy of being in a raid. "Sounds good."

"Sorry it took me so long to be available," said Angel813. "Work's been kicking my ass."

Nighthawk grinned.

"No need to apologize." Kavan shook his head. "This is only a game."

"Yeah, same here." Rallek flicked a finger, which caused the orb circling his hand to disappear. "Been getting stuck late at the office too damn often."

Kavan opened the star map in a large floating display panel and pointed at a glowing peach-colored swirl a few inches left of the middle. "Our objective is to take on a pirate corvette operating under the designation *Scarlet Saber*."

"Can we just blow it up?" asked Angel813. "I hate boarding missions. So cramped."

"That *is* an option." Kavan tapped his fingers on the table.

Fawkes brushed her hand over the polished steel, noticing for the first time it felt cold. She'd gotten used to the game world not having all the sensations and smells of reality due to bandwidth limitations... but with the Neurona 4, it had taken a leap forward, scarily close to reality. Even her new gun pressed into her side uncomfortably. Her equipment had never done that before.

Maybe this upgrade was a bad idea. She chuckled mentally.

"There's slaves though," said Nighthawk, sounding urgent. "Bonus objective is to rescue them."

Rallek nodded. "Yeah. According to this guide I read, one of the slaves is the start point for another quest that's worth a shitload of XP."

Nighthawk laughed at Rallek, earning a smirk from Kavan.

"They're not really slaves," said Angel813. She summoned a dark maroon alien-cat-thing with massive almond-shaped onyx eyes. The vanity pet, a harmless 'decorative' companion, trilled and mewled as she petted it. "Just pixels. If we take the *Scarlet Saber* out in a space battle, we get the experience in a quarter of the time. We could do some other mission and make more experience in the same time than fighting through the hallways of an enemy ship on foot."

"How in-character of you," quipped Rallek with a wink.

"I dunno." Nighthawk fidgeted. "Feels bad to blow the ship up with innocent people on board."

"They're not people. They're computer code." Angel813 shrugged. "Half an hour after we blow it up, they'll be back."

"Yeah, but in the reality of our timeline, we'll have blown them up." Nighthawk glanced at Rallek. "I wanna board. Besides, buttload of XP from that other quest."

Fawkes flicked her hair back over her shoulder. While she saw the point of efficiency, she also often cried when characters in movies or books died. Pixels or not, if they blew the ship up with slaves on board, she'd be glum thinking about how sad it would be to get kidnapped, sold into slavery, and die while unconscious in a stasis pod, never knowing what hit her. A black cloud would hound her over it for days. "Yeah. We board. Besides, I got a new drop earlier I wanna try out."

Nighthawk looked at her. "Why are you giving orders? Kavan's the captain."

"I'm inclined to agree with her. Besides." Kavan gestured at her. "I can't argue with that wide-eyed innocent face."

Fawkes flipped him off.

Kavan laughed.

"Ooo. New weapon finally? What'd ya get?" asked Nighthawk.

She held up the laser. "CL32."

"Badass. Almost as good as mine." He grinned.

Fawkes inspected him, her attention going straight to the equipped-weapon box. He had a pair of identical Raven Model 5s, level 44 blue laser pistols with a damage range of 175-262, both giving a +5% bonus to critical hit chance, and a +2 to the dexterity stat. "Damn, where did you get those things?"

"Gunslinger class quest at level forty-three. Spent most of the afternoon working on it."

"Every 'slinger from level forty-three to their early fifties carries those things." Rallek shrugged. "Unless they get a lucky purple drop on a group quest."

"Oh." She smirked. "So the game basically just hands them to you."

"Well he is a *gun*slinger." Rallek poked her in the arm. "Wouldn't be very useful without decent weapons. That's the whole point of his class."

"Okay, so we board." Kavan thumped his fist on the table like a gavel. "Everyone cool with us taking off now?" When no one raised an objection, he stood. "I've already got the jump plotted. It's about ten minutes to fly there."

Fawkes stood. "I'll go preload some ship buffs."

"I wanna tinker with the Gremlin," said Nighthawk. "Read about a new spec. If I shift a couple points out of Reactive Shields to Overcharge, I should be able to blitz down even a bomber-class fighter in one volley."

Kavan raised both eyebrows. "True, the cooldown from Overcharge could do that, but is it worth having no shields up for twenty seconds? You'd make a debris cloud out of one bad guy, but if he has friends, you're toast."

"They'd still have to hit me first." Nighthawk struck a heroic pose. "Besides... I'm not *that* stupid. I wouldn't use it when I had someone on my butt."

"You know..." Rallek tapped a finger on his chin, smiling. "If you swung close enough to the *Stormbringer* for a moment, I could hit you with *Symbiosis*..."

"What's that?" asked Nighthawk, looking back and forth between Rallek and Kavan.

"A spell," said Rallek.

"Duh. Obvs." Nighthawk sighed. "What's it do?"

"It lets you use your primary class special abilities for thirty seconds with a ship... or other vehicle." Rallek winked.

Nighthawk's expression hardened with deep thought, but Kavan whistled right away.

"That's a hell of a combination," said Kavan.

"What?" Nighthawk stared at him.

Kavan smiled. "You just got that *Showdown* ability, right? Thirty seconds where you don't even have to maneuver. Just hang there and shoot."

Showdown let a gunslinger stand in the middle of the open like something out of a cheesy western movie. As Nighthawk realized the implication of that talent affecting his Gremlin fighter, he broke into a massive grin.

"It also lets Kavan's *Dig In* ability work on the big ship," said Rallek with a raised finger.

Everyone let out an awestruck whistle, even Fawkes. *Dig In* temporarily tripled a tank's health points to give healers a chance to catch up during damage spikes.

"Okay, maybe I don't think magic is that silly anymore." Fawkes winked at Rallek.

Still grinning from ear to ear, Nighthawk got up and jogged off to the access hatch for the fighter bay.

Kavan headed for the bridge. Fawkes grabbed Rallek's ass and squeezed. He spun into an embrace, kissed her for a moment, and leaned back to smile. She teased a finger at the shock of bright violet in his otherwise jet-black hair.

"If I'd known you were in this kinda mood I would've stopped by in person." He nodded toward the bunkrooms. "We got a couple minutes..."

Fawkes shifted her weight from one leg to the other. "I'd prefer to do that in a world where my underwear isn't glued on."

He laughed.

Players could remove all clothing except for the standard drab underpants, and in the case of female characters, sports bra. Of course, the modding community reacted to this atrocity by releasing no less than forty-seven nude patches within hours of the game's release, though she hadn't bothered installing one. If she wanted to get off, she'd invite Eric over for real… or take matters into her own hands. Considering the staggering amount of porn on the net, why people would bother modifying a game boggled her mind. A person could find skin anywhere online, but here, you could blow shit up with lasers.

She kissed him again before jogging off to the engineering room. Between her level and the *Stormbringer's* displacement (corvette), she had four 'buff slots' that would hold pre-made boosts. Whatever she put in there, Kavan could access as the pilot. During a space battle, she could use her tools to tweak at the various components in this room, the engineer's way of participating in combat.

"Hey Kavan," said Fawkes. "Do you know what kind of loadout the *Scarlet Saber* is packing? Are we looking at lasers, particle beams, neutron beams, or mass drivers?"

"Four heavy neutron beams and EMF torpedoes," said Rallek over the comm link. He let the game use his real voice, so hearing Eric distracted her into thinking about quiet time with him in the real world. "They're pirates, so they want to disable ships without tearing them apart."

"You *know* this or you're guessing?" asked Angel813.

"Read up on the mission last week when we got it," said Rallek.

"Research? She don't know what that means." Kavan's voice carried a hint of chuckle.

Rallek groaned. "I hope she starts reading strats when we get to raid content."

"Lay off her," said Fawkes. "She's super busy in the real world. Besides… Eric's got all the strats memorized already. He can tell her whatever she needs to know."

"Lazy," muttered Nighthawk.

"I don't need to read the strats," said Angel813. "Nine times out of ten, my job is going to be standing there spamming heals. You guys have to worry about running the encounter."

"True enough, but sometimes they make the healers jump through hoops, too," said Rallek.

Fawkes slotted two 'polarity reversal' buffs, which would make the shields temporarily resistant to neutron beams at the expense of becoming worthless against any other attack. Neutron beams functioned on spaceships like stun rays on people. They'd knock stuff offline and cripple a ship without doing permanent damage—perfect for a pirate. They also tended to do quite a bit more 'damage' per shot than other weapons, since their effects were temporary. In the third slot, she put a countermeasure that let the communications suite broadcast chaos to confuse incoming torpedoes. The *Stormbringer* had normal countermeasures, but her buff version had a 100% chance to work, making the ship immune to guided missiles for sixty seconds. The fourth slot got the usual, a Recharge ability that 'healed' the ship's shields for half of their normal maximum value. She adored that one since it had saved them from being blown up quite a few times.

That done, she grabbed a giant yellow screwdriver and poked it at the engine component. A momentary surge of acceleration made her lean a bit to the side. "Let me know when you're about to engage. Giving us a twenty percent speed boost until then."

"Copy that," said Kavan.

"How much longer until you can unlock Arcane Bridge?" asked Rallek. He'd been nagging her about that ability for days. With it, she could double the range of his technomancy spells in space.

"That's a level forty slot. Two levels away."

"Oh, hey, grats on thirty-eight."

"Thanks," she muttered.

She rattled around the engineering bay while the ship flew toward the quest destination. A few minutes later, a bright flash announced the warp jump and brought on a full-body sensation of pins and needles. Fawkes shrieked and swatted at herself. Rallek gasped over the comm link, as did Kavan and Nighthawk.

"Whoa, that was weird," said Nighthawk.

"My balls are tingling," said Rallek.

Nighthawk laughed.

"Must you?" asked Kavan.

"What?" Rallek's portrait on the comm panel shrugged. "They are."

Kavan grumbled.

"It must be some 'special effect' for jumping. These new helmets are something else, all right. Do they do anything *good*?" muttered Fawkes. "What do you think, Angel?"

"Not sure. I didn't upgrade. Waiting for a sale. They're a bit steep right now."

"Are they?" asked Fawkes. "Eric got me one."

"Look at Mr. Moneybags," said Angel813. "Someone's getting some tonight."

Kavan coughed. "We're approaching the target."

"How much are they?" asked Fawkes, a twinge of guilt in her voice.

"About five big ones," said Angel813.

"Shit, Eric, you spent $1000 on this game?" asked Fawkes, her mouth open.

"Well, the helmets aren't *just* for Axillon99," said Rallek. "But yeah. And don't feel guilty. I ain't hurtin' that bad. Call it an early birthday gift."

Fawkes grinned. "Okay. I think I might have something for you later tonight."

"Battle stations!" yelled Kavan.

She smirked. They still had a few minutes of flying left. Kavan wanted to change the subject as he always did whenever topics got interesting. She pitied him for being the world's biggest prude. "Hey Kav, why do you always get uncomfortable whenever we talk about sex-type stuff? Are you like a priest or something?"

"Dude seriously needs to get some," said Rallek.

Nighthawk cracked up laughing so hard he sounded like he'd choke to death.

Kavan remained quiet.

Four minutes later, Rallek said, "Activating the transponder."

The mission came with a transponder item that made the *Stormbringer* appear on sensors as a large, slow, unarmed freighter. According to the quest, they needed to fly to this system and activate the device. That would lure the *Scarlet Saber* out to attack, thinking them a juicy target for a pirate. Boots clanked on metal in the hall from Rallek and Angel813 running to turrets, one along the top of the ship, the other at the bottom.

The *Stormbringer* had a relatively sleek design for a corvette. From the nose, the sides curved outward in a bullet shape, became straight until the one-third point, then flared out to a delta wing. It had a fairly thin profile from the front, rear, or side, which made it a difficult target in a fight unless the opponent approached from above or up from below. As ships of it size class went, it ranked about mid-grade for armor and weapons, low on cargo space, but high on maneuverability, essentially being the most 'fighter like' of the medium ships.

She stopped boosting speed, tossed the 'screwdriver' shaped tool back on the table, and grabbed an electric gizmo with two waving antennas. When she pointed it at the shield generator, a soft thrum permeated the whole ship. A twenty percent boost to shield points would help in the event of an ambush.

Overhead speakers crackled to life with a cocky male voice with a hint of nasality. "Jettison your cargo if you want to li—Oh... you're not a freighter. Never mind that then, there's no living for you."

"Contact," shouted Kavan.

Fawkes opened a spectator window, which allowed players inside the ship to watch the space action from a 'chase camera' view. The *Scarlet Saber* had appeared in the distance with a pair of fighter ships flying escort.

Four bright green beams in two pairs streaked across space toward the *Stormbringer*. Kavan rolled the ship so the attack passed harmlessly above and below. An air-blast noise announced Nighthawk launching his fighter.

Rallek yelled some nonsense words, ad-libbing his magic while tossing the *Symbiote* spell through the *Stormbringer's* hull into the departing Gremlin. "You're enchanted, 'Hawk."

"Awesome. Yeah I see the buff icon."

The arrowhead-shaped Gremlin flew straight toward the enemy ships, offloading a blistering array of particle beam fire. Scintillating orange-red streaks shredded one of the smaller escort fighters in seconds, sending it into a spiral tumble that culminated with a dazzling explosion more like fireworks than a spacecraft's death. Incoming fire passed within inches of the Gremlin, but nothing could touch him.

Kavan whistled. "Wow. That's almost like cheating."

"Everyone says that about gunslingers," said Rallek. "Why do you think people assume everyone who plays one is like twelve years old?"

"I'm not twelve," grumbled Nighthawk.

Kavan hit the booster, which kicked the ship forward for a brief but severe moment of acceleration. The *Scarlet Saber*, being a more cargo-oriented corvette, had about half again the armor and shields of their ship, but also the maneuverability of a box. While Nighthawk and the other fighter went after each other, Kavan flung the *Stormbringer* into an aggressive dive, triggering Fawkes' shield modification. He flew straight into a barrage of neutron beams, exploiting the thirty seconds of near-immunity, and settled in on the larger ship's tail.

"Holy cow, that's a corvette. It's not supposed to be able to fly like that," said Kavan, ad-libbing the lines their computer-controlled opponent would never say.

Rallek and Angel813, in the turrets, peppered the *Scarlet Saber's* shields with red pulse lasers since Nighthawk kept the other escort fighter well away from their ship. The *Stormbringer* lacked the specialized 'crippling' weaponry of the pirate vessel, but any ship could try to do enough damage to a target's engines to shut them down. Once a craft drifted dead in space, they could dock and board it for the on-foot part of the mission.

Kavan fired blast after blast from the main laser cannons into the back end of the *Scarlet Saber*. Dark sapphire-hued beams pelted the ungainly ship, which couldn't swerve fast enough to evade. With each shot, scintillating bursts of light in the shape of shield domes flickered over the enemy craft, along with purple-pink wisps of flame. The pirate swerved side to side, twisting and climbing, but succeeded only in making Kavan miss once.

"Bring it in closer and I'll hit him with *Fail*," said Rallek.

"Oh, they're already covered in fail," said Nighthawk.

"No, it's a spell. It'll shut their ship off for a few seconds."

"Workin' on it," Kavan's strained voice leaked past his teeth. "He's really pushing that thing. It's gotta be modified. Heron class corvettes aren't supposed to turn this tight."

"It's a quest boss. Probably has cheated stats," said Angel813.

The Gremlin raced by, strafing particle beams across the *Scarlet Saber's* nose.

"Engines, engines, engines," yelled Kavan.

"Gotta get through the shields first. Doesn't matter where I aim until the shields are down," said Nighthawk.

Kavan pulled in close, lining up a perfect shot at the back end of the pirate vessel. An instant before he fired, the enemy ship's rear exploded in a fireworks flower. Six anti-ship missiles spiraled out, leaving a pinwheel pattern of energy trails. Fawkes mashed the button for the guidance-scrambling buff while both turrets started firing at the incoming weapons.

All six torpedoes went around the *Stormbringer*, detonating harmlessly a good distance behind it.

"Holy shit," muttered Kavan. "I wasn't expecting that... who loads rear-mounted missile tubes at all, much less six of them?"

"A quest boss," muttered Rallek. "Guarantee that ship doesn't actually *have* that weapon on it if we were to steal it."

Fawkes blinked. "That's an option? You can just board and take a ship?"

"Sorta. We'd be able to fly it until we docked somewhere... then the 'authorities' would confiscate it."

"Oh, that's lame," muttered Fawkes.

"Yeah, well, if players could just steal ships, it would be too easy to get them." Kavan clucked while putting a barrage of particle beam into the rear end of the pirate vessel. "They gotta make us work for it."

"Or buy it," said Rallek.

"Touché." Kavan laughed. "I regret nothing. I got this game for the flying, and skipping three months of crappy quests only to be given a wind-up toy of a ship was worth it. Nothing sadder than a pilot without a ship."

The *Scarlet Saber's* shields faltered and collapsed, sending a ghostly disc of white light expanding into space. A sudden eruption of red lightning crackled around the walls in the engineering room and filled the air with the flavor of questionable eggs.

Fawkes screamed. "Something just hit us!"

"Relax," said Rallek. "That was me. Targeting buff."

She shied away from the crackling mass of electricity, gagging on the stink of it. "It reeks! Isn't sulfur demonic? And why does a buff smell *bad*?"

"It smells?" asked Rallek, sounding surprised. "Oh, how about that. It does. Smells like ozone to me."

"Smells like your socks," said Nighthawk over the comm.

"You're not even in the ship!" shouted Rallek.

The *Stormbringer* hummed as the main laser cannons fired. In the spectator window, the *Scarlet Saber* rocked from an explosion at the rear end by the row of four round engine ports. Three of the glowing blue spots went dark, leaving one engine functioning. Fawkes staggered to the left when the ship decelerated rapidly. The pirate hung 'dead in the water,' vulnerable to a boarding attack.

"Coming in," said Nighthawk.

Kavan guided the *Stormbringer* into docking position, hovering over a port at the midpoint of the pirate ship's underside. The two vessels came together belly to belly with a frighteningly loud *clank*. Answering creaks and groans in the frame sounded like the protests of a submarine going below crush depth.

"Is that normal?" yelled Fawkes.

"Yeah," shouted Kavan. "You should do your override thing now."

"Right!" Fawkes hopped on a terminal, and with a few clicks, began a technological attack on the pirate vessel.

The hacking mini-game came up, and she raced the red line to the hostile CPU node. Her character's skill allotment made it a trivial task. So easy, in fact, she hit all six bonus nodes, picking up an extra 2,800 credits and two *Worm* modules, one-use disposable software helpers that functioned somewhat like buff spells, except program code instead of magic. The *Worms* didn't impress her that much. Since she'd focused on hacking skills, she rarely needed the temporary boosts to succeed, so she'd stocked up a large amount of them.

As soon as her green line hit the CPU, she got into the enemy ship's computer. This opened a control interface for the other ship. She shut down the weapons and navigation controls, unlocked the boarding hatch, and opened all the interior doors.

"All gift wrapped," said Fawkes. "Let's do it."

Everyone met in the main room by the round table. Angel813 didn't look happy, but didn't exactly seem pissed off either. Kavan led the team down the corridor to the airlock access. A blast of freezing air came by as the door opened, making everyone shiver except Angel813.

"You know, I'm starting to wonder if the new helmet is an advantage or not." Fawkes rubbed her hands up and down her arms, shivering. "Damn... it's seriously cold in here. I could legit cut glass right now."

Nighthawk stared at her with a note of confusion in his expression.

Kavan shouted, "Come on," and charged down the boarding tube.

A device on his shoulder projected a forward-facing energy shield around his rifle. The outer hull door of the *Scarlet Saber* opened with a simple button-press, as Fawkes had already neutered the security system. They advanced into a surprisingly clean hallway of polished steel.

"Hmm. Guess space pirates gotta keep the place tip top for guests," said Rallek.

Kavan glanced left and right. "Let's deal with this pirate, then check the cargo hold."

At mutual assent from the other four, he faced to the right and advanced toward the bridge. Nighthawk hovered close behind, his guns up. Rallek reached out as if to grab something out of thin air. A half-length staff appeared, metal and covered with glowing circuitry lines. Two puzzle-cubes orbited the head end. So far, he'd been the only one in the crew to get a purple weapon drop, and much to Fawkes' annoyance, it had been an item for a magic user.

She walked side by side with him behind the two pilots.

Angel813 brought up the rear, carrying a clear shield in her left hand that looked like a flimsy piece of plastic. Tiny medical bots, floating four-inch spheres, hovered around her, awaiting commands. She'd put most of her levels into medic, but threw a few into technomancer for some synergistic bonuses to her medical equipment. According to the mechanics of the spell, the little medi-bots counted as 'summoned minions,' so she could buff them.

A hatch on the left side of the corridor twenty feet ahead opened, and five man-sized robots clambered out, raising weapons. Kavan activated a wider group shield to give the party cover from incoming laser blasts while simultaneously firing a sweeping full-auto barrage in an effort to concentrate all the enemies' attention on him.

Fawkes used *Flicker* to insta-hide. By the time her *Shadowblink* ability teleported her behind the robot attackers, Nighthawk had already demolished two of them. She lined up a shot on the far-left robot since it kept trying to shoot past Kavan to hit Angel813. The middle one launched a small rocket, which detonated into a large swath of burning ground under the other four characters. Fawkes' ambush attack struck the robot going after the medic in the back, blasting it apart into a spray of parts. A large red '954' appeared above it, flashing to indicate a critical hit.

Holy shit!

Nighthawk stood still, continuing to shoot at the remaining two bots while everyone else backed up out of the flames. Angel813 grabbed and threw her small orbs at everyone. The tiny flying robots zoomed into orbit around the other characters, projecting green 'healing beams' at them. Two on Nighthawk kept his health bar from going down, hovering at about forty percent. She added a third heal bot, and the line began to creep up to full.

"Damn, did you just hit that one for like nine hundred?" yelled Nighthawk.

"She's got like a 3.5 times multiplier on critical hits from ambush," said Rallek as he waved his staff. Both remaining bots went still, heads bowed as if they'd fallen asleep on their feet.

Kavan, Nighthawk, and Fawkes peppered them with laser fire, destroying them before the paralysis spell wore off.

Fawkes did a little victory dance, hugging her weapon. "I *love* this thing. Holy crap did you see that hit!?"

"Yeah," said a rather sullen Nighthawk, jamming his pistols back in their holsters.

"Hey man." Rallek clapped him on the shoulder. "Don't hate. She's gotta hide to do that kind of damage, and she only gets it once or twice in a whole combat. Takes her three times the effort just to keep up with a gunslinger. In the time she did 900, you hit four times for 320 or so."

"Oh." Nighthawk smiled. "Yeah, right."

Fawkes grinned to herself. *Level forty-eight and I'll become one with the shadows.* She daydreamed of pulling off huge ambush attacks with impunity, wondering what sort of whining would come out of Nighthawk when that day arrived. Granted, she'd never have the multi-target abilities he would, but area-of-effect didn't kill raid bosses… unless they had tons of summoned adds.

Angel813 shot Nighthawk an annoyed look while topping off his health bar.

They fought their way past four more sets of robots to the bridge door, where the captain of the *Scarlet Saber* waited with his crew as well as his cheesy overdone suaveness and large chin. His hair even sparkled whenever the light hit it at a certain angle.

"Well, it seems I underestimated your piloting skills," said the pirate, patting the guns on his hip. "Perhaps we can come to a lucrative arrangement."

Crap. He's a gunslinger. Fawkes edged behind a control console and dropped into stealth.

"I don't see that happening," said Kavan.

The pirate's four friends fidgeted with weapons. A skinny guy in back had a medic's kit on his belt, so he became Fawkes' primary target. Next to him stood a dark-haired woman with an eyepatch and a facial scar. Her armor looked light, and she carried a pair of energy blades instead of guns.

"They have an assassin," said Fawkes over party chat. "Eric, watch Angel."

"You got it." Rallek nodded at her.

Angel813 retreated a few steps, putting her back against the wall.

"How much can I offer you to walk away?" asked the pirate.

"Release the slaves in your cargo hold and maybe I'll think about it," said Kavan.

"I'm sorry, I didn't quite catch that." The pirate tilted his head.

"He's only going to respond to a number," said Nighthawk.

Kavan glanced over his shoulder at the crew. "Is it possible to talk this guy down?"

"Nah," said Rallek. "Even if we give him a number he agrees to, he's going to backstab us when we try to leave. This is a simple mission. Combat or combat."

Fawkes tried to creep into the room, but an invisible wall blocked her. "Ugh, that's cheap. I can't get in position until the fight starts."

"Hah." Nighthawk grinned. "Getting around behind them before the fight *is* cheap. But yeah, I guess it's lame to have a barrier."

"Sorry, pal," said Kavan. "I'm afraid your pirate days are over."

"Really?" asked Rallek. "When did we wind up in a B movie?"

Nighthawk snickered.

"I guess you didn't understand me," said the pirate. "What's your price?"

"Aww, hell with this." Kavan shot him in the chest.

The green laser dispersed in a blast of light on contact, leaving a small char mark and dropping the pirate's health bar by about eight percent. The background music shifted gears to an energetic 'combat' track. Their assassin disappeared into thin air, the other three dove for cover behind consoles, and the pirate shimmered with a faint glowing effect while pulling his pistols.

"He's using *Showdown*," yelled Nighthawk. "Don't bother trying to shoot him for like a minute."

"Ugh. I hate boss fights," muttered Angel813.

"That's because you don't read the strats," said Nighthawk, while firing at a rifle-bearing crewmember.

Fawkes scurried around the room, keeping her head down as laser bolts streaked back and forth. The pirate laughed between firing off shots, standing impervious in the open to incoming attacks. Nighthawk had taken cover, likely saving his *Showdown* for once the pirate became vulnerable. Rather than go for their medic, Fawkes circled back around to the outer corner that offered her a clean view of her crew. On one knee, she raised her CL32 and aimed in the general direction of Angel813.

Their white-haired medic lobbed orb bots into the air like a coked-up juggler. Rallek waved his staff around, his defensive spell allowing him to control ambient energy and bend the constant barrage of incoming lasers into the wall. Kavan stood his ground, holding up his shield while trading fire with the pirate's heavy trooper. Except for Fawkes (who remained hidden), everyone's health bar fluctuated up and down too fast to keep track of.

A few seconds later, the female pirate appeared out of nowhere next to Angel813, her right hand extended forward in a throwing motion. At a flash of bright energy in the face, their medic took on a zombie-like posture and began to stagger around while 'stunned' animation bits orbited her head.

Before the assassin could move behind Angel813, Fawkes fired.

The shot critted for 900 damage, knocking the assassin to four percent health in one hit. The pirate medic switched focus from their heavy trooper to her, raising his hand and projecting a golden beam of light into the woman's chest. Her health bar raced upward. Fawkes fired as fast as she could, but no longer being hidden, her attacks only did around 170-200 points per shot. The assassin leapt at Angel813's back, slashing at her twice with energy daggers. The first hit knocked off two-thirds of her health and caused her to drop to the ground.

"Shit, she's crippled," yelled Fawkes, still firing as fast as she could.

The boss pirate raised both his guns and fired a barrage that raked over the entire party. A sensation like a pelting of snowballs accompanied the loss of fifty-five percent of Fawkes' health points. Since Angel813 had been lying on the floor, the attack passed over her; otherwise, it would've killed her.

Nighthawk wheeled around and opened up on the assassin. With three guns pelting her, the incoming heal from the enemy medic stalled to a stalemate, leaving the pirate woman stuck at thirty-three percent health. The assassin sprang again at Angel813, but Rallek summoned a wall of techno-junk around her that provided a pool of temporary armor points. Energy knives struck the orbiting barrier with a series of metallic *clanks*, but the assassin didn't inflict enough damage to break through.

"Do something about that medic!" shouted Kavan.

Fawkes *Flickered* into stealth and *Shadowblinked* to the far side of the bridge, nearest the viewscreen looking out to space. As fast as her brain could reorient itself after teleportation, she drew a bead on the pirate medic and fired.

A 1026-point crit caused the man's head to explode. The healing beam ceased, allowing Nighthawk to mow the assassin down in seconds. Angel813 moaned and dragged herself upright, still surrounded by a ring of floating random junk.

"I fucking hate being stunned!" she shouted.

Kavan glared at her.

Nighthawk grinned.

Angel813 pulled three orbs off her belt and set them flying in front of her, then waved her hand over them. Amid a spray of magical energy, the little robots doubled in size and radiated continuous light. One zipped over to Fawkes, hovering at her shoulder while projecting a stream of green energy into her. Her health bar rushed to the right, filling. The other two went for Kavan and Rallek.

Rallek hit the pirate boss with a spell that made his laser pistols stop working. At the same moment, Nighthawk leapt out from cover and activated *Showdown*. He fired so fast at multiple targets his weapons appeared to be throwing off three separate streams of fire. Yellow damage numbers filled the air over the remaining enemies. A rifle-toting pirate dropped in seconds. The boss dipped to below thirty percent health, and their heavy trooper's life bar fell a little below half.

While Angel813 took a three-second break from wrangling heal bots to stab Nighthawk in the back with a comically huge syringe that have him bonus temporary health points, Fawkes fired at the boss from a blind angle. Positional advantage let her crit for 416, not quite as good as full stealth. The hit was, however, enough to get his attention. The boss pirate spun to face her and switched from his temporarily dead guns to a bright red sword.

"Don't get hit by that," shouted Rallek.

Fawkes backed off to the right. "Wasn't planning on it."

"That's the Scarlet Saber. It's a one shot kill if you're not a tank." Rallek cast another spell, which caused one of the control stations to break apart and reconfigure into the shape of a humanoid robot, which leapt in front of her.

The pirate swung the sword at the summoned creature, slicing it in half in a single stroke.

"Eep!" yelled Fawkes. She couldn't *Flicker* again for another thirty-five seconds, so she did the next best thing: hauled ass.

He chased her around the bridge, evidently not programmed to climb over consoles. She leapt from one computer desk to the next, using the terrain to keep the AI-controlled death machine far enough away that he couldn't swing at her. After about ten seconds of that, he stopped, put the sword back in its scabbard, and switched to his pistols.

With a deep groan, the pirate heavy trooper succumbed to Nighthawk and Kavan's attacks. He collapsed to the floor, out of hit points.

Roaring, Kavan faced the pirate captain and zoomed forward as though propelled by a rocket. He plowed shoulder-first into him, stopping dead and sending the smaller man over backward. The pirate fired both guns from the floor, shaving most of Kavan's health points off in a single barrage.

Angel813 let out a squeal of alarm and ran up behind him, stabbing Kavan with a big metal cylinder that spiked his health bar back up to full.

Fawkes ran to the left, trying to circle around behind the boss while firing at him. Moving and shooting caused her to miss about half the time, but between her, Kavan, and Nighthawk all attacking at once, plus Rallek lobbing energy balls from his staff, the pirate captain dropped, only managing to get Kavan's health down to eighteen percent.

"Holy crap," said Nighthawk. "That was a lot harder than I expected."

"I hate boss fights," muttered Angel813.

"Damn fine heals," said Kavan.

"Not bad for a medic." Rallek winked.

"What's that supposed to mean?" asked Fawkes. "She kicked ass."

"A lot of players give up on medics because they're complicated. Auramancers are much better single-target healers, and their AOE isn't bad either. It takes a lot less skill to be decent as one of them." Rallek patted Angel813 on the shoulder. "Medics are the best group healers in the game, but they have trouble keeping tanks alive through a hammering. Fortunately, we have a damn good medic."

Angel813 sighed. "Thanks. Wouldn't have been so bad if I didn't get stunned like that." She glanced over at Fawkes. "Would've been a lot worse if I went down. Thanks for covering me."

"No problem." She grinned.

"Good call there," said Kavan. "Their medic was less important than making sure that assassin didn't get ours."

Nighthawk twirled his guns around his fingers in a fancy display of dexterity. "Might not have been pretty, but we won."

Kavan stooped to search the pirate, and opened a loot box. "Hmm. Key card, a set of light boots, and... ooh. Blue belt with +8% crit on it."

"Mine!" yelled Nighthawk.

"Hey, what about Fawkes?" asked Rallek.

Nighthawk spun on him. "But, she's a rogue! She gets criticals automatically when she's shooting from behind. If she's 'rogueing' right, crit chance is a waste for her."

"Whatever." Fawkes shrugged. "He's kinda got a point. Let him have it."

Kavan, being the group leader, allocated the drop to Nighthawk. "Done. Anyone want these?"

An icon of the boots appeared. Of the entire crew, only Rallek used light armor. One advantage the medic class had over the auramancer—they got to wear medium. Rogues and gunslingers also went for medium armor, and Kavan wore heavy.

"Umm." Rallek examined them. "They're statted for an auramancer. Wouldn't do me much good. Sell 'em and split the cash."

"Done." Kavan sent them to the ship's storage hold. The next time they landed on a planet or docked at a station, the boots would become 3,500 credits.

"Drat. Was hoping that sword would drop," said Nighthawk.

"Yeah right. I think it's just a middle finger." Rallek shook his head.

"What?" asked Nighthawk. "A middle finger?"

"He only pulls out the sword if he's somehow prevented from using his guns. It does ridiculous damage. Heck, it would take Kavan down to ten percent in one hit and he's a tank. I think it's basically a 'screw you for taking the gunslinger's guns away' mechanic. Like a punishment from the game developers more than a weapon."

Everyone chuckled.

Kavan led the way out of the bridge and down the main central corridor to the cargo hold. With the pirate captain dead, no security robots spawned to challenge them. Minutes later, they stared open-mouthed at a huge cargo hold full of coffin-sized pods, each holding an unconscious human or alien in the basic 'underwear' outfit.

"Wow..." Fawkes whistled. "There's got to be five hundred people here."

"Glad we didn't murder them," said Nighthawk.

"They're computer characters." Angel813 shook her head.

"This one's a child," said Rallek. "Like twelve or so."

The medic sighed. "All right, all right. I'm glad we saved them."

"Which one gives the quest?" asked Kavan.

"Umm." Rallek stared into space for a few seconds. "Fifteenth pod on the left side." He pointed at one with a yellow aura surrounding it. "See? It's interactable."

"Interactable's not a word, dumbass," muttered Nighthawk.

Rallek frowned at him.

Nighthawk kicked at the ground. "Sorry."

7

DON'T STAND IN BAD

Fawkes approached the highlighted stasis pod, swept her pink hair out of her eyes, and took a knee to peer through the clear lid. Within a cloud of cryogenic fog lay the willowy form of a young woman with cobalt blue hair. A metal collar kept a boxy enclosure with a slow-flashing red light tight at her throat. She appeared somewhere between fifteen and eighteen, and slept peacefully.

"Hmm. I think she's wearing a bomb. Is that going to blow up if I open this?" asked Fawkes.

"One sec. Reading." Rallek kept quiet for a minute or so before closing a floating window and shaking his head. "Nope. It only blows up if we try to take her off the ship without killing the pirate captain. She's some kinda princess. The quest she gives is taking her home to her parents."

Everyone groaned.

"It's not that bad. A quick flight. Really easy." Rallek grinned. "It's worth a lot of XP because it's an easy quest to miss. Most people just open the first slave pod they find and let them go, then leave. If no one talks to her specifically, she acts like any other slave being freed."

"Right..." Fawkes hacked the panel and hit the open button.

Cryogenic mist receded into vents, and the interior color-shifted from frigid blue to a warm orange. The lid motored open, as did the lids of all the other pods.

The girl's eyes fluttered. She sat up and smiled. "Thank you for rescuing me." She bowed her head, sniffled, and started to walk into a group with the rest of the people who'd climbed out of pods.

"We're here to take you home," said Fawkes.

The girl ignored her.

"Don't you wanna go home to your family?" asked Nighthawk.

"Uhh, how do we start the quest? She's not reacting," asked Angel813.

Rallek glanced at the small hovering screen again, reading for a second. "You look sad. Is something wrong?"

The girl's dejected expression evaporated to a hopeful smile. "Yes! I know you have done so much already, but I would ask another favor of you. My name is Siana Marchand, daughter of King Marchand of the planet Antimedes. My parents will reward you greatly if you were to see me safely home."

Nighthawk stared dumbly at her. "Wow, she's pretty."

Siana looked at him and blushed. "Thank you. I am sorry for being so poorly dressed. The people who kidnapped me took all my equipment and weapons. They are in a storage case nearby."

Fawkes examined the detonator collar, which had a tiny keypad and code lock. "Let me get this off you first." She took her override kit from her belt and plugged its wire into the collar's jack.

"Oh, thank you!" Siana beamed at her. "I don't like having a bomb around my neck. It's scary."

Rallek leaned toward Kavan and mumbled, "Who writes this dialogue?"

Kavan snickered.

A mass of people, an even mix of men and women plus a handful of children, gathered around. Only Siana had a bomb on her throat, probably intended as another clue of a hidden quest.

"I see the trunk," said Angel813. "It's all the way on the other side of the cargo hold."

"Why do we have to go open it?" asked Nighthawk. "Can't one of them do it?"

"They're NPCs," said Rallek, starting to walk for the storage box. "They don't do quests. We do."

With a *beep*, the bomb collar popped open and fell to the ground.

Siana let out a squeal of delight and hugged Fawkes. A faint flower-scented perfume surrounded her, and her skin had a surprising amount of warmth. The embrace felt so genuine, like she really had her arms around a terrified teenager, that Fawkes choked up a little.

"Intruder alert," said a painfully loud electronic voice.

The former slaves screamed and scattered like roaches to hide behind the empty stasis pods.

Earthquake-level shaking rumbled the ship. Fawkes peered up over Siana's shoulder, gawking at a twenty-foot tall robot emerging from a previously hidden compartment in the wall behind the storage trunk. Two backward-jointed legs supported a main body shaped somewhat like the nose end of an attack helicopter. Angled doors on either side of the center looked frighteningly like missile bays. Rather than arms, it had a pair of stubby extensions with long laser barrels on each side.

"Shit," said Rallek.

Nighthawk stuck his tongue out at Kavan's back when he glared at Rallek.

"Geez. I feel like I'm at work all over again," said Fawkes.

Siana screamed in terror.

"Work? Huh?" asked Kavan.

"Every time I swear, my boss yells at me. You just gave Rallek the stink eye." Fawkes scooped Siana up and set her on her feet behind cover. "Find somewhere to hide."

"Keep that thing pointed away from the pods," yelled Rallek. "It'll kill these people, too."

"Dammit." Kavan hurled himself into a shield charge at the giant robot. The force barrier emanating from his left forearm flashed and sparked on contact as he bounced off its right leg and stumbled between them. Once past, he whirled to face the room and fired a red laser blast up into the robot's rear end.

A defensive-specialized soldier's *Rush* ability forced the target to attack only them for about ten seconds, enough to make the machine turn around, limiting collateral damage.

Siana ran in among the pods and crouched.

"Everyone get in front of it so it doesn't melt down the civilians," roared Kavan.

Fawkes dropped into stealth and stayed put while sending, "I'll move in front after I get off an ambush," over the party chat.

Everyone else scrambled forward.

The robot opened up on Kavan with lasers so large they belonged on a vehicle. The first shot torched his personal shield and went halfway through his health. Angel813 threw a health grenade at him in the brief pause between its first and second shots. The explosion of green positive energy and subsequent laser blast left Kavan at twelve percent health.

"Damn," muttered Rallek. He hurled a spell that surrounded the bot in red light and made it swoon a little.

Kavan grunted and pounded his fist on his knee. His shields came back up, and a mass of techno-spaghetti ran down his legs into the floor, fusing him to the spot. Another health bar, pale grey, appeared above his green life points.

"Die!" yelled Nighthawk, as he activated *Showdown* and stood there firing as fast as he could pull the trigger. Orange pulses streaked across the dim cargo hold, leaving glowing spots in the robot's armor plating. Its health bar chipped down bit by bit.

Where the hell should I aim on this thing? After a short pause to consider, Fawkes took a shot for the middle of its back. Her dark blue laser beam slammed into it for a 990 point critical hit that made a deep, reverberating *clonk* and knocked the giant walker forward half a step. The machine whirled around to aim at her, but before it could line up a shot, she *Flickered* back into hiding. Rather than risk it melting down the innocent, she hurried as fast as stealth allowed to a better position closer to the robot.

It fired at Kavan again, though this time, the laser blast only took away a third of his grey bar. After that, the angled doors on either side of the main body opened, and a rain of small missiles pelted the area around the whole party, creating four distinct patches of burning flames.

Kavan couldn't go anywhere, since while his *Dig In* ability greatly reduced incoming damage, it rooted him in place. Rallek and Angel813 moved enough to get out of the flame patch, but Nighthawk stood there and burned, merrily firing away.

"Hawk, get out of the damn fire!" shouted Angel813, while scrambling to throw healing orbs at him and Kavan.

Both of their health bars sank alarmingly fast.

"If I move, my DPS will plummet," shouted Nighthawk, still firing. "Just heal me through it."

"You're not a goddamned tank," shouted Angel813. "You have five seconds to move or I'm going to let you die."

"Don't be like that," said Nighthawk.

"Dude, just move," yelled Rallek. "She can't keep your ass alive without losing Kavan." He summoned three small humanoid robots, which hurled themselves at the big one, attacking its legs with energy blades.

Fawkes stopped about twenty feet behind the robot and took her second ambush shot, which critted for 1150. Again, she got its attention, but darted forward before the robot could fire and send stray death into hiding slaves. She hit her *Evasion* cooldown, which gave her a +90% bonus to dodge for fifteen seconds. Brilliant green laser beams as thick as her arms drew glowing trenches in the metal at her heels as she ran around in circles, screaming in genuine terror at the heat.

Sometimes, full immersion sucked.

"You hit it where it hurts," shouted Kavan, before tossing a lightning grenade at it.

The charge went off with a bright blue-white flash, sending creeping sparks up the giant machine's legs. It twitched and shuddered in place, momentarily stunned. Fawkes' tongue tingled with the flavor of ozone.

Rallek waved his arms, throwing energy bolts made of wires and circuitry. Upon impact, they caused muted *clanks* to come from the robot's hull.

"This is BS," yelled Nighthawk. "How is he doing so much damage? We're almost even."

"It's a robot," said Rallek in a deadpan tone. "My *one* direct attack spell only works on mechanical enemies. It does inflated damage because I can only hit machines with it."

By the time the lightning stun wore off, the robot had lost interest in Fawkes. Its upper body swiveled to the right too fast for anyone to react to.

One blast of its lasers put Rallek down. His ghost stood over the inert character, sighing.

Angel813 said something in Chinese. Kavan still glared at her.

"You understood that?" asked Fawkes.

"Some words are universal." Kavan fired a burst from his laser rifle into the robot's nose, making it vibrate and emit a mechanical growling noise.

Fawkes slipped into hiding again and scooted around for another back shot. Angel813 rushed over to Rallek, yanked a pair of glowing paddles off her backpack, and mashed them into his chest. The body erupted in a shroud of sparks, convulsing and twitching. His ghost melted out of existence. Two seconds later, Rallek opened his eyes.

The robot got tired of the constant pelting from Nighthawk and let him have a double blast, but the gunslinger remained on his feet—albeit at six percent life.

Angel813, still on one knee by Rallek, winged a flurry of heal orbs at the gunslinger.

Kavan fired another barrage from his plasma rifle; it didn't do much damage, but the robot growled again at the taunting attack. He got an energy shield up barely in time to absorb a volley of small missiles. The string of detonations chewed through the energy shield, stripped off the last of his special armor (causing the roots holding him in place to break) and went two-thirds into his health points.

"I'm not liking this thing," said Kavan. "Hope that princess is worth it."

Angel813 wailed in annoyance. She sprinted over and stabbed him in the back with another syringe, then cast a spell on it that made it glow green. Kavan's health bar raced up to ninety-two percent.

Fawkes took cover behind an empty stasis pod, her position offering a clear shot at the giant machine's back—but she waited, watching lasers fly back and forth for a few seconds. She tuned out the shouts of her teammates, focused on the missile pod door. The instant they sprang open, she fired at the inner surface studded with rocket heads.

Her shot went true and hit for a 1,840 point critical before setting off a secondary detonation that did another 100,000 points. On top of the damage the robot had already sustained, the ammo explosion finished it.

The boss swooned around like a drunken rooster, staggered a few steps to the right, then collapsed in a smoking heap. Both of its huge laser cannons crimpled when it crashed to the ground.

Nighthawk marched up to Fawkes. "How the hell did you do 100K in one hit?"

"Shot it in the missile bay when the armored door opened." She walked over to the hulk and pointed. "I guessed it might be a vulnerable spot. Bosses like this usually have a weak point."

"Oh." His irritation melted away to awe. "That's cool."

"Damn that thing hit hard." Kavan stretched. "I think my armor's getting old. Time for an upgrade."

"You need to level up, man." Rallek patted him on the shoulder. "That robot was level forty. A same-level tank would've laughed at it."

Kavan frowned. "Yeah. You're right. Guess I should be glad we have an awesome healer."

"I swear"—Angel813 jabbed her finger in the air at Nighthawk—"if you stand in bad again, I'm going to let you die."

"But... I lose DPS if I move." He flailed.

"The damage meter can go to hell." She scowled. "Dead gunslingers do zero DPS. If it's a choice between keeping your prima donna ass up or losing the tank and all of us dying, you're going to go down. I refuse to rip my hair out trying to keep you alive when you insist on standing in a damage patch over a stinking meter."

"Point is made," said Kavan, a calming hand raised. "Nighthawk will move out of fire from now on."

Nighthawk hung his head. "Okay."

"And by fire, he means acid, lightning, freezing... anything. Not *just* fire." Angel813 narrowed her eyes at him.

He nodded.

"Wow, thanks for the rez," said Rallek. "I didn't think medics could restore the dead. That's kind of supernatural."

"*Defib* works if it's been ten seconds or less, and it requires touch." Angel813 smirked. "Stupid angels can rez you an hour later from across the room."

"Not *all* auramancers are Niath," said Rallek.

Angel813 gave him a look like he'd just said humans breathed water.

Kavan reached down and opened the glowing white loot box. "Oh, for the love of..."

"What?" asked Fawkes.

"It dropped a light armor robe." Kavan held up a blue-grey garment with a couple of composite resin panels attached to flexible fabric. "Bonus intelligence and focus."

"Aethermancer crap," said Rallek. "Again. It's like the game knows we don't have one and keeps taunting us."

"Why does a giant robot have a robe?" Fawkes laughed. "That makes absolutely no sense."

Rallek shrugged. "Gotta love random loot drops. Killed a Vos Dur warlord a couple days ago, and he dropped a really femmy tiara with a bunch of Aethermancer damage boosts on it."

"Oh, you totally should've worn that." Fawkes grinned. "It would've been cute on you."

He laughed, shaking his head.

"Right. Sell bait." Kavan teleported the robe into the *Stormbringer's* storage box.

The rescued slaves emerged from hiding among the boxes.

A sudden trumpet blast made Fawkes jump and draw her pistol.

Gold letters appeared in midair:

Achievement Earned - Savior of the Lost.

She poked the placard. "Saved all five hundred captives aboard the *Scarlet Saber*."

"Oh wow," said Nighthawk. "Cool! We didn't lose any."

"You're welcome," said Angel813. "Two of them kept peeking out to watch the fight and I had to throw orbs at them to make sure they didn't die."

"It never fired backward," said Kavan.

"Splash damage from the missiles." Angel813 examined her fingernails. "You may worship me at your convenience."

Everyone chuckled.

"You should've gone Niath," said Nighthawk.

"Nah." She shook her head, making her long, white hair dance. "Too easy. I'd fall asleep."

Siana emerged from a gap between two rows of vacant stasis pods and walked up to stand nearby with an eerily placid expression. The other former slaves crept out into the open, but stood in place looping small fidgety gestures.

"Damn that's kinda creepy to watch a hundred people all scratch the same way at the same time," said Rallek. "They gotta work on the NPC's idle animations."

Fawkes opened the storage box at the end of the cargo bay, which appeared empty but triggered a quest status update. All the former slaves went from standing around in their irremovable underwear to being dressed in an array of garments from civilian clothing to armor. A few seconds later, 499 of them said 'thank you' at the same time. Siana, now in a set of medium armor of white and violet, stared pleadingly at the group and repeated her request for them to escort her home.

"Yeah," mumbled Fawkes, eyeing the huge group that had spoken in unison. "Just a *little* creepy."

8

COMPLEX

The amount of gunk that could build up inside a coffee grinder over a twenty-four hour period never ceased to amaze Dakota. She perched on a chair, elbow deep in one of the big units, wiping down the chamber while daydreaming about winning ten million dollars and never having to be elbow deep inside a giant coffee machine again.

Some people would say ten mil wouldn't be enough to stop working. She thought those people were stupid. They'd probably burn it all on fancy cars or a giant house, and wind up homeless in four years. Nope. Not Dakota. If she won, she'd take her two-mil cut, or however much remained after taxes, and stick it in the bank. The interest would have to come close or even beat what she got paid now; she'd spend only what she needed to cover rent and bills. She had no need of fancy swag. No longer being chained to a day job would be enough.

"Someone's happy today," said Blake.

"Huh?" She pulled her head out of the machine and looked back at him.

He had a blender jug in each hand, both dripping from being washed. "You're humming."

"Oh. Didn't notice." She grinned. "Yeah, I'm feeling optimistic."

"Nice." He nodded and continued walking over to add the jugs to the stack of eight others. "Hope whatever it is works out for you."

Yeah, me too. She sighed. "It's a long shot."

"That contest in the game of yours?"

"I found the item that starts the mission and got all happy until I figured out that it's pretty easy to find it. The mission itself is impossibly hard."

"Ahh." Blake waved his hand about. "It's like those call-in contests with radio stations. I don't think they're real. My whole life, I've never gotten anything but a busy signal when calling them."

"Oh, ye old man of what... twenty four?"

"Not yet, hon. I'm only twenty-one." He struck a pose. "Don't rush me into the grave just yet."

She laughed and pulled a formerly white towel out of the machine. "Ugh. This machine is the devourer of towels. This is the third one and it's still coming out like I soaked it in brown paint."

Blake tossed her a clean towel. "Don't obsess. The dust is just more coffee. You don't have to get the hopper immaculate as long as you've de-gunked the teeth."

"I guess." She put the grinder module back in and hopped down from the chair.

Blake zipped over to deal with a drive-through customer while she grabbed a large sack of coffee beans and refilled the machine. That done, she resumed her place leaning on the counter and staring at the empty room. Between 2:00 p.m. and 4:30 p.m., the place tended to be dead, though today, she dealt with a scattering of drone orders.

Her brain couldn't let go of the prize mission despite the astronomical odds of actually winning. She kept thinking back to the message in the data pad that mentioned a strange star system with three suns. Via her smartphone, she hopped on the web and started searching. All the posts she found appeared to be people asking if anyone had seen a star system like this, but no one had. Then again, if someone actually *did* find it, why would they post about it? That would be helping nineteen million other people chase down a prize that you'd gotten one step closer to. No, if anyone had already located that star system, they'd been smart enough to keep it quiet.

"Grr," she muttered.

A few people did post the message in the data pad naively asking for help figuring it out. She read it over and over again, but other than referring to a three-sun system where the center one had a blue tint, it offered no additional clues other than a string of randomness at the bottom.

...GYA4865505052454957ZGH32FZR7090555552455156GHR...

After almost an hour of staring at it, she started to wonder if the apparently meaningless line was the real clue. Excitement surged in her blood. She hunched over the screen, staring at the text, more convinced than ever it might have more importance than some 'flavor text' illustrating a communication link failure.

She plugged in her headphones and called Eric.

"Hey, babe. What's up? You still at work?"

"Yeah. I was just thinking about that mission. Can't find anything about a three-star system."

"I dunno," said Eric. "I'm starting to wonder if CSI announced the prize as an advertising gimmick and they don't really want to have to actually give the money away."

"Still, I'm trying."

Eric muttered something too low to make out. "Yeah, well. If anyone found it, it's not as if they'd share. Pirates don't give away their treasure maps."

"Right. So I was staring at the text in that datapad. I think that random string at the bottom might not be so random."

"What do you mean? They put that sorta thing all the time at the bottom of text messages that get cut off."

She nodded, not that he could see. "Yeah, I know. But... that's a great way to hide something by putting it in text everyone will dismiss as being there only for flavor. People are all scrambling to find the three-star system but that could be a total misdirection thing. What if this string is the real clue?"

"Hmm. Hang on, let me pull it up."

She stared at it. The middle part stood out to her. ZGH32FZR. The string had three letters in the beginning, GYA, and three letters at the end, GHR. *Hmm... that's weird. What if*—she gasped with realization. "The letters are formatting!"

"What?" asked Eric.

"There's three letters at both ends and in the middle surrounding 32." She shifted her lips back and forth while thinking. "32 is an ASCII space. Maybe this is two values separated by a space. The alphanumerics in this string are placeholders or separators. Ignore them, look at the numbers?"

"You think they're using ASCII code?" Eric laughed. "Babe, it's 2031. Who would bother whipping out an ancient set of character codes."

"A company with ten million bucks on the line and a habit of making Easter eggs about ancient computer games. That's who." She grabbed a napkin and a pen and wrote down the string. "You said CSI was going to make this a bitch, right? Who in their right mind would even think of ASCII codes?"

"Language, please," yelled Hal from the back room.

"Sorry," shouted Dakota while jotting down numbers. *Ignore the GYA. 48 ASCII is a 0. 65 ASCII is, umm, capital A. 50 is 2... twice in a row. 52 is 4, 45 is a period, 49 is 1 and 57 is 9, then more letters.* "Eric, does 0A224.19 mean anything to you? It almost looks like coordinates or something."

He remained silent for almost a minute before blurting, "Holy shit you're right! That matches the format for a grid reference to the star map. Or at least half of one. Where'd you get that from?"

She explained the translation while continuing to jot down the rest of the string.

"Damn!" said Eric. "The string is a map reference. Wow I'm rusty as hell with ASCII."

"Aren't you a programmer?" she asked, raising one eyebrow.

He laughed. "No, I do tech support. I haven't even looked at ASCII since school. Let me pull up a chart."

"No need. I've finished. I was right. The letters are just spaces to separate the ASCII codes. It's 0A224.19 FZ774.38."

"Okay, the star map," said Eric. "It's numbered by X/Y axes starting at 01, counting up to 09 before going to 0A through 0Z, then 10, 11, 12 etcetera to 1A, 1B and so on. 0A is the tenth row down from the top. FZ in the X coordinate is almost all the way on the right side, so we're looking at going pretty much to the far southeast corner of known space."

"Long ride then..."

"It's worse. That's the home area of the Kazalor."

She cringed. Player characters could choose them as a race, but if many people did, they didn't often travel far. Fawkes couldn't remember ever seeing a player-character Kazalor. However, they turned up often enough as hostile NPCs. Their society emphasized strength and warfare. They walked erect on two legs but had four arms, each with three fingers. Tough, alligator-like hide covered them from head to toe. The average Kazalor stood close to seven feet tall with wide shoulders. Most annoying of all, their gemlike eyes reacted to heat as well as visual light, making them the most difficult race to hide from.

While not 'evil' per se, they had a highly aggressive nature and used combat to solve even the most trivial of problems. Not to mention, they tended to regard humans as an inferior species, akin to the way a person might regard a talking dog. Dealing with them in large numbers would *not* be fun. If Axillon99 had been reality, even ten million bucks wouldn't have been enough for her to go anywhere near their home world. She'd rather die than wind up as an alien's 'pet human.' Of course, enslavement never happened to player characters in a video game. Also, death in a virtual world didn't hurt much, and didn't last long.

She squealed and bounced on her toes.

Blake stared at her.

Dakota pointed at him. "Erase that sight from your memory. I did *not* just squee like a tween."

Blake tilted his head.

"I mean it!" She stomped her boot.

"Fine, fine. I did not just see a little girl receive a unicorn for her birthday."

She glared at him. "I did not squee *that* loud."

Blake wandered off to the back room, whistling to himself.

"So, okay. Don't email this to anyone. We'll share with the group the next time we're all online."

Dakota grinned. "Yep. Don't want someone at the NSA stealing our prize money. Oh wait, they already heard this phone call."

"Paranoid much?"

She tapped her fingers on the counter. "Just being pragmatic, and a bit sarcastic."

"A bit?" Eric's voice conveyed a giant smile.

"Dakota, are you on the phone?" asked Hal.

She jumped at having been snuck up on, whipping around and planting her butt against the counter, hand over her chest. "Crap, you scared me."

Hal folded his large, muscular arms.

"Yeah. Sorry. Place was empty." She leaned her head closer to the mic on the wire by her right breast. "Gotta go."

"Later, babe," said Eric.

Hal's stern look softened. "Try not to make a habit of it. Yes, I know the place was empty."

"Sorry, Hal." She stuffed the phone back in her pocket.

"Incoming." The boss nodded toward the door.

A thin, pale guy with a narrow face and sharp nose entered and sidled up to the counter. His long, black coat looked expensive.

Dakota smiled. "Good afternoon. Can I get something started for you?"

He stared at her. "Well, you've already got *me* started. What's a beautiful girl like you doing in a place like this?"

She kept up her plastic smile while daydreaming about pickpocketing limpet mines into this douchebag's briefcase. "Making coffee."

Hal edged closer like a protective dad.

The man leaned back. "Uhh, flat white with an extra shot."

Dakota twitched at the word 'extra shot,' remembering the idiot from two days ago. Still, she kept on smiling while tapping the order into the terminal. "Can I add anything else for you, or is that it?"

The customer's mouth opened. He glanced at Hal, closed his mouth, then said, "No, that's it, thanks."

"$9.85." Dakota smiled for real.

After the man paid and wandered off to the left awaiting his drink, she thought of limpet mines and made a soft explosion noise.

9

REALISM

Despite knowing that she wouldn't be able to make any progress on her own with the prize quest, Dakota still couldn't wait to get home from work so she could log in to Axillon99. Believing she'd figured out the first clue charged her with enthusiasm and made her want to be in the game world even if she wound up doing random crap.

The urge to log in made the last hours of her shift feel like she'd been there for since the dawn of recorded time. As 10:00 p.m. approached, each new customer that walked in triggered a progressively stronger internal groan of annoyance.

At 9:38, a thirtyish man with long brown hair in a blue wool coat and cap glided in the door. He shot a cursory glance around at the shelves full of decorative mugs, snacks, coffee beans, and other kitsch before approaching the counter and nervously smiling at her. A fringe of beard—a sad attempt at a goatee—surrounded his mouth. It looked more like he had little ability to grow facial hair and hadn't shaved in weeks.

"Hey," said the man. "I'm Michael."

"Hi, Michael. Welcome to the Amazon Café." Dakota tried to stop thinking about the game and give the customer her full attention. "What can I get started for you?"

He rocked heel-to-toe for a moment while looking over the menu screens along the wall behind her. "Are you eighteen yet?"

She blinked. "Umm, what?"

Michael shifted his gaze from the menus to her. "I mean, you're really pretty. If you're too young, I don't want to think certain things."

Okay, that's completely effing weird. Freaks come out at night.

The muscles in her back tightened. She cast a furtive glance sideways, hoping Hal heard that and would walk out to the front. He didn't usually work the closing shift, but they had a regional manager coming by in a few days for a routine inspection. For a moment, she considered claiming to be sixteen, but chickened out at the worry this creep might actually be hoping she *was* under-age. The more she looked at him, the more uncomfortable she became. He seemed like the kind of thirty-something who still lived in his mother's basement—and buried the bodies in her backyard. Her hand edged to her hip, where the CL32 heavy laser pistol wasn't.

"Nah, I'm a couple years past that point," she said with a fake chuckle. Hopefully, if she played along, the guy wouldn't snap and do something crazy. Again, she shot a glance at the door to the back room. *Come on, Hal.*

"You look good then." He smiled, leaning one elbow on the counter. "Got any plans later? I know this nice Italian place."

She shifted her weight from leg to leg. "I, umm, already had stuff to do."

His stare raked over her chest and slid downward, as uncomfortable as a physical touch. "I understand. Another time then?"

"Can I get a drink started for you?"

"It's all right. I don't think you'll get in trouble for being friendly." The man started to reach for her hand, but froze as the back door flapped open.

Hal wandered out, deliberately not looking at them, carrying a huge tub of ice as easily as if he held an empty Styrofoam cooler. The man might've been short, but he had biceps the size of a normal person's thighs. He strolled past Dakota to the end of the counter on her right, set the tub up top, and began scooping ice into the hatch. Usually, everyone dumped it in to save time. She mentally grinned at him and shifted her attention back to the creep.

"Did you decide on anything yet?" asked Dakota.

"Uhh, let me get an extra-large dark roast, light and sweet." He turned enough to move Hal out of his field of view, but his body language had stiff-ened to match Dakota's nervousness.

She hurriedly prepared the coffee and rang it up. He paid with cash, including a small scrap of paper with a phone number on it. She pretended not to notice it and stuffed it in the drawer with the money before handing him change. He winked at her while walking backward two steps, then turned and took a seat at a table by the entrance.

Dakota took a step to her left to hide behind the giant coffee grinder.

"You okay?" half-whispered Hal.

She crept over to stand beside him with her back to the room. "There's something off about that guy. Thanks."

He nodded, continuing to scoop ice into the freezer under the countertop.

She stood close to Hal for a moment or two before her hands stopped shaking. With the place closing in fifteen minutes, she ran around cleaning up. At one point when she looked up at the seating area, she caught the guy aiming his cell phone at her.

"Fucking creep," she whispered, and ducked.

Hal whirled to stare at her. He apparently noticed the cell phone as well. Rather than harp at her language, he dropped the ice scoop and stormed out from behind the counter. Dakota huddled out of sight behind the espresso machine.

"Sir, I'm going to have to ask you to leave," said Hal.

"Uhh, yeah man. No problem."

A chair scraped the tiles. Sneakers squelched across the room, and the front door squeaked. Dakota peeked up over the counter, watching the guy walk off to the right while Hal stood inside the door with his arms folded over his chest. Once the creep walked past the end of the windows out of sight, Hal returned to the counter, shaking his head.

"Some people..." He angled his head toward her. "You okay?"

"Yeah. Little on edge, but, nothing that hasn't happened before."

Hal sighed.

"Sorry about the F-bomb."

He chuckled. "Exigent circumstances. Figured you did that on purpose so I'd look and catch him."

"Brazen son of a—"

Hal's eyebrows went up.

"Biscuit." She winked.

Hal's baritone laugh followed him into the back room.

At least Trini's off tonight. Wondering if that guy would've gone after the actual teenager made her skin crawl—never mind that the girl was both innocent and skittish. Dakota broke down the milk foam machine to clean the parts, all the while thinking about that alley in the game and how much it had reminded her of the street where she'd nearly been date raped. She started slamming parts around as fear gave way to anger.

Hal emerged from the back, pushing a broom. At a loud *clank*, he gave her another 'you okay?' look. She sighed, nodded, and tried to calm down. That the game so closely matched *that* street unsettled her almost as much as this guy had. It had taken her two years, but by eighteen, she'd thought she'd gotten over it.

Eventually, happy thoughts of winning a crapton of money distracted her back to looking forward to getting home and immersing herself once more in the virtual world of Axillon99. She finished cleaning the machines while Hal scrubbed down the tables out front.

Soon, she had her coat on and went outside. Hal leaned past the door to the back room, reaching to kill the lights before following her and locking the door.

"Night, Hal. See you tomorrow."

He looked around. "You want me to walk with you?"

She considered it, but didn't spot any signs of trouble. Hundreds of times, she'd walked the few blocks back to her apartment building without a problem. He had a forty-minute drive home. Though he meant well, she cringed at his implication a woman couldn't be safe without a man around. "I should be okay; it's only a couple blocks."

"I don't mind. You sure?" He summoned a fatherly smile.

"Yeah." She patted him on the arm. "Thanks for chasing him off."

"All right. Be safe."

Dakota started off to the left. "Thanks. You too."

Walking the four blocks down and two over to her apartment had been something she'd done over and over again without even thinking twice about it. Getting hit on by guys at work had happened before, irritatingly often, but none of them had been so unsettling. Her mind ran away with itself, conjuring up a waking nightmare of everything from him slipping her a drugged drink for a one-night conquest to winding up trapped in a basement sex dungeon.

"Ugh." She rubbed her face. "I've been watching too many bad movies."

When she reached the first cross street, she glanced around for cars. Her heart about stopped when she caught sight of Michael approaching from behind. He had his head down, eyes on his phone, but an unsettling quality to his body language made it clear he'd followed her. She scurried across the street, moving up to a brisk pace a little shy of jogging.

At 10:08 p.m., the moonlit streets had far more shadows than people. The strike of her sneakers on the sidewalk went off like cannon blasts in the silence. His scuffing footfalls increased in speed to match hers.

Dakota fidgeted at her hip, desperate for the CL32 to be real. They hadn't quite been able to produce laser pistols outside of video games and movies yet, but an ordinary firearm would've been just fine. At that moment, she didn't much care how difficult the process of buying one had become in New York. Almost no civilians had one legally. She tugged out her cell phone and sent Eric a ‹Someone's following me› text.

Before panic built to the point she broke out in a full on sprint, she made a random left turn down a street that didn't go toward her apartment building. Finding it devoid of people made her gut sink like a lead weight, but she kept going. Her mind raced for something to do.

I'll duck into a random building so he thinks I live there. She gazed around at the high-rises. *Will anyone hear me if I scream?*

Michael's dark-coated form appeared at the corner, but he kept going straight, still staring at his phone, not even looking in her direction for a second.

‹Babe, you ok? Need 911?›

Confused, Dakota stopped, and stood with her back to the wall of a building, staring at the intersection where the guy had walked right on by. It took her a moment to find the courage, but she crept back to the corner and peered around.

He'd gone another block down by the time she got eyes on him. She clung to the cold stone, watching him, barely breathing, as he wandered over to a black BMW and got in. Doubt swirled around her head. Had he followed her or had they merely been going in the same direction? But why would he still be there, behind her, fifteen minutes after he'd been kicked out of the café? *Of course* he had to be following her.

She looked down at her phone and typed with her thumbs. ‹Nah @ 911. He's gone.›

Dakota waited motionless, huddled in the shadow of the high rise until the BMW went by. She imagined having a gun, pointing it at the guy if he tried to grab her. Combat in the game had enough realism to it that she felt pretty confident in her ability to handle a firearm. She'd read a few posts about players whose characters had martial arts skills, and the players wound up learning it, too. The line between game and reality had become quite thin. Some places had even started using the Neurona helmets for training—especially pilots, cops, and soldiers.

She gripped a nonexistent weapon and clutched it to her chest, daydreaming about being Fawkes, who didn't fear stupid creeps following her home. Fawkes would've *Flickered*, appeared behind him, and put a knife to his throat. She'd have scared him so bad he'd never have done anything like that to another woman.

Grinning, Dakota aimed her non-pistol at the street. Lasers had no recoil, and hit wherever the weapon pointed. Bullets didn't quite do that, but if she had to shoot someone for real, it's not as if she'd be sniping someone from far off. No, she'd be close enough to have the creep's hand at her throat when she pulled the trigger.

When the BMW disappeared around a turn some ten blocks or so away, she let off a slow exhale of relief. The idea of trying to get a real gun didn't seem like such a bad one. Of course, the way things always went down, someone would try to attack her and she'd be the one who landed in jail for defending herself. It always seemed like the woman wound up getting punished.

Grumbling, she ducked out of her hiding spot and hurried home.

10

FARMING

Over the next two days, Dakota's hypervigilance while going back and forth to work lessened somewhat. It helped that she had opening shifts Wednesday and Thursday, 6:00 a.m. to 3:30 p.m. Going home in broad daylight eased her nerves. Much to her relief, she hadn't spotted Michael again, nor did she mention it to anyone other than Eric. The only person she had in a close enough circle of trust was her brother Nebraska, but if she told him about it, he'd grab his boys and go roaming around to kick the ass of some random dude in a black BMW.

Eric stood right at the edge of that circle. On one hand, she wanted to confide in him how freaked out she was about the whole thing, but hesitated out of not wanting to weaken her 'counterculture fringe girl' persona. She laughed to herself, wondering where Dakota Marx ended and Fawkes began. Or for that matter, how a barista at an Amazon Café with a computer science degree wound up as some crusader for the people against greedy corporations.

She'd done a few things out on the net in the name of the little person, mostly defacing corporate websites and wiping out a database or two. Back in college, she'd gotten into a group that called itself Anonymouse—a nod to the more famous hacker group, but one specifically focused on making life annoying for a particular company that started off as an animation studio and then tried to buy the rest of the world.

About the legally worst thing they did wound up being somewhere between leaking financial reports that played small havoc with stocks and launched a handful of insider trading investigations, and publishing the home addresses of some Big Oil policymakers who they believed responsible for a massive pipeline spill that left about twenty-four percent of the state of North

Dakota uninhabitable. The rest of her group didn't care to go after the oil companies because they all figured fossil fuels would run out by 2040 and then humanity would have no choice but to do something else.

After all, said a guy she had only known as Specter, *there had been only so many dinosaurs.*

So, for two frustrating days, Dakota suffered a seemingly endless work shift followed by a scary jog home only to be unable to pursue the prize quest due to the absence of Kavan and Angel813. Nighthawk showed as online every time she logged in, which got her wondering if he might be an advanced AI. He'd been with Kavan from the start, and the two were always together. Since Kavan's player, William, had enough money to buy a ship with real cash, maybe Nighthawk was some kind of rare helper bot you could purchase.

She dismissed that idea. A helper NPC wouldn't go off questing when Kavan was offline, nor would he hang out with her. Plus, she'd never seen any advertising for anything like that. If the game had that option, it would be spammed everywhere.

Conversationally, Nighthawk always had seemed a bit off, but not so much so that the AI theory gained ground. A lot of her jokes sailed over his head, and he always laughed at crude humor, swear words and fart jokes. It drove her crazy not to share what she'd discovered with the map coordinates, but she and Eric had agreed not to bring it up until tonight, Friday night.

Wednesday after work, her frustration at not being able to go anywhere with the 'big quest' boiled over into a bizarre random tangent. She created a second character, a female Niath auramancer. The starting city, a floating platform full of winged angels nestled in a vast sky of purple-pink clouds with only small bits of visible terrain below, made her feel as though she'd switched genres from a spaceship/sci-fi game to a fantasy MMO. She opted to do the 'learn how to be a Niath' quest, which started her character off as a six-year-old child and ran through the basics of control. After about a half-hour of quests as a little kid, she advanced to stage two (around twelve years old by human standards). A teacher led her class up to the roof of a three-story building to practice flying for the first time. Adjusting to having two extra limbs that obeyed her mental command had been surreal enough, but when she jumped off that roof, the realism of the interface kicked her square in the frontal cortex. She lost all sense of anything but 'holy shit I'm falling!' and screamed until she blacked out.

When she regained consciousness, she found herself staring at the green letters 'session interrupted' floating in a field of black. She'd fainted for real. Annoyed at herself, she logged back in to find her tweenaged Niath safe in the arms of a teacher, who carried her back up to the roof to try again.

Nerves rattling, she approached the edge and let her toes curl over it. For whatever reason, the Niath had a super-casual relationship with clothing, and wore airy, thin garments that didn't cover much. Staring down at a child-body she hadn't seen in about ten years felt so bizarre she used that to distract her from the concept of willingly jumping off a building. Jaw clenched, she spread her wings, let gravity pull her forward, and jumped like a kid learning to dive into a pool.

The wind caught her wings; falling became gliding. Before smacking into the street, she pulled up and glided higher, feeling out the interaction between physically moving her wings and the game responding to her simple desire of wanting to go in a particular direction.

Eventually, flying became as automatic as walking. When the tutorial ended, her adult Niath stepped into the city to begin her journey of leveling. Dakota felt 'unclean' at having made a character who used magic, and being level one again stank. However, the newness of the environment plus flying, plus relying on magic instead of a laser pistol and stealth was so different and intriguing that she stayed up too late.

The next day, she shivered constantly, her brain not quite having been able to divorce itself from the feeling of wearing Niath-style clothing that universally left her back exposed. Most Niath men went bare-chested unless they wore armor, the women had garments that attached to a neck ring and covered their front. Some of the Niath armor protected the back, but having to accommodate wings made it expensive.

As a starting auramancer, she had a few neat spells: a temporary armor buff, one that put enemies to sleep for a little while, and a couple different forms of healing, along with a fairly weak attack spell based on 'un-healing.' Fawkes had to struggle to deal with a group of three or more enemies at once when alone, but despite the weaker damage output, the auramancer simply put the extras to sleep and whittled down the one while self-healing. It took three times as long to kill anything, but felt super easy. Also, the auramancer's spells would get more potent as she gained levels, which made her less dependent on equipment. She wouldn't be as crippled as Fawkes had been while stuck with a crappy gun.

On Thursday night, Dakota contemplated buying passage to the nearest civilized planet around where the coordinates pointed, but the info text showed the starting quest there as level fifty, plus the population breakdown of ninety-two percent Kazalor scared her off. It didn't strike her as likely Fawkes ran any risk of winding up on the end of a leash. She figured having a character locked up would be a sure way to piss players off and make them cancel their subscriptions. Mostly, she didn't feel like dealing with NPCs talking down to her constantly.

The highlight of the past three days at work had been a news report on the TV about a group of super-hardcore Axillon99 players who wore adult diapers and binge-ate so they could play for extreme stretches. She worried for a bit that crazies of that magnitude would run off with the prize money, but the interview never mentioned it—only their drive to be the first ship crew to beat Tetratheon, the current 'big bad' tier two raid boss.

Friday, she rushed home after work and spent the next twenty minutes warming and eating a ramen packet while trying to decide between doing missions as Fawkes or playing around with the Niath, Triani (she had not mentioned this to Trini at the café) to kill time until everyone showed up.

Right when her butt hit the bed, a lingering bit of ramen flavor still in her throat, she decided to focus on Fawkes. The crew wanted to raid someday, so she figured she'd get one character to sixty before throwing large amounts of time on another one. So, she hopped in on Fawkes and burned two-ish hours running around the city of Prosperion (where the crew had last landed), doing missions. She wound up getting one that unexpectedly turned into an 'assault a room full of bad guys' situation when a little NPC boy she had to rescue from a pack of mercenaries proved impossible to do with stealth alone. The instant she took the child out of the little room the mercs kept him in, the whole place erupted like a smacked hornets' nest.

Ugh. I really goddamn hate this bullshit. Like these guys are all psychic and just know *I let the kid out of the room.*

At least this boy followed her in silence. Not like a similar quest a few planets back where another kid screamed her head off the whole time, attracting the kidnappers right to them. Of course, her being a preprogrammed NPC, no amount of 'shut up kid' worked. The developers had designed her to keep screaming to force several combats along the way.

Fawkes sighed.

The small son of a local wealthy executive looked up at her with silent innocence on his face. Fawkes peered around the doorjamb of the little room he'd been locked in at a warehouse with about fifteen armed and armored people, including two Kazalor. Their armor stood out as unmistakable due to the overdone pointy bits. That they stood a foot taller than humans helped too. And well, the four-arm thing was pretty obvious. Blocky jaws with bony spikes made her hope dearly that the developers did not program what it felt like to experience their bite. With any luck, it would just use the 'you've taken damage' wiffle bat smack.

She opened a crew chat box, focused her attention on it (which would keep her voice out of the ambient game world) and said, "Hey Nighthawk, you busy?"

The over-handsome face of their gunslinger/fighter pilot appeared a second or two later. "Umm, just grinding a bit, why?"

"I'm stuck on a mission. Gotta get this kidnapped kid out of a warehouse, and there's like a million level forties in my way."

"Oh, sure, no problem. Toss me an invite. Be right there," said Nighthawk.

She poked the virtual holographic display to send a group invite. Her portrait appeared in the top left of her vision with a small green star at the corner indicating group leader. Nighthawk's somewhat smaller portrait appeared below. She figured Angel813 spent most fights staring at the party list watching health bars go up and down. While playing her Niath, she fell into a random group and learned that abilities other than firing a weapon could be targeted at the portraits. That made it easier during chaotic fights to be able to find allies.

That had been *weird*. Fawkes never had people begging her to group with them to do lowbie missions. She couldn't walk within a quarter mile of a village as a Niath auramancer without being spammed. The first time she broke her 'I quest alone' rule happened purely to wind up in a group so the incoming requests would stop. The soldier she'd teamed up with killed things way faster than she could, so she focused on healing him and using crowd control. It wound up being *much* less tedious than soloing, so she kept going.

"Oh, wow, you're not that far away," said Nighthawk over group chat. "What's going on now?"

"I'm hiding in the room they had the kid locked in. Soon as I finished the 'Hey I'm going to get you out of here and bring you home' dialogue, all the mercs went on high alert."

Nighthawk made an *ahh* sound. "Oh, you're doing *that* mission. The Prince of War or something, right? His mother owns that company that makes space fighters and weapons."

"Yeah."

"No wonder. That's a soldier mission. They force you to go all commando to get the kid out, but the little guy's a dumbass. You're *supposed* to shoot your way in. I bet you snuck in, didn't you?"

"Yeah." Fawkes grumbled.

"More dudes spawn as soon as you activate the kid. That's why you have so many roaming around at once. It's difficult because he just stands next to you and gets shot by accident."

"Ugh. Why do they make the NPCs so stupid?"

"Easy though in a group. Hang out in that room and I'll clear the dudes out of your way."

"Umm, okay."

Nighthawk hummed to himself. "Oh, the mission reward's not going to be any good for you, but if you wanna save it for my—I mean Kavan, I'll give you credits for it."

"My?" asked Fawkes.

"My buddy." Nighthawk grinned. "We live near each other."

Fawkes waited. She tried to make small talk with the boy, but the maybe-eight-year-old's dialogue consisted of 'Thank you for helping me,' 'Are we there yet,' and a whiney 'I wanna go home.'"

Fortunately, the way he'd been programmed, no matter what happened, he'd not stray from her side, so she hunkered down inside the storage closet. After a few minutes, she glanced down at the boy. He looked *so* real. It bothered her like an itch beneath the skin she couldn't scratch that he acted so much like a computer program. His dark brown hair and roundish face somewhat reminded her of Nebraska when he'd been that age. Her brother also went through a period of rather bad nightmares at the time. Despite only having three years on him, she still wound up playing Mom.

On a lark, she picked the boy up. The game's physics engine allowed it, and the kid didn't protest being carried. He even clung like a small boy should. Perhaps the 'child' flag for his character did that.

Hmm. He's quiet enough... I wonder if I could sneak out with him.

She engaged stealth and her body went semi-transparent, but the boy's didn't.

"Damn. They'd probably shoot at him."

With a resigned sigh, she dropped stealth and paced around inside the little room.

A few minutes later, Nighthawk said, "Okay. I'm outside the building."

She opened the minimap in the top right corner of her field of vision. Sure enough, a blue diamond indicating a friendly party member showed up by the warehouse door. "Cool. So, umm. What's the plan?"

"Well, if you just want to be done with this quest, I figured I'd clear the room for you and you could walk out. These dudes are four levels under me."

She blinked and glanced at his portrait. "Holy crap you hit forty-four already?"

"Yeah." He shrugged.

Fawkes put the boy down on his feet. He dutifully stood by her side, staring up at her with a 'please help me' wide-eyed face. "If I ever spawn for real, and my kid makes this face at me, I'm so screwed. I'd give him whatever he wanted."

"Huh?" asked Nighthawk.

"The way this kid's looking at me is making me feel super guilty and I haven't even done anything."

"Oh. Okay. Here I come."

Fawkes dropped into stealth and peeked out of the room.

Nighthawk, in a new set of shiny dark-grey armor with red highlights—and a cowboy hat—strolled in the door with a confident swagger. A whitish shimmer around him appeared when he activated *Showdown*. "Howdy, boys. Don't take this personal like."

He drew his pistols and waved his arms back and forth, sending a withering rain of red laser fire into the air. Answering green and blue streaks of energy streamed back at him, but nothing hit. Eight of the fifteen mercenaries dropped within seconds. Red critical-hit damage numbers appeared over most of them. Nighthawk advanced in a slow, purposeful stride, picking off the remaining mercs with two or three shots apiece.

Fawkes sniped one in the back, her ambush taking him out in one hit. Since Nighthawk had gotten all the mercs' attention, she didn't lose stealth and managed a second ambush before he finished off the rest of them. The instant the last mercenary 'died,' the boy's pleading 'help me' expression changed to a more natural neutral one.

She walked out from the back room with the boy hovering at her side, the child oblivious to the spread of corpses lying around. "Holy shit…"

Nighthawk spun to flash her a silly grin. "Umm, what?"

"You wiped the room in like fifteen seconds."

"New cooldown. *Six and Six*," said Nighthawk. "I can hit up to twelve targets and get automatic head shots. Can only use it once every twenty minutes though. Dunno why they called it six."

"Probably a reference to Old West six-guns."

"Huh? Oh… right."

She whistled at the destruction. "Still nice. 'Slingers are amazing at AOE. I don't get anything like that."

"That sucks," said Nighthawk.

"Yeah well. My single-target's a little better… eventually. Thanks for the assist." She held up the boy by one arm like a sack of potatoes. "Gonna go turn this in and head back to the ship. Almost time for the others to log in." She lowered the boy back to stand on his feet.

"Cool." Nighthawk nodded. "See you there."

He summoned a silver motorcycle and zoomed off. Fawkes activated her bike, and the boy climbed on behind her without being prompted to. She drove back to the Security Force building where she'd gotten the mission from; evidently, those mercenaries had been too well armed for the local police to bother with—or so said the quest story.

Upon turning the quest in, the boy gave her a huge hug. "Thank you for saving me!"

The joyful look on his face choked her up a little, despite his artificiality.

As Nighthawk said, the mission reward took the form of a nice blue-quality heavy-armor chest-piece. The game offered a choice between the same armor with stats for a tank or stats for a damage-dealing soldier. She picked the tank one, which appeared in her inventory. The interface showed it with a sell value of 11,500 credits, but she'd give it to Kavan anyway. By the time he hit level forty and could do that quest for himself (or its equivalent on some other planet) he could take the damage-statted version and wind up with both.

The experience reward left her a little past halfway to thirty-nine.

Normally, quest rewards like that couldn't be traded to other players 'just because.' It didn't make any logical sense in reality that she couldn't hand it to someone else, but she figured the developers put it in to prevent twinking (loading a low-level character up with high-end gear). However, to encourage people into forming starship crews, that loot rule didn't apply among members of the same crew.

She headed back to the *Stormbringer* and used the food printer to create a decadent dark chocolate mousse cake. Being able to eat anything and everything without caring about calories had been the best part of the game—until she'd tried flying as a Niath.

Eventually, Rallek logged in and appeared out of thin air in the next seat. "Hey."

"Hey yourself." She stuck a giant forkful of sin in her mouth.

"You tell anyone yet?" asked Rallek.

"Nope. Bitchin' hard keepin' my lips sealed." She grinned.

Kavan's name lit up in the roster when he came online. He walked in from the corridor leading to the bridge soon after. "Hey guys. How goes it?"

"It goes," said Rallek. "We've got something cool to share once everyone's here."

"Oh?" Kavan's eyebrows went up. "Something to do with that money quest?"

"Yeah." Fawkes nodded.

Kavan barely suppressed an eye roll. "You know that in all probability, that whole thing is a BS gimmick."

"Here." Fawkes made a gesture like she pulled something out of her pocket, and a full-size combat armor breastplate appeared in her hand.

Kavan took it. His initial surprise shifted to an expression of *OMG* after he examined the stats. The white-plastic looking armor in his hand swapped places with the dull olive-drab chestplate he had been wearing, and the old one vanished into his inventory. "Damn, Fawkes... this is ten levels better than what I had... and a blue."

"You may express your adoration for my awesomeness at your leisure." She held out a hand like a queen awaiting a kiss on her ring.

Rallek and Kavan chuckled.

Nighthawk walked in from the boarding ramp and hit the food printer for a monstrous bowl of chicken nuggets and fries. When Kavan smirked at him, he shrugged. "What? It's fake food."

"Great," said Rallek. "As soon as Christina gets here, we can start."

"Who's Christina?" asked Nighthawk around a mouthful.

"Angel813," said Fawkes.

"Oh. Cool. You guys traded real names?"

She nodded.

"I'm Shawn," he said.

"Dakota," said Fawkes.

"Eric," said Rallek.

In a shimmering swirl of blue squares, Angel813 appeared in the main room. Up until now, Fawkes had always assumed the 813 had some personal significance to Christina, but after playing the Niath, she figured there'd been 812 other people at the time who had tried to name their character 'Angel.'

"So what's this announcement?" asked Kavan, still admiring his new chest armor.

"Right." Rallek stood. "We—mostly Fawkes—have figured out the clue in the datapad."

Nighthawk's eyes bulged. "Really? You found that three-star system?"

The skepticism in Kavan's expression lessened a little.

"Possibly," said Fawkes. "But that could be a red herring."

"A what?" asked Nighthawk.

"Fake information." Fawkes grinned, and explained how the apparently meaningless string of numbers at the end of the message made sense in ASCII as a map reference. "I'm not sure if there's a trinary star system at that location, but a coordinate is a lot more to go on than trying to find some blue star."

Even Angel813 appeared interested. "Wait, you're serious?"

Rallek nodded. "Yep. The bad news is, it will send us into Kazalor space."

"Hmm." Kavan tapped at a control console on the giant, round table and opened a star map display. "Give me those coordinates again?"

Fawkes read them off her notes.

With a faint chirp, a small crosshair appeared in the lower right corner of the map. The view zoomed in on a brownish planet inside a blue circle highlight.

"AG148," said Kavan. A text box appeared indicating the planet as an agriculture world. The 'economy,' 'law,' and 'danger' ratings all showed a dreadfully tame planet.

Nighthawk yawned. "That place looks boring as hell."

"Hmm." Rallek opened a floating window and attacked it with a flurry of finger pokes, typing. "Some people play this game as a trading thing, moving cargo from planet to planet. Buy food on an agricultural world like this, sell it on an industrial planet, and so on."

"Bo-oo-rring," singsonged Nighthawk.

"AG148 appears to be a randomly-generated world by name, but it also has a mostly human population despite being deep in Kazalor space." Rallek looked up from his screen. "The capital city is Prakash."

"So?" asked Angel813.

Rallek laughed in Eric's voice. "One of the game's creators is named Prakash." He shifted forward in his seat. "The capital's surrounded by a forested area with fast-respawning hostile aliens. There's a bunch of posts about it being a prime spot to grind kills to level up from thirty to forty for people who hate doing quests. Takes *forever* but it's simple. A couple villages around the edge of the forest all have repeatable 'go forth and kill fifty bad guy' type quests, so you can get mission experience on top of the kill XP."

"So..." Fawkes grinned, licking chocolate off her spoon. "This planet is good for farming in more than one way."

Kavan groaned.

"I think that city being named after one of the primary designers is a giant clue." Rallek pointed at the star map. "We should check it out."

Kavan shrugged. "We don't have a ship mission right now, so... Up to you guys. I still think this prize crap is a load of hooey."

"Oh, come on, William." Fawkes winked. "I know Angel and me are innocent girls, but you can still use bad language in our presence."

"I'm in," said Angel813. "If nothing else, we can kill a couple hours grinding XP. If the farming grounds are as good as Rallek says. Mindless slaughter is a nice break from running around trying to figure quests out."

Nighthawk shrugged. "Sure, why not. But the planet looks like solid boredom."

"Solid boredom?" asked Fawkes.

"Yeah." Nighthawk held his hands up as if cradling a softball. "If boredom existed as a solid... this planet is made out of it."

Rallek laughed. "That could be on purpose. No one would think the place is worth going to."

"Okay then." Kavan stood. "I'll go fly us there."

"Be right back." Nighthawk got a distant look in his eye. "Gotta pee."

He vanished.

FAWKES STOOD BEHIND THE PILOT'S CHAIR AS KAVAN BROUGHT THE *Stormbringer* down into the atmosphere of AG148. The trip into the star system had been nail biting. Six groups of Kazalor pirates rushed toward them, but broke off after a scan revealed no cargo. The potentially hostile ships ranged in level from twelve to forty-five, but the game had enough sense for the pirates to ignore a pointless target. As much as the lore suggested the Kazalor would've abducted a human crew to sell as pets, Fawkes' opinion proved correct. That fate appeared limited to NPCs.

Despite appearing brown on the star map, the visible surface in the viewscreen filled with verdant greenery. Silvery geometric shapes spotted the vegetation here and there, wherever a settlement had sprung up.

They flew for a while, heading for the capital city, Prakash, which jutted up from the vast field of trees and farmland like a mass of crystalline daggers jammed into the ground. A narrow strip of smaller buildings surrounded a city heart of about 150 high-rise towers made from mirror-like crystal. The star port here, despite the size of the city, amounted to a dirt field where pilots put down wherever they felt like it. Fortunately, the *Stormbringer* represented the only player-controlled ship in sight.

Kavan landed in a rectangular patch of brown dirt near a refueling station. "Well, we're here. Now what?"

"Well the clue could be anything," said Rallek. "I'm sure it's going to be in or near this city. Pretty sure this is a static world, but they wanted it to *look* like a randomly generated one."

"Or it *is* random and the city being called Prakash is pulling from a database of names," said Fawkes.

Rallek shot her a 'you traitor!' stare, then laughed.

She strolled down the boarding ramp, boots clanking. A breeze that smelled of manure and vegetation flipped pink hair across her face. "Ugh, this place is *charming*."

"Eww," said Nighthawk. "It smells like crap."

"Welcome to a farm world." Kavan took a deep breath in his nose.

"I don't smell anything," said Angel813.

"Hooray for upgraded helmets," muttered Fawkes. "Remind me again what the upside of these things is? So far it's only been bad smells and uncomfortable chills."

Nighthawk patted his guns. "Special effects are cooler looking, especially for spells."

"Well, the food's better. Login's faster... I'm sure once we get into raid content, we'll appreciate the wider data throughput. No lag when there's a lot of stuff flying around." Rallek followed her down the ramp to the dirt.

"Oh, yeah I guess." She walked out from under the *Stormbringer*, turning as she moved to survey the environment. "Wow. This place looks like a cake slice of New York City dropped square in the middle of uhh... Kansas or something. It's so weird to have big city turn into hayseed farmland so abruptly."

"Yeah." Rallek gazed at the not-too-distant wall of blinding mirror. "Looks like they copied and pasted a section of Thaeleos."

"Hey you're right." Fawkes studied the profile of the building tops long enough to get a sense of nostalgia for the capital city of the human starting planet, where she'd spent her first forty-or-so hours ever playing the game. "I guess it's just the 'human' style of architecture or something."

"It's out of place here." Angel813 shielded her eyes, squinting at the high rises. Her waist-long snowy hair flowed in a graceful wave off to the side. "Every other settlement on this planet is just a collection of portable pods. How did they construct advanced buildings like this?"

"Well, for one thing, this is a video game," said Kavan. "While your logic would make sense in reality, the lack of materials or construction equipment isn't a limiter here."

"But that also makes it stand out more," said Fawkes.

"Hey guys, look!" Nighthawk, a little ways off to the left, pointed at the sky.

Fawkes glanced at where he indicated, and her jaw hung open. A brilliant point of blue light hung over the horizon, flanked by a pair of orange specks. "A trinary star system with blue in the middle!"

After a minute or two of staring at a floating screen, Kavan exhaled, making his lips flutter. "There's nothing on the star map in that direction that's even close."

"Maybe it's not *on* the map?" asked Rallek.

"Let's check it out," said Angel813.

"Right on." Fawkes jogged back to the ship.

The others clambered in behind her, everyone going straight to the bridge.

Kavan powered up the ship and brought it into the air only a few feet, rotating toward the trinary orange-blue-orange system on the horizon. Acceleration pinned bodies to seats as the *Stormbringer* shot skyward, leaving the planet's atmosphere a minute or two later.

"Huh," said Kavan. "That's weird."

"What?" asked Rallek, looking up from an internet window.

"It's gone. I don't see it anymore."

Fawkes leapt out of her chair and ran to the viewscreen, cramming herself as close as she could in the pilot's nook, her hip bumping Kavan's armrest. The trinary system had disappeared. "It's gone..."

"I just said that." Kavan shook his head.

"Systems don't just disappear!" yelled Nighthawk.

"Calm down, it's only a game." Angel813 patted him on the head.

He frowned. "I'm not upset. I was quoting Admiral Torellian from *Fleet Strike*."

"Clearly, none of us have seen that," said Angel813.

"It's not a movie, it's another game." Nighthawk rolled his eyes. "Geez. Only the most popular space sim before Axillon99 came out."

"The space stuff is cool, but I'm more of a raider," said Rallek. "Used to play *ROI*."

"You know, Realms of Infinity is *still* active," said Fawkes.

"What class?" asked Nighthawk. "I played Realms, too."

"Had a level 180 necromancer, and I got a planerunner up to like ninety something."

"Cool." He nodded.

Rallek grinned at him. "Let me guess, you had a hunter no-pet spec?"

Nighthawk's expression went blank. "Yeah, so?"

Angel813 suppressed a giggle.

"Oh, just saying it fits the sort of player who goes gunslinger is all." Rallek winked.

"What's that supposed to mean?" asked Nighthawk.

Kavan glanced at Rallek, a faint note of warning in his expression.

"Oh, just an uncomplicated-to-play ranged damage class is all." Rallek smiled.

"Hang on!" yelled Fawkes. "What if the star system isn't really a star system, but a visual anomaly in the atmosphere?"

"Once more in English?" asked Nighthawk.

"It's not real!" yelled Fawkes, bouncing like a giddy tween. "It's a mirage in the sky pointing us toward something *on the planet*."

"Babe, I hate to break it to you, but *none* of this is real," said Kavan.

She smirked. "You know what I mean."

"Right. Back down we go." Kavan brought the *Stormbringer* around in a 180-degree flat turn and dove once again into the atmosphere.

"Don't land right away," said Rallek in a tone more asking than ordering.

"Can you bring us in to a hover near Prakash, point at the trinary system, and fly that way?"

"Yeah easy." Kavan nodded.

A few minutes later, they glided in as if to land in the same section of star port, but the ship hung in midair about twenty feet off the ground. Kavan swung the nose around until the orange-blue-orange dots appeared on the horizon, and accelerated in that direction. For about twenty minutes, everyone stared in silence at endless rolling plains of wavering grass. Distant mountains grew millimeter by millimeter, shrouded in a canopy of fog and snow.

When operating in an atmosphere, starships behaved more like airplanes than spacecraft. Going past Mach 2 didn't happen often since the ships would break apart. They could only use about 1/100th of the speed they pulled out in space. Kavan and Nighthawk got into a grumbling match about how a ship as sleek and as 'airplane-shaped' as the *Stormbringer* ought to be able to go faster planetside than a boxy one. Nighthawk indignantly pointed out that *Fleet Strike* took a ship's design into account when determining its handling characteristics within an atmosphere. Kavan agreed with him and they both complained about Axillon99 slacking off on design.

"Well, that other game is *only* ship combat. There is no character content really," said Rallek. "CSI's trying to find a balance point between the two, so corners got cut I guess. The game's only been out two years, so give them time. I'm sure they'll add a ship realism patch in at some point."

Fawkes, who hadn't taken her eyes off the viewscreen, caught a glint of metal amid the endless greenery. "What's that?" She pointed.

"Umm." Kavan pushed a series of buttons on the console, which caused a smaller display box to appear at the bottom of the big viewscreen, containing a zoomed-in image of wreckage. "Looks like a crashed heavy fighter."

"Check it out?" asked Rallek. "Kinda weird that it's still sitting there. Player crashes disappear in like a half hour. It's gotta be a quest at least."

"Maybe it's what we're supposed to find," said Fawkes.

"A crash site?" Angel813's eyebrows went up. "Seriously?"

Fawkes faced the crew. "Most of you want to ignore it, right? I bet that's exactly what the designers expected. Precisely because it looks like a waste of time, I think it's the big quest."

Kavan slowed the *Stormbringer* and dropped altitude. "It won't take long to check it out. Who knows? The kid could be right."

"I'm not a kid. I'm twenty-two," said Fawkes.

"You're a kid," said Kavan.

Fawkes leaned on him. "Are you playing a grizzled old pilot Kavan as a character or are you really a grizzled old curmudgeon?"

He laughed while flicking at a silver highlight in his black hair. "Well, Kavan's well into his forties, but I've still got a couple years to go."

"So, like thirty-nine?" Fawkes winked.

"Seven." Kavan brought the ship to a midair halt, extended the landing pads, and brought it straight down to land in the meadow not far from the crash site.

"Stay alert," said Rallek. "If this *is* part of the big quest, investigating this spot could trigger a combat encounter."

"Nothing online about it?" asked Angel813.

"Nope." Rallek shook his head. "Another reason I think Fawkes might have a point. If anyone *did* find this crash site, they haven't made it public."

"There's a leaderboard already," said Kavan. "Shows the five closest crews or players to completing the mission, but no indication of how far on they are. It's only got two names on it and they're marked tied."

"But millions of players have gotten the data pad drop. Aren't we all tied?" asked Nighthawk.

"I doubt just getting the quest in your log counts," said Fawkes. "So at least two groups beat us here."

"You sound so serious, like you really think we have a chance at winning that money." Angel813 shook her head. "It's going to go to the kid of someone who's best friends with a bigwig at CSI."

"Don't the contest rules say employees and family aren't eligible?" asked Rallek.

"Yeah, but the CEO's best friend's kid isn't an employee or family." Angel813 walked around pressing an autoinjector into everyone's arm. The inoculation caused an extra inch of health bar to appear for everyone. "This'll last twenty minutes."

"Neat." Nighthawk pulled his guns, twirled them, and stuffed them back in the holsters. "Let's go."

Kavan led the way down the boarding ramp into waist-high grass. The crumbled remains of a heavy fighter, a small ship barely 1/5th the size of the *Stormbringer* lay slumped about fifty yards away at the end of a quarter-mile of flattened grass.

"Either this thing crashed only an hour ago, or it's part of the mission." Rallek pointed at the swath of ruined vegetation. "Grass doesn't stay crushed forever."

Fawkes let out a cheer at the sight of the tail fin art: an orange-blue-orange trinary star system. "Guys, look at the logo on the tail."

"Whoa..." Rallek jogged over. "Sneaky."

They spent a while searching around the wreckage with little success. Fawkes went for the cockpit, but found it locked. Opaque gold canopy glass gave her a nice view of her distorted reflection, but not a clue as to what lay inside. She plugged in the override kit which started up the hacking mini-game, and displayed a 'network map' full of level eight and nine nodes.

"Holy shit," said Fawkes.

Nighthawk laughed.

"What?" yelled Rallek from beneath a flange of armor some distance behind her.

"Trying to get the cockpit open and... this node. It's an eight. I've never seen one this hard before."

"That's what she said," muttered Angel813.

Nighthawk looked at her in confusion while everyone else except for Kavan laughed.

"Oh, sorry... aren't you and Rallek..." Angel813 gestured back and forth at them.

"Yeah," said Fawkes, staring at the node map while trying to pre-plan the route she'd take to clear it. Three geodesic spheres representing security nodes would send out red lines in an effort to chase her down. If those lines touched her blue one or made it to the CPU node before her, she'd fail the hack and get locked out. "I think I may need to use some software on this one."

"What, you guys are like dating?" asked Nighthawk.

"Yep," said Rallek.

"Cool." Nighthawk squatted to pick up a fragment of electronics with dangling wires. "This is messed up. The ship's bent and damaged and stuff, but there's no burning. It looks like a fake crash."

Rallek abandoned his slab of armor and walked over to the gunslinger. "Probably because this ship didn't crash. They put it here pre-crashed. The game engine didn't render scorching and damage in real time."

"Isn't that a lazy mistake?" asked Angel813.

"Not if they intended it as a clue." Kavan set his hands on his hips and gazed around the crash site. "But this could be us overthinking it."

"The trinary star logo's a bit hard to dispute though," said Rallek.

Fawkes decided to ignore the 'bonus data' nodes that could give cash rewards, start quests, or drop random one-use software hacking tools. She already had a mountain of unused boosts, so missing a chance to get more didn't matter. It irritated her beyond belief to have something called software be a consumable item, since no one except some virus people wrote programs that self-deleted after execution. However, the gamer in her understood the rationale behind them being temporary boosts.

She triggered a *Crypto* soft, which reduced the network's overall level by 1, then a *Freeze* soft for a six-second head start before the security system would start hunting her. With one finger poised over an *Ice Hammer* (another soft that could instantly take over a node without the usual countdown but set off the security), she tapped the first node away from the start point.

The blue line crept up to that node and began filling it up. By some miracle, she didn't set off the security pulse, so the red line remained dormant. Her hacking skills were high for a level thirty-eight character, being at rank seven. Not since she'd first started playing had she dealt with hack equal—or higher than—her skill. Especially after the game-wide nerf that made hacks easier due to player whining.

She tapped the next node on the path to the CPU, and it started to fill in. At the three-quarter mark, the security pulse went off, which would normally start the red line racing outward from any defense nodes, but her *Freeze* kicked in, delaying it by six seconds. The instant the second node became hers, she *Ice Hammered* the next one in line, taking control of it in an instant without having to wait the ten or so seconds a normal capture required.

When the fourth node in the path was halfway hers, three security lines raced out from their starting points, each one taking ownership of any node in its path. They moved way faster than normal, but then again, Fawkes had never tried to hack a level eight terminal before. Maybe that speed *was* normal.

She burned another *Freeze*, which halted the security lines for six more seconds, then spent three *Firewall* softs on unclaimed nodes in the red lines' path. She didn't need to take them over to reach the CPU, but raising their defenses would delay the security pulse by forcing it to capture them instead of simply passing through.

Fifty-two seconds after starting, the CPU finished filling in blue with a red security line maybe ten pixels away from 'zapping' her.

'Access Granted' appeared on the screen along with an 'open/close' switch.

Fawkes sighed with relief and draped herself against the fighter ship. "Wow, holy crap."

"That looked easy," said Rallek, standing alongside her.

"I used up like twelve softs. That's ridiculous." She laughed. "I haven't even used one since level ten. I almost started selling them off. Glad I didn't."

"Well they don't take up any inventory weight." He shrugged. "No reason to sell them."

"They're expensive, even to an NPC vendor." She smiled. "Star Auction is better, but players don't buy hack softs."

He nodded. "Yeah, not many people bother with the hacking system. Their loss."

"You know..." Kavan scratched his head. "I wonder if they did that on purpose to be pricks?"

"Did what?" asked Rallek.

Fawkes smiled, adoring the irony. "Yeah. The developers knew everyone whined about hacking since putting points in it took away from raw combat power... so they made hacking required for the prize money. A giant middle finger to the meter-kiddies."

Angel813 groaned. "Ugh, I hate them."

"Wait..." She squinted at their white-haired Chinese medic. "You know what meter-kiddies are, but you're all into vanity pets?"

"The reason I'm a casual is because I used to be a serious raider." Angel813 rolled her eyes. "Got tired of dealing with the jackasses. This is a game. As soon as it felt more like a second job, I walked. I already *have* a job."

"What guild?" asked Rallek.

"Army of One," said Angel813.

Rallek and Kavan both stared at her as though they'd stumbled across a celebrity at a random coffee shop.

Fawkes' eyebrows flattened. "What?"

"They're the number two guild in the game," said Kavan. "Pro sponsorship and everything. People in that guild basically get paid to play this game."

"Well that explains why she's so damn good," said Nighthawk, a note of awe in his voice.

"Aww, thank you." Angel813 made an 'autograph-singing' gesture. "Really, it's not as fun as it sounds. I could hang with them, but way too much pressure. No one with a day job lasts long."

Fawkes pushed the canopy glass up, exposing a single-seat cockpit containing a skeleton in a flight suit.

"Gah!" Fawkes yelled and jumped back, not mentally prepared to come nose to hole with a skull.

"What?" called Rallek.

"Dead pilot." She clasped a hand over her chest and took a few breaths. "Just caught me off guard."

"What else did you expect to find inside a crashed ship?" Kavan shrugged.

Angel813 peered in. "I'm afraid the pilot's beyond my skill to help."

Everyone chuckled.

After a little rooting around, Fawkes found a data pad in the pilot's jumpsuit. She hit the button on the side, activating a six-inch tall hologram of a thirtyish woman.

"We've spent months tracking these damned pirates, but we're too late. They got their hands on a prototype battlecruiser with a new type of warp drive. Everyone else gave up, but I managed to track the *Reckoning* to a system deep within Kazalor space. I was able to approach undetected, but one fighter isn't going to stand a chance. Their network defenses are surprisingly low for the tech level of that ship, but maybe they just don't know how to use it. The data I recovered points at a research facility at CF204.18 HH313.51, which may hold some clues for discovering how to track this crazy drive. Now, I just need to get out—"

The blue hologram face flashed red along with a warning buzzer.

"Damn. They've noticed me. Fighters are launching. If I don't make it and someone"—another, louder, alarm went off—"finds this recording, bring it to Dar Cevu on Bauthen 3."

A loud *whump* accompanied the holographic head breaking apart into static, then cutting off with a loud woman's scream.

"Well, I guess she didn't make it," said Nighthawk, gazing at the wreckage.

Fawkes tried to stave off the sadness by concentrating on the thought this woman never existed. *She's a storyline in a game. No person ever died a desperate death trying to stop pirates. It's just backstory.* She exhaled out her nose.

Kavan looked around at everyone. "So, should we go to those coordinates or do we try to find this Dar Cevu guy?"

"Yeah," said Nighthawk. "Now what?"

The ground rumbled, and six giant alien insects erupted, surrounding them. Glossy shells in vibrant colors caught the sunlight and gleamed. The biggest of them would make a semi-truck cab feel tiny while the other five had bodies the size of compact cars.

"Now..." Fawkes hit *Flicker* to leap into stealth. "We try not to die."

11

ONE STEP CLOSER

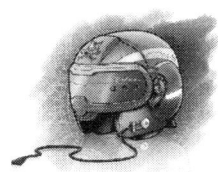

Kavan rushed at the huge bug. The stream of oversized 'fireball' projectiles coming out of his rifle announced his low-damage-high-threat attack designed to get a creature's attention. While the boss alien focused on him, the smaller bugs ran at random characters. Fawkes fought the temptation to go for the big, juicy target and again decided to protect Angel813.

Rallek used a technomancy shield to give himself extra armor. Nighthawk kited one of the bugs going for him, running away while firing back at it. Fawkes lined up her gunsights on a yellow-plated bug seconds away from springing at Angel813.

The ambush shot critted for 1113 damage, knocking its health bar down about halfway. Fawkes' body went solid again, indicating loss of stealth, making her grumble. One annoying quirk with the game and stealth: in boss fights, ambushing always kicked her out of hiding. Shooting open-world mobs in the back didn't do that.

"Oh, shit. These things are tough as hell!" shouted Fawkes.

The one she ambushed whirled around and hissed at her, machete-sized mandibles twitching. It spat a shower of dark green liquid, which she some-what-dodged. A pattering sensation as if she'd been pelted with a machine gun throwing ping-pong balls accompanied three-quarters of her health points disappearing.

A purple-plated bug slammed its jaws into the wall of techno-junk orbiting Rallek. Lightning crackled from the impact point, doing a little damage to the bug. Kavan instinctually moved to the side, pulling the giant one around to put its back to the party. Some of the group mission bosses had spray type attacks that could hit everyone, and did way more damage than a non-tank could handle, so he'd gotten in the habit of making anything boss-like face away.

Angel813 hurled a pair of medi-orbs at Fawkes. Green light streaming from the tiny flying robots got her health bar sliding back toward full. The bug that sprayed her charged. Fawkes ran like hell, chased by two baseball-sized bots and a bug as big as a Prius. She weaved side-to-side avoiding streams of acid. One attempt to peer back and squeeze off a shot ended with her chickening out and running harder when she realized how close the mandibles were to her rear end.

Fortunately, rogues had an innate foot speed bonus over other classes. With that, she could go fast enough to keep the bug from biting her, but she didn't get any farther away from it.

Laser blasts filled the air behind her, but she couldn't focus on anything other than the bug coming for her. Something exploded in the distance, triggering an idea. Still at full speed, she pulled one of the limpet mines from her inventory and set the timer to ten seconds before triggering it. Fawkes held it out in front of her so she could see the timer ticking down as she ran. When it hit two seconds, she dropped it.

Boom.

The concussion wave from the detonation hurled her off her feet. Fawkes landed on her chest in a forward slide under a torrent of warm bug guts. She clamped her mouth and eyes closed, abandoning her body to the flood of slime. When motion ceased, she put her hands down and pushed herself up out of a small lake of muck. Clear, intestine-like tubes draped off her arms, dripping with yellow goop that had the consistency of raw scrambled eggs.

Feeling it plus seeing it nearly made her throw up. It didn't have a smell, likely the only reason she managed not to vomit. Paralyzed with disgust, she stared at her friends. Kavan appeared to be holding the big one's attention, though it still hadn't taken significant damage. Two bugs, one red and one pink, lay dead already. Nighthawk peppered the remaining pair of smaller bugs with laser blasts while they chewed on a group of rudimentary androids that Rallek must have summoned. Angel813, free and clear of imminent attack, frantically threw healing at Kavan, who's health bar fluctuated so fast between twenty percent and full, the green line looked more like a stereo equalizer on a dance track than a health indicator.

She dragged herself out of the knee-deep muck and loped up to a jog, moving closer. Since they appeared to have the last two small bugs under control, and her class had been designed to work single-target damage, she slipped into stealth and moved into position behind the gargantuan bug. If the crashed fighter sprouted legs and started walking around, it would've been smaller than this monster.

Rallek backed away from the android fight, throwing a stream of pale magic light at Nighthawk. The instant the bolt hit him, his pistol's laser blasts got brighter and thicker.

"I'm gonna dig in," yelled Kavan. "This thing is tearing me up."

"Thank you!" screamed Angel813. "I'm running out of supplies!"

Magic users had mana pools to power their spells. 'Tech' healers like the medic had an approximation of 'supplies,' which worked exactly like mana using a different name.

An explosion of creeping black techno-roots grew out of Kavan and sank into the ground, covering him in a network of crisscrossing strands. The grey 'bonus armor' bar appeared above his health points, which stopped bouncing up and down.

Fawkes ducked low in the tall grass and aimed at the huge bug's ponderous, pulsating abdomen—a pod-like structure covered in segmented chitinous plates sticking up from the bug's midsection. She'd spent enough time avoiding the first bug and recovering from the slime bath that *Flicker* had become available again. She fired, *Flickered*, and fired again too fast to process that her first shot critted for 6640 damage, and the second for 8260. While her jaw hung open from seeing such massive numbers, it ratcheted closed in horror at realizing the insect's health bar barely moved.

Despite the huge hits, the bug didn't flinch toward her. Kavan had been pounding on it long enough to build up a huge threat lead. She stayed low in the grass and fired as fast as she could click the trigger. Even not using stealth, her shots were hovering around 2,000 damage per pull.

"Nighthawk, get around behind it!" shouted Fawkes. "It takes extra damage if you shoot it in the abdomen."

"The what?" yelled Nighthawk.

"Big pulsing pod thing sticking out of its back," shouted Fawkes.

Considering she fired at a target the size of a large passenger car, she didn't bother looking over the gunsight and watched Nighthawk and Rallek take down the last two bugs. Kavan's bonus armor dropped at an alarming rate, which got Angel813 resorting to shouting in Chinese.

"What?" yelled Kavan.

"I'm just swearing," said Angel813. "We gotta do something quick. I'm almost dry."

Nighthawk bolted off into the field at a full sprint, leaving Rallek to handle the last bug alone. Much to Fawkes' astonishment, Rallek didn't seem annoyed or even surprised.

"What are you doing?" shouted Fawkes. She gawked at the fleeing gunslinger for all of three seconds until she realized he ran towards the *Storm-bringer.* "Oh, shit," she whispered. "We're outside!"

She shifted targets and snapped off an ambush shot into the side of the last small bug's abdomen at the same instant it bit the head off the last of the summoned androids. Its rear end exploded in a shower of raw-egg goop, and the screaming bug collapsed in place. Rallek faced Kavan and threw another spell at him, which caused his armor to start glowing in random places. Whenever the big bug bit into Kavan's arm-mounted shield, a few tiny lightning bolts zapped it in retaliation.

"Thanks, but I got plenty of aggro already," said Kavan.

"It's still a bit more armor rating." Rallek shifted toward Angel813 and hit her with two spells.

"Ooh! Thank you!" she cheered. "I hate that they buried that so damn deep in the tree."

It took Fawkes a second to notice her 'supplies' bar had gone up a bit. Technomancers had access to the only ability that could restore mana to technical resource classes.

Rallek nodded. "Yeah, they don't want medic mains to branch into that for unlimited mana. Gotta be a pure technomancer to reach it."

"It's not unlimited mana." Angel813 scowled. "You use mana. It would just be converting mana into supplies."

"Fawkes, get out from behind it!" shouted Kavan. "Now!"

She sprinted to the right, pumping her arms, grass blades whipping at her thighs. The *Stormbringer* glided straight up and tilted forward. Four bright blue streaks of energy connected the midpoint of the ship's wings to the giant bug, setting off a huge cloud of bug-gut-steam and a horrible insectoid screech. The brief pulse of energy lingered in Fawkes' vision, seared onto her retinas.

Still squealing, and down to a little more than half its health, the giant bug forgot all about Kavan and charged at the *Stormbringer*. It fired glops of sticky goo from an opening at the back end of its abdomen at the ship. The greenish slime splattered uselessly on the hull. Many bosses had abilities to ground Niath who tried to fly and get away from combat, but they didn't work on a starship.

Nighthawk fed it a full barrage again; all four laser blasts melted holes in the enormous insect's shell. The fragrance of a slightly overcooked omelet rolled by, making Fawkes gag.

Down to ten-ish percent health, the giant insect teetered to a stop and swooned. Its shell split open, red light pouring from the cracks. Quivering, it swelled up in size and emitted a roar.

"Shit, it's enraged!" yelled Angel813.

Nighthawk blasted it again, and the titan crashed dead to the meadow, shaking the ground.

"And it's dead," said Rallek.

Fawkes stood there for a moment gawking in horror at the idea of that thing doing half again extra damage during an enrage phase before her brain rebooted, accepting the fact of its death. She slumped with relief and put her weapon away. Everyone gathered around the head of the dead bug while the *Stormbringer* drifted over to land nearby.

"Something on your shoulder," said Rallek.

"Huh?" Fawkes looked up at him.

He reached over and plucked a length of clear, rubbery tubing away from her. "Think it's a piece of bug. Kinda looks like a giant gummy worm."

She went to clamp a hand over her mouth to hold in vomiting, but stopped herself realizing her hand had a coating of yellow slime. "Ugh. This is so disgusting. I feel like I went swimming in raw egg with giant udon noodles."

"Eww," said Nighthawk.

"It'll disappear soon." Rallek smiled. "Fight's over."

"Damn good idea." Kavan nodded at Nighthawk. "That thing had so many damn hit points I think they intended for it to take on a ship."

"Nah," said the gunslinger. "If it was meant for a ship fight, it wouldn't have died so fast."

Angel813 shook her head. She summoned a pair of puffy peach-colored alien dogs that bore a resemblance to Pomeranians with three eyes and little pink antennae. The dogs leapt at each other, yipping and playing. "I think they meant it for a twenty-person raid group."

"Who knows?" Rallek shrugged. "Where's the loot box?"

"Maybe it didn't count as a kill because we used the ship?" asked Fawkes.

"Well, whatever it was... we killed it." Kavan kicked a piece of shell.

The ubiquitous white loot box finally appeared, around the same time the bug guts coating Fawkes vanished. A pillar of white light rose around everyone, a pair of rotating gold orbs leading the way. The *bwong* noise of leveling up approached deafening with five characters all going at once.

"Ooh, grats all!" yelled Fawkes.

"Whoo hoo!" shouted Rallek.

"Double grats," said Nighthawk.

She blinked at Kavan. He'd leapt from level thirty-four to thirty-six. "Damn... Guess you were technically too low for that kill." She'd gone into that fight halfway to thirty-nine. Her XP progress bar now showed forty-four percent of the way to level forty.

"Oh, it just took the game a moment to realize we killed it." Nighthawk chuckled. "I don't think they expected someone to use starship cannons on it."

"Or a group of five to take out a twenty-person raid boss." Angel813 laughed.

"I think this fight was supposed to be a wipe, springing a raid boss on an unsuspecting crew." Fawkes frowned. "Something to slow down the contest mission by a week."

"A week?" Kavan tilted his head. "We don't stay dead for a week. That's a raid lockout."

"Group wipe to a non-instanced outdoor raid boss could lock these characters as 'dead' for a week. Or maybe just keep us stuck on this planet until the reset." Fawkes scrunched up her face, trying to remember how the game handled that. "I think."

"They should've thought of that, having it outside like this." Rallek gestured at the ship. "Only idiots would've stood there trying to take that thing on in personal combat. By the time we had the adds under control, Angel was almost out. We would've wiped if we tried to do it 'the correct' way."

"She's right." Angel813 groaned. "Army of One required everyone to have a raiding alt so if we wiped on an outdoor boss we wouldn't be sidelined. We'd have been stuck as ghosts until reset."

"We killed it." Nighthawk shot finger guns at the dead bug. "That *was* the correct way."

"So... umm. Let's get out of here before someone notices us," said Fawkes.

Rallek and Kavan glanced at her.

"Expecting a problem?" asked Angel813.

"No, just general paranoia." She shrugged. "If the developers put that fight here to force a wipe and lockout, killing it might've broken something or at least been noticed."

Kavan opened the loot box. "Hmm. We'll that's yours." He tossed a set of black leggings to Fawkes.

She caught the flying medium armor pants and examined them. Purple quality level forty, with a whopping +30 bonus to agility and +10% stealth chance. "Holy shit. Sorry all. This isn't waiting."

Her existing pants disappeared, leaving her in the dingy brown irremovable panties for a few seconds until she dragged the new armor into the corresponding inventory slot. Of course, anyone who went to the beach saw more skin than the 'basic underwear' revealed, so she didn't even feel embarrassed. That and, well, the character avatar wasn't really her body. The new pants looked and felt like wearing thick spandex, but didn't reflect any light, making her legs appear to be an absence of reality.

"Whoa. That's trippy." Rallek poked her in the thigh. "I read about some stuff like that on the 'net. Carbon nanotubes or whatever. Super black."

"Who wants this?" said Kavan, while holding up a frilly one-piece garment: a black bikini top and a skimpy bottom with a useless gauzy see-through loincloth over it. "Rallek, this has your name all over it."

"If a giant robot carrying a mage robe was messed up, what about this bug having a Victoria's Secret obsession?" asked Angel813, still playing with her alien dogs.

"It doesn't go with my eyes at all," said Rallek in an overacted feminine voice.

Fawkes scowled. "It's freakin' 2031! Why do game developers continue putting that sexist shit in games?"

"What?" asked Angel813. "I'd wear that. I'd totally rock that thing. Especially in PVP. Distraction, sweetie."

"In public?" Fawkes stared at her, mouth agape.

"This isn't public. This is a video game." She picked up one of the dogs and made kissy faces at it. "I'd be way too chicken to wear something like that for real, but in the game? Sure, why not?"

"This is almost pushing the boundary of what ought to be in a game without an age restriction." Kavan frowned, and tossed it to Rallek. "Look at the stats. You might change your mind and wear it anyway."

"I could always pay for a character modification and make Rallek female," said Rallek. He studied the armor for a moment before his eyes bulged. "God dayum!"

His armored trenchcoat disappeared, replaced a second later with a suit that blended Victorian style with high tech panels, glowing purple runes along both sleeves. Both arms had forearm guards full of techno-gadgetry.

"*That's* the same garment?" squeaked Fawkes. "What misogynist bullshit is this?"

"Hang on." Angel813 reached for him. "Let me see it?"

Rallek went bare-chested for a second before his old armor appeared. He handed a generic-looking black T-shirt item to Angel813.

Her medic armor disappeared. Soon after, the racy 'combat bikini' with transparent loincloth appeared on her. The outfit exposed more skin than the game's underwear did. "Guess it changes if a girl wears it."

"Whoa, that's kinda messed up," said Nighthawk, a hint of blush on his face. He didn't quite look directly at her. "But I guess it would be more messed up if it still looked like that when Rallek wore it."

Rallek laughed.

Angel813's green and silver armor reappeared. She handed a frilly item back to Rallek, which once again became the gothic Victorian/techno armor suit when he put it on.

"Ooh!" Fawkes fumed. "I'm really pissed off now. I ran into a Niath played by like a ten–year-old. It's not right to make kids wear something that reveal-ing. It's not right to force women to either."

"Check the options screen, hon." Angel813 winked. "They put in a selector to change it. Under social/outfits, they've got a one-to-ten slider for armor sexiness."

Seconds later, Rallek's clothing all but vanished, leaving him standing there in an almost-nonexistent super-tiny bathing suit with glowing purple arcane writing on it.

"Whoa!" shouted Nighthawk. "Not cool!"

Kavan shielded his eyes.

"I guess it *does* work on guys, too." The frilly techno-Victorian suit reappeared.

"Hmph." Fawkes folded her arms. "Still feels like they're being sexist."

Rallek raised an eyebrow at Angel813. "That means you've got your sexy slider all the way up."

She winked at him. "PVP hon. The boys can't shoot straight if they're staring at boobs."

"Oh, there's a tank weapon in here. Anyone care if I nab this?" Kavan held up a boxy assault rifle. "Damage is way better than mine and the stat bonuses are all constitution and willpower."

"Go for it," said Fawkes.

Everyone else nodded.

"Well that's the lot of it." Kavan closed the loot box, which disappeared. "So... the *Reckoning*."

"It's a world boss," said Rallek.

"Which world?" Nighthawk looked at him.

Rallek gestured both hands out to the sides. "I mean a universe boss that can appear literally anywhere out in space. It spawns randomly and moves every half hour. It could be anywhere on the star map and go from one corner to the opposite corner instantly."

"Damn." Kavan whistled. "That would take us hours of game time to pull off that trip."

Angel813 sighed, holding up a small cat-like alien with three tails. She scratched under its chin and made cooing noises at it. "That's why I don't pay attention to that stuff. It's not worth the hassle."

"Exactly how many vanity pets do you have?" asked Nighthawk.

Angel813 opened a small floating window and read for a second. "289. I'm only a third of the way done collecting."

"You're way too good at playing a medic healer to be casual," said Rallek.

"She's not a casual," snapped Nighthawk. "She's former AOO."

"If she's from a big time raid guild, how come she never reads any of the strats?" asked Kavan.

Rallek smiled. "Lazy healer?"

"I have a real job." Angel813 tucked a lock of her hair behind one ear. "If I'm not in the game, I'm usually reading stuff for work."

"So do I... have a real job that is," said Kavan. "And I can still take ten minutes to go over a strategy write up."

"I've got a job, too, but I wouldn't call it real," said Fawkes with a sigh. "Just a barista."

"Hey, don't undervalue that." Kavan pointed at her. "Without you, I couldn't work."

Everyone chuckled.

"It's not a big deal for you. You can read strats at work, Mr. Programmer." Rallek grinned. "I can't. I'm stuck on a damn phone all day trying to explain to people why they can't use garden hose to wire up their computer network. I had one dude think the internet would be faster because the hose was fatter than the network cable."

"Who uses cables anymore?" Nighthawk blinked at him. "That's *so* last decade."

Fawkes glanced at Nighthawk. "How do you have the time to read strats, work, and still be five levels over us all?"

"Six levels." He winked. "Just special I guess."

"Well... we know who's unemployed." Fawkes winked.

Nighthawk stuck his tongue out at her.

"So you guys really want to try and find this impossible-to-find raid boss ship?" asked Angel813. "Army of One still hasn't been able to track it down... and they've got at least forty crews. We're *one* crew. Even if we could find it, we wouldn't stand a chance."

"I hear beating that boss drops an exclusive vanity pet," said Rallek.

"Oh?" Angel813's eyebrows notched up. "Are you serious or just messing with me?"

Rallek opened a terminal window, typed for a moment, and moved so she could see. "Nope, I'm serious. Blacklight Phoenix pet. The only way to get it is to take out that ship. No one in the whole game has it yet."

"That's because no player has even laid eyes on it." Kavan gestured at another display panel hovering by him. "Not one."

"Ooh!" Angel813's facial expression became that of a six-year-old girl staring at a birthday pony. "He's so cute! I want him!"

"Yeah..." said Fawkes, "But not only do we have to find it, we have to figure out how to kill it."

"Wait." Nighthawk scratched his head. "People know about the *Reckoning* already?"

"Yeah. AOO is hunting for it," said Angel813. "That ship has been around since the game started."

"But do they know it's part of the *big* quest?" asked Fawkes.

"Doubtful." Rallek shook his head. "It's been a world boss since launch. It's older than this prize quest. I bet they made that ship part of it because no one's been able to find it yet."

Kavan laughed. "Is it no one's been able to or no one's bothered because it's too much of a pain in the ass."

"Either way." Rallek held up the data pad from the crashed fighter. "They don't have this. At least for the purpose of this quest, we might not have to take the boss on. The developers can't be that sadistic to force a forty-ship raid for this prize. Having to share the prize money with that many people wouldn't make it worth bothering with. Maybe they just refer to the *Reckoning* as backstory, yanno? No one's said we have to kill it."

Murmurs of agreement spread around.

"Come on." Kavan tromped off toward the *Stormbringer.* "It's only seven. We still got a good two hours or so, can knock out a ship mission if everyone's up for it."

"Might as well," said Fawkes. "Or we can go check out these coordinates."

"Let's do that." Rallek pointed at her. "It's going to be a long flight anyway."

12

LIVE SUPPORT

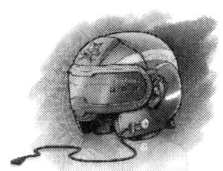

Saturday after leaving the café, Dakota hopped an Amazon Lyft™ car to Dover Street, where Nebraska's 'people' had built up a section of space under the Manhattan side of the decommissioned Brooklyn Bridge. Between the MagTube transit system, telecommuting, and the general decline of the area, the city stopped maintaining the bridge in 2030. Officially, people weren't allowed on it, but the cops seldom bothered enforcing that. Radicals tried to install solar panels along the surface to 'reclaim wasted space,' but of course, the power companies sent the cops to shut that down.

Corrugated steel panels splashed with graffiti and chain link fence walled off the area below the bridge superstructure. The orange glow of fires within steel drums illuminated the interior. Two young men somewhere between seventeen and twenty, both in yellow wool caps and openly carrying small UZIs, gave her the stink eye. Barring a situation like a severe malfunction of an auto-driving vehicle leaving a rich person stranded here, the cops rarely set foot within three miles of this place.

She pulled out her phone, logged on to Amazon, and ordered two forty-packs of Disney Castle burgers. Twenty years or so ago, it had been White Castle, but the rush of buyouts reshaped the world. About ten minutes later, the buzz of approaching fans pulled her attention skyward. The drone carried a thermal bag, in which her eighty hamburgers sat snug and protected from smog and pigeon shit. Every so often, someone who ordered coffee would complain of a splatter on the cups, usually from a drone-to-bird collision during the delivery. The Castle delivery drone looked like a veteran of the million-pigeons-war, or a Jackson Pollack rendered in bird poop. Fortunately, the burger cartons remained clean.

After retrieving the food, she approached the armed punks. Their hard-faced glowers of derision eased back to confusion, then recognition when she got within speaking distance.

"Oh, hey girl. Didn't recognize you," said one she thought might be named Leon.

"Brass here?" asked Dakota.

"Yeah. Go on in."

She hefted the boxes. "Brought you guys some food."

"Right on," said the other guy.

Dakota didn't care for this place much. The dying bulk of the old Brooklyn Bridge hung overhead like the Sword of Damocles, thousands of tons of concrete and steel that could collapse without warning at any minute. Her brother saw it as an impregnable fortress. A scattering of oceanic cargo boxes served as enclosed rooms for the higher-ranking members of the gang, several even boasting large television sets and gaming consoles. They boosted a couple PlayStation 7s off the back of a truck a while back and kept three.

Black oil barrels here and there radiated heat. Whatever burned inside them gave off a foul stink like engine degreaser from a heavy truck. She wrinkled her nose at the fumes but kept on walking around concrete lane dividers and old patio furniture. They'd set this place up preparing for a siege that never came. One day, the 'social crusaders' hoped to do something significant for the people, set off an event that would alter the course of civilization and probably trigger a bullet-riddled standoff with authorities.

Some of them longed for that day, hoping to go out as martyrs of change, but they still had a secret exit on the other side. While they all talked a big game, only about a third would be likely to follow through with the whole fighting to the death thing.

Nebraska wound up somewhere in the middle of the hierarchy. Not particularly influential, but loyal and dedicated enough to where he had earned respect. He, along with a dozen other young people society had no further use for, congregated around a cluster of battered sofas where someone had rigged an overhead projector up to play movies on a giant screen. Three rag-clad children under ten, two boys and girl, sat on the floor by the middle couch, enthralled in a car-to-car gunfight on the screen.

"Kota!" Brass leapt from his seat on the sofa arm, and hurried over. "What's up?"

She hefted the boxes. "Brought you guys some food. I wanted to make sure you were eating. What's with the little kids? Kinda young to join up huh?"

"Oh, they're not joining." He rolled his eyes. "They live in the building out front. Just here to watch TV."

"That movie's a little R rated for them. Are they even nine yet?" She shook her head.

"Yo! Food!" Brass held up the boxes. "Sis, *life* is too R rated for little kids."

The barefoot girl shifted her weight to stand, giving Dakota a glimpse of a small handgun strapped to her thigh under her tattered dress.

"Gracias por la comida. ¡Eres agradable!" The child scrambled over and hugged Dakota before grabbing a bundle of burgers and scooting back to her spot on the floor.

Dakota stood back while the two boys and the other gang members helped themselves. Brass wolfed down six of the small cheeseburgers in eight seconds, stifled a burp, and approached to throw an arm around her back.

"Workin' on something. I should be able to pay you back a bit of the cash you loaned me soon."

She smirked. "Don't rob a place, okay? I don't need money back from you bad enough to put you in jail."

Nebraska shook his head. "Ain't like that. Hey, since you're here..." Dakota started to suck in a breath, but he raised a hand. "No, I ain't gonna ask you for money."

"What then?"

He grinned. "A chance to remember who you are and do some of that stuff you went to school for. AmeriBank has been a giant pack of douchebags lately. We want to hit their website."

"Hit their website?"

"Yeah, Franco's got all the graphics and stuff ready. The files are good to go. We just need someone a little better at this shit to get them on the official server."

A slow, predatory smile formed on her lips. She'd had a special hate on for AmeriBank after they'd foreclosed on the house she'd grown up in. Though she knew it had been a scam, neither she nor her parents could afford a lawyer good enough to prove it. Her parents had enabled automatic payment of their mortgage from the bank account, also with AmeriBank, so they hadn't consciously thought of making payments for years. A year and a half ago, a huge scandal erupted involving tens of thousands of foreclosures that all correlated to areas where property developers wanted in. The bank falsified records to make it appear that the mortgage hadn't been paid. They took the money for three months in a row so homeowners wouldn't notice anything strange in their balances, then when they moved to foreclose, the missing payments reappeared in the accounts and any record that the transactions occurred had vanished.

As blatant a scheme as it was, somehow no prosecution had ever occurred. Her parents, and hundreds of other families, lost their homes. The house she'd grown up in was gone, reduced to a dirt lot that still remained blank four years later. Construction crews labored to convert real estate that once held over a hundred normal homes to thirty or forty giant estates for the wealthy. Or maybe a mall.

She fumed inside. "Sure. You still got that sniffer?"

"Yep. Still has your cat sticker on it, too."

"Oh, come on. I was fourteen."

Nebraska held his hands up in surrender. "Hey, I didn't mean that in a bad way."

"All right. Give me a few minutes."

She followed him to one of the ocean-transport cargo boxes, which had been set up like a bedroom complete with a computer desk. They'd tapped a fiber line somewhere for free high-speed internet, with Wi-Fi throughout their little compound. While she got to work using a 'seen better days' desktop, Nebraska ran off to fetch her old laptop since she'd need it for this. Better it hide here among these people than she have it at her apartment where it might get found by the authorities. Some hardware could land a girl in jail for merely having it.

As irritated as she'd become at her parents for taking their conspiracy theory nonsense too far, she spared a moment of gratitude. She'd never been 'eight-year-old with a gun strapped to her thigh' desperate at any point in her life. For that, she at least owed them thanks.

After some time poking around the net and slipping in and out of the dark web, she found information on AmeriBank executives. Brass arrived with her old Dell laptop, still bolted to the extra case with the military-grade Wi-Fi unit and sniffer. A huge Hello Kitty sticker adorned the lid. Seeing it made her nostalgic. Not that she wanted to be thirteen again, but she missed a life where she had all day to play online before adult responsibilities.

He sat on the naked mattress behind her, watching as she hunted down addresses and phone numbers.

"Okay, got a couple places to try. You have any transportation?"

"Yeah. Come on." Brass handed her the laptop and stood.

She followed him deeper into the bridge compound and out a gate on the other side to a parking lot full of concrete rubble and a beat up cargo van with so much graffiti that it blended into the urban decay like camouflage. He called out and two more guys, one black, one Chinese, came running, along with a woman around her age who appeared to be a mix of black and Hispanic.

"Tito, Larry, and Gina," said Nebraska.

The new arrivals all nodded in greeting.

"Where to?" asked Gina.

Dakota read off the first address in Brooklyn Heights, where the SVP of marketing lived. "Marketing exec probably has access to web content, but I bet he never touches it himself."

"Wouldn't it be better to go after, like, their head of network?" asked Tito.

"No way. They'd never fall for part two." Dakota shook her head. "We need someone who has access but no clue."

"Oh," said Larry. "Cool. Cool."

Gina hopped in behind the wheel. Dakota took a mid-row seat. Nebraska sat next to her and fumbled a power adapter out of the junk piled up in the middle of the floor. Tito rode shotgun with Larry in the rearmost bench. He huddled against the side, keeping his gaze out a broken back window. Dakota tried not to let the sight of a cut down AK47 in his lap unnerve her too much, but couldn't contain her worry.

"Dude, he's got a damn assault rifle. If we get pulled over, we're not going to do small time." She bit her lip.

"Relax. You're too important to get taken." Nebraska fished handcuffs and a black bag out from the pouch behind the passenger seat. "If we're gonna get nailed, you were kidnapped." He packed the terrifying items back out of sight.

"No way," said Dakota. "That'll put you away for the rest of your life! I can't do that to you."

"I wanna be kidnapped, too," whined Gina. "Or just bring those toys with you when we get back." She winked at Nebraska.

He grinned back.

Scarlet-faced, Dakota opened the laptop and refused to look at him. "Uhh, it's dead."

Wordless, he handed her the plug end and ran the other side to the cigarette lighter port up front. She watched him crawling forward until Gina squeezed his ass. Soon after she averted her eyes, her Dell powered up. While the van trundled over rough-paved streets, she booted up the nearly ten-year-old laptop. All the stuff she needed ran under Linux, so old hardware didn't matter. It didn't make one bit of difference how fancy or plain one's screen appeared. Beneath all the flashy graphics of modern operating systems, everything still boiled down to ones and zeroes going out in Ethernet packets.

Eventually, they parked near the target house in Brooklyn Heights. Dakota fired up the WiFi module and polled for active networks. It took her a little while, but based on signal strength, she narrowed it down to two that appeared to be transmitting from inside the marketing executive's house. Since one had 'Brandon2020' as the SSID, she figured it had been set up for the guy's son. She focused her attention on R1V3nd3ll.

"I almost feel bad. This guy's a fantasy geek, too." She poked a couple keys and frowned. "And he's smart enough to password protect his network." Another finger tap started a brute-force intrusion module.

"So we're screwed?" asked Nebraska.

"No. If this thing doesn't crack his network password, I can capture all Wi-Fi traffic, then filter down by this SSID and extract the MAC address of his client's network card. From there, it's just a matter of grabbing the data burst with the info we need and letting the decryption routines chew on it."

Her brother leaned in close, staring at the screen. The dumbfounded look on his face struck her as cute. "How long will that take?"

"Well, if I have to attack the encryption, probably a couple of weeks of leaving this thing powered up and running. Odds aren't great that he won't have changed his password by then."

"Oh." He frowned.

The laptop beeped.

"Well, our guy's smart enough to put a password on his Wi-Fi network, but he's not smart enough to use a *good* one. My caveman has a leet-speak dictionary. He had a one-word password with some of the letters swapped to numbers. We're in."

"Cool. So you own his network now? And what's a caveman?"

She smirked at him. "It's my brute force proggie. Custom by the way, and no, I can't just see the traffic... or we could use his internet connection. Now for the hard part. Everyone stay quiet."

Dakota loaded a softphone client and dialed the guy's home number.

Six rings later, the voice of a prepubescent boy said, "Hello?"

"Hi," said Dakota with overly forced cheerfulness. "Is your father home?"

"Uhh, who is this?" asked the boy.

"Is this Brandon?"

"Yeah," said the kid.

"Hi Brandon. It's Kelly from the bank. I need to talk to your father for a minute or two. It's important, but not bad."

"Umm. Okay, hang on. He's taking a dump."

Tito snickered.

Dakota almost laughed. "Okay."

For a minute or three, tinny video game sounds came back over the phone.

"He's out. Hang on," said Brandon before muffling the phone and yelling, "Dad?"

Murmuring preceded a man saying, "Hello? This is Mr. Snyder."

"Good afternoon, sir. I'm sorry to bother you on the weekend. My name is Kelly. I'm from the information security team at AmeriBank. There's been an attempt to access your account. We need you to log in over the VPN as soon as possible and change your password. Don't tell me what it is. Remember, no one from the IT group will ever ask you for your password. It's important that you change it though, so whoever compromised it can't get back in."

"Oh, I see," said Mr. Snyder, sounding alarmed. "Hang on. I'll do it now. Do I need you on the line?"

"I can wait with you if you like, but I don't have access to see your password so it wouldn't make a difference either way," said Dakota using her Amazon Café customer service voice.

"All right then, uhh. Gimme a minute and I'll get it changed. Did they cause any damage?"

"Nothing we've seen yet. We caught it early and kicked them out." Dakota started recording all traffic on his Wi-Fi network.

"Good. All right then, I guess I should go do this. Thanks for the warning."

"No problem sir. Have a great rest of your weekend."

"You too."

She clicked off the call.

"Whoa, you gotta call people to hack?" asked her brother, wide-eyed.

"Yeah. It's called social engineering. It's not all hiding in the basement and working black magic through a keyboard." She poked him in the side. "You watch too many movies."

"So... what did that accomplish?" asked Gina. "By the way, you do a really good cute voice."

"Thanks." She chuckled. "Well, at some point within the next few minutes, Mr. Snyder is going to log into the AmeriBank VPN and change his password. I'm capturing all the data going over his Wi-Fi network, so somewhere in that garbled mess of information is enough to tell me what VPN software they use, what those credentials are, and what his new password is. Once I decode all this shit and install the correct VPN client, I should be able to waltz right onto the AmeriBank network."

"Awesome. I have no idea what the hell you just said, but awesome." Nebraska grinned.

"What now?" asked Tito.

"Give it another five minutes, and we go... umm... home." She glanced out the window at the beautiful house, and sighed. No hate on those people, but she couldn't help but feel more than a little jealous at the sort of life she'd never be able to have. *Ramen and tiny apartments for me.*

Almost two hours later, Dakota extracted the password from the decoded network packets around the same time the Pulsar Secure VPN client software finished installing on a desktop system the group used for cyber-attacks. She couldn't help but roll her eyes at the 'off-the-shelf' DDOS client her brother's associates had on it. She'd advanced beyond that bullshit by age twelve.

It took a little finesse to handcraft a cryptographic login token using the information she'd gotten from Snyder's system, but after a tense few seconds, the effort paid off with a green indicator light and a good connection to the AmeriBank corporate network. She fed it Snyder's username and pass-word—the new one he'd just changed—and the man's desktop appeared, complete with a picture of a cute little boy with straw-blond hair. Brandon, she figured, from a few years ago. It surprised her they didn't have a two-factor token authentication, but perhaps the system would only prompt for that if she tried to access account information or get into any applications involving money. For that, at least, she felt grateful. No one had to break into his house to steal the code generator or try to pickpocket him.

Her guess proved out. Snyder had access to the web development folders. Nebraska handed her a USB stick with the altered files on it. Evidently, one of their people had cloned the bank's website, and their team of artists and goof-balls had spent the better part of the last week making a mockery of it.

Chances are, the bank would have everything back to normal from backups in four or five hours, but for a little while, they'd look foolish. The attack amounted to little more than a juvenile prank, but this was also the same bank that tried to sue children for writing 'Save the Earth' with sidewalk chalk near one of their branches, calling it 'criminal vandalism.' Of course, their parents had been protesting the bank's financing of oil-drilling projects and put the kids up to doing it, but sidewalk chalk? One light rain shower and it's gone, and these corporate pigs had the gall to term it 'vandalism.'

She sighed, and with an imperious frown, mashed the enter key to begin the upload of website files. "In thirteen minutes, there will be an epic amount of penises on their website."

Nebraska blinked. "You changed the files?"

"Huh?" She glanced at him. "No, why?"

"There's no penises. It's political stuff. Our slogans, evidence of the bank's fuckery and crap like that. Where'd you get penises from?"

"The last time I saw you and your friends commit an act of political disobedience, you—"

"Yeah, yeah... I was like fifteen." He rolled his eyes.

While waiting for the file transfer, she started poking around the network. A folder ATM_REG caught her eye. She skimmed a listing of ATMs in the area, complete with their model number, software version, and IP address.

"Oh, hey..." She grabbed his shoulder. "Screw these guys. Can you send a crew to the ATM by Fulton and Williams?"

"Sure, why?"

"It's about to puke money."

"What?" He gawked. "You can do that?"

"I think. It's an old Model 880. They have a feeder test routine that cycles the cash handler to make sure it works. If there's any bills in it at the time, they go flying."

"Whoa, that's serious."

"Nah, at most it would only gonna be a couple grand." She poked her finger into his chest, staring into his eyes. "And it better go toward food and clothes. Not booze or drugs."

"I'm clean," said Nebraska. "No more heroin. I swear. Been off that shit for six months."

Tito nodded. "He's legit. Dude still drinks like a mofo though."

"Dick." Nebraska thumped him in the leg. "This is my sister."

"What?" Tito rubbed his thigh. "I ain't like sayin' 'nice tits' at her."

Nebraska hit him again.

Tito leaned around to make eye contact with Dakota. "Nice tits, girl."

"Thanks," she muttered with a smile, knowing he only said it to tweak her brother.

"Stop that!" Nebraska hit him again. "She's my sister. That's like, really uncomfortable."

She glanced at him. "Oh, like me hearing Gina talk to you wasn't just as bad. And you're really going to... do stuff with her later. Tito's just messing around."

"'Do stuff?' Geez, Kota stop treating me like I'm twelve."

"As soon as you stop living like you are." She squeezed his arm.

"Oh, shit. Here it comes." Tito shook his head. "Get a job, apartment, girl, have kids, etc. You didn't tell me your big sis was part of the routine."

"I'm not 'part of the routine.' I just don't want my little brother to get himself killed."

"I love you too, sis." Nebraska patted her on the back, a little too hard.

She waited there in the cargo box while Nebraska, Tito, and Gina ran off. Eight minutes later, a new instance of a softphone client on her laptop rang with an incoming call.

"*Hola, tengo un conejo muy esponjoso,*" said Dakota.

Gina's voice came over the line with uncontrolled laughter.

"*¿Tu conejo es esponjoso?*" asked Dakota. "*Lamento que tu conejo no sea esponjoso.*" Gina laughed harder.

The phone crackled. "Hey, what are you saying?" asked Tito.

"Oh, nothing. Just nonsense." Dakota grinned. "You guys there?"

"Yeah," said Tito. "What are we looking for?"

"One sec."

She ran the ATM diagnostics client she'd downloaded while waiting for them to get in position. After plugging in the IP address of the machine at their location, she clicked to connect. The progress wheel spun for a few seconds, and miraculously, it worked. She snickered to herself, muttered, "*Ka-ching*," and clicked the button to test the cash dispenser.

"Whoa," yelled Tito. "This thing just exploded."

"Stay calm, stay calm," rasped Dakota.

"We good," said Tito.

Dakota closed the ATM diagnostic program and disconnected from her VPN connection to Norway. Then, she disconnected the VPN connection to Munich. The initial VPN link from the local network went to Moscow. With any luck, the bank's IT people would blame Russian hackers and think the branch to Manhattan had been misdirection.

"Dude, this is like four grand," blurted Tito over the phone. "Big time."

"Bah," said Dakota. "The company blows more than that on balloons for stupid corporate events."

"Yo, Kota, thanks... This shit is serious, yo. You're a lifesaver."

She sighed. "More like life support. You're dying a slow death out here."

"It's what I need to be doing." Nebraska let out a long, slow sigh. "Someone's gotta stand up to these people."

She stared at the black screen and primitive ASCII bar graphs fluctuating in time with sound levels on the softphone line. Being against 'the corporate man' was cool and all, as long as it didn't involve her brother winding up dead somewhere in the street. Dakota hated getting older. Already, doubt crept in. Did that happen to everyone? Would she cave in and just flow with society like everyone else by twenty-five? Thirty? At what point had what Nebraska gotten himself involved with gone from being awesome to stupid and dangerous? It wasn't as though the two-percenters would ever start caring about the poor. For that matter, short of an actual second revolutionary war, the people in the middle would never demand change. They'd keep right on arguing over political party, race, religion, women versus men, whatever the two-percenters could think of to keep isolating people with. While all the little guys bashed each other over bullshit, the elite sat on their hill and laughed, watching the 'serfs' battle like some socioeconomic MMA pay-per-view. Only here, the fighters paid to put on the show. She'd lost hope somewhere along the past few years that things would ever get better. The wealthy did far too good a job keeping the poor at each other's throats, so they never looked up at the steady drizzle of bird shit falling from on high.

"The best we can hope for is a wide enough umbrella," said Dakota, her voice weak.

"Huh?" asked Nebraska.

She bowed her head and sighed. "Nothing. I'm just tired. Look, I need to get home."

"No probs. We'll drop you off."

A half-chuckle slipped out past her wistful smile. "All right."

13

THE FERAL

Nebraska had tried to give her $500 of the haul from the ATM, but she declined since he needed it more. He wouldn't back down, and she eventually settled on accepting $300. Concerned that the bank might somehow trace the bills' serial numbers, she insisted that he stop at a handful of shady check cashing places to get money orders in varying amounts before cashing them elsewhere. Better to dump the bills before the bank noticed them missing and started hunting.

Dakota trudged into her apartment and locked the door. The whole ride back, she stared down the maw of her slow but inevitable slide into normality. Teenage idealism might've lasted longer if her little brother wasn't at risk. Truth be told, at nineteen, she'd been every bit as gung-ho as him. She couldn't decide if she was 'coming out of the fog' and growing up, realizing it pointless to fight corporate power... or if the machine had won, sapping her will to fight it.

Stuck somewhere between the idea of taking a shower and actually doing it, she sat on the edge of her bed naked for a few minutes, feeling like a close family member had just died in her arms. Stealing $4,200 from an ATM barely registered at all. As a teen, she'd faked out prepaid gift cards and stolen $100 here, $50 there, and usually wound up terrified for days afterward that she'd get busted, but no one ever found her. Stealing four grand should've freaked her out, but everything had become numb.

She started to reach for the game helmet, which made her think about Eric's quip of sending him a 'wearing only the helmet' pic.

The tiniest of smiles happened.

She put the helmet down, showered, and slipped into a tee and sweat pants. While blow-drying her neon blue mane, she devoured a box of pizza rolls after microwaving them. One in three retained frozen cores, while a handful napalmed her mouth.

Once finished, she snugged the helmet on, reclined, and threw herself into Axillon99. There, she didn't have to worry about a sick society, poor children with guns under their dresses, a stupid little brother living on the street, or the off chance she might go to prison for stealing from a bank.

Frustrated at no one else from the crew being online—surprisingly enough, even Nighthawk was off—she logged on Triani and spent a while flying aimlessly around the pink clouds. Except for not getting tired, the game did an amazing job of making it feel like she really had wings. The new helmet completely blocked off all sensation of lying on her bed, allowing the touch of the wind creeping into all the gaps in the scanty Niath garment to lift her out of reality.

It wouldn't take much effort at all to wish away the real world and embrace this life among the clouds.

Eventually, she resigned herself that yeah, maybe she had let her conspiracy theory parents push her off the deep end. What she thought had been reasonable compromise might have still been 'edgy.' Maybe she had grown up a little. Slinging coffee at an Amazon Café wouldn't give her the sweet life, but it at least gave her *a* life. An apartment, all the ramen she could eat, and wearable clothes. She had it better than quite a lot of people in the world.

Still, she'd give it up to be a Niath living primitive in the Celestia Forest.

Right. She glanced at a '44' by pending messages. Some people she'd grouped with before wanted to know if she'd join them for missions. Anyone below level twenty at this point was either levelling an alt, a little kid, or a genuine casual player. She messaged a male Niath, Avalon42, back, remembering he'd been a pleasant conversationalist at least. Probably educated, maybe even a teacher from the way he spoke.

The rest of Saturday slipped by in a pleasant haze of pretending to be a space angel.

SUNDAY, SHE WENT BACK TO WORKING ON FAWKES, AT LEAST UNTIL 3:00 p.m., when Eric came over for real. They hung out for a bit before he took her out for dinner, an Italian restaurant nice enough that her neon-blue hair got disdainful stares. On a lark, after they ate, he brought her to an interactive exhibit for the 2027 Mars Colony mission. The science center designed it mostly for older children, but he thought it would be fun to compare real spacecraft to what they played with online.

Dakota lost herself, zooming around the exhibit for a while like a teenager. When a security guard called her 'young lady,' she lost it and cracked up laughing. The reaction hadn't amused the guy, but the worst thing she'd done was make noise, so he didn't throw her out. From there, they returned to her apartment and threw on a movie.

While cuddling, she decided to tell him about the guy who followed her home.

He pulled her close. "You should carry something to protect yourself."

"That's what I was thinking, but I'd be the one who goes to jail for shooting a rapist."

Eric sighed. "You don't necessarily need to go that far. Hang on." He leaned up enough to get his cell phone out and fiddled with the Amazon app. "Here, what about this?"

She took the phone and looked at a photo of a black canister with a bright red end. "The Habanero Hammer? What the hell is that?"

"Pepper spray from hell. Hit a dude in the face with that shit, he'll be crying for his mother. Wears off eventually, and won't kill."

"Hmm."

He took the phone back and committed the order. "There. Decision made."

"Pepper spray? I dunno. Don't some guys eat that stuff on purpose?"

"Well, only a bullet is a hundred percent effective, but that's got other problems."

She laughed. "Yeah." Her mirth died quick. "I went to visit my brother yesterday. Saw this little girl. She couldn't have been older than eight and she was carrying a gun."

"Jesus," muttered Eric. "Why?"

"That's what I'm wondering. What could make a kid that age want a gun?"

He raised both eyebrows. "Maybe the Girl Scouts have resorted to more aggressive marketing for their cookies."

She poked him in the side.

"Ow."

"That's not funny. This kid was practically in rags. Barely affords clothes, but she's got a little gun."

"Might not even work. Maybe she found it? Could be a toy she hopes will fake someone out?"

Dakota shrugged.

Eric's phone chimed, indicating a drone had just dropped off the package on the apartment building's stoop. "Be right back."

He ran out into the hall, returning a few minutes later with a box. The Habanero Hammer can wound up being bigger than it had looked online, like the handle of a full-sized Maglite.

"Damn, this thing is heavy. Should I spray the creep or club him with it?" She read over the instructions. "Flick the safety cap up and push the trigger. Stream's got a fifteen-foot reach."

"Go for the face," said Eric.

"Right." She got up and put the can in her bag. "So, you wanna do the sex thing or log into Ax?"

Eric scoffed. "Good grief, woman, you have to ask?"

She grinned and slipped her thumbs under the waistband of her skirt.

He pointed two fingers to the right. "I'll grab my helmet."

Dakota gawked at him.

"Hah! Your face." He strolled up to her. "Just kidding, Babe. Ain't nothing I'd rather do than be with you."

She leaned up to kiss him. "There will be retribution for that."

Eric grinned. "I expect nothing less."

She dragged him across the apartment to the bed.

DAKOTA WOKE UP, DRAPED OVER ERIC. THE WARMTH OF THEIR NAKED bodies pressed together shrouded her in a degree of comfort that came dangerously close to loss-of-job. She snuggled into him, fully ready to tell the Amazon Café to go to hell; she'd rather stay in bed.

She didn't quite manage to drift back to sleep by the time the alarm went off.

"Ngh, what time is it?" moaned Eric.

"Five thirty," said Dakota. "I'm opening."

"Damn, girl. Even the devil ain't up at this hour."

She gave him a squeeze. "You saw my horns last night."

He grunted.

"Ugh. I'd tell my boss to screw off, but I like Hal. What time do you have to go in?"

"Gotta be there at nine."

"I'll reset the alarm for eight."

Eric emitted a moan that sounded like an attempt to convey thanks.

She rushed a shower, got dressed, and jogged the four blocks to work.

MUCH TO HER PLEASANT SURPRISE, KAVAN AND ANGEL813 LOGGED IN LATER that day around 6:00 p.m. She'd had a good few hours of solo mission running on Fawkes and got her experience bar within spitting distance of hitting level forty.

Eric usually logged in around seven since it took him about a half hour to get home from work. She rushed back to the *Stormbringer*, hoping to talk the others into chasing down that next map location. While chatting, planning, and waiting for Rallek to show up, Kavan found a ship mission not too far out of the way that he wanted to do on the way to investigate the second set of coordinates. They discussed taking the datapad to that Dar Cevu guy, but Fawkes didn't trust it.

"Should be pretty easy, little extra experience," said Kavan. "Check out a distress beacon."

Fawkes shrugged. "Okay, cool."

"Ugh," said Nighthawk. "Those missions always turn into a huge ship full of aliens that jump out at you. I hate those."

Kavan bowed his head with a slight nod. "If it's one of those, we can skip it."

"Cool." Nighthawk smiled.

Rallek phased into existence at 7:08 p.m. "Hey all. Wow, everyone's on."

Angel813 stretched in her chair, yawning. A pastel blue puffball with dragon-like wings appeared in her hands. After a moment of gazing round at everyone, it took flight, orbiting her. It had a long, prehensile tail, and made cute tweeping coos. "Yeah. I took some time off work. I need to de-stress. Had a ninety-year-old man grab my boob yesterday, and before you say adorable, he knew exactly what he was doing."

Fawkes frowned. "Once a perv..."

"Yeah." Angel813 waved as if flinging crumbs off a table. "So, I took a week off. Maybe he'll be dead by the time I go back."

Nighthawk laughed.

Fawkes stifled a giggle. "Wow, dark."

"He's ancient." Angel813 examined her nails. "And he's an asshole. Not saying I *want* him dead, but at that age, waking up in the morning is an achievement."

Kavan explained the mission he wanted to do, and showed on the star map how minimal a detour it would be from the coordinates they found on the crashed fighter. Everyone agreed, so he jogged off to the bridge.

The flight out to the location of the distress beacon took about twenty minutes. Nighthawk used the time playing the in-game auction system, buying and selling items for profit. Rallek read over several different build compositions for technomancers. Soft chirps and tiny giggles emanated from around Angel813 as she summoned a legion of small vanity pets. Some resembled normal cats, but the vast majority were outlandish: a pink-furred thing with giant ears and bigger eyes looked like the physical embodiment of cuteness. She had a few rabbit-ish critters, one with grey fuzzy antlers, and a handful of furballs-with-eyes.

"Heads up," said Kavan over the PA system. "We're approaching what looks like a derelict starship. We're also about a four-minute flight away from your coordinates."

Fawkes ran to engineering. Rallek and Angel813 darted up and down ladders to the turret pods, and Nighthawk hauled ass for the fighter hatch. Once she skidded to a stop by her engineering table, Fawkes attacked the subsystem control panel and rerouted some power from shields to sensors. A brief but intense detection pulse revealed nothing cloaked. Her sweep wouldn't have shown the exact position of any hidden ships, but she would've known that cloaked vessels existed nearby.

"I got nothing on the screen," said Fawkes over the comm. "Just a"—she glanced at the readout showing a silhouette of a large loaf-shaped ship with numerous sections flashing red—"Cassini class passenger ship. Looks like the engines are dead, and it's sustained quite a bit of hull damage. Probably pirates or something hit it."

A small indicator light winked on.

"Incoming transmission," said Fawkes.

"Wow, you guys really get into this, don't you?" asked Angel813. "When did I walk onto the set of *Star Trek*?"

Kavan laughed. "Well, this game is pretty damned immersive. Feels like we're really here. Might as well sound the part." He cleared his throat. "Put it on the viewscreen, lieutenant."

"Wait, Fawkes is a lieutenant?" asked Nighthawk. "I'm a fighter pilot. I should be an officer."

Rallek's chuckling came over the comm as well as echoed in the shaft up to the turret.

"Help me, please," said a young female voice. "I'm Anastasia Hayden. My father is Frances Hayden of the Galactic Senate. Please don't leave me stranded on this ship."

"I smell bullshit," said Rallek.

Nighthawk snickered.

"What's a senator's daughter doing on a shot-to-hell passenger ship out here? And how is she the only survivor?" asked Rallek.

Kavan dropped the starship captain voice. "What happened down there?"

Fawkes opened a viewscreen, patched into the feed. A dark-haired girl of around twelve in a clingy blue light-armor suit, her face smudged with grime, stood in a smoke-filled room where furniture lay scattered about and small fires burned in the background.

"Something attacked the ship. I heard the shooting and screaming, so I crawled into the vents to hide. It was awful! Everyone's gone! There's a couple androids still here, and they're mean, but they can't get in here. I hacked the door."

"Androids attacked that ship?" asked Kavan.

"No, they're our androids. Whoever attacked us made them go crazy."

Wow. This AI's pretty natural. A lot more so than most quest NPCs.

The girl leaned closer to the camera, her face filling the screen. "Will you please help me? I want to go home."

"You must admit, Anastasia, that it's a little strange for a senator's daughter to be on a commercial ship at all, much less be the only survivor," said Kavan.

"I know." She looked down. "You must think this is a trap or something.

Please, scan the ship. You'll see I'm the only person on board. I booked passage under a false name. A body double was on our private ship as a decoy."

Fawkes dialed up a scan of the derelict. Sure enough, she read forty-seven active androids and one human. "Scan checks out."

"All right. Hang on kid, we're coming in."

Anastasia clutched her hands together at her chin and beamed. "Oh, thank you! Please be careful."

The massive passenger liner had a docking bay large enough to carry a small army of corvettes. Kavan swung the *Stormbringer* around toward the starboard aft and approached the gaping hole where a door had once been.

"We're gonna need bubbles for this," said Rallek.

Everyone's armor had the ability to project atmospheric-retaining force fields around the head. Players referred to them as 'bubbles' due to their appearance. While not terribly realistic, the developers opted for that rather than bulky space suits for 'fun' reasons.

Of course, they had a downside in the form of a time limit from power consumption. A player could handle being out of atmosphere only forty-five minutes before the 'battery' ran out and they dropped dead.

Fawkes grumbled internally, arguing with herself between the amount of time this mission appeared ready to consume and the sorrowful face of a young girl in danger. She usually got emotional over fictional characters, so that didn't surprise her. But saving this nonexistent kid cut into time that could be used racing other players to ten million bucks. Well, two million, after the split with the crew. Probably more like 1.2 after the government stole their share.

They disembarked the *Stormbringer* into a cavernous hull full of chewed-up shuttles and a handful of fighter craft. Broken bits glided around, spun in place, or caromed off walls, still in flight from the explosion that destroyed them.

"Crap, I hate zero gravity," said Angel813. "So hard to dodge."

Everyone's armor included a basic set of 'maneuvering jets' that the game controlled in much the same way as walking. A player had only to think of using them, and they worked. After messing around with a Niath, Fawkes took to the zero-g maneuvering with ease since it shared much of the same 'feel' as flying. While the winged alien handled like a sports car, the motion control thruster system steered more like a box truck.

They made their way to a large door on the inner wall. No sooner did they open it than a pack of rickety androids attacked in a flurry of laser blasts. Flashes and sparks snapped from the wall over her head from near misses. Fawkes yelped, ducked, and ran for cover behind a bulkhead strut, unable to engage stealth due to the intense brightness of the light plus the narrow confines of the corridor. She popped out and took a shot that hit a plastic-shelled android in the shoulder, knocking it away from its cover to the floor.

Nighthawk peppered it to death before it could even sit up.

"That innocent little girl is going to be some kind of space demon I bet," said Rallek. "It's going to be 'Oh, thank you for saving me; now die!'" He roared.

"Hah. Yeah, she was rather... pleading," said Angel813.

"If I was her age stuck on a ship like this, I'd be whiney and beggy, too." Fawkes popped up again and shot an android square in the face. The one next to it pivoted and tagged her in the chest with a burst. The annoying-but-not-painful hit slammed her into the wall. Her health bar dropped by twenty percent. "Oof. Well, these guys aren't *too* bad."

The familiar whir of one of Angel's medi-bots glided up behind her.

They made relatively short work of the ambush, and proceeded down the hall toward where the sensor sweep had picked up the lone human occupant. A third the way up the length of the passenger liner, they found a still-operational door with intact atmosphere on the other side.

"Good," said Kavan. "No more time limit."

One hallway full of combat androids led to another hallway full of combat androids. The fights never quite felt dangerous, but didn't reach boredom levels of ease. About twelve minutes after disembarking the *Stormbringer*, the crew reached a locked door.

"Your show," said Kavan, glancing at Fawkes.

She plugged in the override kit and accessed the hacking mini-game. "Oh, easy."

Forty seconds later, she reached the CPU after grabbing enough side captures to make an extra 900 credits and score two *Worm* software modules plus a *Freeze*.

"Totally owned that," said Fawkes.

The door slid open with a soft hiss, revealing a twelve-year-old girl in a miniature set of light space armor. Eyes full of terror and anger stared over a laser pistol she clutched in both hands. Upon seeing the crew, she lowered the weapon and went from angry to sobbing.

Rallek kept pointing his technomancer staff at her. "No funny business, kid."

"You made it!" She darted forward at Kavan and leapt into a hug.

He held her, his armored glove clicking on her gloss-blue armored back as he tried to be reassuring.

Angel813 glanced at Fawkes. "Wow," she muttered. "CSI stepping up their AI game."

Anastasia lifted her head away from Kavan's chest to glance at Angel813, confused for a moment before shifting her attention to the man holding her. "Thank you so much." She sniffled and wiped her eyes. "It's been days. I've been so scared."

"Crazy demon alien any second," muttered Rallek.

"I'm not a threat," said Anastasia. "But there is a complication."

"I knew it," muttered Rallek.

"What sort of complication?" asked Kavan.

She let go of him and took a step back, clasping her hands in front of herself. The look on her face would've been perfect for a kid telling her father she took the car without permission and accidentally wrecked it.

Rallek tensed, raising his staff.

"Oh, please calm down." Anastasia glanced at him. "I'm not going to attack anyone. I'm just a child. The complication is a moral dilemma."

"Whoa," muttered Fawkes. "That kid is reacting to stuff that I've never seen NPCs react to."

The girl glanced at her, but said nothing.

Nighthawk stood half in a daze, evidently entranced by her.

"Okay, I'll bite." Kavan folded his arms. "What's the moral dilemma?"

"You wondered why I was on this passenger ship instead of an official diplomatic vessel."

Kavan nodded. "Yeah."

"I am... or was... running away." Anastasia plucked a data pad off her belt. "My parents divorced when I was six. I found out three months ago that my father sent my mother away and threatened to have her killed if she tried to make contact with me. I was told that she abandoned us and hated me." She held her head high. "My father is not a nice person. I would rather you help me get to my mother on a planet not far from here, Atheos. I will be much happier there, but we won't be able to pay you as much of a reward as my father will."

"Okay..." Kavan rubbed his chin. "If that's true, why would you even give us the choice of where to bring you? Just tell us about your mother."

"Probably has to because of the quest," whispered Rallek. "Bringing her to Mom is more XP. Dad is cash."

"That makes dad the evil option," said Angel813. "The heel path always has a bigger payout."

Anastasia made a face like everyone started talking a foreign language. "Well, I wouldn't feel right if I wasn't honest with you. There is a chance that my father may learn that you helped me run away and... pay people to hurt you."

"It's okay, kiddo." Kavan picked up the blue helmet on a nearby table and tossed it to her. "Getting you off this tin can and to your mother is the easy part. If you can somehow pack all that hair of yours into that helmet, *that* will be impressive."

Anastasia grinned, and giggled. "You guys rock."

That NPC just reacted to a quip about her appearance. Fawkes' mouth hung open.

Everyone stood in stunned silence as the girl put her voluminous brown hair up and got the helmet on without a single strand showing.

The walk back to the docking bay felt like it took only seconds, surprisingly without a single combat.

"This kid is weird," said Rallek over group chat, so the girl wouldn't hear.

"Yeah. She's so damn real." Angel813 shivered. "I'm almost scared if that's an AI."

Fawkes twisted to peer at the medic. "What else could she be?"

Rallek shrugged. "Dunno, but consider me officially creeped out."

"Wow, is that your ship?" asked Anastasia once they reached the docking bay. "It's soooo pretty."

"Yeah. Keep your head down, kid. There's junk whizzing around in here." Kavan hesitated for a second, and took her by the hand. "Come on."

Fawkes grinned to herself. *He must have a kid.*

They ran, ducking the flying debris, not slowing until they reached the entry ramp of the *Stormbringer*.

Kavan hauled himself up the ladder from the cargo hold to the main deck and jogged to the bridge. Everyone else took their time moving to the main room as the ship lifted off and eased out of the dead passenger liner.

Anastasia removed her helmet, sat at the big round table, and behaved way too much like a genuine twelve-year-old for everyone's comfort level. A constant undercurrent of tension hung in the room, with the crew exchanging 'WTF' glances every few seconds as she asked them about their adventures. Nighthawk seemed to have an easy time talking to her, and monopolized much of her conversation.

The hop to Atheos didn't take long. From space, the planet appeared as a beautiful marble of blues, greens, and white, with a hint of rich teal at the deeper parts of the oceans. Kavan flew down into the atmosphere, following the child's direction to the city of Cerna Prime. There, he came in for a gentle landing on a pad at the starport. All around them rose a massive city of gleaming high rises and loopy elevated maglev tracks. Anastasia used the ship's system to make a video call to a rather ordinarily-dressed woman who bore a noticeable resemblance to her.

"Mom," said Anastasia, choking up. "It's really you! I'm okay. I made it! These people helped me."

"Oh, I'm so glad to see you, dear!" The woman grinned, acting much like a normal NPC. "I'll be right there."

The girl hung up the call and faced everyone, still wiping tears. "My mother will be here to pick me up soon. You guys are awesome!"

Unease persisted among the crew as she made her way around hugging everyone. Eventually, the sensors reported a small vehicle approaching the landing pad. Everyone armed up and tromped down the ramp to the landing pad, but the expected ambush turned out to be a forty-something woman in a compact car.

Anastasia ran to her, clamped on, and burst into tears.

"Hello, dear. It's so good to see you are okay." Mom smiled in the general direction of the crew. "Thank you for finding my daughter."

Anastasia hurried back over to the crew, grinning. "I can't believe I really got away from him and found my mother. I wish I had something to give you, but... I'm not rich anymore."

"Umm. You're welcome." Kavan set his hands on his hips and glanced up at the underside of the *Stormbringer.* "That was... a lot easier than I expected."

"Well, not every mission ends with a three-story-tall bug," said Rallek.

Anastasia blinked. "Three stories tall bug? Eww. Seriously?"

Mom stood patiently waiting by the car, wearing the standard 'content NPC' smile.

"Okay, what gives?" asked Fawkes. "Why are you so real?"

Anastasia bit her lip. "Well, since you finished saving me, I guess I can talk now."

Rallek raised his staff.

"Oh, calm down." She rolled her eyes at him. "I can't say too much or I'll get in trouble for breaking character, but I'm a real person. I'm not really twelve though."

Fawkes biffed herself in the head. "I knew it."

"I'm fifteen." Anastasia grinned. "It's a project for school. I'm in the accelerated drama program at Westfield, and they're have this thing going with CSI. Kids from my group get to play bit parts like this."

"Oh, that's cool." Fawkes grinned.

Rallek relaxed.

Nighthawk fidgeted.

"Thank you again for saving me. I need to go home." Anastasia hugged everyone again before running to the car and getting in.

"Well how about that," said Kavan. "CSI's using real actors now."

"One class in one performing arts high school?" Rallek shrugged. "Odds are high we'll never see another one of those. This is a huge game."

"What's wrong with you?" Fawkes poked Nighthawk in the side. "You look like someone shot your dog."

"She's real."

"Cool down there, bud," said Rallek. "Little young for you."

"What?" Nighthawk looked over at him. "Uhh, no. Not that. I mean, she looked so sad. I'm just... whatever." He hurried back onto the ship.

Rallek shot a questioning glance at Fawkes.

"Well that was weird," said Angel813.

"Yeah. Come on, we've got some coordinates to chase down." Fawkes jogged back up the ramp.

Thirteen minutes later, they dropped out of warp in the system specified by the datapad they'd found on the crashed fighter craft. Coordinates CF204.18 HH313.51 led them to an earthlike planet designated AN7145.

"Huh," said Rallek. "Looks like a rando world."

"Info sheet shows a scattering of small cities. Trade broadcast is showing mostly textiles and agriculture products," said Fawkes. "Though, there's a lot of narcotics for sale down there. Whoa, wait... No, 2,455 credits a cargo-box, this is where you'd *sell* the narcotics."

"Hot damn," said Kavan. "Last time I saw narco on the sell list it was like 780 creds per box. I'm half tempted to note this place for future reference."

"Don't do it," said Nighthawk. "If we start trading drugs, we'll get flagged as smugglers and then the cops will attack us every time we go to land on a planet with a high law rating."

Another sensor screen flashed orange. A sub-screen expanded to reveal a near-space map and an approaching ship. The Helm-class corvette had a horseshoe shape, its bridge at the middle of the curve between two extending side pods.

Fawkes yelled, "There's another ship approaching us," into the comm. "Its shields are up and weapons armed."

Green borders around her engineering console displays went yellow, indicating that Kavan had armed their weapons as well. Flying around with them 'off' served mostly to send a message to other ships as to one's intentions.

"They're hailing us, captain," said Fawkes, hamming it up.

"Knock it off," moaned Nighthawk. "You guys are so lame."

"Put it on the main screen," said Kavan.

"I guess I'll go give emotional advice to Rallek," said Angel813. Something meowed.

"No, that's the counselor. You're the doctor." Fawkes snickered.

"Argh," yelled Nighthawk.

A pleasant-looking man with short, curly brown hair and a smile appeared. "Greetings, I'm Veras Kalé of the *Feral*."

"Hey. Guess that makes me Kavan of the *Stormbringer*." He chuckled. "Sounds like a character that belongs in ROI."

Heh. Geez, I haven't thought of that old game for years.

Veras nodded in greeting. "So rare that two ships meet in a universe so vast, is it not?"

"Depends on what system you're sitting in," said Kavan.

"Indeed." Veras chuckled. "What brings you out to this particular middle of nowhere?"

Kavan shrugged. "Oh, just running a quest to collect the testicles of an Andilusian stag. They're native to this planet. Big purple suckers, but the drop rate's not good. Gotta kill like thirty of them to find one with balls."

Nighthawk broke into a fit of giggling.

Veras' eyebrow ticked upward. "Oh. I've never seen that quest. Are you sure? How odd."

"Yep. Pleasure meeting you. Now if you'll excuse us, we got some balls ta snip."

Veras offered a slow nod. "Happy, umm... questing."

Once the comm went black, Kavan grumbled. "Weird finding another player ship out here. Got the feeling he was milking us for information?"

Nighthawk continued cackling in the background.

"Cripes man," said Rallek, "It wasn't *that* funny."

"Down we go." Kavan emitted a laugh worthy of an evil mastermind, and accelerated toward the planet.

"What are we even looking for down here?" Rallek edged closer to the viewscreen, which soon became opaque with clouds.

"Some kind of facility," said Angel813, "where they made that warp drive."

"Be right back, bio break." Nighthawk disappeared as he logged out of the game.

"So, did anyone else think our gunslinger was looking at that kid a bit creepy weird?" asked Rallek.

"Ain't nothin' to that," said Kavan.

"Are you sure?" asked Angel813. "He was like, infatuated with that girl."

Kavan swung the pilot chair around, his expression firm, but calm. "Trust me. Nothing to worry about. I know him outside the game, and it's nothing at all to be concerned with."

"Okay, okay," muttered Fawkes, hands up in a placating gesture. She walked with Rallek and Angel813 down the hall from the bridge to the main room and flopped in one of the chairs around the big table. After an awkward minute of silence, she half-whispered, "I know it looked like he thought her cute, but maybe, I dunno... something else happened. Dude might've had a kid get sick and die and he was feeling all messed up about that."

"Could be." Rallek shrugged. "If you ask me, it was creepier how he seemed disappointed when she said she was fifteen and not really twelve."

"Maybe his kid wasn't that old, and he got sad because she wouldn't ever be." Angel813 stared into the table, stroking the longhaired purple vanity pet in her lap, a six-legged cat with fox ears and ruby-gem eyes. "Okay, well, now I made myself want to cry." She clapped her hands together. "Let's do something fun."

Fawkes opened an internet window and searched for information about the *Feral*. "That other ship is bugging me."

"Back!" yelled Nighthawk. "Where are you guys? Oh..." He trotted into the main room and headed right to the food printer. "Anyone want anything?"

"Chocolate ice cream," said Angel813. "With fudge."

"Hey Fawkes," said Kavan via the comm. "Are you going to scan the surface or should I?"

"Gimme a sec. I'm checking on that ship."

She looked over the crew profile on the Axillon99 main site. Another group of five players, though they ranged from 44-48 in level. "Little higher than us, but their ship is comparable to ours. Helm-class corvette." The other ship lacked the sleek design of the *Stormbringer*, but then again, how maneuverable could a flying horseshoe be? It did, however, pack more firepower in the side pods, carrying a heavy particle beam cannon and two Class 3 lasers on each side. Armor and shield points generally matched between the two ships.

Nothing remarkable there, so she clicked off it. The third link on the page behind led to the contest leaderboard.

Grand Designs (Tied)
Feral (Tied)
The Stormbringer (Tied)

"Eeeek!" squealed Fawkes. "You were right, Kavan!"

"What?" he yelled over the comm.

"Look at the leaderboard! We're on it and so are they. All tied!"

"Son of a bitch," muttered Rallek. "I bet they followed us here."

"The coordinates in that message weren't hidden. We found it, so did they. But I bet they're stuck not knowing where to go on this planet." Fawkes scratched her head. "I better keep an eye out for that ship. If they see where we go, we won't have any advantage over them."

"Holy crap guys, are we really like in the running for that prize money?" Angel813 shivered while inhaling an overburdened spoonful of ice cream.

Nighthawk sat at the table with a huge basket of chicken nuggets and fries. "Yep. We're closer than nineteen million other people, and dead even with two other crews."

"I'm gonna pass out," said Angel813. "I can't believe it!"

He pointed a chicken nugget at her. "If we win that money, would you still be a nurse?"

She looked at him for a long minute of silence. "You know, I think I would. At least until I get old enough where it starts to hurt more than its worth."

"Screw that coffee thing. If we win, I'm *so* out. My butt's gonna live off interest, but I might look for a programming gig."

"You're a programmer?" asked Kavan. "Send me your resume. Maybe I can get you in the door at my place. We're always looking for new blood."

She scrunched up her nose. "Don't you write like accounting software?"

"Yeah it's terribly exciting stuff," he deadpanned, "but it pays better than pouring coffee."

Fawkes bit her lip. "You make a good point."

"That's awesome though, we're on the high score list," said Nighthawk.

"Not really." Rallek let out a long, slow exhale. "That's just put a giant target on our asses."

Fawkes shrugged one shoulder. "So? It's only a game."

"Hey Fawkes, you got any kinda sensor stealth?" asked Kavan over the comm. "The *Feral* is tailing us."

14

KEEP STABBING IT IN THE TOE

Fawkes ran to the engineering station in the back, her home for almost all ship-to-ship combat situations. Since Kavan had tagged the *Feral* in the navigation/tracking system, one of the sub-screens showed a view of it above and behind them.

"This is where that physics shit would be nice," muttered Fawkes.

"Which 'physics shit?'" asked Rallek.

She opened a list of possible tech mods and scrolled down, looking for something useful. "That thing Nighthawk was talking about the other day. Atmospheric differences on flight speed. Their ship is shaped like a giant cartoon magnet. We're much more aerodynamic... we should be able to outrun them planetside."

"Oh, right."

"Yeah," yelled Nighthawk, from the upper turret. "Their weapons are offline. Guess they don't want to spook us into a fight."

"No," said Angel813. "They probably saw us on that leaderboard and want to know what we know that they don't."

Kavan laughed. "Problem is, we don't have anything. I'm going to fly around in random circles."

Line after line of temporary performance boost scrolled by at the behest of her swiping finger, but nothing looked helpful. The *Feral* had gotten too close for sensor masking. Even if they managed to disappear from the other ship's instruments, the pilot could still see them.

"Ugh," said Fawkes. "If only the ship could..." She whipped around and stared at Rallek. "That spell!"

He leaned back, one eyebrow raised, a sly grin starting across his lip. "Can you vague that up a little more?"

"The one you used on Nighthawk." She grabbed the front of his fancy armor and shook him. "That lets player abilities work on the ship."

"Oh, yeah that one. What about it?"

She let go of him and grabbed the engineering desk. "Get ready to hit me with it." She raised her voice at the console. "Kavan, look for a mountain or something we can slip behind to break line of sight with them for a few seconds."

"On it."

"What are you gonna do?" asked Rallek.

She shook her head. "For a magic user, you're not thinking. I'm a rogue. We're trying to hide."

His jaw hung open. "I... don't know if that'll work. Stealth is a base ability, not a cooldown. Hang on, let me read the description of *Transference*. Rallek's face tinted blue in the light from a floating screen.

"Got a mountain up ahead about a minute away," said Kavan's voice from the console. "What's the plan?"

"I'm going to try to hide the ship." Fawkes widened her stance, gripping the console with both hands.

"You're being dramatic," muttered Rallek. "All you need to do is touch the ship and you can't help but do that while inside... unless the artificial gravity shuts off."

"Well, this feels like a dramatic moment." She shrugged. "So is it gonna work?"

"Nothing in the way it's worded makes me think it wouldn't... it's just—well, if it did work, you'd think people would have done it already and gotten it nerfed."

She growled. "Don't get me started on that. Besides, no one mixes techno-mancer and rogue. It would be a cool idea, but all the low-level stuff in TM is debuffs and summons. Nothing I'd even want is in the tree until ten levels deep and at that point it's too much of an investment."

"Five seconds," said Kavan.

Rallek held his hands up and muttered some of his ad-libbed gibberish. Faint white light radiated from his fingertips and surrounded her. "Okay. Spell's cast."

Fawkes didn't feel any different, but she prepared to try. A chase view on one of her screens showed the *Stormbringer* enter a left-banking turn around a mountain. As soon as it looked like the *Feral* could no longer see them, she flexed the mental button that activated stealth.

The ship lurched forward from a sudden slowdown, and the floor became transparent.

Angel813 and Nighthawk screamed in panic.

"What the damn hell did you do?" shouted Kavan. "We just dropped to half speed!"

"Yes!" shouted Fawkes, grinning like an idiot. "It worked! We're in stealth."

Roaring engines thundered overhead as the *Feral* shot past them, still a good ways above. Angel813 kept screaming about her fear of heights. Nighthawk's terrified wail gave way to cheering and proclamations of how 'cool' it was to see the ground through the floor.

"What happened to my ship?" yelled Kavan.

"It's because we're in stealth." Fawkes stared down at her fingers gripping the edge of the console. She, too, had become semitransparent and didn't want to move for fear the connection might break. "That's normal. My character looks like that, too. It's how the game tells you hiding worked."

"Oh," said Kavan, then laughed. "They're swinging back and forth, hunting for us."

She remained motionless while they flew in the other direction and kept low to the ground. Thirty seconds later, the ship became solid again.

"Spell wore off," said Rallek.

"Right." She grabbed a weird fictional tool halfway between a wrench and a soldering iron and poked it in one of the cabinets. That combination of tool plus location created a sensor-blocking effect. "There. We're at seventy percent shields, but won't show up on anyone's sensors unless you arm weapons."

"Excellent," said Kavan. "Now, does anyone have any damn idea what we're looking for on this planet?"

"A research facility," deadpanned Angel813. "Somewhere."

Fawkes pored over the sensor console, trying to bring up a list of structures and settlements. Nighthawk walked around the ship in an endless pattern, occasionally muttering, "Boredboredbored."

She glanced at him as he passed her, heading toward the bridge. *He's not even trying to help. Fighter pilots are such prima donnas. Like oversized children.*

"Huh, I think I've been staring at this map too long," said Angel813 perhaps forty minutes later. "I'm starting to see animals. That brown spot looks like an armadillo." She laughed.

"Wait, what?" said Rallek, running out from the engineering deck toward the main room. "Did you say armadillo?"

Fawkes, curiosity piqued, followed, since the scanners weren't helping. A huge widescreen map floated over the round table, tinting the whole area dark brown-red. Swaths of greenish forest separated bands of open crimson sand, a bit like Mars. The planet had white polar caps on both sides and millions of large lakes, but nothing big enough to count as an ocean.

"Yeah." Angel813 pointed at one of the larger bands of vegetation where a group of brown spots close together created the shape of a half-curled armadillo. "Right there."

"Kavan, go to this point." Rallek stuck his finger into the map hologram. An answering chirp came from the bridge computer.

Angel813 leaned back, eyebrows up. "Mind explaining the magic armadillo?"

Rallek gestured at the air and a slab of bright green hologram opened. He tapped at the floating terminal window, a 'net access client, and pulled up the main page of Cognition Systems International. The top left corner of the page had a blue square with the letters CSI in white, and a logo of an armadillo perched on top of the C. "It's their company symbol."

"Oh..." Fawkes' eyes widened. "Wow that's subtle as hell." She grabbed Angel813's arm and gave her a congratulatory shake. "Nice find!"

The medic brushed her fingernails off on her armor while making an 'I meant to do that' face.

For sixteen minutes, everyone kept their eyes out for any sign of the *Feral*, but they'd either gotten bored and given up or searched the wrong part of the planet, far enough away not to see them.

"Got something up ahead," said Kavan. "This spot doesn't really look much like an armadillo. Only on the map."

Rallek tapped a finger to his chin. "It would be a lot easier to notice that way. The map doesn't match the terrain. Proof CSI wanted to make this place difficult to find."

Fawkes bounced on her toes, giddy with anticipation. She leaned on Rallek, daydreaming about a life where she didn't have to spend eight hours a day on her feet getting bitched at about how much espresso went into a cup of milk.

"What is it?" asked Nighthawk.

"Building. Pretty big from the looks of it. Gotta be abandoned. There's holes in the wall full of vegetation. I'm going to land as close as I can." Kavan sounded unusually optimistic. "Let's check this bad boy out and see what's here."

Fawkes held on to the wall until the ship came to rest on its landing pads and stopped shaking. One nice thing about being a space explorer in a video game compared to reality: most planets had human-friendly air.

The crew gathered on the cargo ramp, riding it down as it opened with Kavan leading the way. A blast of wind washed over them, carrying an overwhelming smell of 'vegetation' with a few subtle notes of rust and industrial chemicals. They'd set down at the edge of a brown patch of bare dirt where nothing grew, a veritable moat surrounding a massive all-metal structure about fifty yards away. The plain rectangular building looked large enough for the *Stormbringer* to fly around inside it. A pair of towers jutted up from either end, shaped like upside-down kitchen waste bins—if kitchen waste bins stood twenty stories tall. Comparatively thin spars spanned between the towers, suggesting where a spacecraft might have once hung while being constructed.

Huge gaping holes in the wall fringed with greenery peered in on smashed technology and office furniture. Fawkes looked up at it, whistling in awe at the sheer scale of the structure.

Kavan followed the ghost of an old access road that curved around to the left end by one tower's base and connected to an enormous trapezoidal entrance. The door, two immense slabs of metal with interlocking teeth, appeared stuck a quarter of the way open.

"Whoa, that's a big door." Nighthawk whistled. "I could fly the Gremlin through that."

"It's not that wide," said Rallek.

Nighthawk pivoted his hand sideways. "I'd roll it ninety degrees."

"Wow..." Fawkes craned her neck back to stare up at the crenelations running up the edge of the door on her left. Each cutout looked big enough to stack three cars in, the metal ten feet thick from outside to inside. "Slamming your thumb in this door would hurt so bad."

"I don't think it's moved in quite a long time." Rallek kicked at dirt in the track the doors slid in.

The room beyond appeared to be a staging area for spaceship parts. Boxes, stacks of shipping containers, and the heavy machinery needed to move them around littered the place. Fawkes stared up at the interior of the tower and felt like a mouse dangled over a trashcan. Platforms jutted out of the walls, approximating a floor at every story, though most of the space up the middle remained wide open, save for dangling machinery that might've been used to lift chunks of starship up to the top. Gazing into twenty-stories of mostly open space overhead caused a jolt of vertigo that made her stumble.

"Well, this is definitely some kind of facility," said Kavan, creeping forward with his rifle poised.

A shimmer of red light appeared on the ground in front of him with the profile of a speed bump.

Fawkes shouted, "Wait! That's a—"

He stepped on it.

"Trap." She let her arm drop.

Everyone spun to face her, but before any words could fly, the titanic door behind them slammed closed, sending a spray of dirt into the air. Fawkes screamed (not that anyone heard) and collapsed under the ridiculously loud *boom* of six-story tall steel slabs crashing together.

Disturbed dirt left a waist-high haze of pale brown fog around them.

"Little more warning next time maybe?" asked Nighthawk.

Fawkes got annoyed and jumped upright, pointing. "It *just* appeared. The game only let me notice it right as he was stepping on it."

"You know, it most games, the party lets the thief go first to find traps," said Angel813.

"I'm not a thief. I'm a rogue."

Kavan tilted his head at her. "What's the difference?"

"I'm a stealthy spy-slash-ambusher. I don't steal."

With an ear-splitting screech of scraping metal, a huge pile of stacked boxes slid aside to reveal a twenty-foot-tall humanoid robot, bristling with guns and missiles. It had a glowing red stripe for eyes, big enough to be a window into the pilot's compartment in the head—but this thing looked like an android, not a vehicle. Parts of its arms and legs somewhat resembled a heavy fighter craft, including folded wings jutting out of its back.

"Oh, shit," said Nighthawk.

Kavan swatted him on the arm.

"Don't care. Giant battle mech is an 'oh shit' moment." Nighthawk pointed at it.

"Kinda looks like a Transformer," said Kavan.

"A what?" asked Nighthawk.

"Old toy." Kavan rushed forward a few steps to take cover behind a huge metal box.

The rest of the crew followed suit.

"Maybe it didn't see us," whispered Rallek.

A blue laser beam as thick as a man's thigh burst out of the metal container and hit the floor, leaving a neat hole in the steel with flaming edges.

"Or perhaps it did," said Rallek. "Hey, look at the upside."

An explosion in front of the cargo box everyone hid behind pushed it back ten feet, knocking Nighthawk on his ass.

"There's an upside?" asked Angel813 between coughing on smoke.

Rallek flashed a shit-eating grin. "It's a robot. My best spells will work on it."

"Well, looks like we've got two choices. Kill it or die." Kavan readied his energy shield. "Here goes."

He ran out into view, dashing up to the thing's giant boot-shaped leg while firing his attention-getting shot. Angel813 peered out from behind the cargo box, grunted in annoyance at his getting out of her range, and rushed after him, plucking medi-bots from her harness in preparation to launch them.

Fawkes ducked into stealth and slipped around to the left. She waited at the corner hoping Kavan would continue his habit of rotating bosses away from the party. After a few more blasts from his rifle, he ran between its legs. The huge robot shook the ground as it pivoted to follow him, exposing its back and a massive double rocket booster 'jetpack.'

"If that thing turns into a Starfighter, I'm going to give the hell up on this prize," said Angel813.

Fawkes crept closer. Nighthawk stood in place, pelting it with a steady barrage of laser fire the same way he did during most boss battles. She couldn't help but snicker at Eric's assessment of Nighthawk's play style: high damage simple-to-play classes. Then again, most players considered auramancers the 'easy healer.' Having played one for a while messing around, she decided that not having to strategize combos to be effective was relaxing. Part of her enjoyed the complexity of the rogue, even if she had to work three times as hard to keep up with Nighthawk's gunslinger... but taking a break with an 'easy' class made the game into a game again, something to do for fun.

Not to mention even an awesome medic couldn't match an auramancer for single-target healing output unless they had a significant gear advantage. The big guilds always had one or two auramancers dedicated to keeping the tank alive.

Rallek lobbed spells at Kavan, likely buffing him up to make Angel813's job easier.

"Barely hurting it," shouted Nighthawk.

Once Fawkes got in range, she fired an ambush shot. One nice thing about huge bosses, she didn't have to worry about missing. The ambush hit critically for 180 points. "Whoa, this damn thing is energy resistant."

"Ya think?" yelled Nighthawk, who'd been pelting it for a steady stream of about twenty points a shot.

Fawkes ran closer to the huge metal boot, skidding to a stop about ten feet away. Lasers and missiles flew overhead, showering her with the occasional blast of dust or fragments of blown-up cargo box. She plucked her override tool off her belt and activated its wireless mode, targeting the giant robot.

"Heads up!" shouted Angel813.

With a great *whoosh* of rocket engines, nine missiles flew from the boss' shoulders in graceful arcs to the ground in a mostly random arrangement. Wherever one exploded, it left a fifteen-foot wide patch of glowing green goop. Naturally, at least one missile landed on top of everyone except Kavan.

Fawkes yelped at the sensation like an army of two-year-olds smacking her in the shins with wooden spoons. Every second, her health ticked down by eight percent. She scrambled out of the glowing patch.

Nighthawk leapt into a flying somersault, leaving his 'patch of badness' behind. He rolled back to his feet and kept on shooting. A medi-bot floated up to Fawkes and began spraying her with healing. She looked back down at the override kit and the hacking mini-game. Not caring about wasting unneeded temporary buffs, she invoked a *Freeze* soft, and an *Overclock* (which increased the speed of her blue line). Nothing quite made burning a 5,000 credit cooldown feel trivial like trying to hack in the shadow of a giant robot.

She looked up for a second when Angel813 screamed. Kavan lay flat on his back with five percent health left. The robot reared its hand back to pound him again. Angel813 grabbed two thermos-sized syringes from her belt and ran at him. She dropped into a slide and crashed into him, hitting him with both needles.

His health bar leapt to 120 percent.

The fist came down with a thunderous crash, leaving him with eighteen percent health and also taking Angel813 down to five percent.

She scrambled back, launching a trio of medi-bots around herself.

"Stay out of melee," yelled Rallek.

"No shit," shouted Angel813. "My big heal's touch ranged! I had no choice."

Rallek cast a spell that projected a stream of wires and glowing circuit lines into the robot's back. Its health bar chipped down enough to notice, and the robot started to turn toward him. "Crap! I got aggro!"

Kavan roared at it, and the robot again seemed to want him dead the most.

The override kit chimed as Fawkes took the final node with a big lead. Stats appeared in a list, plus she applied a ten percent debuff to the robot for hacking it, reducing its health and damage output. Unfortunately, being a 'boss,' she didn't have the option to take control of it. She skimmed the stats, noticing it had a ninety percent resistance to energy damage, but a vulnerability to physical attacks.

"It's weak to physical damage!" shouted Fawkes. "Lasers are worthless on it!"

Nighthawk whined. "I don't have bullet pistols. Ammo's annoying."

"Annoying beats dead," yelled Angel813.

Kavan put his rifle away and pulled a broadsword off his back. The edges glowed with blue light once the vibro-blade kicked on. He glanced at the boot-shaped foot taller than him, and wagged the sword at the party. "This is ridiculous. What am I going to do to that thing with this? It's like trying to kill someone with a penknife."

"Keep stabbing it in the toe," said Rallek, grinning. "It's just damage."

"It's silly!" Kavan slashed at the huge metal boot, leaving a gouge in the armor and causing a noticeable chip in its health bar. "Wow this is so stupid. There's nothing vital in its foot, but it'll still die if I hit it enough."

"Incoming," shouted Angel813.

Another barrage of goo missiles went off, plastering the floor with nine more circular zones of glowing green death. Fawkes started running before her missile struck, suffering only one tick of damage from the edge of the disc. She flailed her arms to keep her balance when she stopped short at the start of another patch. Areas of clean floor between the glowing splats wouldn't be there for long if it kept launching those things.

"This whole room's going to be toxic!" shouted Fawkes. "How long do the patches last?"

"Probably until combat ends," said Angel813.

"Go up!" yelled Kavan, pointing his blade at the open floors around the walls. "Second story!"

Nighthawk and Rallek sprinted for a stairwell.

Fawkes put her CL32 away and pulled out a pair of vibro daggers. She whined at them being level twenty items. Still, despite their shitty damage (20-40), they'd probably hit harder on this thing than her laser due to its resistances. Unfortunately, they also required getting close. Generally speaking, melee attacks did more damage than ranged. It didn't exactly make sense, but close-in attacks took more effort than ranged combat, not to mention almost every boss in the game had special short-range attacks to screw over melee people.

Still, she could be useless at range or take a risk and maybe do something close in.

Fawkes sprinted forward, earning a 'what the hell are you doing' look from Kavan. She stopped on the other side of the robot's leg and raked her daggers at it as fast as she could swing them.

"Welcome to melee," said Kavan. "I didn't know you specced for it."

"I don't." She kept slashing, involuntarily grunting with the effort. "But it's laughing off my laser pistol."

Vents on the sides of its legs opened, spewing a green, noxious cloud that expanded to fill an area about ten feet in all directions from the robot, where it mysteriously stopped.

Jolts just shy of painful whacked her from all angles. Yelping, Fawkes jumped backward to get out of the cloud and wandered into a green slime circle. Her health dipped below twenty percent for a second before three medi-bots appeared around her. She jumped clear of the floor patch and glared hatefully at the haze of green hanging low around the robot's legs.

"How am I supposed to melee it with that poison cloud?"

"In and out," said Angel813. "Bosses do that all the time. AOO's got a melee coordinator that calls movement. When the cloud fades, go back in. Time how long it takes to do it again, and jump out the next time *before* the gas comes."

Fawkes groaned.

"Dammit." Kavan pounded it in the foot over and over again with his vibro-sword while ducking and weaving around a car-sized fist trying to flatten him.

Rallek, now on one of the second floor tiers, hit the robot with a direct damage 'tech bolt.' The instant the bot took damage, another panel on its chest opened, spraying a barrage of dozens of tiny missiles. In seconds, the entire second-story area glowed with green poison goo.

Screaming in alarm, Rallek and Nighthawk rushed for the stairs while Angel813 frantically hurled medi-bots at them.

"It's boot is taller than I am. Why do they have to make bosses so damned big?" yelled Kavan.

Fawkes and Angel813 simultaneously deadpanned, "Compensating."

15

VENOM SHROUD

The instant the poison cloud faded, Fawkes ran back in and resumed chipping away at it with her knives. Kavan's sword seemed to be pissing it off the most though, which gave her a small cushion of safety. She *Flickered* into stealth and double-stabbed it, pulling off an 888 point critical. A three-millimeter section of its life bar fell off.

Rallek wailed in the distance as Nighthawk's, "Crap, crap, crap" took on a strange echoing quality.

"Shit!" screamed Angel813. "You guys got too far away!"

Fawkes glanced at the party list. Both Nighthawk and Rallek had died. Spinning green coin icons with skulls in them hovered over where they went down, Rallek near the top of the stairs and Nighthawk a few steps behind him, still on the second floor walkway.

"This isn't going well," said Kavan.

For about six minutes, Fawkes pulled a woodchipper on the robot leg, ducking in and out of range to avoid the poison cloud whenever it sprayed. She'd at least gotten that timing down. Out of every sixty seconds, the cloud existed for fifteen. If only the tank stood in melee range, the robot didn't even use that, which meant her attempt to be useful caused more damage to hit Kavan. Almost the entire floor had been coated in lime green death at that point, leaving nowhere to stand without taking constant poison damage.

Once Angel813 pulled a laser pistol and started firing, Fawkes figured the wipe imminent.

Sure enough, Kavan went down four seconds later. Before Kavan's body even finished collapsing, a massive robotic fist pounded Fawkes' body away from her ghost, swatting it fifty or sixty yards across the room. She hit the wall with a loud *smack*, stuck for a second, and peeled away before falling face down on the ground. Unable to heal herself, and with nowhere to stand, Angel813 dropped to the poison on the floor.

"Really?" shouted Fawkes' ghost. "Can't just kill me, you have to make me look stupid, too?"

The robot stood straight, no longer in a combat pose, and calmly walked back to the spot where it had emerged. All the boxes and crates that had concealed it rushed back into place, making it appear to be an innocent stack of resources. Patch by patch, the green ooze circles faded away.

Ghosts of the crew wandered together, assembling by the spot of floor with the trap pressure plate.

"Well, that sucked," said Kavan, his spectral voice echoing.

Angel813 stared down, her expression a confusing mixture of anger and guilt.

"Hey." Rallek patted her on the shoulder. "That wasn't your fault."

The medic shrugged.

"Seriously. We were not ready for this. No one here is blaming the healer."

"Thanks." Angel813 begrudgingly peeled her gaze off the floor. "Still feels like I screwed up."

The room blurred.

Everyone appeared standing outside the facility, no longer ghosts.

"Damn, the doors are still closed." Nighthawk put his hand on them by the seam. "Oh, dammit. We're shut out of here for a week."

"Is that supposed to be a raid, or do we just suck that much?" asked Fawkes.

"Well." Kavan paced back and forth. "For one thing, we're energy heavy. None of us have current-level weapons that inflict physical damage. And none of us really have our elemental resistances up."

"No one needs ER until level sixty," said Rallek.

Fawkes pointed at the huge door. "That's a raid and it's not level sixty."

He flailed his arms. "They don't even stat gear with resistances until level fifty-eight or so."

"Wait." Nighthawk raised a finger. "There's a poison shield mod reward from this quest on Epsilon2. It's hard for a level thirty-five quest, and the reward is only that mod, so most people skip it."

"What's this mod do?" asked Fawkes.

"It's for a PFF, uhh, personal force field." Nighthawk tapped his belt at the left hip. "We'd kinda have to get those, too. Basically, extra wearable hit points."

"They're like twenty grand," said Rallek. "And only add 250 points. No one bothers with them since they go down so fast."

"Right." Nighthawk nodded. "But this mod is ninety-five percent poison resistance."

"Oh, that makes sense." Kavan rubbed his chin. "The PFFs aren't intended to be used for absorbing general damage. It's got to be a mechanism to let players selectively tweak elemental resistance for certain boss fights."

Fawkes looked at Angel813. "Does Army of One do that?"

She shrugged. "Yeah I think so. I, umm, didn't bother. You know that whole 'too much like work' thing? I kinda figured being a healer would let me coast a little."

"Guess not," said Nighthawk.

She laughed. "No, I got rotated out for a damn Niath auramancer. I'm a better AOE healer, but that other girl did all the farming and read the strats and stuff. No big deal. Whatever. I'm here to have fun, not bust my ass. Getting through content eventually is good for me; I don't have to be first."

"Well." Kavan folded his arms. "Since it's going to be a couple days before we can get back in there, we might as well go farm up that shield mod... and buy some PFFs to put it in." He poked Rallek. "Maybe you could go on a weekend-long farming bender and scare up something useful."

"Hmm." Rallek crossed his arms, rubbing his chin. "Medics can craft a performance enhancing serum that increases physical damage dealt. It's meant for melee characters, but the coding is stupid so it buffs bullet damage, too."

Fawkes laughed.

"Best I can do is some arcane elixirs that increase the bonuses provided by tech armor," said Rallek. "But I know where to farm the materials for that... and the serum."

Angel813 blinked. "Wait, you're serious? You spent a whole weekend farming herbs?"

Rallek nodded. "Not a *whole* weekend. Like a fourteen-hour bender. I pulled in seventeen full stacks of Lotari leaf."

She whistled in awe.

"Damn, dude." Nighthawk blinked. "You could've sold that for mad bank."

Rallek grinned. "I did sell a couple stacks."

"Okay, so... new plan." Kavan walked off toward the *Stormbringer.* "Get that mod. Get shields. Get potions. And we try this again."

Fawkes raised a hand. "We all need to get physical weapons, too. The poison patches are a time wipe mechanic. If we don't kill that robot fast enough, there will be nowhere left to stand."

"And going up won't work either," said Rallek. "It auto-floods the entire second story with nasty poison. Basically the developers saying 'No, no, no, don't do that.'"

Everyone filed up the ramp into the ship.

"We have a plan." Kavan nodded. "Next time, that robot's going *down.*"

"It goes without saying," added Rallek. "None of us should talk, post, or comment about this fight anywhere."

"Next stop: Epsilon2." Kavan tromped off to the bridge.

16

A LITTLE HELP

The shield mod quest had more reason than difficult opponents and an apparently lackluster reward to make it distasteful. Slogging through a mile and a half of sewer tunnel while waist deep in alien fecal matter would haunt Dakota's nightmares for months. Especially the part about the Simarin poop being insanely slippery.

She'd slipped and gone under about ten times.

Some worthless slob of a programmer had to either research or invent what it felt like to have warm, slippery, oily, slime covering a person. After logging off for the night, she took a long shower in the real world, trying to scrub away the feeling. Its stench bothered her the most. The summer she'd been eleven, she'd gotten caught trying to hack the school computer. As punishment, her parents made her clean out a deep freeze cabinet in the garage that had conked out. Five pounds of once-frozen salmon left to steep in its own juices for two months created a yellow-pink sludge that stank with such aggressive awfulness that she'd thrown up twice before her brain could even ascribe a sense of smell to it. Somehow, that alien poop had the same molten-plastic/fishy rot smell, as if the game knew what the worst smell she'd ever experienced was.

Hours later at the Amazon Café, Dakota still randomly shuddered whenever her brain tortured her with that memory. To make matters worse, the sewer-slog didn't even result in the shield mod reward; only a data pad drop that started another quest intended for a starship crew, and *that* mission appeared to give out the shield mod. At Rallek's insistence, the group didn't all run the sewers at the same time, in case the competition might be following them. She got her quest link last night, as well as purchased a PFF to put the mod in when they eventually got it. Kavan completed the quest an hour after she ran it. Rallek and Angel813 would suffer the smelly mess tonight, and Nighthawk would do it sometime earlier in the afternoon.

A black-haired woman in her mid-thirties walked into the café with two tween girls. Both kids remained nose-deep in their smartphones, giggling back and forth with each other while hovering behind their mother.

"Hi. Welcome to the Amazon Café. What can I get started for you?" asked Dakota.

"Ooh, her hair is so cool," said the slightly smaller girl. "Mom, can I get that color?"

"No," muttered the woman. "Blue is not an appropriate color for hair."

Dakota's smile turned fake until the taller girl stuck her tongue out at her mother.

The woman stopped short of frowning at Dakota's near snicker and stared up at the menus. "Let me get a large caramel latte. A small coconut latte, and a small mocha latte."

"Umm..." Dakota's eyebrows inched up.

"Yes, I'm fully aware those are coffee drinks. I'm not about to have some teenage flake with blue hair challenge my abilities as a parent. Clearly, you haven't had a good example of parenting in your life. Please refrain from commenting and just pour coffee like you're paid to."

Dakota blinked. *Just think about all the time I'd have for Axillon99 if I quit right now.* Her jaw tightened.

The smaller girl mouthed 'sorry' without making a sound.

I'm such an addict. I'm addicted to having a roof over my head. Her smile more plastic than ever, Dakota set to the task of assembling the drinks. A few minutes later, she set the three cups on the pick-up counter.

The older daughter grabbed the mocha and made eye contact with Dakota. "Don't mind her. She's been pissed off at the world ever since Dad left for a woman half her age."

"Ashley Nicole!" roared the woman. "How dare you!"

"See what I mean?" asked Ashley. "All bitch all the time. It's not your fault."

The other sister clamped both hands over her mouth, her eyes bulging.

Mom stormed over and glowered at Ashley. "I'll not be made a fool of by my own daughter."

"Too late." Ashley looked up at her. "You made a fool of yourself by biting off this lady's head for no reason. Stop letting Dad win. Why are you always so angry?" Calm as can be, Ashley took the other small coffee, walked around her mother, and joined her sister at a table.

The dumbstruck woman stood there for a second or two staring at Dakota.

"Can I get you anything else, ma'am?" asked Dakota, electing *not* to release any of the five or six wiseass comments circling her brain.

"Some ice for that burn," said Ashley.

"Stop it," whispered the other girl.

The mother shook her head and sighed before collecting her coffee and joining the girls at the table. Whatever murmured conversation went on between them failed to reach Dakota's ears. She fantasized about a quest to take the two girls away from their horrible mom and ferry them across the galaxy to a loving-but-absent father. Blake glided by and shook his head with a 'geez, some people' eye-roll.

A short while later when the little family left, Ashley waved goodbye.

Dakota spent the next few hours slipping thoughts of Axillon99 in between dealing with people. At every lull, she hopped on her smartphone and hunted for missions that offered a ballistic firearm as a reward. As a general rule, projectile weapons did more damage than lasers, but came with the downside of relatively expensive ammunition that weighed a ton. By way of comparison, her CL32 got 250 shots on a single e-pack, which she could recharge for free. A ballistic handgun of the same level and quality would get only 20 shots or so per magazine, at a cost of like thirty credits per reload. Granted, a blue slug thrower of the same level hit harder, averaging 175-250 damage instead of the 142-213 of her CL32. But... basically unlimited ammo made a *strong* case for going laser—unless one ran into a boss like the giant robot that took inflated damage from physical attacks and almost nothing from energy.

The more she read up on it, the more she realized that few creatures had resistance to physical attacks while energy resistances were common. A handful of creatures that *did* possess physical resistance had tons of it, which probably started players thinking 'bullets are useless' after one bad encounter.

It might not be a bad idea to keep a backup weapon up to date.

Of course, anything good would have to be a drop. The weapons and armor available from stores represented the lowest baseline of gear for a given level range. Only someone who'd just re-specced their character and needed completely different stat allocations would ever bother with store-bought gear.

She looked up as the door emitted a *ping*. A somewhat pudgy pale guy with an old winter coat, long stringy hair, and a creepy, vacant look in his eyes wandered in. He approached the counter and stared at her.

"Hi. Welcome to Amazon Café. What can I get started for you?" asked Dakota.

The guy remained silent for a long few minutes, his mouth slightly open. She debated asking him if he had special needs while wondering if he'd suffered brain damage in the past, but aside from the not-all-there look in his eyes, he didn't have any physical abnormalities.

Blake muttered the banjo riff from *Deliverance* as he shuffled past her.

"Sir? Can I help you with anything?" asked Dakota.

"Coffee, please."

Okay, he can talk. "Plain coffee? A latte? Espresso?"

He broke eye contact finally, and peered up at the menu screens. "Let me get a chocolate one, large."

"Large mocha latte?" asked Dakota.

The man nodded.

"Be right out. Nine eighty-five please."

He pulled his hand out from the jacket pocket and deposited a severely-crinkled ten-dollar-bill on the counter. Dakota picked it up, barely managing to suppress the cringe at touching the warm, sweat-soaked paper. She dropped it in an empty section of the till to keep it away from other currency before plucking a dime and a nickel out for his change.

"Your drink will be out in a moment, over there." She nodded to the counter at her right.

The man remained close by, up on tiptoe to peer over the counter. He stared at her the whole time she assembled the latte, obvious and creepy enough that Blake approached and hovered right next to her, though that didn't dissuade the guy in the least.

She set the drink on the counter. "There you go. Have a nice day."

He picked the coffee up, but didn't walk away.

Ugh. What is it with creeps! She tried not to look at him, busying herself with rearranging pitchers, cleaning the foam nozzle, checking flavored syrup levels and so on. Every time she risked a peek up, she made eye contact with the guy who *still* stood right by the counter watching her.

The fifth time, she opened her mouth to ask what his problem was, but before she could say a word, he walked off to a table.

"The fuck is wrong with that guy?" muttered Dakota.

"Language," said Hal from the back room.

Dakota blinked. She walked over to the flapping plastic door, and stuck her head in. "Hal? What's up with the language thing? It's like you're more offended someone might use a dirty word than, oh, this customer wants to throw me over the counter and tear my pants off. You're basically implying they can steal and rape all they want, just don't swear, 'cause swearing's worse."

"Say what?" Hal stood and walked over, peering out the window of the door at the room. "Some dude givin' you trouble?"

She sighed and murmured an explanation of the guy staring at her for a full five minutes. "Really felt like he wanted to jump on me."

Hal scratched his head. "Maybe the guy's autistic or something."

"I guess that's possible, but I don't think so. This felt legit creepy. Autistic people don't radiate malice."

"Hmm." He started to walk out, but she didn't back up. "What?"

"Why are you so hung up on bad words?"

He shrugged. "It's just not the sort of thing decent people want to hear."

"Oh? You know I read a study that said intelligent people swear more."

"Yeah, well, studies say a lot of things." Hal smiled. "I find it rude, and I prefer to operate a business where people shouldn't have to hear that if they don't want to."

"I get that, but... dude was undressing me with his eyes and you're all about 'Oh noes, a bad word.'"

"C'mon." He nodded at the door. "I'll see what's going on."

She backed up, letting Hal out into the area behind the counter. The creepy guy had taken a table near the window, but he kept watching her. Dakota hurried over to the terminal when a group of people entered and formed a line. The whole time she took orders and rang people up, the guy kept staring at her. He didn't make any weird faces, but the total lack of emotion unnerved her more than any lewd tongue gesture could have.

Hal went out from behind the counter and approached the guy. Between a nasal-voiced man reading her a list of fifteen drinks for his office, she caught snippets of Hal ejecting the guy under threat of involving the police.

The creep got up and left without protest. She stared over the office-worker's puffy curled hair, tracking the old winter coat off to the left until he vanished beyond the window.

"Did you get that last one?" asked the office guy.

"Umm, sorry. I missed it."

The man started to heave a sigh.

"This creepy dude was staring at me, bad. I'm sorry. Not easy to focus when someone's giving me a look like they want to kill me."

"Oh." He twisted around to peer at the window. "No problem. So it was a large peppermint latte with two extra shots and a squirt of caramel syrup."

The terminal beeped as she keyed it in. "Got it."

Hal walked back around, clapping his hands off like he'd thrown out the trash. She smiled at him, debating asking if he'd walk her home later.

"Blake, gonna need a hand here. Big order and there's a line," said Dakota.

"Coming," shouted Blake from the back room.

Dakota took everyone's order, and once they had eighteen drinks in queue plus two food items, she and Blake scrambled to put everything together. Trini arrived, a few minutes early for her four-to-nine shift. Dakota sent her straight to the blenders to get the cold drinks going. The seventeen-year-old dove into the fray like a pro without a squeak of complaint.

The rush took her mind off the creep for a bit, but once things quieted down, she caught herself staring at the windows. She didn't see a trace of the guy, so she returned to hunting the internet via her phone for a ballistic firearm.

Four cops came in. Normally, she loved having them around. After poking the AmeriBank ATM, and having $280 of stolen money in her apartment (even if it had been filtered through a money order), she couldn't help but feel nervous in their presence. Of course, it would be next to impossible for anyone to trace it back to her personally. About the only way that could happen is if someone in Nebraska's gang ratted her out. A determined enough investigator might track the login all the way back to Manhattan, but they had an illegal splice connection, so no registration with the ISP. It would take the provider testing the line to determine how far along the run the tap was, and from there, authorities would probably be able to find the gang. All of that seemed like too much effort for a $4,200 theft, but that bank had been the same one to sue children over chalk.

Hal's younger brother was on the force, so he had a thing where uniformed officers could get a large plain coffee for free once a day. He liked having plenty of cops in and around the café as it tended to keep the criminal element away. Three of them opted for the free large plain coffee while one got a mint latte. If the police went for something beyond a basic coffee, they got the employee discount. She debated talking to them about the creep, but didn't want to get thought of as the 'overly delicate' girl who complains about everything. If she bugged them with every jackass that made her uncomfortable, they'd start ignoring her. Preferring not to be the 'Girl Who Cried Perv,' she let it go.

Hal took off at 7:04 p.m., having tickets to a game that started in an hour. Dakota bit her lip as he ran out the door, but the creepy guy hadn't reappeared, so she tried not to think about being alone for the walk home.

Trini left at nine when her dad rolled up outside in a minivan. She liked him, even though he had such a thick accent she couldn't understand a word coming out of him. Blake spent the last hour between nine and ten on the phone with his friend Neal. Dakota felt pretty sure the two of them were a bit closer than simple friends.

By the end of her shift, she'd researched a couple possibilities of blue-quality guns. The best option appeared to be the Warhawk Model 3, a drop from a five-person group mission rated at level thirty-nine.

Right. I know what I'm doing when I get home. She hummed to herself while wiping down the counter. *Farming that instance over and over. Hooray for random group finder.*

She and Blake cleaned out the machines after locking the doors. He ran around with a mop and rag doing floors and tables while she scrubbed the counter area. By 10:10 p.m., she set off toward home. An echo of a shoe scuff made her look back before she reached the end of the block. The blood practically gelled in her veins at the sight of the creepy guy in the old winter coat ambling toward her.

Dakota scooted up to a brisk walk, darting into the street past the corner despite the light going orange. Two cars beeped at her, but she didn't acknowledge them. More horns went off after she reached the sidewalk. Figuring the guy had also decided to ignore the traffic light, which had gone red to them, she stuffed her hand in her bag, gripping the canister of pepper spray Eric bought her. She clutched it like a lifeline, working her thumb at the safety release while her index finger curled around the trigger. With her bag tucked under her left arm, she had to look like she feared a purse-snatcher.

A few blocks later, she made the left turn toward her apartment, but cursed in her mind for letting her need for the security of home distract her from taking a decoy route. The last thing she wanted was to lead this guy to her actual door. Sure enough, he followed her around the corner, walking faster, almost jogging.

She squeezed the canister and hurried faster.

The guy jogged up behind her. "Hey..."

Dakota spun toward him, a nanometer from ripping the can out of her purse and hosing him down.

"You're on the *Stormbringer*, aren't you?"

Dread and panic smashed into a wall of confusion. Her eyebrows crept together. "What?"

"The ship?" asked the guy. "*Stormbringer?*"

She took a half-step back, not quite as on edge. "You're stalking me over a video game?"

He stuffed his hands in his coat pockets. "Uhh, sorry. I kinda guess it is stalky. Didn't mean that. I, umm, wanted to ask you about the big mission. Saw you guys on the leaderboard. I got the intro drop, but I can't figure out what to do with it. Any chance of a clue?"

"It's a puzzle." Her heart began to slow back to normal, but she didn't let go of the canister. "You're supposed to figure it out."

He swayed side to side, wagging his head. "I know. But I'm stuck. Come on, help a guy out a little? Small clue?"

"Look, you seem like a nice enough guy," said Dakota, trying not to sound as false as she felt. "Normally, I'd have no problem throwing spoilers at someone who wanted them, but this isn't exactly a normal mission, yanno? It's a competition to a big prize. My friends would kick my ass if I helped someone beat us to the prize."

"I'm not asking you for everything. Just a little clue what to do with that stupid data pad."

She backed up another step. "Sorry, man. It's a puzzle."

He lunged forward, grabbing her arms. "It doesn't make any sense. Tell me something!"

"Dude!" shouted Dakota. "It's a game. Chill out!"

"It's ten million bucks. Come on!" He shook her by the arms. "You gotta give me a clue. It's driving me crazy!"

She struggled to get away from him, but he had a death grip on her coat. "Get off me!"

"Where's that blue star system?" His fingers squeezed tighter. "Give me something... anything."

"Three seconds," said Dakota, too terrified to shiver.

"What? Three seconds? Huh?"

When he didn't let go, she yanked the canister out of her purse, flung her arm up, and squeezed the trigger.

A stream of red liquid shot out the end, spattering all over his face. Since he had enormous nostrils, she aimed for them, sending a half-second's worth of Habanero Hammer straight up into his sinuses.

The guy howled and reeled back, clamping his hands over his face while shrieking. He tripped over his own feet and crashed to the sidewalk, gagging and choking. Dakota pounced, swiped the wallet out of his jean pocket, and took off running.

He babbled incoherent nonsense between wails of agony.

Dakota sprinted past her apartment building, the man following her a long ways back like a drunken version of Jason Voorhees. Bright fluorescent lights of the 7-11 three blocks from her apartment drew her like a moth. Even better, a police car had parked out front. She scrambled in the door, found the cops by the coffee station, and skidded to a halt.

"A guy..." she wheezed. "A guy tried to grab me."

The officers turned toward her.

Dakota pointed the spray can at the door. "He's chasing me. I maced him."

A zombie-like wail outside happened as if on cue.

The tall cop, a black guy who could've been Hal's *very* distant cousin, took a step toward the door.

His shorter partner, still a few inches over Dakota, grasped her shoulder and pulled her aside. "What happened?"

The creep appeared out front, shambling toward the entrance, his face bright orange, eyes puffy. Snot and blood ran from his nose, forming tendrils that dangled from his chin.

"Holy shit," said the short cop. "A goddamned zombie!"

The tall cop hurried over as the creep stumbled in and collapsed. When the man lapsed into convulsions, the officer squeezed his shoulder mic. "Dispatch, I need an ambulance to the 7-11 on East Fourteenth Street ASAP."

Dakota cringed away as the guy lapsed into a perfect impression of a fish on dry land. He looked quite incapable of harming anyone in his current state. She almost felt a little guilty. *Maybe I shouldn't have shot it up his nose.*

"What did you hit him with?" asked the short cop.

She sheepishly held up the can. "He grabbed my arms and wouldn't let go of me."

"Habanero Hammer?" asked the cop, wincing. "Damn, that's some heinous shit." He took out a pad. "All right, give me the whole story from the top."

"Okay." She leaned against the coffee table, rubbing her hands up and down her arms while going back over everything, including how he'd been in the café earlier and kept staring at her.

When flashing red lights outside announced an ambulance pulling up, she trailed off, watching the EMTs rush in. They swarmed over the creep. In less than a minute, they stuffed plastic tubing down his throat before loading him on a gurney and rushing him outside.

"So, this guy accosted you over a video game?" The short cop blinked in disbelief. "Seriously?"

"Yeah, but it's not as stupid as it sounds."

"Oh, I can't wait to hear this," said the tall cop.

She took a few breaths to calm down. "The company's got a contest for ten million dollars. My friends and I made progress with the contest, and this guy wanted me to tell him what we did."

"Hmm. Well, that's somewhat more understandable," said the shorter cop. "Maybe a little overkill hosing him down with that stuff?"

She fidgeted. "He had me by the arms, shaking me, demanding I tell him what to do. He was at the café before, just staring at me for an hour like some creepy serial killer before Hal kicked him out. And a couple days ago, I had a different creep follow me, so my boyfriend got me this spray."

"Oh, you work at Hal's place?" asked the short cop.

"Yeah. How many blue haired girls are there around here?" The taller officer grinned.

"Actually... kind of a lot," said Dakota, managing a nervous giggle.

17

LEVEL UP

The cops dropped her off at Eric's building and even walked her up to the door to make sure someone let her inside. For a few tense minutes, it seemed as though she'd have to go with them somewhere else, but Eric eventually opened the door with a telltale 'just logged out of VR' disoriented expression.

"Oh, hey, Babe. What's up?" He peered out at the cops.

"Creep issues. Didn't want to be alone."

Eric wiped his eyes. "Shit. Yeah, come on in." He waved in greeting at the police.

"A detective will be in contact soon," said Tall Cop.

"Thank you." Dakota smiled at them and headed inside.

Eric pushed the door closed behind her and locked it. "What happened?"

She wandered over to the sofa and sat, not bothering to take her coat off. She couldn't even figure out how to talk until Eric sat beside her.

"That stuff worked."

"Huh?" asked Eric.

"The spray. I think it worked *too* well. Guy had to go to the hospital."

"Dayum, babe. What happened?" He slid an arm around her back. "Same dude?"

"No." She leaned into him and recounted the story again. He gasped when she mentioned shooting the stream up his nose.

"Ouch." He grabbed his face. "That's... shit, babe. Remind me never to piss you off."

A nervous laugh leaked out of her.

"Well, that dude'll never want to come near you again." He shook his head, still rubbing his nose. "Christ."

"A man attacked me over a game."

"Not just a game. A lot of money." Eric rubbed her shoulder.

"That doesn't make it acceptable."

"No, but it's less psychotic at least." He shook his head. "How the hell did crazy dude even find you?"

She shivered. "I dunno. He knew I'm on the *Stormbringer* though. As soon as I get over wanting to curl up in a ball and suck my thumb, I'm going to find out." She patted her jacket pocket. "Nabbed his wallet."

"You pickpocketed the dude?" Eric blinked. "I guess you didn't mention that to the cops."

"Nope. I wanted his information for other, more nefarious reasons. Besides, if the cops ask, I'll say I grabbed it to get his ID and was too emotionally rattled to remember I had it."

He pulled her close. "You're literally shivering."

"I'm emotionally rattled." She let out a nervous laugh. "I'm going to become phobic about walking home in the dark. Umm. Is it okay if I spend the night?"

"Damn sure it's okay." He smiled. "I can crash on the sofa."

She shrugged. "If you want."

"If?" He pursed his lips. "Is our relationship about to level up?"

"Oh, I dunno." She finally allowed herself to relax. "That might take a bit more grinding."

Eric glided closer and rested his hands on her hips. "I think I can swing that." He stood there for a few minutes, drinking in her presence. "You are damn near perfect, my epic loot drop."

She leaned in so their foreheads touched. "*Near* perfect? What's stopping me from being a legendary?"

He slid his hands around to squeeze her butt. "Booty's a touch small."

Dakota grinned. "Small? Contrary to your opinion, I actually do have an ass."

"You have an ass in theory, being that all humans do, but it's in stealth." He pulled her close, still squeezing her backside. "Ain't like you can help it though. It's a white girl problem like that whole pumpkin spice thing."

"Ugh. I can't stand that stuff. It's not a 'white girl' thing, it's a *basic* girl thing." She let out a long, quiet sigh of relief. "Thanks for being here."

"You know it, babe. Any time."

"So, about that couch..." Dakota grinned. "I'm too scared to sleep alone tonight."

18

OUTSIDE THE LINES

A detective showed up at the Amazon Café the next day. She'd already copied down the driver's license info and social security number for one Jonathan Miles Parker, age twenty-nine. Though the wallet contained two credit cards, she didn't bother with them.

When Detective Smalley, a fortyish guy in a white shirt with brown hair, asked her to go over the events of the previous night again, she handed over the wallet—and showed off some faint bruises on her arms below the shoulders, where the guy had grabbed and shaken her.

The detective used his cell phone to snap some pictures of the bruises.

"I took it in case the creep got away, but I'd been so scared out of my wits, I forgot to give it to the officers in the 7-11."

Detective Smalley looked it over. "All right. One moment, Miss Marx. Since our conversation will be the longest, let me make the rounds first."

Dakota nodded.

He spoke to Blake and Hal, confirming that Jonathan had indeed been staring at her for about an hour before being kicked out of the café, then walked back over to her. "The suspect hasn't been able to make a statement yet. That stuff you hit him with got down his throat. They had to jam a plastic hose in there so he could breathe."

She cringed. "Oh, shit. I didn't even think about that... I was scared shitless at the time, just sprayed."

"Given the circumstances, I doubt there'll be any criminal liability, though there's always the chance the guy will try to go after you in civil court."

"Ugh." She hung her head.

He patted her shoulder. "The guy has no prior record. Neighbors say he more or less never goes outside. Probably spends all day on the computer. I wouldn't consider it likely that he'll bother you again, but... if he does, please let us know."

"Yeah, I will. What happens now?"

"Well... sounds like a case of simple assault. Once he's regained the ability to speak, I'll have a better answer for you."

She nodded. "I really thought he was about to break my jaw or something. He got really angry when I wouldn't tell him how we got past the first part of that mission."

Detective Smalley shook his head, chuckling. "Over a video game."

"Ten million dollar prize more like." She gestured at the samovar. "Want a coffee?"

"Heh. Sure. And yeah, people do crazy things for big money."

She shuddered internally at the memory of wading stomach-deep through a river of alien shit. "Yeah, they sure do."

DESPITE HER SHIFT ENDING THAT DAY AT 3:30 P.M., HAL WALKED HER home. She gave him a thank you hug and headed inside. After a feast of Hot Pockets, she changed into sweats and flopped on the bed to log into the game.

Grumbling at Jonathan ruining her prior night's plans, she hopped in a random 'group finder' queue for the instance she'd wanted to run. Alas, being a rogue, she had a bit of a wait. Tanks and healers always got in fastest, but eventually, the notification popped.

The system teleported her to a dingy alley peopled with homeless humans and one vagrant Kazalor with an eyepatch. Four other players faded in around her, a Draath tank with a literal shield in his left hand and a sword taller than her character in his other. His body resembled one of Michelangelo's statues—if he'd carved one of a ridiculously over-muscled bodybuilder—rendered in amethyst crystal brought to life, with glowing red eyes. Everything about him embodied the concept of 'I do not take damage.'

They drew a human medic, a tall woman with dark skin and blonde dreadlocks, as well as a Zhavir gunslinger. The Zhavir, a relatively rare race, were frail of build and about the size of humans. They had four all-black eyes, backward knees like the rear legs of cats, tiny horns, needle-like teeth, and hooked bone spurs at their elbows. The race had big bonuses to agility and dexterity, and often wound up as rogues or gunslingers. While theoretically possible, she'd never seen a Zhavir soldier going the tank route, since they had such a big penalty to constitution.

The fifth member of the random party turned out to be a Cika rogue. She had to fight her instinct to pick him up and squeeze him. The Cika only stood about waist-high to an adult human. Big eyes and round faces made them highly cute, as well as either cat or rabbit-style ears and long fluffy tails. This particular Cika had the rabbit ears, and the buckteeth to match. He wore a dark armored suit and carried an array of knives—another rogue, but he'd gone heavy melee spec.

"Hi," chirped the Cika.

"I'm sorry," said Fawkes, right before scooping him up and squeezing him. "You're too damn cute."

"Hey, stop that! Put me down!" chirped the Cika, his tail puffed up like a terrified cat.

She set him back on his feet, laughing.

"All right," said the tank, in the slow, deep voice common to the Draath.

The mission involved running an instance, a self-contained map full of enemies and mini-bosses.

"Dibs on the Black Edge," said the Cika.

Fawkes looked down at him. "Sure. Dibs on the Warhawk."

"Oh, wow." The Cika's ears drooped back as his eyes widened in surprise. "You're a ranged build?"

"Yeah."

He peered up at her. "Sounds like it would be annoying always having to hide to attack."

"It's work, yeah. But the giant hits are worth it. Be even better when I unlock *Master of Shadows*. And I don't have to deal with 'screw the melee' boss mechanics."

Melee rogues didn't hide, at least not in boss fights. They just got behind something and stabbed as fast as they could move. Instead of abilities to enhance hiding or teleport around, they got evasive bonuses and up-front damage boosts. Some melee rogues could even tank bosses for short periods while their cooldowns made them impossible to hit. Of course, unlike a real tank, all it took was one shot landing and down they went.

Fawkes ran the instance with the random group, often breaking out into laughter as the Cika hurled himself at the creatures like a psychotic furry wood-chipper. The high-pitched "Yaaaaaagh!" that accompanied him flinging his little furry body across the hallway got her giggling every time, despite blood flying from NPC thugs. His character name, Monty, made sense once she remembered an old-ass movie with a murderous rabbit.

This medic, unfortunately, reinforced the awesomeness of Angel813. Fortunately, the Draath tank was over-geared for the instance and didn't need much attention from the healer. When the final crime lord boss went down and dropped a crappy set of light armor pants, both Fawkes and the Cika growled.

"Hey not bad," said Monty. "You're right on my heels on the meter."

"Meter?" asked Fawkes.

He opened a display screen with bar graphs. "Damage meter. Tracks who does damage during a run so we can find slackers."

She'd wound up in second place, a few thousand damage points behind him with the gunslinger a more distant third, lagging her by 12,000 or so.

"If you didn't have to keep bouncing around that cyborg with the rotary cannon, you'd have been way ahead of me," said Fawkes.

He shrugged. "Still not bad. Damn, that knife didn't drop."

"Again?" asked Fawkes.

"I'm out." The healer nabbed the pants and disappeared.

"Sure," said the tank.

The gunslinger nodded so fast his head blurred. The bizarre feline-insectoid quality of the Zhavir unsettled her, but the guy seemed friendly enough. She didn't even try to pronounce his character name, Xrrystln.

On the second run, the randomizer gave them a Niath auramancer for healing. A third of the way through, she complained of being bored, which got a, "You're welcome" from the tank. The space angel threw damaging spells between heals, and made the second run feel like they had a cheat code active. No one ever appeared to take damage.

Holy crap. Maybe I should level my angel up some more. This is so damn easy.

When the end boss dropped the second time, a wicked black knife with a thin, stark silver edge appeared.

"Woo hoo!" shouted the Cika, doing a little dance.

The Niath healer won the loot roll and took the knife.

He stared at her, ears drooped.

She tucked her wings in, walked over, and handed it to Monty. "I only rolled on it to make sure it went to the knife spec. She's ranged."

Ooh, bitch. Fawkes narrowed her eyes.

"It's okay," said Monty. We already worked it out. She's after the Warhawk."

"Oh." The Niath woman gave her an apologetic look. "Sorry. I'm just used to rogues being greedy. Nice to meet some decent people finally."

Monty pointed over his shoulder at Fawkes. "Wanna run it some more so she can get her gun?"

"Sure." The Niath smiled.

"I got one more in me," said the tank.

They reset and ran the same instance a third time. Repetition allowed Fawkes to anticipate spawns and enemy movement. She weaned herself of target fixation and started attacking whatever had its back to her when she couldn't get into stealth. Back shots boosted damage, but not as much as an actual ambush.

The third time the end boss went down, the Warhawk pistol dropped.

"Awesome!" shouted Fawkes, while hitting the 'need' button for the loot roll.

The Zhavir gunslinger beat her by two points. "Cool. Peace."

He disappeared before she could scream.

"Argh!" Fawkes fumed. "Asshole. He only heard us talking about that gun for the past three runs!"

Monty's two-foot-tall rabbit ears folded out sideways. "Prick. If you're up for another run, I'll go."

"Wow. What a... I hate people like that." The Niath folded her arms. "Yeah, I can go again."

"Oh, okay..." The tank rolled his head around, cracking his neck with a crunch like rocks grinding together.

The randomizer gave them a human aethermancer for the missing damage dealer, which made Dakota sigh with relief. No competition for the gun... if it dropped again. She spent the whole run muttering 'pleasepleaseplease' to nothing in particular.

Four mini-bosses and an end-boss fight later, she stared at the white loot box and shivered with anticipation.

When the Draath tank touched it, and the Warhawk pistol appeared again, she shrieked with glee.

"Holy crap!" Fawkes bounced and mashed the 'need' button.

"Hey, shoot me a message in a couple days huh?" asked Monty. "Let me know how the bullets compare to that CL32."

She cradled the big handgun to her chest like a teddy bear once it appeared in her possession. "Yeah, I can do that. Thank you everyone!"

The others bowed. Murmurs of "Thanks for the group" and "Take it easy" went around as everyone dropped out, their portraits disappearing one by one from the edge of her view.

Fawkes stood alone next to the dead body of the former crime boss, holding a gun that looked a hair ridiculous in size for her. "Well, might as well test this sucker out."

AFTER BUYING SOME AMMO, SHE EQUIPPED THE WARHAWK AND RAN A couple missions. Initially, going back to fighting normal creatures as opposed to the amped up ones inside an instance intended to face groups made her feel like a goddess. Once she realized the stuff she'd spent hours killing inside the instance had six times the health as normal NPCs, she deflated.

Still, the Warhawk hit damn hard. She couldn't help but hear a cash register sound every time she fired, knowing she'd have to re-purchase ammo. The modest uptick in damage over the CL32 wasn't worth the expense, so she'd save it for fights against things where resistance or vulnerability made a big difference. Also, its deafening *boom* when fired would knock her out of hiding even when not dealing with a boss battle.

Around 7:00 p.m., the crew reconvened in the main room of the *Stormbringer*. The ship had attracted a small crowd of curious onlookers, which blossomed into an influx of other players swarming the planet.

"Damn, look at them all," said Rallek, glancing over a list showing all player characters on the planet. "There's over 8,000 people here."

"They're probably trying to figure out what we're doing." Kavan spun a small metal orb on the table. "Stupid of them to post a leaderboard."

"On purpose. They want other players to mess with the front runner." Angel813 fussed with her hair. "Anything to make winning that money harder. I guarantee if we get closer, we're going to have people shooting at us. We have to be ready for that."

Fawkes shivered. "Oh, it's starting." She shared the story of Jonathan attacking her for real.

Nighthawk stared at her, wide-eyed. "Umm... wow. That's not cool at all." He glanced at Kavan, seeming afraid.

"How'd he find you?" asked Kavan.

She sighed, teasing a spoon around her orange sherbet. "I'm still working on figuring that out."

"Probably clicked the roster for our ship. The leaderboard links to our crew profile page, and you put something there about slinging coffee in Manhattan under hobbies. That guy probably went to every Amazon Café in Manhattan until he found you." Kavan turned the floating panel to show her something she'd typed in while half-awake two-ish years ago. "Might want to change that."

"Shit," muttered Fawkes, opening a window to do just that. "Gotta vague that up a lot more."

"Okay, so tonight, we go for the shield mod. Everyone's got the mission now, right?" asked Rallek.

Nods went around the table.

"Cool. I probably don't have to say this, but prepare for a shitty night. This is going to suck." Rallek folded his arms.

Nighthawk grinned.

"Guys, mind the swearing?" asked Kavan.

"Why? You sound like my boss." Fawkes chuckled.

"I have my reasons." Kavan pulled a huge star map display open over the table. "So, as Rallek was saying. The mission objective is to obtain a set of plans from the primary computer system inside a pirate space station. It's a mixed mission involving both space combat and doing stuff on foot."

"We've done those before," said Angel813. "What makes this one so annoying?"

"This quest is designed to be done by a group of two or three crews." Rallek gestured at the map. "The pirate station is protected by cloaked corvettes. One of them is an even match for us without being invisible. We could easily wind up having two or three on us at once. Kavan's a pretty good pilot, but the odds of us getting through that aren't great."

"So we find a group?" asked Fawkes.

"If we want to risk the entire Axillon99 community knowing someone on the leaderboard is interested in this mission." Rallek tapped his fingers on the table. "It's a catch twenty-two. If we try to find help, we're basically giving away the advantage of us knowing this anti-venom thing is important."

"The Venom Shroud," said Nighthawk. "It's a purple mod, named."

"Right. What he said." Kavan gestured at him.

"There's more than one way to work a quest." Nighthawk stood, wagging a chicken nugget at everyone while he walked in a circle around the table. "We've got an advantage over everyone else."

The ship hung in rapt silence as he ate the nugget.

"Out with it, man," said Rallek.

"Easy." Nighthawk held his arms out to the sides, smiling. "You guys have the best fighter pilot in Axillon99 on your crew, and Fawkes is really damn sneaky."

"And so humble." Rallek rolled his eyes.

"Stealth?" asked Fawkes.

"Well sorta. Hear me out." Nighthawk went back to his chair and munched on another nugget. "NPC ships have an aggro radius. The bigger the ship, the bigger we have to be to trigger it. A single fighter can slip past their defensive fleet... with a little help from our technomancer."

"Don't forget I'm a techie, too." Fawkes patted her electronics pack. "The fighter's got two slots for buffs... I'm just not usually on board."

"Right." Nighthawk pointed at her. "But you're important for something else."

"You can make your own sandwiches, Nighthawk," said Angel813.

Kavan and Rallek stifled snickers.

He froze, shifted to look at her with a mask of complete confusion on his features. "What? Sandwiches? We have a food printer. Why would she make sandwiches?"

"Forget it. Geez. You grow up in a bubble?" asked Angel813.

"Umm. Whatever." Nighthawk looked at Fawkes. "You, me, and Rallek pile into the Gremlin. I fly us past the screen. Get close. You sneak into the space station. Instead of us fighting our way to the control room, you stealth it. We don't *have* to kill anything... just get the plans. It's not an instance, so if you get killed, we don't get locked out."

Kavan's eyebrows went up. "That's so damn crazy it might just work."

Nighthawk leaned both hands on the table. "I know I can pull it off."

"Better than revealing information to the competition." Fawkes grinned. "Since there's no lockout, we should try it."

"Okay. I'll just sit here and sip coffee then." Kavan winked.

THE *STORMBRINGER* CAME TO A FULL STOP A SAFE DISTANCE BACK FROM THE pirate space station. Amid a belt of asteroids, some bigger than Earth's moon, floated a huge cashew-shaped rock with an octagonal metal plate in the center of the curve. The front face of the pirate installation glimmered with thousands of little lights, but most of the facility occupied areas hollowed out inside the asteroid. At both pointy ends of the 'cashew,' nests of superstructure moored a handful of fighter ships and corvettes. The enemy ships looked held together by bandages and hope, all with a 'junker' aesthetic.

"I'm going to fly in from the side," said Nighthawk. "Installations like this always concentrate the defenses in front and back, directly up and directly down. We head for the mooring structures on the right tip."

"Won't they see you coming?" asked Kavan.

"You're too into it again." Nighthawk smiled. "NPCs only react to stuff that gets close enough, even if a normal person should be able to see it. They're not real people with eyes, just programs reacting to players crossing boundary lines. One fighter won't set off the corvettes on defense... I hope."

"Well, it's just a respawn, right?" Rallek shrugged. "Let's do it."

Nighthawk hit the button on the wall to open the floor hatch, exposing the ladder down to the tiny bay where the Gremlin waited, like a full-size SUV crammed into a garage made for a small car. He climbed down the ladder with Fawkes and Rallek going one after the next.

Once her boots hit the metal floor, she did a double-take at the giant particle cannons on either side of the ship. The Gremlin had a silhouette similar to a guitar pick with a notch in the front when viewed from above. Giant particle cannons mounted to the frame near the back of the wing, their nine-foot-long barrels hanging unsupported for most of their length.

"How do those guns not snap off as soon as you turn?" asked Rallek.

Nighthawk shrugged. "It's a video game." He climbed up a foldout ladder and slipped into the forward seat. "You guys can share the back seat. is the Gremlin's a medium fighter with guns that belong on a heavy fighter."

"Yeah, looks it," said Fawkes.

She let Rallek go up first and lowered herself into his lap.

"This is... intimate."

Fawkes grinned at the warm breath on the back of her neck. "Yeah, it is. Hey 'Hawk, you wouldn't mind if we got it on back here while you fly, would you?"

"Got what on?" asked Nighthawk.

"Way to kill a joke, dude." She sighed. "Do these things have seatbelts?"

"Harnesses," said Nighthawk. "But it won't work with two people in the same seat."

He hit a button and the canopy closed around them, making the space feel even smaller. Every little creak or shift in the ship made her twitch.

"Wow, this is like *too* realistic. I'm legit scared right now."

Rallek threaded his arms around her and held tight. "Just a game."

"You know I hate those stupid rides at the amusement park where you go up this big tower and they droaaaaaaa!"

The Gremlin plummeted straight down out of the bay with a loud rushing hiss. Fawkes continued screaming as thrust kicked in and her body crushed back against Rallek, who grunted. More stars than she'd ever cared to see spiraled around above her. With only a thin canopy between her and the vastness of space (however fictional it may be), she wound up breathless with fear. It didn't help that with the Neurona 4 helmet, the icy chill of outer space brushed at her face through the glass.

"Whoa, calm down," said Rallek. "We're not doing this for real."

"Could've fooled me." She grabbed his hands, where he'd interlocked them at her stomach. "Holy crap this is intense."

"Oh, that was merely launch. That's not intense," said Nighthawk. "What we're about to do is intense."

She whined.

"I'm kidding. This isn't going to be half as cool as a six-on-one dogfight. That probably would've made you pee your pants."

"Ha ha."

Rallek chuckled, and muttered, "Pee your pants?" over a private whisper channel.

Fawkes shrugged. "Maybe they live in a repressive religious commune or something and can't curse."

"People in repressive religious communes wouldn't be playing this game. You know, science and learning are evil and all that... so's technology."

"Fair point. Guess he's just a strange guy."

Rallek nodded. "Or he's trying not to swear in front of the delicate lady."

She sent him a text middle finger.

"Here we go!" Nighthawk shoved forward on the throttle bar, and again, the force of acceleration crushed her into Rallek. "Okay, dude. Hit us with a spell to keep us off sensors."

Rallek rested his hands on the two side consoles, both aglow with various gauges and flashing lights, most of which meant nothing but decoration. He cast a spell, again chanting his pointless nonsense words.

"Okay, done. We got five minutes before I need to re-up it."

Fawkes messed with the console in front of her until she found the engineer's interface. Since the Gremlin lacked the physical space of an engineering bay, she didn't need to run around with fictional tools. Instead, she simply selected options from a menu. "I added a sensor mask, too. It should have appeared in your hotbar. While it's on, shields are reduced a bit."

"Cool," said Nighthawk. "We are space ninjas."

She bit her lip. *What is he, twelve?* "Yeah, sure. Something like that."

Nighthawk got quiet, seemingly mesmerized by the passing starfield. He steered to the left, taking a wide berth around the pirate installation until one end of the distant cashew-shaped asteroid rotated enough to block the view of its front face.

"You okay?" asked Rallek.

"Shh. I can kinda see the cloaked corvettes," said Nighthawk.

"Really?" Fawkes leaned up to peer past him. "What ability is that?"

"No ability. 'Cause we're moving, the stars blur a little at the edges of the ships. It's hard to see, but I can do it. I was right... they don't have anything watching the side."

Fawkes leaned back, not minding Rallek's hand squeezing a bit close to her rear end. Minutes of tense silent flying passed, her gaze drifting off into space. One star seemed to bend backward like a two-dimensional sticker being rolled off a sheet onto a flat wall. She stared at the spot, and noticed another speck of light move as if someone pulled 'space background' wallpaper over a corner.

"T-there's a ship right next to us," whispered Fawkes.

Nighthawk snapped his head to the left. "Crap. Hang on. It hasn't seen us yet."

He banked to the right and accelerated. The Gremlin pitched and twisted like a rollercoaster. Fawkes couldn't tolerate watching the asteroids rush by and swim in circles along with the sensation of inertia pushing her around, so she closed her eyes.

"This looks hard, but it's not so bad," said Nighthawk. "Imagine a three-dimensional minefield, where the enemy ships have blobs of detection. I gotta fly in the dead spots between the blobs, and we're gonna make it."

Minutes slid by, Fawkes' stomach churning.

"Rallek, kill that, quick!"

She opened her eyes. Nighthawk pointed at an approaching blinking light, a more or less spherical probe made of apparent scrap metal, studded with antennas.

Rallek gestured at it. The dumpster-sized probe rocked as if it hit something, and went dark.

"No funny words?" asked Fawkes, grinning.

"No time." He repeated the gesture, but nothing happened. "It's dead."

She turned her head, tracking the sparking lump of metal as it shot by on the left. "Why didn't you just blast it?"

"Sensors will pick up particle beams. They won't react to magic." Nighthawk rolled to the right and accelerated. "Almost there."

A pair of meatloaf-shaped corvettes phased in out of cloaking, both less than two hundred meters ahead. He emitted a strangled squeal and nailed the thrust boost. Fawkes' head rocked back into Rallek's face. The corvettes blurred as the Gremlin zoomed down a narrow canyon between them, nearly as tight as the distance between neighboring houses. Nighthawk swerved about, dodging turrets and protrusions. Four seconds later when they shot past the end of the corvettes into open space, Fawkes screamed.

"We're in." Nighthawk clapped and cheered. "One sec, gotta find an open door."

They skimmed along the outer curve of the cashew-shaped rock for a little while before cresting the point and gliding in among the hundreds of metal spars sticking out of the stone like whiskers. Broken fragments of larger spacecraft, probably victims of piracy broken down for parts, drifted about, tethered by mooring lines.

Nighthawk slipped the Gremlin between two spars sideways, rolled over, and tucked into an open docking bay.

"I feel like a piece of bread in a toaster," said Rallek.

"Yeah... that was a little tight." Nighthawk hit a button, which filled the cockpit with five seconds of mechanical thrumming before a heavy *clonk*.

"What was that noise?" asked Fawkes.

"Landing pads." Nighthawk nudged the ship to the left, out of the path of the door, and put it down. "Okay, we're in."

"You landed in their launch bay," said Fawkes. "Seriously?"

"Looks like a launch bay, but it's a giant empty room." Rallek gazed up and around at the bare steel.

"Yeah." Nighthawk grinned. "They're NPCs. They don't actually have dudes on foot running to get in fighters. Why animate all that when they never expected anyone to be here to see it? The ships just appear out of thin air and launch. It's kinda cheating, but we could sit here all day powered down and they'd never notice us."

"Looks like it's your show now." Rallek patted her on the butt.

"You're so sure I can pull this off?" asked Fawkes.

"Yep." Nighthawk nodded. "This place is going to use the same design as most buildings. There's gonna be vents. I bet the exact layout of this base is copied dozens of times for all sorts of missions. All you need to do is get to the primary computer terminal in the command room and use it. Since you're on the quest, it'll automatically give you the plans."

She relaxed. *Right. Just a game. I don't actually have to call the head pirate and trick him into giving me his password.* "Okay."

Everyone put their bubbles on. Nighthawk opened the canopy and she climbed out.

The two guys remained with the ship while she scurried across a hundred yards of bare metal littered with stones toward a hangar-sized door on the innermost wall. At the halfway point, a junker fighter appeared out of thin air above her and shot out the docking tunnel.

Roaring ion blast knocked her to the ground in a tumble. Fawkes scrambled upright again and sprinted for the airlock. Unsurprisingly, the door refused to open. She plugged in the override kit and attacked a hacker mini-game. The level four network made her laugh with its simplicity, and in twelve seconds, the panel went from red to green.

She punched the button, and a pair of doors big enough for the *Stormbringer* to fly through slid open a few feet. After ducking past, she found herself in a featureless metal corridor. Since it contained neither defenses, pirates, nor even any sort of cosmetic decoration, she decided to run.

Fortunately, video game characters didn't get tired. Though, by the time the half-mile sprint wound to a halt at the end of the passage, her brain and legs had fallen off speaking terms. Consciously, she thought she *should* be tired, but her legs ignored the past few minutes of hard work as though it never happened.

Another hack got her past the much smaller door at the interior end. She opened it enough to peek inside, and cringed at a hallway dotted with men and women in crude armor. None stood close enough to the door to catch her if she hid, so she dropped into stealth and crept inside. Her eyes on the floor to monitor the red vision cones panning around, Fawkes hurried over to a square hatch at floor level twenty feet away from the door.

She got down on her hands and knees by it. Somehow, six people wandering around didn't notice her kneeling in the open. At a touch, the hatch slid open on pneumatic struts. Fawkes shimmied into the vent and pulled the hatch closed. In all the time she'd been playing a sneaky character, not once had guards ever reacted to a left-open vent duct. It still bothered her on some deep OCD level, like one day game developers would decide to start programming sentries to notice 'Hey, that vent wasn't open five seconds ago, I should check that out.'

Despite having no idea where the command room was, she felt reasonably certain a right turn at the end of the small spar would take her there. Since her entry point sat all the way on the left side of the base (as viewed from the front) it made sense. The command room likely sat in the middle, at the deepest point. This quest had been designed for a group to blast their way in, which set her on edge. The pirates roaming around inside might be tuned for a raid, with four or five times the health of a normal NPC, and probably higher damage output. That meant she wouldn't have a chance of surviving even a one-on-one encounter.

One nice thing about a game that liked to make stealth important: comfortably large vents. She crawled down a shaft with plenty of room to spare, following a handful of turns closer to the thrum of technology mixed with beeping and tweeping. The bridge of the *Stormbringer* made the same 'generic computer' sound in the background, barely audible over the game's ever-present musical score.

She found herself humming along with the dramatic 'pirate' track as she crawled.

"Hey, how goes it?" asked Nighthawk over comm.

"Vents," said Fawkes. "Still in the vents. This place is pretty long."

"Cool. Cool."

"You okay?" asked Rallek.

Oh, I'm a dumbass. She opened a minimap. The top-down view of the pirate base resembled a croissant more than a cashew, with the ends tapering to points. Inside, a symmetrical arrangement of boxes and rectangles illustrated the interior of the compound. A room at the thickest part of the asteroid, directly opposite the front face, caught her eye. Mostly due to the shape drawn at the back: a curve around a diamond icon. The map didn't give her any indication of what each room contained, but it did show her position as a blue dot. Fair bet, that diamond represented the main computer terminal.

"Fine for now. I just hope the computer works without the boss being dead."

"Crap. I didn't think of that," said Nighthawk with an odd note of sheepishness.

Rallek hummed for a second or two. "I don't think it would... the shield mod isn't part of a major loot drop. It's an incidental thing that also uses this pirate base. There's a ship raid mission to take out this pirate."

"Oh, cool." Fawkes hung a left turn and crawled into a larger space full of multicolored boxes. A square hole in the ceiling made her frown. "Damn. I gotta go up. Hang on."

Having done so many times before on stealth missions, she stacked the boxes into a configuration she could climb, and made her way up to the hatch. Her faint grunt echoed in the upper level vent as she pulled herself through and flattened out on the floor.

"Well if my job as an interplanetary spy doesn't pan out, I can always go into HVAC maintenance."

"Huh?" asked Nighthawk.

Rallek chuckled.

"I spend so much time in damn vents, I could get a job fixing them."

"Oh," said Nighthawk before emitting a forced laugh.

Shaking her head, Fawkes crawled onward, using the minimap to choose turns. She slinked past several slatted covers that looked out into rooms where groups of pirates stood mannequin still. Some robotically walked around between workstations or consoles. Every so often, a random bit of atmosphere dialogue like, "I can't wait for another raid. It's so boring to sit around here" or "any day now, I'm gonna hit it big," echoed around her.

She headed toward the generic computer noise, which progressively got louder than the background music. Soon, her blue map dot approached the room with the curved wall. She shimmied around a right turn and ahead another fifteen feet to the first visible vent cover.

"Yes!" she whispered.

The slats overlooked a room containing the sort of equipment she'd expect to see on the bridge of a massive starship. Desks and consoles with chairs, giant monitor screens, and walls covered with hundreds of decorative-but-useless machinery. Six pirates milled around. One guy in power armor who appeared to be the boss pirate moved about with heavy clunking footsteps.

Her stomach tightened.

If that guy aggroed on her, she'd probably go splat in one shot. Fawkes leaned up to the slats and strained to examine the left side of the room where the map had the curve. Behind a captain's chair setup, a raised dais with a small railing around it held a glowing purple gem two feet tall. She recognized it as a Simarin computer, alien technology based on crystal power. They'd used a generic graphic for it, something she'd seen here and there in various places. That made her feel more confident that this plan might work. When they made it part of the money quest, the developers put the shield mod here to be annoying. It had nothing to do with the pirate fight.

Heck. Maybe the developers even wanted *someone to do exactly what I'm doing.*

She couldn't see an opening to make it across the room without being caught, but that didn't necessarily matter. Hoping that past precedent held true, she eased the vent cover open and backed up, watching. After a while, and none of the pirates reacting to it being open, she crawled back over and hovered a few inches short of the point where vision-cone red crept into the duct. From there, she had a good view of the empty computer area.

Shadowblink teleported her across the room to the right side of the curved walkway. Fawkes scooted forward to hide behind the workstation. As long as she kept low, none of the NPCs down below in the command area should spot her and trigger combat.

She eased herself up enough to see the top of the workstation, and 'used' the screen.

Blue text appeared in midair. Mission Update: Plans recovered.

"Awesome, you did it!" said Rallek, over the comm.

"Whoa. I just got a quest update. What happened?" asked Kavan.

"I'm at the computer," whispered Fawkes. "Now, I just need to get out."

"Well, you could always take the fast way out," said Nighthawk. "Shoot the pirate, die, and respawn at the door."

"This isn't an instance," whispered Fawkes. "I'd leave a corpse inside and have to run my ghost back to it, and then die right away all over again."

"Oh, right," said Nighthawk. "Sorry. We're still here waiting for you."

"Twenty seconds," muttered Fawkes.

She crouched in place, waiting for the cooldown of *Shadowblink* to reset. Every thump of the pirate boss' power armor made her twitch. The game's realism teetered on the verge of causing actual fear of death, though whenever her hands started shaking, she called up one of her many hundreds of memories of character death and running around as a ghost. How was it she'd never felt quite so scared of being killed in the game before? Did the new helmet tweak some deeper emotional response the old Neurona 3 couldn't? Hell, that little boy from the quest the other day triggered the sort of protectiveness she'd had for Nebraska when they'd been younger.

Either I'm getting old and soft, or this helmet is freaky.

As soon as *Shadowblink* cooled down, she crept to the right side of the curved walkway, peeking out enough to see the ventilation duct. A split second after she triggered the stealth teleport, her character went solid and combat music started. A roaming pirate had turned his vision cone over that patch of floor at the same instant she landed on it.

"Shit!" she shouted.

She didn't bother looking back, instead scrambling into the vent before the hatch could close. It did slam shut, but after she'd made it in. Explosions, laser blasts, and crackling lightning slammed the flimsy little vent cover, but it didn't break or even appear damaged.

"Dammit... Dammit... Dammit..."

"What happened in there?" yelled Kavan. "A mosquito storm of fighters just exploded into space outside."

She crawled as fast as she could into the vents while the thunder of NPCs trying to shoot her through the wall continued. "I teleported to the vent, but got seen. Started the boss fight."

"You a ghost?" asked Nighthawk.

"No, I got into the vent before it shut. Just need to wait it out."

Rallek clucked his tongue. "Raid bosses don't give up. You might be stuck in combat until you die."

"Don't think so. I didn't do or take any damage. I think it'll let me go." She hurried to the hole leading down to the stack-o-boxes she built. As soon as she landed on the lower level, the combat music stopped. "I'm clear!"

"Fighters are disappearing. Hah!" yelled Kavan. "I can see where the corvettes are because the fighters are flying into them. Wait. Those two aren't corvettes... they're cruisers."

"How do you know that if you can't see them?" asked Rallek.

Kavan coughed. "Corvettes don't carry fifteen fighters apiece."

"Oh, good point," said Rallek.

"Oh crap!" shouted Nighthawk. "I played chicken with *cruisers*." He burst into riotous laughter. "No wonder they didn't notice us. Way too big."

Fawkes scrambled down the vent, heading for the exit. "Why would they stick that damn mod quest in this place?"

"They probably knew people need it for that stupid robot," said Angel813.

"It *used* to be on the sewer mission," said Nighthawk. "They moved it. Before the contest, it wasn't a big deal. Unless you're doing quests on the Zhavir homeworld, it's pretty rare for things to use venom damage. Fire and lightning are the big ones. If that mod gave ninety-five percent fire resistance, everyone would have it."

"To get on Army of One's main raiding group, a player has to have at least eighty percent in all elemental resistances and be in the upper level of armor value for their class. No stacking up weak armor just for resists," said Angel813.

"Damn. I didn't think it was even possible to get them *all* that high." Rallek whistled.

"It is," said Angel813, "when you've loaded up on all purple items from the first tier of raids."

"They still run the first-year stuff?" asked Nighthawk.

"Yeah. But not like seriously. They'll grab a bunch of Tier 2 players and drag the new people through it to gear them up. They can clear the Coriolis Promenade in forty-five minutes."

Whistles of awe came over the comm.

"Wait, how are you only level forty-one but you used to be in AOO?" asked Nighthawk.

"I umm... Well, the Angel813 you see before you now is a much calmer version of who I used to be. When I got asked to leave... okay, when I got kicked, I was upset. Maybe I deleted my character in a fit of rage."

"Ouch," said Kavan. "Sorry."

"The devs wouldn't restore it?" asked Rallek.

"Oh, they did... eventually, but by the time I got her back I had this medic to thirty and just kept going with it. My sixty is an empath. I like the medic more."

Fawkes poked her head out of the vent entrance she first crawled into. None of the pirates in that hallway had moved from where they pathed before. She engaged stealth and crept from there to the door, then ran down the quarter-mile corridor back to the fighter launch bay. The huge door had sealed itself again, requiring another hacking mini-game to get open. As soon as she slipped past the gap, Nighthawk cheered over the comm and all the little lights on the Gremlin fighter came on.

He lifted off while she was still climbing up over the side. Rallek grabbed her arms and pulled her in, whacking the button to close the canopy before she got herself oriented properly in the seat. She grunted, pinned to Rallek's chest in an upside-down fetal position. Acceleration weakened after fifteen seconds or so, releasing her. She shimmied around to sit up, and almost screamed at the cloud of pirate fighters in front of them.

Two blinding beams of bright orange light shot forth from the tips of the oversized cannons on either side of the Gremlin. The blast atomized the first pirate gunship and sent a second one tumbling out of formation sparking and sputtering.

"Holy crap," said Fawkes.

"Yeah." Nighthawk grinned like a fool. "These guns are huge... and the Scimitars are super brittle."

"Why are we shooting at them and not sneaking away?" asked Rallek, grunting as a high-energy turn crammed them into the left wall.

"No need to stay quiet now." He fired the particle cannons three more times at the unprepared fighters, blowing a hole in the curtain of smaller craft. Debris clanked against the shield bubble around the Gremlin. "These things do like 2,500 damage a shot, and the Scimitars only have 900 hull points."

"Uhh," Rallek gazed up and back at the perhaps thirty remaining Scimitar fighters turning toward them. "How many hull points does this thing have?"

"Two-K on the nose," said Nighthawk.

"So the Gremlin could one-shot itself?" asked Fawkes. "Who designs that?"

"Twice. *Each gun* does 2,500." Nighthawk cackled.

Streams of green laser blasts filled the infinite blackness behind them. A few struck the shield, making a high-pitched crackling squelch with each hit.

Fawkes mentally rolled her eyes at the people who complain about movies where space combat shouldn't have sound effects. *If they were going for realism, there wouldn't be space dogfights at all.*

Nighthawk flung the Gremlin into a spiraling downward turn. Every so often, he fired the particle beams and an explosion went off in the distance. "Uhh, time to go. Cruiser's on us."

He swerved back the other way, rolling under a blue-white energy beam almost as wide as the Gremlin.

"Are you serious?" asked Nighthawk. "What kind of moron fires a capital ship laser at a fighter?"

"I'd say someone who's really pissed off, but they're bots." Fawkes shrugged. "Can we get out of here now?"

"As you wish," said Nighthawk. He hit a button, triggering a blast of acceleration.

Lasers and the errant missile or two chased them for a little while. Around the time the *Stormbringer* came into view, the NPC pirates hit their distance limit and turned back to base.

Fawkes finally started breathing again. "Wow. I can't believe that actually worked."

"Awesome job you guys." Rallek hugged her then leaned forward to clap Nighthawk on the shoulder.

"This is the first time I've ever completed a quest while sitting around doing nothing," said Angel813. "Kinda boring actually."

"Well, call that make up for what you'll deal with when we go back for that damn robot." Kavan laughed. "And no... I am *not* looking forward to that."

"You need a better sword old man," said Nighthawk. "I got that covered. Tomorrow night."

"All right. What about the others?" asked Kavan.

Fawkes smiled. "I already got a bullet gun."

"Did you go for the Warhawk or the Thunderstrike?" asked Nighthawk, guiding them beneath the *Stormbringer's* hull.

"Warhawk." Fawkes gazed up at the ship, marveling at how big it seemed from the outside.

"Ahh. Yeah, I should do that, too." Nighthawk slowed the Gremlin, spinning it to line up with the docking hatch above them. "Been trying for the T-strike. It's an epic in a different instance, but the drop rate sucks."

The fighter came to a relative stop and glided straight up into the bay.

"Wow, you're really good at this," said Fawkes. "If space ships were real, you should be a pilot."

He laughed. "How many times did you have to run for the Warhawk?"

"Took me three tries." She scowled. "Some idiot gunslinger out-rolled me the first time it dropped."

Nighthawk laughed harder. "Three? Wow. That's *such* a pain in the butt."

She narrowed her eyes. "How many runs have you tried for the other one?"

"Uhh, like fifty-two?" He scratched his head. "All day. Over and over. Notice I'm level forty-six now?"

"Fifty two?" She gawked. "How are you not drooling all over yourself?"

"I probably am." He shut down the engines and popped the canopy open. "Haven't taken the helmet off in twelve hours. I'm logged in while sitting on the toilet."

"He lies," said Kavan. "Don't believe him."

Fawkes chuckled. "What time is it for real?"

"About five to midnight." Rallek boosted her up off his lap.

She stood on the Gremlin's delta wing next to the cockpit and reached down a hand to help him up. "Crap. I need to call it a night."

"You and me both." Rallek kissed her quick. "Night, babe. See you soon."

"Night guys," said Fawkes to the comm.

"Great job in there." Angel813 yawned. "See you tomorrow."

Fawkes climbed back up to the main room, fell in a chair by the round table, and logged off with a big grin on her face.

19

LEADERBOARD

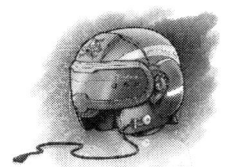

Dakota opened the Amazon Café at 6:00 a.m. the next morning. By 6:10, and no sign of Blake, she got worried and called him. The phone rang a dozen times and went to voicemail. She tried again, and he picked up after five rings.

"Oh, hi, Dakota. What's up?"

"What's up?" She blinked in disbelief. "It's almost quarter after and you're not here. Is everything okay?"

"Doesn't matter."

The unusual depth and slowness in his voice hinted at a serious problem. "What's wrong? You know Hal isn't here yet. If you get here before him, I won't say anything."

"It's... complicated. I... Look, I'm probably not going to be back. Nothing's important."

She bit her lip. "Neal left?"

Blake didn't reply.

"Hey, Blake, it's all right. Things will work out. I know what you're going through. I've been dumped before. If you wanna talk about it, I'm here."

A couple guys in suits and some women in office-type attire walked in.

"Customers here. I gotta go. Please be okay?"

"You knew?" Blake's voice cracked.

"Suspected. It's fine, really. You shouldn't be alone right now. Please come in?"

Blake sniffled. "Uhh, okay. S'pose I shouldn't leave you there to do everything yourself."

"Hi!" chirped Dakota at a guy in a blue suit. "What can I get started for you?"

"See ya soon," muttered Blake.

"'Kay," she whispered, and hung up. "Sorry, co-worker having car problems."

One customer blurred into the next. She scrambled trying to cover the drive-up window, prepare drinks for drone delivery, and handle the walk-ins by herself. It seemed like only twenty seconds before Blake trudged in looking like hell.

She ran over and grabbed his hand. "If you wanna just make shit and I'll deal with people today, that's cool."

He shrugged.

"Thank you for being here." She hugged him. "I'm all ears if you want to talk."

Blake pulled the drive-through headset off her. "I'll get the window."

"You're awesome." She winked and zipped back to the espresso machine.

Hal arrived a little after nine. If he somehow knew Blake had been late, he didn't let on. After about a half hour of back office work, he emerged and took over preparing drinks for the drone orders. The load leveled off to 'tame chaos' at that point, and she focused on the walk-in customers.

Right when her mood began to improve, Mr. Extra Shot walked in.

"Shit," muttered Dakota.

Hal whirled from the drone station and gave her the bug eyes.

She nodded at Mr. Extra Shot stepping up to the counter.

He smirked, but gave her a nod of 'okay, but be careful.'

"Hi, what can I get started for you today?" asked Dakota.

Mr. Extra Shot gazed up at the menu screens. "Peppermint mocha latte, large, with an extra shot."

"Got it. You wanted a peppermint mocha latte with an extra shot, correct?"

"Yes."

She pivoted toward Hal and belted, "One pep mocha with an extra shot!"

Blake managed a smile.

"Right, so that's a peppermint mocha latte large with an extra shot. That's eleven dollars even."

He held up his smartphone to pay.

"The extra shot's a buck seventy-five more." She scanned the barcode. "When a drink's got an extra shot it gets more expensive."

The man narrowed his eyes. "Is there a problem?"

"Not at all." She beamed. "I'm just making sure I have your order correct. You requested an extra shot, amirite?"

He frowned.

She grabbed a cup, pumped the peppermint and chocolate syrups in, and added milk. "Okay, here's the standard espresso." She poured that in. "And one more shot..." She hit the button on the espresso machine again.

"Okay, okay. I get it." Mr. Extra Shot raised his hands in surrender. "Sorry. The coffee just tasted a little weak last time."

Her smile faded from exaggerated to normal. She foamed the milk, gave the latte a nice crown of suds, and set the drink up on the counter. "There you go. Have great day!"

He sipped it, nodded, and walked out in a hurry.

At 11:25, a voice saying 'Axillon99' from the television got her attention. She pivoted around at a pair of morning show hosts flanking a graphic of the game's leaderboard, still displaying the same thing it had last time. The ship *Grand Designs* as first, *Feral* second, and *Stormbringer* in third place, though all had [tied] next to them.

"In a massive online game of over nineteen million players, fifteen people have made tangible progress on a mission worth ten million bucks of *real* money." She looked at her co-host. "What do they call them? Missions? Quests?"

The mocha-skinned guy in a grey suit laughed in an overly false tone that made Dakota roll her eyes. "Quests, I think. But there's no elves in this game."

"Elves? Really? This one's about space and stuff, isn't it? Well, anyway..." The perfect blonde smiled at the cameras. "The company behind the game, Cognition Studios International, has put up a prize of ten million dollars to the first player or players to complete a certain quest. As you can see here, there's three teams who have made progress."

"How do you get fifteen people out of three names?" asked the guy.

"Oh, it's like team names or something." The woman laughed, also forced as hell. "Each one represents five people. The winning team is set to claim the ten million dollar prize."

"Interesting. Who know there was so much money in video games? I may be in the wrong field. Must be nice to just sit at home all day long on the computer and become rich." The man clapped his leg, grinning.

"Oh wow," muttered Dakota. "Prick."

"Well, there's no poking fun at such a big prize no matter if they're quests or missions." The hostess smiled. "It's not too late to try though. CSI just released their next generation gaming helmet, the Neurona 4. And here to walk us through its paces is Alton Stirling, our tech guru!"

A geeky guy with spiked silver hair, a pale blazer, and plaid bowtie appeared on the screen, standing behind a counter upon which sat a Neurona 4 next to a PlayStation 7.

She tuned him out as a middle-aged woman approached and ordered a strawberry-mocha slushie, vaguely aware of the TV discussing data transfer rates, enhanced sensory resolution, and so on. While firing up the blender, she glanced at the screen.

"So, let's give this thing a whirl huh?" Alton grinned and picked up the helmet.

Dakota paused. "That idiot's going to put it on, isn't he?"

"What's wrong with that?" asked Hal.

Blake leaned over and peered at the screen.

"He's standing up..." Dakota pulled the blender jug off the motor and dumped the contents into a giant plastic cup.

Alton Stirling put the helmet on, the blackout visor covering his eyes. "Okay, now I can't see anything. The helmet's going to talk to my brain soon. There it is okay. I gotta hit this button to finish logging in..." He reached up and pushed the small rubber button by his right temple. The man went limp and collapsed straight to the floor.

Dakota burst out laughing as the camera cut back to the two confused hosts.

"We seem to be experiencing some technical difficulties," said the man.

"Here you go, ma'am." Dakota handed over the strawberry-choco-coffee drink. *There's so much sugar in that I think I gained six pounds from touching the cup.*

"Thank you sweetie." The woman smiled and hurried outside.

"Oh, wow." Alton stood back into view, the helmet in his hands. "This thing's got quite the kick. Felt like I was really somewhere else. Maybe I'm supposed to be in a chair or something first."

"Ya think?" muttered Dakota.

"Anyway... congrats to the three crews closing in on that prize. Best of luck!" said the hostess. "When we return from this break, we'll be talking to celebrity chef Misty Simms who's going to share her recipe for super fluffy Angel Food cake."

"Yay," muttered Dakota while jamming a scoop into the ice and closing the cooler hatch with a *thump*. "We're famous."

20

FULLY FUNCTIONAL ROBOT
OF DOOM

In the shadow of the abandoned starship plant's left tower, Fawkes glanced down at the heavy ballistic handgun. Shiny lines of neon blue accented a frame of dark grey. She squeezed her fingers into the comfortable rubberized handgrip, admiring the perfect amount of squishiness.

At her belt, a box the size of a pack of cards offered the hope of a different outcome. A personal force field generator, or PFF, slotted with the Venom Shroud modification gave her 250 extra 'health' against poison damage plus ninety-five percent resistance to it. If the robot hit her for 1000 venom damage, she'd only lose fifty points. Alas, the resistance only applied to the shield's points, not her health. But as long as she had shield points, the venom wouldn't touch her.

She wore two spare magazines for the gun on her belt, but her inventory showed 4000 rounds of ammo. As soon as she pulled one of the fresh magazines from the holder, a new one would appear there as long as she still had more ammo in her possession, so she didn't have to walk around 'wearing' ammo over every inch of her outfit. The game didn't make a big deal of reloading time as much as requiring her to *have* ammunition.

Kavan hefted his new blade, a slightly oversized broadsword named Fury's Edge. The steel had a dark blue sheen and a line of white around the cutting edge that almost glowed. He and Nighthawk spent most of the day working on that drop while she'd been pouring coffee. Evidently, William (Kavan's player) had taken the day off work to farm that thing.

Rallek hadn't had to do much prep beyond the shield mod. His technomancy had already been up to the task, though he did rearrange some microchip slots on his staff for a damage amp against robotics. Some of the higher-end items had slots where players could add different microchips to customize small bonuses. He'd also spent hours farming plants. He handed everyone elixirs that would boost any physical type damage they caused for twenty minutes.

Angel813 had also created serums that boosted max health by twenty percent and gave a base +15% boost to venom resistance, though that would only affect damage to health points. She walked down the line, hitting everyone with the booster shots.

"Okay." Kavan faced them like a general before the charge. "Now that we know what we're going in for, here's the plan. I'll rush the damn thing and get its attention. Give me a fifteen-second lead before you open up on it so I have a good threat cushion. We're staying off the stairs. Everyone spread out, with Angel in the middle. I know we got those shield things, but that's not an excuse to stand in the puddles. Do everything you can to stay clear."

Everyone nodded.

"Potions are ticking down," said Angel813. "Let's get going."

Kavan spun on his heel and marched into the channel between the two massive doors. The cavernous factory looked no different from the way it had the first time. Even the dust on the floor showed no sign of any prior footprints. He stormed straight over to the not-so-innocent stack of containers, where the twenty-foot robot boss concealed itself.

Fawkes dropped into stealth and scooted to the left. Angel813 took up a position about twenty feet behind Kavan. Nighthawk went to the right, stopping at a point roughly opposite Fawkes compared to the medic. Rallek stood at the rear, almost in line with Kavan, since his spells had the longest range of anything in the group. Only DPS soldiers using rifles could outrange a caster.

"Come on you heap o' junk." Kavan kicked the box. "What triggered it last time?"

"I think walking far enough into the room. I got it." Nighthawk jogged off to the right, where the group had gone last time.

Sure enough, once he went another dozen or so steps, the robot woke up and pushed the cargo boxes out of its way. The ambient 'creepy' music slam-shifted to a racing battle anthem.

Kavan sprang into action, swinging Fury's Edge at the enormous metal boot. The blade landed with a sharp *clang* and a shower of sparks. The robot's car-sized fist came down on him, stalling when it struck the energy shield projecting from Kavan's left forearm. The hit still took twenty-five percent of the tank's life off, but Angel813 had her orbs in midair before the hit landed.

"Ten," shouted Kavan, swinging twice more at the leg while ducking between them to get the titan to put its back to the group.

Again, it punched at him, and again, his health took a twenty-five percent hit.

Fawkes crouched in waiting, lining up an ambush shot at its back. Forty feet to her right, Nighthawk had two of the exact same pistols in his hands.

They didn't look quite so oversized on a male character, but she still wouldn't want to try using two at once. Her hand barely made it around the grip.

"Five," yelled Kavan, counting down the 'give me a chance to establish aggro' timer.

Her finger tensed on the trigger. *Four. Three. Two.*

The blast from her shot drowned out Kavan yelling, "Go!"

2040 appeared in bright red letters. She used *Flicker* to hide right away again and ambushed a second time, hitting for 2280. Somewhere to the right, Nighthawk fired so fast it sounded like he had a machinegun.

With a metallic groan of annoyance, the huge robot began to turn toward her.

"Dammit to hell, what did you do?" shouted Kavan. He roared and pounded his blade at the robot's leg, while red flames appeared on his shoulders.

"Crap!" Fawkes reflexively tried to use stealth, but it didn't work while in combat with a raid boss. She did, however, stop shooting.

Kavan's desperate assault on the robot's boot managed to get its attention back before it took a step to attack Fawkes. It pounded him again, knocking his health down to seventy percent. Angel813 kept a steady stream of medibots flying at him. Each hit did roughly twenty-five percent of his health points, and she managed to heal back twenty-two percent or so before the next one, so he steadily declined. She'd already discussed this with the group. Once he hit thirty percent, she'd run in and jab him with the full heal cooldown. This strategy relied on no one else taking spike damage and distracting her with the need for big heals.

Fawkes resumed shooting, landing hits a hair shy of a full 1,000 points from flanking multipliers. Nighthawk fired his pistols empty, reloaded, emptied them again, reloaded, and so on, keeping up a continuous barrage except for when he used his *Sharpshooter* cooldown. For two seconds, he'd take on a dramatic pose, raise one handgun, and squeeze off a single shot. She figured it had to do a lot of damage for him to use it, since it stopped his normal attacks for the time it took the fancy animation to play.

At thirty seconds in, the first wave of green goo missiles fired.

"Shields!" shouted Kavan.

Fawkes started running before the missile came down on her head, mashing the button attached to the box on her hip. A green energy field winked on around her, flickering for an instant as the edge of the poison disc clipped the bubble, doing two points of damage.

"Stand close to the edge of the venom patches," yelled Angel813. "That way they overlap and we have more floor space for a longer time."

"Got it," yelled Nighthawk. "Hey look. I didn't stand in bad."

"You want an award or something?" yelled Angel813.

"That would be cool, yeah." Nighthawk reloaded. "I think I deserve one for being this awesome."

Angel813 rolled her eyes.

Fawkes snickered, and emptied the rest of her current magazine into the robot's back.

Rallek spammed his techno-bolt, adding a steady stream of damage with the occasional pause to mend Kavan's armor bar or throw a spell at Angel813 to replenish her 'medical supply' meter. Once *Flicker* came off cooldown, Fawkes hit it and lit off another 2200-point ambush crit. That got her daydreaming about *Master of Shadows* when she could ambush over and over again.

Reloading a bullet-eating gun proved to be highly annoying. Every twenty shots, she had to grab a magazine off her belt and stuff it in the gun. Admittedly, she had to reload the CL32 the same way with power packs, but only once per 250 shots.

Another barrage of goo missiles rained down. Fawkes had been standing within inches of the first green disc. A little less than half of the new circular patch overlapped area already made toxic by the first one. She scooted left, enough to not stand in damage, and kept firing.

Inch by inch, the huge robot's life bar shrank.

When it hit fifty percent, it stopped punching at Kavan and clenched its fist in front of its chest while shuddering.

"Is it trying to take a dump?" asked Nighthawk.

"That's probably not a bad metaphor," said Rallek. "It's about to take a dump all over us I think."

Kavan kept swinging in an endless *clang, clang, clang* of enchanted steel striking ordinary armored boot.

Three seconds later, vents all over the robot body opened up, spewing green gas. The noxious cloud spread over the whole room in an instant, causing a steady stream of damage ticks on everyone. Fawkes glanced up at the storm of numbers ranging from five to fifteen. After twenty seconds, the cloud dispersed.

"That was a shitload of damage," said Rallek. "Average ten points a second for twenty seconds to a ninety-five percent resistance? Ballpark it would've done maybe ten grand without that mod."

Fawkes jaw dropped. "How the hell do they expect players to survive an attack that does ten grand over twenty seconds? I've only got 1,844 health!"

"We're still standing, aren't we?" asked Angel813, patting the shield box.

She couldn't argue that, and kept on firing.

Rallek summoned an android.

"No! Nothing in melee. Kavan will take more damage," yelled Angel813.

"Oh. I thought it was venom. He doesn't have to worry about standing in goo, so it should be okay, right?"

Angel813 thought about it. "Okay fine."

The summoned android wobbled up behind the big robot and began punching at its leg. Sure enough, the 'screw-the-melee' poison cloud appeared, the same one Fawkes had worked out the timing to avoid. Kavan, having no choice but to be close to the robot, stood there and ate it. It did a little damage to the venom shield, but nothing alarming. The summoned android, being a machine, ignored poison.

At twenty-five percent life, the giant robot arched its back and opened two panels on its shoulders.

A bright red shaft of laser light fell down from above on Fawkes, but didn't do damage. The robot fired a barrage of missiles straight up.

"What the...?" She gazed at the rising warheads.

"Targeting unit. Run like hell!" shouted Angel813.

Fawkes sprinted to the side, darting around venom patches. Deafening whistles went off behind her as a rain of rockets slammed into the ground at her heels, one every second. The red beam tracked her for eight seconds before disappearing. The last missile came close enough to fling her off her feet onto her chest and do thirty-three percent damage to her health, ignoring the shield since the PFF only stopped venom damage.

"Ow," she muttered, not that it really hurt.

The targeting beam reappeared on Rallek. He sprinted, but wound up getting cornered by venom patches and going across one to avoid getting trapped under the barrage. His shield withered down to about twenty-five percent by the time he reached clear ground.

Fawkes picked herself up and resumed shooting at the robot as medi-bots swarmed her. After Rallek's eight seconds, the missile beam came back for her.

"Dammit!" screamed Fawkes, while sprinting hard. "Go after Nighthawk!"

"Hell to the no!" shouted Nighthawk.

Fawkes hauled ass, waving her arms to keep balance as she tiptoed along a one-foot-wide section of clean floor between glowing green patches. That time, she ran fast enough to avoid the splash damage from the eighth warhead.

"Oh, screw you!" Nighthawk wailed in annoyance and sprinted away from the targeting laser.

"It's random," yelled Rallek, hurling a techno-bolt into the robot's back. "It didn't listen to her."

"I was talking to the robot, not Fawkes," shouted Nighthawk.

When the robot's health bar hit ten percent, the aerial bombardment stopped and the two launch bay doors motored closed. Armor plates exploded off its back and chest, amid a ridiculous amount of goo missiles flying in all directions, splattering every scrap of floor space with the inch-deep deadly slime. The whole room turned toxic green with nowhere to go to avoid it.

"Burn phase!" yelled Angel813. "Hit it with everything you got!" She, too, pulled a Warhawk pistol and fired.

The robot had stopped punching at Kavan and simply spewed poison in all directions. The energy shield projecting from his left forearm collapsed, and a second, smaller sword appeared in his off hand. Fawkes clicked the trigger as fast as she could move her finger, cursing the mechanism that limited her to twenty shots before reloading.

Nighthawk sprang into the air, his body covered in white fire. Hanging six feet off the ground, he pirouetted around in a fancy maneuver, then floated motionless while both of his pistols spat bullets. After four seconds, he dropped back to the ground and reloaded. The barrage knocked the robot forward a step and took four percent of its life away.

"What the hell was that?" shouted Fawkes.

"*Blaze of Glory*," yelled Nighthawk. "Sixty shots per weapon that can't miss... but they can't crit either."

"Those guns don't even hold sixty shots," said Rallek.

"They do when I use BoG." Nighthawk laughed.

Right as the venom shield collapsed and the ground started ticking Fawkes for 100 poison damage a second, the giant robot teetered and fell over to the side, dead. She cheered, but stopped when her health kept going down.

"Umm, is this gonna stop?"

The venom got in a few 'cheap shots' after the boss died, but faded before any player went below half health. A faint pale-green fog hovered over the floor for a little while where toxic gel had been.

"Woo!" Fawkes leapt into the air waving her gun around. "We did it!"

"Sweet!" yelled Nighthawk.

"So, umm, what did that do?" asked Rallek.

Fawkes walked over to stand by Kavan, near the dead titan's leg. "Probably a guardian of this facility. Now, we can explore it."

"Wow, that was almost easy that time," said Nighthawk.

"Being prepared for a fight makes a world of difference." Kavan clapped him on the back. "Why do you think I read so much?"

The loot box contained a heavy weapon for a DPS soldier that spewed poison. (Essentially a green flamethrower). Since no one wanted (or could use) it, Kavan sent it to the ship's hold for sale. He picked up a better tank shield, and it also dropped a golden staff that looked like it belonged in a sword & sorcery game. Only the winged medallion at the top having a circuitry pattern broke the fantasy illusion.

"Hmm. Auramancer item. To the hold it goes," said Kavan.

"Wait. Would anyone mind if I nab that for my alt?" asked Fawkes. She could stick it in her 'account storage area,' which any of her characters (if she ever made more than two) could access.

"You have an alt?" asked Rallek.

"Yeah, she's been messing around with a Niath auramancer," said Nighthawk. "It's only level seven though."

"Be a while before you can even equip this." Kavan examined it. "Minimum level is thirty-six."

"Oh. Well, I guess go ahead and sell it then. I still don't know if I'll ever play her that high."

Kavan tossed her the staff. "Go for it. It's a purple drop. Would be nice to have a backup healer around."

Angel813 glanced at her, a hint of a lift to her chin.

"Oh, I dunno. I'm nowhere near as good as Angel."

"Hah," said Angel813.

"I'm serious. I did this rando instance with another medic... holy cow they sucked. If the tank wasn't over-geared, we would've been so dead."

Angel813 smiled. "Okay... I'll accept your sincerity."

"We should get going. With that thing dead, the other crew could get in here." Fawkes jogged around the robot toward the rest of the building.

"Nah." Nighthawk shook his head. "They'll get an instance with a fully functional robot of doom."

Fawkes smiled. "Let's hope."

21

A RIP IN THE VEIL

The crew explored the massive, derelict factory for over an hour, checking every room along the interior. Rusting hallways, broken pipes, and a general sense of malaise got the hairs on the back of her neck on end. A flavor like brackish water and rust settled on her tongue. Every so often, packs of small robots attacked, but they landed firmly in the 'irritating' category, being no real danger. Still, the constant threat of another attack kept the level of tension high enough to get Fawkes jumping at shadows.

"You know," she muttered, "I've never been a fan of watching horror movies. I don't like being *in* one."

Soft chuckling echoed behind her from everyone else.

"Yeah," said Nighthawk in an unusually quiet voice. "I hate stuff that jumps out, too."

She nudged open a door that led to a command type room full of computers. A huge wall of screens stood in front of an array of workstations. "Oh, hey this looks promising."

Fawkes strolled down a short staircase, heading for the center of the room. She flopped in the most important looking chair and attacked the computer terminal. It turned on, displaying a log entry with cryptic notes about the warp drive.

"The QDD-1 has exhibited poor performance when used for short-distance leaps of less than a hundred nav units. However, when operating in blue-star systems, we've noticed an inversion in the energy transfer that results in a successful jump and a net increase in stored power. Our monitoring stations detected that this phenomenon leaves behind an energy trace for up to twenty-four days that is vulnerable to being detected by standard sensor arrays if the operators scan for a particular wavelength. Before the QDD-1 can be certified for military use, we'll have to fix this issue. For the type of service this ship is intended, leaving behind any sign of presence is unacceptable."

Glowing text—Log Updated—appeared in midair and faded.

Fawkes opened her mission log. The prize quest lit up with a new entry. She tapped it.

"Your ship's sensors have been updated with the information you found in the research facility. Sensor sweeps can now detect the energy trace left behind by the *Reckoning's* warp drive and record its location." Fawkes looked up from her personal display screen. "So... we can see where this ship has been now?"

"Hmm." Kavan rubbed his chin. "I'm guessing that they expect us to fly all over and look for these traces. Maybe it'll let us follow the ship?"

Rallek walked around to stand beside him. "How do you follow a ship that blips from one side of the universe to another in an instant?"

"There's gotta be a pattern in there somewhere." Fawkes tapped her foot for a moment in thought. "Maybe we can extrapolate where it's going to go before it goes somewhere?"

Angel813 sputtered. "Who is supposed to win this prize, the NSA?"

Kavan and Rallek laughed.

"Maybe you're overthinking it?" asked Nighthawk.

A faint metallic glint caught Fawkes' eye. She twisted the chair around with a low creak, squinting at a shelf of dusty equipment along the wall at her left.

"What?" asked Rallek.

"I thought I saw something." She kept staring at the spot. When the flash happened again, she darted out of the chair and ran to it. Under a heap of keyboards, computer components, and a broken flat-panel monitor, she found a data pad. "Aha! Don't anyone ever tell me throwing a couple points in perception was a waste."

"What is it?" asked Nighthawk.

"A data pad," said Fawkes.

"Duh. Obviously." Nighthawk rolled his eyes. "What's on it?"

She tapped the button, activating the display.

Text appeared in bright cyan on a blue holographic screen:

Fuck me? No. Fuck *you*. So8agtHRbt! -TURBAN
    BB842.32 HF222.20

Fawkes ran her finger back and forth under the So8 part. "This kinda looks like a password."

"Who the heck is TURBAN?" Nighthawk scratched his head.

She shifted her jaw side to side.

Angel813 shrugged. "One of the head developers is Indian, but I don't think he's a Sikh."

Rallek snapped his fingers. "No! It's not TURBAN... It's T. Urban!"

"What?" asked Kavan. "Give an old man a break here."

Rallek grabbed Fawkes' head in two hands and pulled her into a brief kiss. "Keep on putting points in perception."

"Less kissy more info-y," said Kavan.

"Heh." Rallek pointed at the data pad. "Okay, CSI started off real small, with three main guys, the founders. Vinod Prakash, Gerald Barker, and Thomas Urban."

"I've heard of the first two..." Nighthawk scrunched up his eyebrows. "Not the other guy."

"Right." Fawkes's eyes shot open wide with realization. "Urban left the company right before Axillon99 exploded into the most popular game in the world."

"Rumor had it he got fucked," said Rallek.

Nighthawk cackled.

Kavan winced.

"Uhh, sorry." Rallek flashed a cheesy smile. "All sorts of rumors say Urban got the shaft."

"Look at this." Fawkes pointed at the data pad. "F me, no F you? That's gotta be from Urban. This could be his revenge. Hang on. I have to try something."

She flung herself back into the computer chair and forced the terminal to a login prompt. The game world's fictional Portals14 operating system screen appeared. She entered TURBAN as the username and 'So8agtHRbt!' for a password. A spinning icon appeared.

"Did it work?" asked Rallek.

"It's still thinking about it." Fawkes raised an eyebrow. "But it's doing something. A bad password would've rejected by now unless it's got no connection to the domain controller."

"What?" asked Nighthawk.

"Oh, I keep thinking this is real life." Fawkes groaned and ran her hands up over her hot pink hair. "Come on, girl. Hold it together. Pink hair and background music means game world."

"Invalid Username" appeared on the screen.

"Damn." Fawkes muttered. "Was worth a try."

"Maybe that other thing is the password?" asked Angel813.

"No, that's coordinates." Nighthawk pointed at the numbers.

Fawkes' hands trembled. "Wait a sec. This could be a back door login. This terminal is still fully in game. It wouldn't take a *real* login. This could be Urban's *actual* network credentials for the CSI network."

"Whoa." Rallek leaned back. "So this is or is not related to the big mission?"

She flicked a thumbnail at the edge of the data pad, in a repetitious clicking motion for a moment of thought. "I don't think it's intentionally related, but maybe the 'no F you' part of this is him helping someone get that money. We should check out what's on the other end of that rainbow." She pointed at the coordinates. "But, as far as the mission goes, finding this terminal and getting the sensor unlock I think was it."

"So, we had to fight that obnoxious robot only to get our sensors able to sniff out this ship we have no chance in hell of taking on?" asked Kavan.

"Yeah, something like that." Fawkes grinned.

Kavan frowned.

"Wait... the pirates!" Nighthawk held up a finger. "We snuck in and out of a raid doing this quest and didn't have to fight it. Maybe we don't have to *kill* the *Reckoning*. Finding it at all might be enough. Something might happen, like a transmission as soon as we're close."

"Oh." Kavan's eyebrows both went up. "That's possible."

"Don't give up yet, old man." Angel813 punched him playfully in the shoulder. She had a flirty look to her eye that he seemed oblivious to. A few seconds later, she turned away, disappointed.

Fawkes glanced between them, debating if she should tell Kavan, but she chickened out.

BACK ON THE *STORMBRINGER*, AND WELL AWAY FROM LEADING ANY OTHER prize-seekers to the abandoned factory, the crew convened in the main room with an overabundance of fattening treats. Fawkes did things with her tongue to a portion of chocolate mousse that would've resulted in prison time in some countries. Rallek printed an unhealthy amount of hot wings while Nighthawk went for the usual: chicken nuggets and fries. Angel813 introduced everyone to daifuku, flavored filling wrapped in a gummy, sugary shell made from pounded rice.

"Got it," said Nighthawk. "Those coordinates point to DB224. It's a desolate planet with no natural water."

"Random?" asked Fawkes.

"Again, the name looks random but if Tom Urban is sending us there... Maybe it's not as random as it appears." Rallek inhaled another wing. "You know this game is ruining me for food. These wings taste just like the ones I used to get back home before I moved to NYC. So perfect."

"Mmm," said Nighthawk. "It does the fries awesome, too. They taste like just the ones from sc— I mean the ones I used to get at school years ago."

Fawkes glanced over the table at him.

"So this planet..." Rallek nibbled on a wing while glancing at a floating display screen. "It's got a few lame quests. There's some comments about it having overpowered creatures that aren't worth the experience rewards. People are pretty much all saying don't bother going here."

"Iceland," said Kavan.

"Whoa left field." Fawkes stared at him. "What?"

"Greenland and Iceland." Kavan smiled. "Greenland is an icy wasteland. Iceland is paradise. The people who discovered them named them backwards to keep Iceland for themselves. Maybe it's a similar thing. Urban made the planet unappealing so people wouldn't want to go there—to hide something."

"Well..." Fawkes waved the data pad. "It's not like we're going there looking for quests. We have something amazing."

"Are you sure it's not a trick?" asked Angel813.

She turned the data pad over in her fingers. "I think it's legit. At worst, it's an Easter egg. At best, who knows? Maybe the cash."

"Might as well check it out. It's either that or we fly around at random hunting for sensor traces." Kavan stood. "Gimme those coordinates again."

Fawkes tossed the data pad to him.

22

FRIENDLY RIVALRY

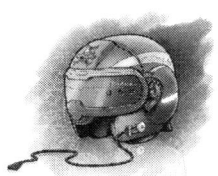

Thin white lines on the viewscreen reduced to individual stars, and the brown sphere hurtling toward them at a terrifying pace stopped cold as the *Stormbringer* dropped out of warp in DB224's star system. The planet, which had been approaching like a cannonball, hung motionless, occupying the middle third of the main viewscreen. Faint striations of beige rolled across the surface beneath a wispy gauze of cloud cover along with a few darker bands.

The crew gathered on the bridge, crowded together behind the pilot's seat.

Bit by bit, the unimpressive brown sphere eked larger.

"Wow. If boring had a color, it would be that," said Kavan.

Fawkes' account pinged. She opened the interface and nearly passed out at the new message counter showing 28,417 unread. "Oh, shit. Is everyone getting spammed or is it just me."

"Crap," said Rallek, staring at a floating window. "What the hell?"

"Oh, wow." Nighthawk whistled. "Thirty thousand messages."

For a second, Fawkes felt a twinge of disappointment at 'the damn gunslinger' getting a higher score, but when she looked back down at the little display screen her count had gone up to 32,044.

"It's people begging for information," said Angel813. "Oh, and about one in ten feel the need to tell me I'm not really a woman."

Biting her lip, Fawkes checked a couple of the first messages. A few offered congrats, most begged for a clue, some cursed her out, and a couple accused her of really being a dude. "Yeah, same here. I wonder if anyone's accused Nighthawk of really being a man yet."

He held up a middle finger.

Rallek laughed. "Watch, he's really a chick playing a dude."

"Am not," said Nighthawk.

"So why the sudden barrage?" Kavan swiveled the pilot's chair around to look at everyone.

"Because of this." Rallek grabbed a display screen like a floating piece of paper, stretching it wider and turning it around to show everyone the leaderboard.

1. The Stormbringer
2. Grand Designs (Tied)
3. Feral (Tied)

"Dammit!" yelled Fawkes. "That's not cool. They might as well paint a giant target on our asses."

Buzzing came from the console.

"Crap. Someone *did!*" yelled Nighthawk, before running down the hall.

The computer locked on to an approaching Cobra class corvette designated *Elite*, a broad flying wedge. It had about half the nose-to-tail length of the spearhead-shaped *Stormbringer*, but twice the width. Red lights indicated the other ship had armed its weapons.

"Pirates?" yelled Fawkes.

"No, not this close to a planet."

"Hello!" A twenty-ish looking guy with a black bowl cut streaked with bands of neon green appeared on the viewscreen. "Nothing personal. We're just hoping to slow y'all down so we have a chance at the prize. Good luck!"

The comm cut out.

"Huh?" asked Fawkes. "The hell is that?"

"If they blow us up, we're stuck on a one-week lockout like we don't have a starship. We'd be stranded on this dung ball doing missions on foot until the reset." Kavan armed the weapons. "Mind giving us a hand back in engineering?"

"I hate PVP!" yelled Fawkes.

"Do you hate a lockout more?" Kavan swung the ship to the left and twisted around in a loop, sliding sideways in a corkscrew that kept the approaching idiot near the crosshairs in the middle of the screen.

"This moron's in a Cobra," yelled Nighthawk. "That's 'baby's first corvette.' Don't worry."

"Ugh!" She bolted down the hall, which lit up blue in the flare from the *Stormbringer's* four laser cannons. Once she skidded to a stop by the engineering station, she slotted a shield booster out of reflex. "What are we dealing with?" she yelled at the comm panel.

"*Elite's* mounting a twin pulse laser and a molecular disruptor," said Kavan from the console.

Her mind raced. Pulse lasers did less damage than normal lasers, but fired rapidly, like a machinegun. *If* a pilot could keep them on target, they could do more damage in less time than the standard lasers. That varied a lot based on your target. With Kavan at the helm, and the agile *Stormbringer*, odds favored those being weak. Disruptors on the other hand did almost no damage to an active shield but they shredded armor. They also created a fairly slow-moving blob of energy, making them short range weapons since any decent pilot could dodge them given a long enough shot.

"Disruptor's going to do jack if our shields stay up. I think I'm just gonna load up four shield boosters."

"That works," yelled Kavan.

The *brmmm, brmmm, brmmm* of the ship's guns going off over and over gave her some hope. If Kavan fired, that meant the *Elite* remained in front of them. The *Stormbringer* rattled as if it hit a patch of turbulence. Heavy thuds went overhead and some panels showed red. Shields dropped to ninety-two percent.

"Come on you bastard," said Kavan, right before inertia pushed Fawkes into a slide away from her station. "Oh, he didn't like that!"

Kavan had to be turning damn hard.

"What's going on?" yelled Fawkes while scrambling into her seat and fastening the belt.

"I don't think he scanned us before deciding to attack. We've got Class 3 laser cannons. Four of them. This guy's still on Class 1 weaponry. I bet he hasn't had his ship for a full week yet. If I get a good shot on him three times, he's gone. I hit him once, and now he's all over the place like a bull with a flea chewing on its butthole."

Nighthawk cackled over the comm. "He probably crapped himself when he saw how much damage we did in one hit. Launching in three seconds."

"This guy thinks he's all sorts of hot shit," said Kavan, "because of his targeting unit."

"Predictive?" yelled Fawkes, as the *Stormbringer* took another barrage of pulse laser fire.

"Yeah. If I fly erratically enough to avoid that thing, I'll never get a shot off."

Rallek laughed like an evil mastermind. "Oh, boys! I got something for you."

All the lights in the engineering bay flickered.

"What did you just do?" asked Fawkes.

The air-blast noise of the Gremlin launching made her clamp her hands over her ears for a second.

Rallek strolled in to the engineering bay. "Hit the *Elite* with a debuff. Almost no one remembers technomancers can affect ships in space battles. They're thirty seconds without that predictive targeting module. He's gotta aim by hand. Now it's a pure twitch contest of who's the better pilot."

"Nice." She gave him a high five.

The engineering station's chase view screen flashed bright orange. Two streaks of particle beam came out from beneath the *Stormbringer*, strafing over the *Elite* and punching through its shield. A pair of black scorch marks appeared on the shiny hull. The Gremlin slipped out into view, accelerating at the *Elite*.

"That damn fighter hits almost as hard as our ship's main guns." Rallek closed his eyes and put a hand on the engineering console. "Bet Nighthawk purchased his ship with real money too, only took a fighter craft instead of a corvette."

The same animation for the techno-bolts he'd been throwing at the giant robot appeared in space, flying out from the *Stormbringer's* nose. It caught the tip of the *Elite's* left side, leaving a patch of sparking blackness.

"Right about now, I bet the pilot of that ship is thinking he made a tactical error," said Rallek.

"Or he's a 'worked-his-way-up' guy cursing us out for having a purchased ship." She shrugged.

"Oh, this is only tier five... they go up to ten. And some of those 'workers' are already into the tier sevens."

"No one got a ten yet?" asked Fawkes.

"Nope. Leveling up ships is more of a bitch than getting a character to sixty. A lot more."

Three fighters popped out of the *Elite's* hull and turned toward them. A rapid barrage of incoming laser fire shaved twenty percent off the *Stormbringer's* shield.

"Crap, you better get in a turret." Fawkes poked a cooldown slot and the shield snapped back up to full.

"On it." Rallek ran off down the central corridor.

Nighthawk wheeled the Gremlin around, chasing fighters. Fawkes poked a tool at the shield generator, using her 'active ability' to boost the ship's max shield by twenty percent. She watched the screen, mesmerized by the veritable ballet of spacecraft. The Gremlin skimmed around the smaller fighters' attacks with apparent inches to spare, almost causing two of them to crash into each other trying to stay in firing position. Nighthawk seemed to be toying with them. The steady ripple of small red laser blips from the *Stormbringer's* two turrets peppered one of the enemy fighters enough to send into a death tumble that resulted in an explosion at the end of a twisty, sparkling trail.

The Gremlin spun over and flipped like something kicked it in the ass, a maneuver that left him leveled off directly behind one of the enemy fighters. A dual blast from the particle cannons incinerated the light fighter in one shot. The last one wheeled around, trying to bring its weapons to bear on him, but he accelerated, keeping the Gremlin a few feet to the right of a steady stream of red laser beams.

"What's the matter dude? Can't quite turn tight enough?" said Nighthawk. "Heh. Okay, I'm bored."

The Gremlin rolled to the right and stopped dead in place, causing the other fighter to zoom straight through where it had been seconds before. He pulled the nose up and melted the last light fighter down with another blast of orange.

"Wow. He's really good at that," said Angel813.

"Are you that good or did those guys just suck?" asked Fawkes.

Nighthawk laughed. "Both. They're only level thirty, so they don't have as many micro-bonuses as I get from my fighter pilot secondary class... but space combat is all twitch. Levels don't really make that much difference. And I am the twitch master."

"Well played," said the voice of the *Elite's* pilot, an instant before the buzz of laser cannons vibrated the hull.

On the chase view, four strands of scintillating blue light connected the *Stormbringer's* outer edges to a rapidly expanding orange fireball where the *Elite* had been seconds ago.

"Wow, I almost feel bad," said Fawkes. "That wasn't even a challenge."

"Don't." Rallek put an arm around her. "It's like being the new guy in prison. Kick someone's ass hard the first day, makes people leave you alone. Word gets around that they tried to attack us and we didn't even go under seventy percent shields, might make more idiots think twice."

"Those aren't the ones I'm worried about." She leaned against him. "What about those people with the tier seven ships? What if Army of One decides they want the prize money more than being the first group to kill the big raid boss?"

He shrugged. "Well... then it gets complicated."

23

THE ARMADILLO

Nighthawk stayed out in the Gremlin, flying escort for the rest of the flight to DB224, docking only a few seconds before they began atmospheric entry. No one else tried to attack them, and Angel813 found an option in the settings to block incoming messages from senders not part of a friend list.

The planet had one major colony and one star port. All ships hard-disabled weapons within two miles of a star port, since no one at CSI wanted to deal with the sort of bitching that would happen if griefers could strafe helpless starships on the ground. An army of players locked out of space for a week at a time would threaten the bottom line. Also, they didn't want the griefers firing starship weapons into cities, incinerating crowds of players.

No amount of map gazing yielded any clues, so the group decided to explore the colony on foot. Drab brown or beige buildings huddled close together on narrow streets paved with dirt or cobblestones. The architecture resembled a blend of the Middle East and Mexico, with a heavy helping of drudgery and little bits of futuristic tech. A change in the background music added stringed instruments and an Arabian feel.

Citizen NPCs in the robes of desert-dwellers roamed about, offering limited dialogue that complained about late water shipments, bad hydroponic crop yields, or missing goats. The missing goat turned out to be a quest, but Nighthawk advised everyone to ignore it as the goats remains lay a short walk out of town surrounded by three massive scorpions. For a measly 5,000 experience points, that fight wouldn't be worth it.

"Can we complain to CSI about that leaderboard," asked Kavan. "It's made us a big target."

"Oh, like the company cares about PVPers slowing us down. They want them to." Fawkes scowled.

"Ooh! I fucking *hate* PVPers." Angel813 fumed.

Nighthawk snickered.

"Don't candy coat it, Angel." Rallek winked. "Let your emotions flow."

"I'm serious." She balled her hands into fists, arms shaking. "Damn PVP idiots are always whining and crying about classes being overpowered because they got owned in PVP, so CSI gets tired of the bitching and they nerf something to shut them up, and that nerf takes a giant shit all over me in PVE."

Nighthawk scrunched up his face. "How does PVP affect PVE? One's killing players, the other's raiding or doing instances."

"Because they cry about abilities. CSI nerfs those abilities to make the PVP kiddies stop crying, and then those same abilities used in PVE start to suck. Like, empaths used to have a level forty-five spell, *Essence Barrier*, that put a big shield on them. It stopped them from attacking at all, but it gave a 2,000 point damage soak and a twenty-five percent boost to healing output. We had a raid strat that relied on me using that cooldown to survive the boss's big enrage explosion at ten percent life. I'd pop that, the bubble would keep me alive while everyone else but the tank died, and then I'd light off *Soul Rebirth* to bring everyone back on their feet. Well, the PVP jackasses cried about *Essence Barrier* being overpowered, so instead of changing how it worked only in PVP, they got rid of the force field. Now it's just a twenty-five percent boost to healing output."

"Oh. That's shitty," said Fawkes. "I hate PVP, too."

"'Cause of nerfs?" asked Rallek.

She laughed. "No. Because I get too pissed off too fast. If I die to an NPC, I know it's either me screwing up or bullshit. When another player kills me, I get insanely angry at them for being better than me."

Kavan stopped walking and shifted toward her. "How do you tell the difference between screwing up or the game cheating when you die to an NPC?"

"If the NPC is five or more levels over me, I screwed up by attacking it." She grinned.

"So, basically, any time you die, it's the game cheating?" asked Kavan.

With an exaggerated tongue-sticking-out face, she nodded rapidly, hoping he'd take it as the joke she meant.

He laughed.

Nighthawk approached another NPC townie and rushed through a dialogue about a missing boy. He shared a quest to find 'Mot.' When they reached the village square, he ran around grabbing twelve more quests, sharing each one. Collect teeth from dust wolves, extract the brains of desert lizards for an alchemist, find a lost toolbox, and so on.

"Why are you grabbing all these quests?" asked Fawkes. "I thought you said they weren't worth it? Most of them are like ten levels under us."

"Habit. I've never done them before. It's cool to see stuff for the story, yanno?" He shrugged.

"That lizard brain quest is stupid," said Rallek. "Only one in like thirteen lizards you kill drops a brain."

Kavan chuckled. "So you're saying these lizards are MMO designers?"

Everyone snickered.

She followed him around for another few minutes as he checked every NPC in the town square for quests. While he discussed with a fruit cart vendor the problem of someone poisoning a poor man's goats, she yawned and looked around. Sun glare made a few of the buildings painfully bright, so she shifted to face back the way they'd come.

This city radiated such a degree of drab boredom that she gave serious thought to logging out and going to bed.

She started to turn back to face Nighthawk when his conversation ended, but stopped at the sight of a small sign mounted to a narrow three-story building on a corner about a block away. The dark brown rectangle had a tan armadillo pattern on it, but no words. Beneath it, one narrow door sat inside a recessed alcove with a curved top.

"Hey. Follow me," said Fawkes, a little over a whisper. "Act natural."

The others muttered amongst themselves, evidently Angel813 and Kavan not having heard her. She walked out of the square, following the street to the suspicious building. Rallek let out a stifled squawk like a stepped-on chicken, no doubt noticing the sign for himself. She strolled right up to the door, grabbed the knob, and opened it.

Inside, the room had the look of an abandoned dwelling. Small cracks ran across the walls near the ceiling. Cheap furniture lay scattered about in front of a smashed fireplace. Plaster fragments and plastic bits crunched under her boots. She approached a small stairwell in the back and made her way up to the second floor, emerging from a hole with no railings into a barren space. Tiny flecks of white plaster dusted a hardwood floor full of gouges, casting long shadows in the light radiating from one street-facing window. White walls with the same hand-troweled stucco pattern as the outside held no paintings, smudges, or any other sign that someone had ever cared about this place.

She stood in silence, trying to make sense of this, until it dawned on her that she experienced total silence.

"Do you hear that?" whispered Fawkes.

The others surveyed the room.

"Hear what?" asked Kavan. "I don't hear anything."

"Exactly." She twisted around, her boot soles squeaking. "There's no background music in here."

Jaws hung open.

Nighthawk's eyes bugged. "Whoa. Yeah. There's *always* background music."

"I can hear my fridge," said Rallek. "Like my real fridge. It's so quiet in the game, reality is seeping into my consciousness."

Fawkes crept forward, tracing her fingers across the rough plaster wall. "There's gotta be something important in here."

"Background music comes back as soon as my head's below the floor," said Nighthawk from the stairs. He peeked up into view. "As soon as I stick my head into the room, it stops."

The group spread out. Rallek walked the other way, feeling at the walls for 'secret doors.' Kavan searched the floor. Nighthawk moved around the edge, kicking the walls, and Angel813 glided about with her eyes turned to the ceiling.

Fawkes brushed her hands back and forth over the wall, noting the texture, coarse and dry. The wall appeared to be hand plastered like something out of the Old World, but it felt like stone.

Click.

Everyone froze at the sound of a pull-chain light switch far louder than a pull chain light switch ought to be.

Angel813 had stopped roaming near the back of the room, two steps from the wall. Her right arm extended up over her head to clutch a thin filament hanging from the ceiling next to a dead light bulb. She pulled on it again and the same too-loud *click* sounded. The light bulb remained off.

"This is something," she said, before pulling it again.

Click.

"It's a broken light." Nighthawk shook his head. "This place is a dump. A broken light doesn't stand out."

"But a click that loud..." Fawkes walked up beside her, staring upward, mesmerized by such an ordinary object.

Again, Angel813 pulled the chain and made the loud *click*. Fawkes twitched, expecting the light to come on, but it didn't.

She inhaled a breath full of the stink of moldy plaster... and a hint of coffee.

"Coffee," said Fawkes. "Did I smell that or is it in reality?"

Angel813 lowered her gaze to the wall, then rotated her head to Fawkes like an android. "What is reality? What if we're a bunch of space adventurers who escape our dangerous life by playing a simulation of society as it was a thousand years ago."

"Girl, whatever drugs you took, share some of that shit," said Rallek. He pursed his lips, tilted his head, and raised his hand. "On second thought, don't."

Angel813's creepy calm cracked, and she laughed. "Sorry. I'm being silly and messing with you."

Fawkes glanced up at the ceiling. "This is something." She reached up and grasped the pull chain. When she tugged it, a faint silver thread glinted in a rectangular shape around the bulb, as big as a door. "Aha! Perception skill for the win."

She pulled harder on the string, and kept pulling. The ceiling creaked. She added her left hand to the cord and dangled all her weight on it. On screeching rusty hinges, a hatch like an old attic stairway opened downward. Instead of a rickety ladder, it morphed into a solid staircase.

"Wow. I know this is a game and all, but that looked freaky as hell," said Rallek.

Fawkes examined a set of white wooden stairs that appeared more modern than the anachronistic colony, but more primitive than a futuristic game. They appeared solid enough, and led to a plain white door even with the third story. She climbed without hesitation and grasped the knob.

The door opened into a mundane office with blue carpeting, bookshelves, a ceiling fan, and a big window with silver blinds. Outside, the scenery appeared to be San Francisco in the late afternoon, the Golden Gate visible in the distance. An ordinary desktop computer sat on the lone black steel desk, next to an expensive padded ergonomic chair.

She stepped around and took a seat.

An otherwise blank screen displayed a simple prompt.

Login:

"You ever have that feeling that you're about to do something *really* bad you probably shouldn't be doing, but can't wait to do it anyway?" asked Fawkes.

Rallek twirled his staff back and forth. "Sometimes."

She glanced at it, then up at him. "You shouldn't spin your scepter. Makes it look like a baton."

He clamped his hand shut, stalling the rotating weapon. "It's a staff."

"More like a walking stick," said Kavan.

"Hey now." Rallek raised his hands. "Don't be talkin' small about a brother's rod."

Fawkes laughed. "Okay, here goes."

She tried the username TURBAN with the password from the data pad. When she hit the enter key, the username changed to a mess of letters and numbers and the screen flickered dark before she could make sense of it.

"Well, that didn't—"

An ordinary desktop appeared on the screen.

"Oh, wow." Nighthawk leaned close. "That's like an Easter egg or something. Looks like the PC I have at home."

Fawkes glanced at a line of dark blue text embedded in the wallpaper image of floating metal plates, something generically artsy. It read: Property of Cognition Systems Incorporated. All activity on this workstation is subject to monitoring. Authorized use only. "Huh... they got the company name wrong, but I think we just found a back door into their real network."

"Wait." Rallek leaned close, his chin hovering by her right ear. "This could be a recreation of Tom Urban's workstation. When he still worked for them, they were 'Incorporated.' They didn't change it to 'International' until after Axillon99 went super-mega."

Kavan leaned on the desk. "What I'm wondering... If Urban got the ax, quit, or whatever... why did his credentials still work?"

"They didn't." Fawkes pointed at the screen. "As soon as I clicked login, the username shifted to a long string of meaningless letters and numbers. The TURBAN username exists only in the game code somewhere, buried as a passkey. When I used it, the game must've replaced it with an actual account on their corporate network. Something he added before he left that they didn't find."

"So you're saying this guy knew he was getting fired and left the keys in the ignition for someone to go nuts inside CSI?" asked Kavan.

She looked up at him. "Yeah, basically."

"Huh." Rallek scratched his chin with his 'staff.'

"Don't break the game," said Nighthawk. "I like it."

Fawkes cracked her knuckles. "I'm not going to break it. CSI hasn't pissed me off. But I am a curious little kitty."

She popped *Reckoning* in the search box. A whole mess of results came back including exterior artwork, text files containing the words spoken by NPCs who might discuss it, audio files of the same lines, and a whole mess of program code. She dragged one of them into a compiler, and started sifting through it.

"Wow, that looks boring," said Nighthawk.

Kavan took a knee beside her and also examined the screen.

They skimmed it, mostly reading comments for the better part of the next twenty minutes before one line caught their attention.

'Random timer teleportation destination algorithm'

"Holy shit," said Fawkes and Kavan simultaneously.

Nighthawk snickered.

Kavan narrowed his eyes at him and grunted.

"Wow. This is... ten million bucks." Fawkes copied that section of code into a notepad file, opened a web browser, and used a throwaway email account to send it to another throwaway email account, then re-sent it to a few more. Once she logged out, she'd go through a couple countries and grab the text in the real world.

"So, what good is that stuff?" asked Rallek.

She leaned back, gripping the armrests of the fancy chair like a victorious queen about to pronounce judgement on a peasant. "Those couple lines of program code are how the game decides where the *Reckoning* is going to tele-port. It's not following a fixed path after all. It's completely random."

"It looks like it's based on a clock/date value, so we can use this to predict where the thing will be at any given moment." Kavan rubbed his hands together like a weasel.

"Can you change it?" asked Rallek. "Send the ship wherever we want it to be?"

"That's more difficult. I don't think so." Kavan shook his head. "At least not without a really good chance of being detected. We'd have to bundle it into an update for the production systems, then somehow trick a CSI network person to apply the patch over all the server farms. Far too much effort for no real benefit."

Fawkes sat up and attacked the file system. "Maybe it's completely point-less. If I can find the quest files for the contest, we might be able to just jump straight to the endpoint."

Everyone held their breath as she hunted among file folders. She first tried searching for 'The Lost Dreadnought,' the overarching title of the mission tied to the prize money. A nest of files that appeared to be the data from which the live production CSI website fed from contained the leaderboard information... a simple text file the game generated.

"You could light the world on fire by changing a text file," said Kavan.

She laughed. "Yeah, but I don't want anyone to know we have this access."

Other parts of the mission like finding the crashed fighter (Trinary) or dealing with the giant robot in the factory (Research and Development) had sub-mission titles. She couldn't search for the parts they hadn't gotten to yet, as she had no idea what they'd been titled.

Nighthawk wandered around the room, fussing with the bookshelves, lamps, and fake plants. Sometimes, he'd mutter 'bored' to himself in various pitches.

Fawkes kept hunting, trying a slew of phrases that referenced a phantom ship, a prize, contest, and so on. When frustration mounted, she tried changing the filtering settings to display hidden files. That revealed a folder named -Armageddon- which she clicked on as a matter or reflex.

Something with that name *had* to be worth snooping on.

The topmost file in the sort, aa_readthis.txt, contained a simple message.

"This folder contains the fruits of my final FU to the two bastards. Hope-fully, two things have happened. 1) Someone is reading this who possesses a high degree of curiosity and a low degree of love for stab-you-in-the-back corporate weasels. And 2) the little routine I let loose has found dirt worth being shown to someone with high curiosity and little love for stab-you-in-the-back corporate weasels. Do with it as you will, but give them a black eye."

"Let's check it out," said Kavan, still hovering close.

"Are we done yet?" asked Nighthawk. "These quests aren't doing themselves."

"Hang on," said Fawkes. "I think we might've just found some real juicy shit."

"Eww," said Nighthawk. "That sounds nasty."

She bowed her head and snickered. "Not literal shit."

Rallek cracked up loud enough to wake Angel813.

"What time is it?" she yawned.

"10:07 p.m." Rallek closed the small display window. "Been here about two hours."

"The silence is *so* weird," said Angel813.

Fawkes dove into the files, which contained program modules, design documents, CAD drawings of helmets, and some email chains. She clicked into one email with 'OMG' as the subject, and started reading.

With each passing line, her jaw hung open wider. One of the engineers from the hardware team working on the Neurona helmets made an accidental discovery related to the technology that allowed the transmission and reading of information directly into the brain. Evidently, they could 'prompt' the brain with stimulus information at a subconscious level and detect locations that responded to it. By reading them, they could effectively query and retrieve information—or in this case, memories. By virtue of this mechanism, CSI had created a way to essentially read the minds of their players based on whatever search criteria they wanted to use.

"Holy shit," she whispered, paging faster and faster into the email system. "They can hack our brains!"

"What?" Rallek looked up from whatever he'd been distracting himself with. "Are you serious?"

Nighthawk stopped boredom-wandering and stared at her.

"Still reading, hang on."

More emails, technical white papers, and testing reports showed the company had perfected this application and built it full scale into the Neurona 4 units. CSI had the ability to not only target individual people while they were logged in, and go fishing for whatever memories or information they wanted, they developed an invasive marketing system that could influence behavior like subliminal suggestion taken to an exponential degree.

Fawkes grabbed her face so she didn't scream. "This is so fucked up..."

"What?" asked Rallek.

"Whoa. They can read our minds," said Kavan. "Find out what stuff we like and target ads based on that. Or even mine passwords, usernames, private information right out of the brain of anyone wearing a Neurona 4."

Angel813 whistled. "Damn. Glad I didn't upgrade then."

"They can influence us too, like to do things we'd never—" Fawkes shivered as a chill fell over her shoulders. She opened a new window and searched for 'Steyr.'

In a subfolder of -Armageddon-, she found more emails, program code, and logs that proved the Gavin Steyr campaign (technically, a super PAC working for him) had paid CSI to prime its players living in New York with the idea to vote for him. Despite that process being prototyped via the Neurona 3 helmets, data corroborated that it had worked, but only at a sixty-two percent uptake rate. Even some staunch opponents who hated the very fiber of Steyr's being had voted for him and not even realized they'd done so. Their bodies had reacted automatically, obeying the implanted notion.

A lump formed in her throat at the idea someone could make her do something against her will. For an instant, she wanted to fling the helmet off and never go back, but she forced herself to calm down.

"The only way to fight this beast is from inside its belly." She took a deep breath and kept digging.

Rallek paced around. "These people are selling our innermost thoughts the way corporations used to sell phone numbers or marketing info. That *can't* be legal."

"It's not illegal until someone makes it illegal." Kavan nibbled on his fingernails. "Look how long it took them to update the law when the internet happened. Most people wouldn't even believe something like this is *possible*, much less actually happening."

"Right," said Angel813. "They haven't made a law against electronic mind reading or control because it's pure science fiction."

Fawkes frowned. "Or not. No wonder that pig Steyr won the election. They literally *bought* it. Goddammit! I might've even voted for him and I don't remember doing that."

"Ugh." Angel813 scrunched up her nose. "Isn't he the guy they caught in a hotel room with like a thirteen-year-old boy?"

"Wasn't that a girl?" asked Rallek. "And maybe younger than—"

"Don't wanna hear that," said Kavan, loud. "Topic change."

Fawkes glanced at him. He didn't seem *too* emotional about it, so she hoped he didn't have any horrible memories to cope with. "Okay."

"You all right?" asked Angel813.

"Yeah." Kavan cast a furtive glance at Nighthawk. "Just not a topic of conversation that belongs in a video game."

"We've gone well past video game here." Fawkes exhaled hard. "We're on the moon. This is some serious bullshit. Ooh!" She clicked into a folder named 'inoculation' that contained a small module of program code that disabled the thought-mining and influence functionality. "We need this."

"Yeah. No shit." Kavan patted her shoulder. "Good find."

Nighthawk made a sour face at Kavan's back when he swore.

"So we compile this and our brains are safe." Fawkes sent the modules off to her throwaway email accounts.

Angel813 gnawed on her finger. "Did anyone notice you get in there? If that's as deep as it sounds like it is, more than our thoughts are going to be in danger if they find out we saw that."

"Maybe we should get out of here." Nighthawk headed for the stairs down out of the hidden third story office.

"Gimme a minute." Fawkes hunched over the keyboard, typing like a fiend. "I can't just walk away from a gold mine like this. I gotta copy this shit. All of it."

"Are you sure you know what you're doing?" asked Rallek.

She peered up at him past a haze of pink hair. "From a technical stand-point, absolutely. From an 'I don't want to get murdered standpoint,' not so much, but I can't help it. This is what I do."

"You think people are going to try to kill you over a contest in a video game?" asked Nighthawk.

"Oh, no... this is way more than that. Some of those documents flirt with the idea of military applications. If the CIA or something gets their hands on this stuff..." She whistled.

Kavan braced a hand on the desk and stood. "How do we know they haven't?"

24

COMPLETIONIST

F awkes knew she'd be up too late tonight, but didn't care. Not like she'd be able to sleep anyway.

The crew sat around a table in a cantina, still on DB224. This planet had nothing to do with the money mission, so sitting here acted as a distraction for anyone trying to follow their footsteps. That they'd spent hours here would hopefully make people think the next part of the mission was on this planet and they hadn't been able to find it yet.

A mission share box opened again, from Nighthawk. She sighed and accepted it.

Kavan logged back in, appearing as a wireframe outline of a person for a few seconds, then filling in solid. He'd been the last to log off and on again to reboot the helmet. The software mod that disabled the 'brain backdoor' had to go into the helmet itself. Technical documentation in the hidden -Armageddon- folder had detailed the process to apply mod code directly to the helmet's firmware that couldn't be overridden by a command from a game. This involved uploading the mod to a mini-USB device, and accessing a port at the back of the helmet under a concealed hatch.

The existence of that interface port hadn't been released to the public. Only CSI engineers and executives knew about it. Granted, telling the universe the helmets had a hidden USB port wouldn't do much but give her away as having been inside their network. The company could claim they added the port for their technicians to diagnose problems, not for consumer use. Make it sound all innocent and whatnot.

A mission share box opened again, from Nighthawk. She glanced at him, but still accepted it.

"So, we found some serious stuff," said Fawkes. Since the cantina held no other player characters, only some NPCs, she went over an explanation of what she'd found for 'those who'd slept through it.' CSI could steal thoughts and memories straight out of a person's head or implant suggestions.

"Like, if some car company wanted to know what people wanted most, they could pay CSI to farm that information," said Fawkes. "Or if they're scummier, they could pay CSI to give people the sudden urge to go buy a car they choose to make people want."

"Companies could read the minds of rivals, steal trade secrets," said Kavan.

"Or get questions before exams," said Nighthawk.

"Or cheat tests, yeah." Fawkes chuckled. "But, I think they'd have darker intentions than that."

"I love these mudslides," said Angel813. "So good. Just like this place near my old school."

Fawkes froze, staring at her and the chocolatey drink in her hand. Her mind leapt back to that frightening section of street that reminded her so much of where she almost been date-raped. "Motherfucker..."

Nighthawk cracked up... and shared another quest.

She mashed the decline button.

He leaned back. "Whoa. Sorry."

Fawkes tucked her hands under her legs to keep them from shaking. "I... They've already been reading our minds. This street... I was doing a mission, and this one street looked like a place where something bad happened to me as a kid. So scary... but they did that on purpose! And the sewer full of alien shit! It stank like bad salmon. The worst smell I could remember."

Nighthawk twisted up his face. "I thought it smelled like puke."

Kavan grimaced. "Ugh. Now that you mention it, couple years ago, I got food poisoning. Spent three days exploding from both ends. That sewer smelled like a mix of crap and vomit to me."

"Babe..." Rallek put an arm around her shoulders. "You wanna talk about it? Maybe, uhh, later?"

She nodded. "Maybe."

"The fries." Nighthawk stared at his basket of nuggets and fries. "They taste just like the way I love them."

"Son of a bitch," muttered Rallek. "This one boss from a solo quest I did last week looked an awful lot like some dude I had issues with in school."

Angel813 squirmed. "Grabbing bits and pieces of stuff to make the game seem scarier or cooler isn't quite as messed up as that other stuff you found, but it's still invasive. There should at least be a warning and an option to turn it off. That could seriously trigger someone who's been through some bad shit."

"Yeah," said Fawkes in a small voice.

Rallek groaned, glancing at a small display screen. "Ugh. Looks like word's out we're here. Players are swarming this place looking for the next step of the prize mission."

"Wouldn't they have to start at the beginning?" asked Kavan.

"You'd think." Rallek chuckled.

Angel813 sipped her mudslide. "Might be trying to find information they can sell to someone on that stage. Like, hey I know what to do next. Gimme three hundred bucks and I'll tell you."

"People do that?" Nighthawk blinked.

"Some no-lifes in AOO level alts up to sixty and sell the characters," said Angel813. "Selling information is a lot easier if you can find it."

Nighthawk shared another quest.

"Dude, what is it with you and these quests?" half-shouted Fawkes.

He shrugged.

"Look, we need to wrap this nasty stuff up in a nice neat little bundle and send it out to the media." Fawkes looked around at her friends. "We can't just sit back and let them do this."

"Never pegged you for lawful good," said Rallek.

"Huh?" asked Nighthawk.

Fawkes smirked. "I'm not. But I love sticking it to corporations."

"Wait on that." Kavan patted her shoulder. "Let's put this on hold for now until the money's out of the question."

"You mean until we win?" asked Nighthawk.

Kavan shrugged. "Until we win or someone else does. I say we keep quiet until we're not going to screw ourselves. It might be a long shot, but we *do* have a chance at winning that money. If this blows up now, it could take CSI down with it and there goes the prize."

"You're saying a prize is worth more than the power to influence people's actions on this scale?" Fawkes blinked at him.

"Not worth more, but worth a short delay at least. I'm not saying we never let the cat out of the bag. Just wait for the best time to do it." Kavan made a finger gun at her. "I dunno about you guys, but I could really use two million bucks."

"I could agree to that," said Angel813, "as long as it doesn't take *too* long. These people could do a lot of damage."

"They already have," muttered Fawkes. "Steyr?"

Angel813 stirred her mudslide. "I'll agree to a month. If the contest isn't over by then, we blast to the media."

Rallek drummed his fingers on the table, creating ripples on the surface of the glowing-green liquid in his fictional cocktail. Dark blue blobs shifted around the base of the glass. "We also have to consider that 'going public' might not do anything. Depends on how connected this is to the three letter agencies. For all we know, the only thing we'll accomplish is letting them know we have the defense mod, and they'll change the code to ignore it. For the moment, I like having my brain protected."

"Okay." Fawkes absentmindedly scratched at her head. The fringe rat in her screamed to blow this wide open without hesitation, but she couldn't in good conscience put her crew at risk without their full consent. "We give it at least a month, and see what things look like then?"

"Crap," whispered Kavan. "Players incoming."

A flood of around forty characters entered the cantina, mostly human with a handful of other races. Everyone stopped what they were doing, the whole bar quiet (except for the background music) when a Draath with violet stony skin in jet back armor thudded in. He took a seat at a table, further proving this place existed as a computer game. A 900-pound alien made of rock should have crushed the relatively flimsy chair.

Among the crew of the *Stormbringer*, conversation shifted to Nighthawk attempting to talk everyone into running quests with him on the planet. Angel813 kept bringing up small things she'd seen or experienced in the past that reminded her a lot of her real life. Fawkes figured that because she had the Neurona 3, the game's ability to read from her was limited, hence drinks, a smell here or there, or music that kinda sounded like her favorite songs.

Sitting on this information felt so wrong, but if anyone got hurt, Fawkes would have the added weight of breaking their trust on top of that. *Argh!* She sank into a torrent of worry and guilt over the information they'd discovered.

"Why hello there," cooed a woman's voice. "What's your name, handsome?"

Fawkes detangled her brain from her inner argument and peered over and up at a bronze-skinned Niath woman standing by Nighthawk and giving him the 'I want to devour you' eyes. So far, most Niath she'd seen had radiated innocence. Not this one. No, this woman radiated the exact opposite in her metal-cupped halter-top, a long loincloth so thin it pushed the character from anime into hentai, and high-heeled armored boots that came up to her thighs.

"Uhh." Nighthawk stared at her chest. "Umm. Hi."

"Hello, 'Hi.'" She laughed and glanced at the shoulder patch on his armor. "Really, what's your name? You're a fighter pilot, huh? How 'bout I play around with your joystick?"

Nighthawk stood dumbfounded, gawking at her. His brain seemed to have shut down.

Kavan fixed the Niath with a pointed stare. Two seconds later, she shifted her eyes onto him instead. Soon after that, her sultry expression evaporated to embarrassment.

"Oh. I'm sorry." She turned on her armored high heel and hurried away, gold-feathered wings rustling.

What did he say to her? Fawkes glanced back and forth from Kavan to the hastily departing woman. She thought about the way Nighthawk had been around the young girl, that lonely, longing look in his eyes. *Crap. Maybe he had a wife and kid and they're dead. William knows him outside the game... probably told her to back off.*

She grimaced.

"So, quests?" Kavan stood. "Looks like we've got about seventeen around here."

"You know they're all like six levels under us, right?" asked Rallek. "But... Cool. I hate unfinished quests."

Kavan adopted the posture of a posh Englishman. "Oh, you dreadful completionist, you."

"At your service." Rallek bowed with a flourish. "Leave no quest undone."

Angel813 yawned.

"You know two of these have vanity pet rewards." Rallek waggled his eyebrow at her.

"Ooh." Angel813 perked up. "Really?"

Everyone laughed at her, but she folded her arms. "So what if I like pets? They're cute."

25

SIDE QUEST

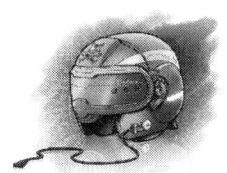

The endless hammering of shrill digital beeping pounded Dakota's skull. Her right eye peeled open and swiveled to point at the offending alarm clock. She tried to ignore it and go back to sleep, but the incessant, awful noise wouldn't leave her alone.

Six minutes after the cacophony started, she dragged herself out of bed and mashed the silence button. For another minute she stood in place, swaying side to side with her eyes mostly closed. Eventually, she stumbled down the hall, heading for the shower. Feeling around for the little handle, she opened the door and stepped in. It took her about three minutes of grasping in search of the faucet before she realized she'd climbed into the broom closet in the kitchen.

"Ugh." She let her forehead hit the wall.

A few forced, rapid breaths woke her up enough to successfully locate the actual shower in the bathroom. Scenes from the fifteen or so quests they'd raced through last night replayed in her mind under the spray of hot water. They'd logged out around one in the morning (a little more than four hours ago). She regretted being tired, but didn't regret staying up. Though she'd logged out at one, she didn't fall asleep for a while after that, too worried and horrified by the information she'd unearthed about CSI.

How much of anything she'd done in the past weeks since she'd started using the new helmet had been *her* idea? Other than voting in the last election, she hadn't made any purchases more major than food, so she clung to the hope that no one had messed with her. But, she *had* bought food. What if they influenced the brands she'd chosen?

"Argh!" yelled Dakota.

The mirror teased her with a hint of her natural color at her roots where it had grown out enough to expose about a quarter-inch of blonde below the neon blue. "Almost time for more AI."

Chrissy, this girl she knew in high school, had jokingly referred to her hair dye as 'artificial intelligence,' since she used it to not be blonde. As much as that had annoyed Dakota at the time, she'd wound up referring to it as AI out of habit after that.

"At least I work at a coffee shop. I'm going to need to drink as much as I sell today."

She dragged herself along the surprisingly difficult task of getting dressed, and stumbled out the door. Her key turned the lock on the Amazon Café at 6:01 a.m., late but not so much so that Hal would give her a hard time. Blake appeared at the end of the opposite block, fast-walking toward the store.

"Guess I'm not the only one who had a rough morning." She waved at him and went inside.

Dakota floated in a haze of customers and coffee for a few hours, functioning mostly on autopilot and not making *too* many errors. When she mechanically took a giant sip from a drink she made for a customer, the man laughed it off. Of course, she made a new drink for him.

She picked up the stray mocha latte. "Mine now. It's a sin to waste coffee."

"What are you doing here?" half-yelled Blake.

"I, umm, work here?" Dakota swiveled to face him, but he stared out the window at the line of cars in the drive-through lane.

"I know that but you said..." He sighed. "I've already given you a minute." Blake pinched the bridge of his nose, his lips quivering. A man's voice murmured in the earpieces, loud enough for her to notice but not understand.

"Okay. Okay. I'm at work. I'll call you later." Blake's slightly-chubby fingers lined up like an army of small sausages as he gripped the counter in both hands and bowed his head. "I promise. I can't do this now. You know I'm at work... you're right in the damn drive-through." He sniffled into a chuckle. "Seriously? Okay." He tapped in an order for a medium peppermint mocha.

Neal, a shortish, skinny blond guy about Blake's age, pulled up in a little grey Honda. He paid for his drink without a word and drove off.

"Anything you want to talk about?" asked Dakota, since no customers waited for anything.

Blake shrugged. "I..." He sighed, and let it out... then started talking. Once the first few words tumbled forth, he couldn't stop.

He'd been dating Neal for almost two years, but had been too terrified to tell anyone about it, being deep in the closet. Even his family had no idea, or so he thought. Dakota decided not to mention that anyone watching him for twenty minutes would know, so his parents had to know, and tried to help him cope. Neal had grown tired of sneaking around and pretending to be his best friend in public, and wanted to make their relationship official. That terrified Blake and precipitated the argument that led to a breakup in the heat of the moment, though she had a feeling neither one of them really wanted it to end.

She leaned close to him and whispered, "Before you can come out to anyone, you have to come out to yourself. You always seemed so happy when you talked about going to hang with Neal. That day you didn't want to come in... you're clearly in love."

Blake wiped a tear. "Yeah. Maybe."

"Would your parents freak out?" asked Dakota.

"Nah." He chuckled. "I think they know already. It's just like one of those things that never gets talked about. You're right. I need to face this head on."

She play-punched him in the shoulder. "Come on, man. It's 2031... not like 2017, right?"

"Hah. I was seven then... I remember on the news, all those politicians saying horrible things about..." He looked around and lowered his voice. "People like me."

"That left a mark." She squeezed his hand, took a deep breath, and exhaled. "When I was sixteen, this guy I went on a date with attacked me..."

An hour went by on conversation about mental scars. Dakota wound up telling him about the almost date rape, and even about one two years later when she hadn't been so lucky to get away. That time, she'd been at a party full of seniors and blacked out. She woke up on the floor of an upstairs bedroom with no pants. To this day, she still had no idea who spiked her drink, or what exactly happened to her while she'd been unconscious. Anxiety and weeks of negative pregnancy tests led to depression, and a wild tornado of drinking, pot, and LSD, which lasted until she fell in with the fringe crowd her second year of college. Her new mission pulled her away from drugs. She couldn't overthrow 'the man' if she couldn't stand without holding onto the wall.

Blake's damage stemmed mostly from bullies, including his father who had intimidated him without even meaning to. Constant encouragement at sports Blake didn't care for, martial arts, paintball, and all sorts of 'man hobbies' caused him to grow up feeling like a perpetual disappointment. It only worsened midway through high school when his father abruptly stopped pushing stuff on him.

"I thought he'd given up on me since I'd been the ultimate disappointment." Blake stifled a sniffle. "Look at me. I'm 325 pounds. I can't sports. I can't change my own oil. I thought he secretly wished I'd go away."

Dakota hugged him. "What if he realized who you were? Talk to him."

"Sorry you got, umm... attacked. You know. Guys can be such bastards."

A couple cops walked in.

She gave his hand a squeeze. "Guess I have two brothers now."

"Thanks for listening. I haven't ever told anyone that stuff. Not even Neal."

"Same here, not even my genetic brother."

They exchanged a moment of eye contact, mutual thanks, before she moved to the terminal to take the cops' orders.

Right as she started foaming the milk for the second latte, the television news mentioned Gavin Steyr, and his introduction of a bill to change state law, eliminating the sex offender registry as it amounted to 'cruel and unusual punishment.' The screen cut to an image of Steyr blathering on and on about how these men can't find gainful employment and their 'lives were over' for 'one mistake.'

Her stomach churned. That piece of shit did not belong in office. He cheated, and she had evidence that might prove it. Evidence she'd agreed to keep quiet for now. Her hands trembled. If that law passed, the worst kind of scum could become invisible again. How many more victims would they create?

"That guy is such an asshole," said one cop. "What about the lives of the victims?"

The other cop emitted a dark chuckle. "He's just setting things up so the system goes easy on him when he finally gets nailed."

She grinned, and snuck both cops a little more espresso and flavor syrup. Hopefully, Hal's profanity detecting senses weren't tuned to pick up an overly generous employee. The cops took their drinks and headed back outside to their car. Dakota bit her lip, one hand braced on her stomach to hold back the nausea at the idea her inaction would make her responsible for everything that creep did.

Get real. It's not like I'd mail that stuff to the Times and he'd be out on his ear in an hour.

Words like 'election tampering' and 'federal crime' danced around her head. Dumping the cash dispenser of an ATM didn't seem like such a big deal anymore. Nor did winning a whole bunch of money. Not when she could stop an evil circus master from setting tigers loose in the lamb enclosure.

Argh. I'll talk to the others tonight. Maybe I can change their mind. She closed her eyes, tapping her shoe on the floor while thinking.

For the rest of her shift, she functioned like an automaton, too worried to even eat anything when her lunch break came and went. Trini arrived at 1:45 p.m. and had things well under control by the time Dakota's shift ended at 3:30. Hal mentioned hiring another person since the morning shift had been picking up and it would increase flexibility for people taking days off.

"Sounds cool." Dakota faked a smile.

Not that she objected to the idea of another person working there, but she couldn't stop thinking about how an entertainment software company manipulated a gubernatorial vote. If they could coerce people to vote for someone as odious as Gavin Steyr, they could do anything. It wouldn't be a big leap to go from that straight to the top.

She hurried out the door, more awake than she had been at any point so far that day. The others would have to see reason. Yeah, the fallout might result in Axillon99 being shut down, or losing so many players to anger, paranoia, or fear that it failed. Perhaps she'd kill full-immersion gaming completely.

Would anyone be willing to use a Neurona helmet at all after the specter of mind reading and control reared its head?

Or, perhaps the company would spin it… turn her into a crazy blue-haired malcontent making wild allegations for her fifteen minutes of fame. Of course, being a woman, they'd make it sexual, drag up everyone who'd so much as held her hand and pay them to say nasty things about her.

She stopped walking, grabbed her head, and sighed.

No. I'd need everyone to support me. We'd have to go public as a group so they can't dismiss me as a lone nut job.

Her nerves prickled at someone approaching a little too close, a big guy in a cheap black raincoat fast-walking down the sidewalk on a collision course. She sidestepped to let him go by without running her down, but he swung his left arm around her and grabbed on while jabbing a painful object into her thigh.

"Hey! Get off—"

The most intense, electric pain she'd ever experienced raced through her body. Dakota tried to scream, but her jaw refused to open. Her legs turned to jelly, and her arms twitched out of her control. Somewhere off to the right, tires squealed. The sidewalk spun into a disorienting blur. She couldn't breathe. Foam dribbled over her chin as bright spots danced in her eyes.

Her hand closed around cloth around where her attacker's balls should be. She squeezed, and the electric pain surged over her a second time. A rapid snapping buzz accompanied the stink of melted fabric. She couldn't see anything but flashes of light on a dark field. Dakota's face struck a car seat and slid forward; a man's weight pressed onto her back.

She tried to scream past clenched teeth, spraying foamy spittle, but had no coordination to resist him grabbing her arms. A car door slammed and an engine revved. Handcuffs tightened around her wrists. Dakota kicked and struggled, but the man pulled something over her eyes and cinched a strap around her head.

Panic exploded into a fit of thrashing.

Fingers clenched a fistful of hair at the back of her neck, forcing her face into the seat to muffle her screaming. She pulled and twisted at her arms, but couldn't get her hands loose. He tried to force something into her mouth, but she refused to open her jaw, turning her head away as best she could with a handful of hair holding her down.

Cold metal pressed against her skull behind her left ear.

"That's a gun. Open your mouth," said a man, eerily calm.

She froze, no longer struggling, too frightened to even breathe.

The object pressed into her skull prodded harder twice.

Dakota reluctantly opened her mouth a little.

He forced a rubberized sphere past her teeth, and snugged a second strap behind her head. Blindfolded, handcuffed, and choking on a ball gag, she about lost control of her bladder. He shoved her off the seat to the floor.

"Stay down and stay quiet, you might see tomorrow. Sit up or get loud, you definitely won't," said the man.

She tried to ask, "Who are you?" but managed only an incomprehensible murmur around the oversized thing in her mouth.

Her captor didn't answer.

With only darkness to look at, she listened to the engine revving and fading. Not hearing music frightened her to trembling.

No background music. This is really happening!

There had to be at least one other guy behind the wheel. She remembered a glimpse of a black vehicle, but couldn't tell if she'd been thrown in a car, van, or SUV. Her weight shifted toward her head on a turn. Whenever they slowed, she rolled into the front seats. Acceleration bumped her against a man's leg. She tensed, but he didn't hit her.

The handcuffs bit into her wrists, too tight for her to even twist her arms around. After only a few minutes, her jaw ached from being forced open so wide for so long. As much as she tried to figure out where they took her, the myriad sounds of traffic and one helicopter wound up more confusing than helpful.

She tried to estimate time by counting, roughly confident she'd accurately ticked off 1,652 seconds by the time the vehicle stopped and the engine cut out.

That's almost a half hour away.

The man grabbed her left arm and pulled her upright. She cried out in pain from the tension on the handcuffs, though the damnable sphere wedged between her teeth kept her voice muted enough that no one threatened her. A second set of hands grabbed her legs, and they pulled her out of the vehicle. A waft of air laced with the fragrance of saltwater chilled her face and her legs through her black yoga pants, leaving her feeling as vulnerable as if she had nothing on below the waist.

Dread at what these men would do to her got her trembling all over again.

Again, she tried to ask, "Who are you people?" and "What do you want?" but her words couldn't get past the rubber ball crammed into her mouth.

Each man grabbed an arm, ushering her forward. She stumbled along, terrified at being blind and fearful of what she might step in. Her squeaking sneakers and the tromp of boots echoed, suggesting a giant warehouse type space or a massive studio apartment. They maneuvered her past a doorway and forward seven steps before taking a left turn.

"Stairs," said the man on the left.

She reached out a tentative foot until she kicked the front of a staircase, and gingerly ascended.

They guided her to the left at the top, paused long enough to open a door, and dragged her into a room that didn't echo as much.

"That was fast," said a lighter-voiced man. "Any complications?"

"Nope." The guy holding her left arm tugged her sideways. "No one noticed."

They spun her around and shoved her into a chair. She curled up, shaking.

"Damn." The lighter voice approached. "Little younger than I thought."

The two guys who abducted her off the street each grabbed a leg, removing her sneakers and socks. She squirmed in protest at the cold air on her bare feet. Cords tightened around her ankles, comfortable by comparison to the handcuffs. While the two men secured her legs to the chair, the one who'd been waiting here pulled a belt around her chest, pinning her to the seatback.

Shoes scuffed around her. She turned her head, trying to follow the motion, not that she could see anything. The crackling *pfssh* of a beer or soda can opening came from her right. She strained at the bindings, but succeeded only in causing a burning spot on her right thigh to flare up. Dakota struggled at the cords on her legs, trying to force her knees as close together as she could.

After an eternity of listening to men move around, drink, and click small plastic objects, a set of soft footsteps approached her. The overwhelming presence of generic scented body spray enveloped her. Fingers traced the strap over her cheek to the back of her head. A buckle clattered, and the tension holding the rubber ball in her mouth released.

She spat it out when he pulled, and worked her jaw around in a weak effort to ease the soreness.

"There. Much more comfortable, right?" asked the lighter-voiced man.

"Who are you people?" She again stretched her jaw. "What do you want?"

"Ahh, that's the question, isn't it?" He dabbed at her face and chin with a paper towel—or something that felt like one. "Little drool there."

She squirmed. "Would you mind loosening the cuffs? Your trained monkey put them on a little too tight. My hands are gonna fall off."

"Well, if you help us out, this won't take long at all. You'd even have some time left to run some missions before you have to go to sleep."

Dakota froze in disbelief. "You guys seriously think I'm going to just go home and play a game like nothing happened after this?"

"You will if you want to go home again," said the deep voiced guy.

She swallowed saliva.

"We're here to find out who you've sent copies of the stolen data to. If you can convince us certain information is secure, then we go our separate ways and everyone acts like none of this ever happened."

The burn on her thigh intensified. She squirmed, gritting her teeth, but couldn't reach it.

"How many copies have you made and where are they?"

"I didn't copy it."

He chuckled. "Oh, we know you did."

She threw her weight at the belt across her chest, but barely moved it. "I mean, I didn't make multiple copies. Just the copy I have."

"Of course you didn't." He sighed. "I'd really prefer no one get hurt. Has anyone ever told you that you're quite pretty? It would be such a shame to change that."

She shivered, momentarily forgetting how to breathe. "Really! I just sent it to myself. No one's seen it!"

"Hmm." The man's voice sank in front of her, coming from lower than her eye-level. Cold metal touched the top of her left foot. "This is a hammer." He traced it around her skin, despite her best effort to pull her vulnerable feet away. "I shouldn't need to explain what happens when a delicate little woman's toe winds up between it and a concrete floor."

Dakota whimpered, "Please don't. I'm not lying."

"How many copies did you send out?"

"Just the one to myself," she half-whispered. "To a couple throwaway email service accounts. I swear no one else has seen it."

He clucked his tongue.

The hammer stopped touching her foot. She thrashed and pulled at her legs, murmuring a constant stream of "Pleasepleaseplease."

Crack! The hammer smacked down on concrete—but not her foot.

She shrieked, jumping so hard the belt holding her chest against the chair crept up a half inch. It took her a few seconds to realize she hadn't pissed herself. When the initial shock wore off, she tried to curl up against the restraints. Involuntary tears and sniffles started, despite her not wanting to look so vulnerable. Dakota got angry with herself for cracking so fast, but that only made her tremble harder.

"Dude," muttered one of the other guys. "Maybe she's not lying."

A hand clapped twice on a jacket, and the deep voice muttered in Spanish, "Come on, man. Torturin' kids ain't what we signed up for."

"Yeah," replied the other one, likely the driver, also in Spanish. "I, umm. I ain't got the stomach for this kinda thing. You wanna pop her nice and clean, let's do it. Not this shit."

She jumped at the clatter of the hammer dropping on the floor.

"Fine," said the guy with the softer voice, the evident boss. "Okay, girl. How'd you get in?"

Sensing a hint of humanity in her abductors gave her brain a tiny ledge to grab. Few things in her twenty-two years had terrified her as much as being blind and tied to a chair, but these guys didn't know about the back door. Her inner hacker snarled in defiance, refusing to give up such a huge prize.

"Sweet-talked someone in your IT department into resetting a VPN connection." She squirmed at the belt over her chest, working it upward millimeter by millimeter. "It's not like they show in the movies."

Metal grazed across her neck beneath her chin, followed by a faint *click*. "Convince me."

Dakota didn't have to act much, despite lying, to tremble. "You want me to wet myself or something? Would that do it?"

The gun fell away from her chin. She started to exhale with relief, but a slap rocked her sideways. If not for the belt crushing her chest against the seatback, the hit would've sent her tumbling to the floor.

She gasped, too stunned in pain to say a word.

"Are you sure? Who's the person you spoke to in IT?"

"Mike," said Dakota, going for the most common name she could think of. "I told him I was a new assistant to Prakash."

Another, harder, slap caught her on the opposite cheek, flinging her head to the side. Despite the blindfold, stars flickered by her vision. She cringed in on herself, whimpering and sniffling, only half an act. A fist hit her in the gut, knocking the breath out of her.

"I can't watch this," said the deep-voiced guy in Spanish, before walking out.

It took her a few seconds to start breathing again. *His accent is weird. Not a native speaker... they must not know I understand them.*

"Please," whispered Dakota. "I didn't even look at the data yet. I just copied a bunch of folders looking for game stuff."

Light voice grabbed her throat and squeezed. "You think we don't know what you found?"

Dakota gurgled, working her shoulders back and forth to nudge the belt upward. *He's bluffing. He's gotta be bluffing.* "It's true!" she wailed. "I only wanted to check out the guts of the game for optimization character building. I swear!"

Again, he slapped her hard across the face; that time the chair tilted up on two legs for a second.

"I think you're feeding me a line of shit. But I get that you're feeling a little stressed out right now." His voice glided away and circled her. "We're going to give you a little time to think about your situation." He leaned over her from behind and patted her cheek twice, right on the tender spot. "I have clamps, needles, and a soldering iron... and you have a lot of beautiful, untouched skin. Think real long and hard about your priorities."

The men walked out, slamming a door that sounded metal. Scraps of Spanish conversation filtered through the wall, mostly the two men who grabbed her off the street objecting to torturing a young woman. It would've reassured her except for the one guy's statement that he'd be totally fine simply shooting her in the head, but drew the line at torturing a girl. They argued amongst each other about how best to proceed.

She wriggled her shoulders in earnest, pushing with her chest at the belt. It crept up, approaching her throat. A little more and it might slip over the back of the chair. *Oh, please don't be watching me.*

Dakota had no idea where she was, if she'd even make it out of the room alive, or what these men would do to her—but she did know one thing.

She wouldn't just sit there and wait to find out.

26

CAUSING TROUBLE

The belt snagged on the back of the chair, refusing to move upward any more. Growling to herself, Dakota lost a few seconds to a panic-induced struggle, futilely trying to reach her cuffed hands up to grab the leather strap across her chest. With each passing second, dread that she maybe had minutes to escape or she'd wind up dead increased.

Sweat dripped off her nose; her heart hammered in her eardrums. No amount of brute force she could muster did any good. One fortunate attempt to jerk her body free caused her ass to slip forward. The belt rode up under her chin, compressing her throat enough to cause a cough. Her brain re-engaged and she focused on scooting her butt forward. The leather snugged into her neck, making her gag. She kept squirming her ass forward, twisting so the strap passed up and over her head. Cord bit into her ankles as her legs bent, but she didn't care about pain.

Living mattered more.

Once she got clear of the belt, she wobbled upright, still with her ankles tied to the chair legs. She stooped enough to grab the front edge of the seat and pulled it up, tugging at the chair until the smooth metal leg pulled free of the cord binding her right leg. She kicked the loose bundle of wire off before freeing her other leg, then paused a few seconds to breathe.

Spanish arguing continued, muted by the closed door and distance. Light Voice called the other two 'chickenshits' for not having the balls to handle a crying woman. Another said he hesitated because 'she looks like sixteen,' which got them debating her age.

She bent forward and wriggled until she got her chained wrists past her butt. *Screw booty! My flat ass just saved my life.* Thinking about the size of her rear end made her think about Eric—and worry that he might be in danger. Dakota shuffled to the side, stumbling when she tried to stand on one leg. Her right foot came down on a painfully sharp object; she recoiled with a gasp and careened over sideways, the handcuffs digging into the backs of her knees. No longer worried about balance, she pulled her legs out one after the other and got her hands in front of her. The instant she reached up, ripped the leather blindfold off, and hurled it to the floor, a rush of confidence came on.

Dingy pea-green walls surrounded her in what looked like a small break room inside an abandoned warehouse. A dead sink on the left held a mountain of trash next to tall metal cabinets with doors so dented they couldn't close. She'd been tied to a hospital-green chair with a metal frame and meager padding. Its three identical cousins stood around a small, square table to her left loaded with scary things like a box of detachable hypodermic needles, razor blades, and an icepick. One solid metal door presented the only exit. Trash and glass fragments littered the floor.

The rambling Spanish voices continued arguing about what to do with her, but sounded distant, like they'd gone downstairs. *Holy shit! They didn't hear me.* She whimpered a little and examined her right sole, but whatever bit of debris she'd stepped on didn't cut her. The men had tossed her sneakers and socks nearby, so she hastily jammed her feet into them and leapt upright. Not far away, the hammer the one guy had been ready to break her toes with lay on the floor beside a stack of old fishing magazines. She reflexively tugged at the cuffs, tight enough that her hands had gone red, and glared. In addition to the torture supplies, the table held Chinese take-out, beer cans, and a rectangular stun gun with two metal nubs—no keys.

"Grr."

She glanced down at her right thigh, where two small holes had burned through her yoga pants. Dakota spent a moment glancing back and forth between the stun gun and the hammer. The stun gun didn't require any physical strength to use, but if they got it away from her, it would be right there for them to use (again) on her. On the other hand, swinging a hammer as a weapon with her hands chained would be awkward, plus all three of them had her beat for strength. Her main advantage seemed to be that they didn't want to kill her—at least not right away—so they probably wouldn't whack her in the head with the hammer if they took it from her.

The burn on her thigh flared.

"Mama wants payback." She grabbed the stun gun in both hands and crept up to the grey steel door, listening.

"You two need to harden up," said Light Voice in Spanish. "They want this information found, and weren't too particular about what happens to the little blueberry. So we break a couple fingers, couple toes, maybe give her a nipple piercing or five. I'm okay leavin' her alive since you two are such bleedin' hearts, but we need the information."

"This girl have a cat or something? Maybe we threaten the cat, she talks?" asked the other guy.

Light Voice sputtered. "What the fuck is wrong with you? Her cat?"

"Hold on." Deep Voice chuckled. "You're all bent out of shape over *threatening* a cat that may or may not even exist, and you're cool with mashing that girl's toes with a hammer?"

"People suck," said Light Voice. "Even cute girls. Animals never screw you over."

Dakota clutched the stun gun tighter. *Time to get out of here.* She shifted the stunner to her left hand and gripped the knob with her right, twisting her whole body as she turned it, like that would make the task quieter. That little part of her brain used to activating stealth mode in the game twinged over and over.

At not seeing her arms go semi-transparent, involuntary tears rolled down her face. *Come on, Kota. Hold it together. This isn't a game. Stealth isn't magic. Just be quiet. Don't freak out.* The door squeaked a little when she pulled it inward, but the conversation downstairs didn't skip a beat. Outside, a small landing offered a stairway to the right next to a water cooler, and a corridor leading left. Her abductors sounded like they were at the bottom of the stairs, so she shied away from the right and hugged the wall heading for the corridor.

More hospital green paint flaked from the metal walls, exposing rust spots. Three doors on the left went to a locker room, a shower, and an area with tall metal shelves loaded with tiny boxes and larger cans. She peered through the window of the only door on the right into an elevated observation area that had control stations for cranes or something mounted to rails inside the main warehouse area.

Dakota stepped with care, avoiding putting her sneakers down on panels of broken glass or kicking empty soup cans. She imagined herself as Fawkes so she wouldn't be afraid of the price of making a mistake. Every time the conversation downstairs paused, her breath caught in her throat. She pushed herself up to go a little faster, heading for the rightward corner at the end of the hallway. If she couldn't find an escape route, maybe she could crawl into some place, hide, and hope the men assumed she got away.

At the end of the corridor, she peered around the corner. A small room had a trio of tall metal cabinets on the right, a couple rotting raincoats hanging on pegs, and a door that led out to the roof. Shivering from fear, she hurried over to the flimsy wood door. Glass that had broken out from its window crunched under her sneakers. The door didn't look like it *could* lock, or even close well enough to keep out the rain. She brushed it open and stepped out onto a massive, flat roof.

From here, she had a good view of a river and dense urbanization on the other side, probably New Jersey. The familiar cluster of high-rises comprising the Manhattan City Center sat way off to the right, so she felt confident they hadn't taken her out of New York.

"Crap," she whispered, still absentmindedly fidgeting at the handcuffs, which had become painful.

She hurried away from the door, hunting for a place to hide. The much smaller second story of the warehouse perched like a building on top of a giant rectangle. Other than the upper floor, the expansive roof offered no cover. Right as she began to panic again, a glint of metal in the sun flashed from the distant edge: a ladder.

Careful not to make noise, she scurried across the roof to where two metal rods looped up and over the three-foot high retaining wall. They braced a simple rung ladder, the lower half of which had retracted upward, a fire escape designed to prevent people outside from climbing up to the roof. She whined out her nose, not trusting the rickety thing, but she feared being caught even more.

I'm only on the second floor. It's not that big a drop. Screw fear of heights.

She threw one leg over and froze, unable to get a good grip on the ladder while handcuffed and holding the stun gun. Dakota clamped the plastic box in her teeth and gripped the rung with both hands before swinging her second leg over and trusting her life to half-inch thick steel rods. Completely focused on not making noise, she lowered herself one rung at a time. It surprised her when her left foot hit pavement. She hadn't even noticed the second section of ladder glide downward.

Yes! I'm out. Shit! Now what?

She spat the stun gun into her hands, then looked left and right along a wide-open stretch of road between old dock warehouses. This whole area had been in decline for the past twenty years. After the political mess with China, most manufactured goods came from Mexico (which didn't require boats) or India, except cars and electronics, which Germany and Japan provided a disproportionate amount of. Oceanic transport all came in via the West Coast due to the president's brother owning a shipping company out of LA.

So, yeah, people in this area who had to do nefarious shit always came to the docks. No witnesses and plenty of room.

Trying to think of the fastest way to be found by the police, she took three steps to the right before stopping. *Wait... no. If I go to the cops, I'll have to confess to accessing CSI's computer network illegally.* She bit her lip. Even if they didn't prosecute her for that, going to the cops would require her to spill everything and implicate the others... or at least put them at risk.

Shit. They're at risk now! Against her better instinct, she ran back toward the warehouse doors. *I've gotta warn everyone.*

She crept up to the edge of a huge cargo door and peered around the wall into a cavernous space. Dozens of puddles covered the floor around a black Lincoln Town Car. Walls far away on the left mirrored the shape of the upstairs floor, blocking her view of the distant half of the warehouse floor. A battered steel door with a sign declaring hardhats as mandatory wobbled back and forth in a faint breeze.

"All right. Let's do this," said a man in Spanish, the voice echoing from behind the door.

Fuck... She ran to the car and yanked open the rear driver's side door. Her purse remained on the floor where it had fallen during the abduction. She dove in to grab it and pulled the door shut behind her. After hunkering down out of sight, Dakota fished out her smartphone.

With the angry shouts of her abductors going on overhead, yelling at each other as much as they called her a bitch or shouted about all the 'pleasant' things they wouldn't have to do to her if she showed herself, she swiped her way into the utilities menu and tapped an icon for a golf simulator game.

Only, it didn't run a golf simulator.

Not that Dakota ever had aspirations at being a car thief, but she *did* have an almost pathological need to possess the ability to do anything and every-thing hack-ish. One of the dark web locations she'd visited a while back had specifications she'd used to concoct a nice little bit of software. A fake golf game screen appeared, complete with a 'could not connect to game server' error. She drew a password glyph on the screen with her finger, unlocking the real program beneath the false game. Its plain black interface had one button: go.

She tapped it.

"Where are you?" screamed Light Voice, overhead.

Oh, yeah, like I'm going to tell you. She rolled her eyes. *Did CSI hire these guys from Henchmen R Us?*

If not for being scared shitless, the idea of a room full of thugs waiting to be hired to go do corporate badness, punching a time clock and taking lunch while abducting or beating people up, would've made her laugh.

The app picked up the wireless in the car, resolving the control frequency in eighteen seconds. Another icon popped up indicating it scanned for the key fob signal. She peered up at the roof, mentally commanding one of the thugs to walk close enough, and be the one who had the key on him.

Twenty-two agonizing seconds of screaming and banging echoed through the warehouse before the phone displayed a full set of buttons to start the engine, set off the horn/lights, or open the trunk. *Hah! Sucker walked in range.*

She slithered between the front seats into the driver's position. As long as she kept the app running, her smartphone acted like the key fob. The car would detect it being present and work.

Dakota pushed the engine start button, and the Lincoln's dashboard lit up. The gas engine wouldn't turn over until she tried to go faster than twenty miles per hour, or the battery died. This, she was totally fine with: it meant silence. She grabbed the shifter in both hands since the cuffs forced her to, and pulled it into reverse.

The driver door whipped open. She snapped her head to the left, staring at a middle-aged guy with slick-back hair and brown skin. He didn't radiate a choking cloud of cologne, so he couldn't be Light Voice. He barked a little cry of victory and grabbed a fistful of her hair at the back of her head, like he scruffed a wayward kitten.

"Sneaky little thing, aren't cha?"

"Yeah." She grunted and spun toward him, jamming the stun gun into the front of his throat before squeezing its only button.

Hot spittle flew out of his mouth. Legs locked rigid, he went straight to the ground like a plank, twitching and convulsing. His death grip on her hair tightened, dragging her out of the car so she fell on top of him. She gave him another zap until his fingers flew open, then leapt back into the Lincoln, pulled the door shut, and stomped on the gas hard enough to make the combustion half of the engine kick on. Tires squeaked on concrete as the Town Car hurtled backward.

Fortunately, the open tarmac between warehouses had enough room that her clumsy effort to steer in handcuffs didn't send the Lincoln sailing rear-end-first into a wall across the street. She had to let go of the wheel to shift into drive, and again squealed the tires when she mashed down on the accelerator. Two men in leather jackets came running out of the warehouse behind her, but had no hope in hell of catching a car on foot. One pulled a gun, but didn't shoot at her.

She turned at the first possible chance to go right, away from the water, and accelerated down a narrower road flanked by forklifts, racing past warehouse after warehouse. The area on the left opened into a massive field of transoceanic shipping containers stacked ten or so high on a lot big enough for three or four football fields to stand abreast.

A handful of gang punks emerged from dumpsters and junk trucks, reacting to the sound of an approaching car. None did anything more than make bewildered or startled faces at her as she careened on by. The road curved around to the left, bringing her past a row of semi-trailers up against a building. She spotted a gate out to a city street and planted her hands on the wheel, spinning it around like a suicide knob.

"Fucking hate handcuffs..." She grumbled, and let out an "oof" when the Lincoln hit a speed bump at near 60 MPH that sent her head flying into the roof.

By some miracle, no cop appeared out of thin air when she squelched the tires in a hard left turn that left a haze of white smoke in her wake. For a while, she drove taking random turns, too freaked out and mentally fried to comprehend where she went. Gradually, the idea that she'd stolen a car, or possibly pilfered an already-stolen car seeped into her brain. It didn't seem likely one of those men would've used their personal car for abducting and torturing someone. They also probably didn't rent one because... paper trail.

"Yeah, they stole it. Crap!"

Some twenty minutes after she started the engine, she managed to slow down enough to drive like a normal person who hadn't just been kidnapped. With each passing traffic light, her fear of getting busted for stealing the car grew. Sure, perhaps the cops would let that slide if she told them the truth, but that would take her right back to confessing to interstate digital break in, which would go straight to the FBI. The police would take the kidnapper's handcuffs off her only to put a shinier set on in their place. And though her yoga pants had a couple of little holes in the leg, she still preferred them to an orange jumpsuit.

"Fuck," she muttered.

At the next traffic light, she pulled a right turn and parked in the first open spot of street, not caring about the no parking sign. After tucking the stun gun into her purse, she pulled out a moist towelette packet, and used it to wipe down the start button (pushing it hard enough to shut down the car) as well as the whole steering wheel and the inner handle on the driver's door she'd used to close it. She opened the door with her foot, kicked it closed, and wiped down the rear door handle she'd first touched.

Reasonably confident her fingerprints didn't exist anywhere on the Lincoln, she clutched her purse in both hands and hurried off down the street, twisting away whenever anyone came close enough to possibly notice her wearing handcuffs. She had an 'asshole boyfriend' line ready, which may or may not be helped along by facial bruises from her 'chat' with Light Voice.

She hurried three blocks over and ducked into an alley, taking a seat out of sight behind a dumpster and fishing a paperclip out of her purse. After bending out one strut to use as a handle and biting a crimp into the narrow end, she wedged it into the keyhole on the cuff around her left wrist. A little twisting (and a lot of swearing) later, the cuff popped open. She unlocked the other side and spent a while rubbing her wrists and flexing her fingers to let blood flow into them again.

Her emotion zoomed from elation to fear to anger and back again. She stood, tossed the cuffs into the dumpster, and ran back to the street. Randomness pulled her to a shifty-looking bar named Lenny's a few blocks down on the opposite side. She ducked in and hurried to a cramped booth table in the back, near a pair of beat-up pool tables. Her seat gave her a good view of the front door. There, she pulled her phone out and dialed Eric's number.

"Yo, Babe. What's up?" His voice radiated a huge grin.

"Eric," she half-whispered. "I'm in deep shit. We're all in deep shit. Please, I need you to pick me up, but I'm not sure where I am..."

"Whoa, slow down. I'm still at work for like another hour."

She curled up, hunched over the table. "Eric, please... people tried to kidnap me. I got away and I'm freaking out."

Eric didn't respond for a few seconds. "Holy shit, are you serious?"

Dakota's sniffly, "Yeah" sounded too much like a scared child for her liking. Angry at herself, she cleared her throat. "Yeah... I'm... CSI I think. Hang on a sec." She checked a map application on her phone. "I'm at this bar... Lenny's in Carroll Gardens. Please, Eric. This isn't a joke."

"All right. I'll tell the boss it's a family emergency. On my way."

She bowed her head against the phone, smiling and shaking in equal measure. "Hurry, please."

"Sure thing, babe."

When he hung up, she sank low in the seat, staring at the door. The bartender shot her a curious look, but didn't approach or say anything. The odds of those thugs finding her here at some random tiny dive bar were pretty slim, but she couldn't shake the dread those men would walk in at any moment.

She slipped a hand into her purse, hunting for the stun gun, and found the can of Habanero Hammer. The rigid steel canister felt good in her grasp. Fourteen ounces of pure unadulterated awfulness ready to be unleashed at her command. She held it tight, not the least amount of hesitation in her mind at using it.

If she saw one of those guys again, she'd definitely put him in the hospital with burns all over his trachea.

27

REAL LIFE

For a touch past twenty minutes, Dakota sat in a ball, staring between her knees over the table at the door. The bartender, a pale, black-haired guy in his middle thirties, eventually wandered over.

"Hey, kid. You okay?"

She'd seen him coming out of the corner of her eye, so she didn't jump. "No, but I'm okay."

"You're not okay but you're okay?" He scratched his head, one eyebrow raised. "Need me to call the police or somethin'?"

"I got a friend coming, thanks."

"Someone assault you, hon?" He leaned to the side, trying to get a better look at her face.

She turned her head toward him. "Why, does it look like it?"

"Yah. Little bit of a bruise there, an' you seem kinda scared shitless."

Dakota tried to dial back the pitifulness radiating from her, and sat up straighter. "Some creep tried to drag me into an alley but I got away. I didn't get a good look at him. Ran here. The cops'll just tell me they can't do much if I can't describe the guy. No point bothering them. I'm not a kid either, I'm twenty-two."

"All right." The guy nodded, taking a step back. "I'm Nathan. If you need anything, let me know, 'kay?"

"Actually... can I get a Corona or something? I need to relax."

"Sure." Nathan smiled. "Can I see some ID?"

She fumbled her wallet out of her purse and showed her card. "Thanks."

"Thanks?"

"For thinking I look young."

"Kid, that's not a compliment until you don't actually look like you're eighteen." He nodded at the ID card and handed it back to her. "Nine bucks."

She paid cash, and nursed the beer to dull the edge of her nerves.

The door chime made her jump and look up, but Eric—not a kidnapper—nosed in, as if unsure of having found the right place. Dakota perked up in her seat and caught his eye. He slipped past the door, closed it, and hurried over. She leapt up into a hug, clinging to him for a little while until her mouth decided to obey her brain.

"Holy shit it's good to see you." She held him tight for a moment more, and took a step back so she could look him over. "Are *you* okay? Did anything happen to you?"

"Uhh, no..." He raised an eyebrow. "What's going on?"

Dakota pushed him into the booth seat and climbed in beside him. "I'm still not sure. Look." She held up her arm to show off the red mark around her wrist. "I was walking home from work and some guys grabbed me."

"Shit..." he whispered, listening as she clung to his arm, recounting as much as she could remember. "Where did that come from...?"

"I dunno." She raked her hands through her hair. "They knew who I was, but they didn't know how I got into that data." Her toes curled inside her sneakers at the thought they might've been smashed one by one until those men finally believed her. "The only thing I can think of is that the system, the helmet, read my thoughts when I saw that information about the vote manipulation or the thought influencing. Maybe the game engine is constantly scanning for 'forbidden' information."

"What about that mod? Our helmets are shielded."

"Yeah, but we didn't install that until *after* I spent like an hour reading over that shit with my jaw on the floor. Plenty of time for the thought police to flag the no-no information in my head and send out the dogs."

Eric lifted her left arm into his grip and gently rubbed the line of bruise over her wrist. "Did those fuckers touch you?"

"Not like that, no. Couple slaps, stun gun. I'm really surprised I didn't get groped. Maybe they thought I was underage."

"Maybe. They say terror shaves years off the face."

"Oh." She poked him in the side. "My stealth ass saved me. If I had a real booty, I'd probably wouldn't have made it out."

"Huh what?" He stammered, almost chuckled.

She reached around and squeezed his butt. "My 'white girl' non-ass didn't trap my hands behind me."

Eric laughed. He cradled her head, pulling her into a firm embrace. "Damn, girl. If I ever pick on you again for that, tell me to go straight to hell. I can't lose you."

Whoa. She tightened her fingers, gripping his polo shirt. It had been a long time since anyone gave off such strong feelings of protectiveness, not since before her father went all conspiracy kooky.

"We have to warn everyone," said Dakota. "I've got emails for Christina and William... but I don't have any idea who Nighthawk is."

"Who the heck is Christina?"

She looked up at him. "Really?"

He nodded.

"Angel813. She's not too far from here I think. William is Kavan."

"William said he lives near Nighthawk, maybe he can get word to him. Or you could hack CSI again, check his account info. Dude's gotta have a cush job where he can play from work, or he doesn't have a job."

"Uhh, let's try William first." Dakota finished the last half of her beer, and set the bottle down hard on the table. "You drive."

After she stood up out of the bench seat, Eric slipped past her and led the way outside, down half a block, and stopped next to an older Nissan Sentra.

"Oh, wow. I didn't even think to ask if you had a car." She hopped in the passenger side.

"I don't. This is my mom's." He flopped in behind the wheel.

Dakota emailed Christina with, "Hi, this is Fawkes, if you don't remember giving me your email. Serious BS just went down. I need to call you. Urgent." After sending it, she sent the same email to William.

Eric drummed his fingers on the wheel, waiting, giving her an expectant look.

A bit over a minute later, her phone pinged with an incoming email. Christina sent back, "OMG what happened?" and a phone number.

Before she could click over to the phone, William also replied with his number.

Dakota decided to conference call the pair of them at once, and put it on speaker.

"Bill Decker," said a voice matching Kavan from the game.

She'd never seen so much as a photo of him in real life, but his voice made him sound tough and confident... just like Kavan.

"What? How'd you call me?" asked a woman with a mild Chinese accent.

"I called you," said Dakota. "Hi guys, it's me Dakota... or Fawkes. Look, this is serious. Like two hours ago, some guys kidnapped me and dragged me to this abandoned warehouse. They knew about what we saw, and they also knew that other people saw it, too. You guys need to be extra on guard. I got away from them, but they might be going after you. Maybe even *right now*."

"Whoa, slow down, hon," said William. "What happened?"

"Are you okay?" Christina asked, her voice drenched in worry. "Did you go get checked out?"

Dakota shook her head, not that they could see her. "No. Nothing. Just hid out until Eric found me. That's Rallek."

"Hey all," said Eric.

She squeezed his hand. "I can't go to the cops or I'd have to confess to breaking into CSI's network, and probably dragging all of you with me. We agreed not to make this public, so I didn't want to do anything until I had a chance to talk to everyone." She took a breath and gave them the five-minute version of her ordeal. "My wrists are a little sore, but that's about it."

"Stun guns can cause other problems. You really should get checked out," said Christina.

"I'll worry about that when I'm not looking over my shoulder for a black Lincoln Town Car." She peered at the rearview, giving the nervous eye to an approaching Latino in an army coat. He passed by without incident, and she resumed breathing. "William, I don't have any contact information for Nighthawk. You said you live near him, right? Can you warn him?"

"Yeah. No problem. I got that covered." Metal clicked in the background.

"Is that a gun?" asked Dakota.

"No, it's a rifle." William chuckled. "I did eight years in the Army. Had to pay for school somehow."

"Oh, awesome. We have our own Green Beret." Dakota laughed nervously.

"Nah, just an infantry grunt here, but I know which end gets pointed at the bad guy."

"Charming," muttered Christina. "So, what are we supposed to do if we can't call the police?"

Dakota thought that over for a moment. "I... Wait. How about we steal Tom Urban's mindset? F me? No... F you."

"Which means what exactly?" asked Eric.

"We take the fight to CSI... or something. I dunno, can't really think right now. But I know where we can go and be safe for a little while." Dakota glanced at Eric. "Are you guys willing to meet up for real and lay low?"

"Do you have any proof of anything?" asked Christina.

"Just red marks on my wrists from being handcuffed and a stun gun burn."

"And a couple of bruises on her face." Eric leaned closer to the phone. "I've known Dakota for a while now, and for what it's worth, I ain't never seen her so freaked out. I believe her."

"Well, if only so I can at least check you over." Christina gave an address in Hartford, Connecticut, which Eric keyed into the GPS.

"Little bit of a ride," said Dakota. "But that's okay."

"I can keep an eye on things for a bit. Got a feeling Miss Lee isn't armed. You go on and get her first. I'll be here." William rattled off an address in Philadelphia.

She glanced at Eric. "Is your mother okay with us using the car for such a long trip?"

"Yeah. She only keeps it around for emergencies. Don't use it much." He dropped it in drive and pulled out into traffic.

"What about Nighthawk?" asked Dakota.

"I'll let him know. Don't worry about it," said William.

"Okay, we're on the way."

"This place you're thinking of," asked Christina, "does it have net access?"

"Yeah. Pretty decent connection too, for the area."

"For the area?" asked William.

"It's, umm... off the grid. But safe. My brother is there. Why would we need our rigs?"

Christina chuckled. "Well, if we're going to be laying low, we'll need something to do instead of sitting around bored."

"Yeah." William chuckled. "And since we've got nothing better to do, we might as well hunt down that prize. Or, we go back into that little hidden spot and kick CSI in the balls so hard they won't come near us again... or near you."

Dakota nodded. "I like the sound of that. See you both soon."

"Be safe," said Christina.

"Don't rush. Anyone comes through my door without an invite, they're going to have a bad day." Two metallic rattles followed, like William patted his rifle.

ERIC PULLED TO A STOP IN A FIRE LANE BY DAKOTA'S APARTMENT BUILDING. No suspicious black cars lurked anywhere in sight, but she didn't fully trust it.

"This is so stupid. My apartment is the *first* place they'd look." She shivered.

"They probably think you went straight to the cops. Those dudes are halfway to Mexico by now I bet."

"I didn't even see them. Only the one guy. Damn blindfold." She exhaled into her hands, warm breath over numb fingers. "I've never been so fucking scared in my entire life... except once." Her brain forced an old memory in the way to distract her.

"Do I want to ask?"

She grinned. "It's funny now, but I almost shit myself back then."

"Let's go get your stuff, explain on the ride."

"Okay."

She darted out of the car. Eric ran after her into the building and up the stairs to the fifth floor. It took her six minutes to pack the helmet and Play-Station in a duffel, and toss in a couple spare bits of clothing and a few extra sets of panties.

"Wow," said Eric. "They tossed your apartment and didn't even touch the helmet."

Dakota pulled the zipper on the duffel shut. "Huh? No one tossed my apartment."

He looked around at the clothes on the floor, the monolith of Chinese take-out containers on the desk, and the general state of disarray. "Oh."

"This is clean for me." She winked and pulled the duffel up onto her shoulder. "Maybe they couldn't find my address, just traced me back to an ISP. I don't have much of an on-grid footprint. Probably why they nabbed me so close to the café, and not out of my bed in the middle of the night."

Eric put an arm around her. "We need to take this to the cops. As soon as we cook up a decent enough story to keep you sounding innocent."

She stifled a laugh. "Yeah. Well, I could always say I thought it was part of the game. Cops might buy that given how TURBAN set it up. Most gamers would've thought that was a side quest."

"Speaking of side quests, how much XP was the kidnap mission worth?"

She slugged him in the shoulder. "I don't want that experience. I freely surrender those memories."

He held her close for a moment, softly rocking her side to side.

"We should get going," said Dakota, her cheek mushed into his shoulder.

"Right."

Once they'd returned to the car and got moving again, she let out a long sigh.

"So, umm, what was that scary thing?" asked Eric, grinning.

She chuckled. "I was like six years old. My dad's a high functioning autistic, I think. Something's not quite right with his social abilities. Anyway... what do you get a six-year-old girl for her birthday?"

"Whatever she's into," said Eric. "He get you dolls or something when you wanted computer stuff?"

Dakota grinned. "Wow. Right answer. But, no... he got me a toy fire truck."

Eric laughed.

"I definitely wasn't into fire trucks." She shrugged. "But he tried. Anyway, this fire truck wound up in cabinet at the foot of my bed. Thing made siren noises with flashing lights. So, fast-forward a couple months. Somehow, it shorted out and in the middle of the night, turns itself on. The batteries had run down, so it didn't come all the way on. Instead of a siren and flashing lights, the little headlights glow like the eyes of a demon and it makes this *Mrrrrrr* sound like a zombie cat."

"Shit..." Eric whistled.

"I almost did. I screamed my damn head off." She grinned. "By the time my mom woke up and came to check on me, the thing had stopped making noise. I start ranting and pointing that there's a monster in the cabinet, and of course Mom is rolling her eyes and trying to get me to go back to sleep so she can go back to bed. Well, the damn fire truck turns itself on again... and my mother jumps behind *me*, like I'm going to protect her."

Eric cackled. "Oh damn. Too bad you didn't have that on video."

"Yeah..." She glanced out the window at the passing buildings, daydreaming about how her mother was before she cracked. "You know, I spent the past few years thinking my parents took an express train to Crazy Town with all that conspiracy stuff."

"Damn. Sorry."

She turned her head to look at him, half-smiling. "CSI is selling access to people's brains. Maybe Mom and Dad were right after all."

28

RETURN FIRE

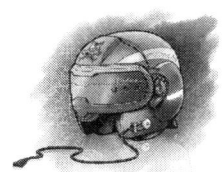

Two hours and thirty-eight minutes later, Eric pulled into an apartment complex on the outskirts of Hartford. They drove past five rectangular two-story buildings each with eight doors, four at ground level and four along a second-story walkway. From the size, she figured each building housed sixteen apartments, with another eight doors on the opposite face. When they spotted Unit F on the right, Eric stopped in a parking space between a brown minivan that looked like it narrowly escaped a post-apocalyptic wasteland and a brand new Toyota Camry.

Dakota pushed her door open and stood. A group of people hanging out by the building, some up on the second-floor walkway, some in groups at ground level, all stopped talking at the same time and stared at her. A guy in his sixties working a barbecue grill and two twelve-ish boys with him stared curiously at her from the left-most door on building F. A pack of six young men, possibly Chinese, congregated on the walkway running along in front of the second-story apartments. They approached the banister to watch her, their expressions a mixture of suspicion and territorial aggression.

Trying to ignore them all and act casual, she approached the door marked F3. As soon as she passed under the overhead walkway, the men resumed muttering in not-English. She stepped up onto a shallow concrete porch between a pair of white plastic chairs and rang the bell. Eric stopped beside her, hands in his pockets, and attention on the area around them.

The door opened, revealing a twentysomething Chinese woman in a tank top and jeans, barefoot. "Oh, hi. You must be Fawkes."

"Dakota actually, but if you want to call me Fawkes, that works." She shrugged and offered a hand. "Christina?"

"Yep. That's me." Christina pulled her arm close and studied her wrist. "Hmm. That doesn't look too bad, but there's some cuts. Come in, let me swab that with some disinfectant."

Dakota bit her lip. "I dunno if we have time, but... I gotta pee anyway."

"Bathroom's right down the hall. How long do you expect we'll be away? Should I ask my mother to watch after my cats?" asked Christina.

She hurried down the hall toward the indicated white door. "I really don't know. Might not be a bad idea to ask her."

A patch of pink on a small table in a bedroom at the end of the hall caught her eye, a 'Happy 35th' birthday card. Dakota blinked. *Wow. She looks like she's my age.* Mildly jealous, she stepped into the bathroom. A pair of all-grey cats with piercing teal eyes zoomed in before she could close the door. Both sat like statues watching her pee.

"What?" asked Dakota.

Neither cat reacted.

"Your cats are weird," she said in a loud voice.

Christina chuckled.

She let her head sag, enjoying the brief respite from being in a car plus the relief of finally unloading her overfull bladder. Eric and Christina's conversation murmured in from out in the hall, mostly talking about the ride up. The cats continued staring at her all the way up until she flushed. She checked herself out in the mirror, having been in too much of a rush when she'd been home to do so. Some bruising showed on her cheeks, worse on the left from the heavy slap, but they looked more like shadows and would probably be gone in a day or two.

When Dakota returned to the kitchen, Christina dabbed at her wrists with an alcohol pad. She also checked out the burn on her thigh. Considering the woman a medical professional, and Eric her boyfriend, she dropped her pants.

Eric gave her a surprised eyebrow lift.

"I'm sure a nurse has seen much more of people than panties," said Dakota.

"Oh, that doesn't look *too* bad. Is it still sore to the touch?"

"A little, but only the two dots, not the whole red oval." Dakota snarled. "That sucked *so* much. My legs just went out instantly. I couldn't even move."

Christina dabbed some burn cream on the spot and peppered her with questions about pain, soreness, dizziness, muscle weakness and so on.

"No not really. My wrists are sore and my jaw hurts a little, but mostly, mental damage. I'm gonna be on edge for a while."

"That's totally normal for what happened." Christina re-capped the tube of burn cream. "You really ought to go to the police with this."

"Eric said the same thing." She folded her arms. "And I will. After I've had a chance to get back in there and get everything I can get. They messed with the wrong woman."

"Right on." Eric clapped her on the shoulder.

Christina fidgeted.

"A day or two, tops. If we don't get anywhere, I promise I'll get the police involved."

"All right. Let me collect some things and call my mother about the cats."

Both cats trailed Christina back into the apartment.

"Oh, shit." Dakota pulled out her phone and called Hal.

While Christina packed some things, Dakota explained a brief version of events to her boss, that some men tried to abduct her, but she escaped.

"I'm gonna miss a couple days, okay?"

"You go to the police?" asked Hal.

Why is everyone obsessed with the police? Tell someone you were kidnapped and it's like the first thing they say. "Not yet. I'm... not quite in the right emotional space for that."

"Well, you need ta do that soon. Don't wait. You take the time you need. I'll cover it." He chuckled. "But don't be a stranger, you hear? If you're not back in a couple days, call me and tell me how you're doing, deal?"

"Yeah, definitely. Thanks, Hal. You're the best."

"Go to the cops."

Dakota fidgeted. "I will." *Just not yet.*

"I'm here if you need to talk, you know."

Her voice faltered. "Thanks... I'll probably ask you to walk me home for a while once I'm back."

"Done."

"I'll call you in a couple days."

"And call the police. Take care."

After she hung up, she used the phone to take pictures of the handcuff marks, the stun gun burn, and her bruised face. Evidence couldn't hurt...

Christina walked out from the hall with a backpack and a small, wheeled suitcase. She'd also put sneakers on. "All right. My mother's going to check on the cats. I'm still not sure how I let someone I just met talk me into a spontaneous road trip, but I guess I'm ready when you are."

"Technically, we didn't just meet." Dakota rubbed the red mark on her left wrist. "You use your real voice in the game. I'm sorry. I know it's a lot to ask but it's possible that *all* of us could wind up in deep legal shit for that back door. Before I roll those dice with the cops, I'd prefer to have a little time to maybe think of a better option."

"You use your real voice, too." Christina set her bag on the floor and scooped up both cats. "Okay you guys, Mommy's going to be away for a day or two. Be good to Grandma when she stops by to check on you."

The grey cats squirmed and pawed at the air, clearly eager to escape being hugged.

"You talk to your cats?" asked Eric.

Christina set them down, stood back up, and nodded. "Oh yeah. All real cat parents do."

"Right..." Dakota headed outside.

Eric followed.

She stopped to wait a few steps away from the tiny porch while Christina locked the deadbolt. A squeal of tires made her look up and to the left at a small black SUV tearing across the parking lot. The dark-tinted passenger side windows rolled down in front and back, exposing a pair of men in ski masks with submachine guns.

Dakota didn't even have time to scream before Eric flew into her from behind. Rapid *cracks* of gunfire erupted from her right. Christina crashed against her side a second before they both ate hedge bush, with Eric's weight coming down on top of them.

Another fusillade of gunfire went off directly above them. *Pings* and *clanks* came from everywhere. Beneath the din of shooting, an engine revved. Tires peeled out. Gunshots slowed to a trickle, then stopped.

Young men shouting in Chinese filled in the subsequent silence.

Dakota spat out a mouthful of leaves and dirt. She'd landed in the mulch beneath a row of greenery beside the porch. Eric's right arm encircled her, squeezing her almost painfully into Christina. "What are they saying?"

"Things a girl shouldn't say." Christina spat a few times. "What the hell was that?"

A young voice shouted, "Take that you dumbass mother fuckers!" and two more small gunshots went off.

"Jesus H." Dakota muttered. "That kid's got a gun..."

"Looked like a drive by," said Eric. "Lucky for us you have some interesting neighbors." He shifted his weight onto his knees and got up off the women, then reached down to help them stand out of the bush. "Anyone hit?"

One of the boys who couldn't have been older than twelve stuffed a little handgun in the back of his jeans while walking from the curb across the lawn to the old guy by the barbecue grill. The elder clutched a shotgun and appeared to be struggling with it.

"Damn, Grandpa," said the second boy, still holding a handgun, "ya can't get the damn safety off."

Dakota glanced at the parking lot where only a scattering of brass remained. "I'm not hit. Holy shit! How did they find me?" She stuffed her hands under her armpits to hide the shaking. "And how the fuck are you so calm?"

"It's not *that* bad," muttered Christina.

"Easy. This isn't real. We're still plugged in and playing a game." Eric winked.

"Oh, don't even go there." Christina dusted herself off. She took a few steps away from the building until she could see past the overhead deck, and called out in Chinese.

The men up top waved and nodded at her. Dakota got the sense she thanked them for the help.

"Also, I don't think this is about you, babe." Eric hugged her from behind. "No way in hell would they be able to know we'd come here. They were going for her. I think you're right. We're all in danger."

Christina glanced at them, a little paler than before. "Eric, you're bleeding."

"Shit." He twisted to look at his arm. "Where?"

"Graze on your left side, right above the elbow."

"Let's get out of here before the police show up." Dakota hurried to the car and got in.

"They won't." Christina hopped in the back seat. "We get one or two of those a week here. Cops occasionally roll by to look for bodies, but that's about it. To them, it's just the undesirables thinning themselves out."

Eric leapt into the driver's seat, started the engine, and looked over his shoulder at her. "Why the hell do you live in a place where goddam twelve-year-olds pack heat?"

"Random gun violence works wonders on rent." Christina's eyes betrayed her fear, but she continued acting nonchalant. "The guys upstairs look out for me because I help out whenever they get themselves injured. Let her drive, you sit back here so I can take a look at that wound."

"Shit that stings." Eric glanced at Dakota. "You got a license?"

"Not technically, but I do know how to drive."

He groaned. "If you wanna stay out of jail, we better not tempt fate."

The guys up on the second floor deck nodded or waved at them as Eric backed out of the spot and drove away. Christina shifted forward and attempted to look at the injury, but the gap between the door and seat didn't offer enough room.

"You're bleeding," said Christina.

"Yeah, I noticed." He grimaced. "I'll find a place we can stop soon."

Dakota glanced at him. The reality of having been shot at gradually overwhelmed the adrenaline of the moment, leading to her whole body shivering. "I'm sorry. This is my fault. I've put everyone at risk."

"We all went in there," said Eric. "Did you do anything with that data yet?"

She swallowed hard and shook her head. "No. Nothing more than compiled the mod for the helmets."

"Well, then you haven't put us at risk any more than we all already did to ourselves." He patted her leg. "Hell, this might not even be CSI. Maybe those thugs work for Steyr, and they're trying to keep us quiet."

She covered her mouth with both hands, trying to warm her fingers. "I'm pretty sure the guys who grabbed me worked for CSI. They seemed hesitant to kill me. Heck, two of them weren't even too interested in torturing me." She glanced sideways at him. "I guess they either know I'm the one with the data and want to keep me alive until they are sure it didn't go anywhere, or you're right and *these* guys work for Steyr and wanna kill us."

"You are dripping on the door," said Christina.

"All right. All right, fine." Eric changed lanes to the right. "I'll stop at that ZonGas station coming up. Need to fill this thing anyway."

A moment later, the car rolled to a stop by the pumps.

Dakota got out to deal with the fuel while Christina made Eric take his jacket off so she could get to his arm. She logged into the pump with her Amazon credentials before connecting the nozzle and standing there staring at the ground, wondering when her life decided to go off the rails over a video game. Eric gasped and groaned as Christina applied an antiseptic wash.

"Aww, damn that hurts." He cringed.

Dakota fixated on her sneakers, the laces still untied. Bits and pieces of her struggle to get off the chair flashed in her mind. Unable to decide which event (being kidnapped or shot at) to freak out about more left her numb and calm. Shoelaces hadn't even registered to her then. Hell, she'd barely forced herself to spend the time to recover her shoes. Probably because of all the broken glass on the floor in that place. A barefoot escape wouldn't have gotten far.

"Not so bad," said Christina. "Little Dermaglue and you'll be okay. Just a graze. I think you did more damage to us when you drilled us into the ground."

"Sorry," muttered Eric.

"No sorry." Christina chuckled. "I have a severe lead allergy."

After cleaning the cut out, she took a plastic tube from her bag and dabbed some clear gel on the spot, then pinched the skin closed.

"Gah!" Eric stifled a yell and pounded his fist on the steering wheel.

"Oh, this hurts a lot less than actually taking a bullet." She winked.

Dakota jumped and nearly screamed when the pump stopped with a *clank* and beeped to indicate the tank had filled. She kept her head down as if she'd done something wrong and hoped no one saw her while unhooking the fuel line and getting back in the car.

"Thanks, doc." Eric examined his arm. The gel had hardened into a plastic-like substance that held the wound closed. "Feels weird, but it's not bleeding anymore."

"I'm not a doctor. They get the money; we do most of the dirty work." She winked.

"So where now?" asked Eric.

"Philly." Dakota picked up the GPS and plugged in William's address. "And we hope he's still alive."

29

UNDERGROUND

T hey'd left Christina's apartment around 5:30 p.m. The GPS estimated their arrival in Philadelphia at 9:28 p.m. Dakota huddled low in the seat, occasionally risking a look out the windows for signs that anyone followed them.

Christina broke the silence at 8:40 p.m. "Would you guys think I'm crazy if I complained about being on the road instead of in the game?"

"Heh." Dakota fiddled with her shoelaces. "Me too. I'd rather be home working on hitting level sixty."

"You two are addicted," said Eric.

"It's an addiction to want to be home safe instead of hiding out from thugs?" Dakota kept twirling her finger around and around the shoelace. "Fawkes is confident. She wouldn't be so scared. She wouldn't have run away; she'd have killed all three of those guys."

Eric glanced at her. "Fawkes also gets back up if she dies."

"Yeah. That's true." She chuckled, unable to help but feel irritated at the loss of game time. If those men hadn't grabbed her, she'd have gotten home a little before three and had like seven hours to while away in Axillon99. "Yeah. She's right. The nerve of those assholes, taking up my game time."

Christina laughed.

"Ooh." Dakota fumed. "Now I'm conflicted. Half of me wants to burn CSI to the ground, but if I do that, I won't be able to play."

"There's other games," said Christina.

"Oh, yeah. Realms of Infinity, right? I guess I could deal with elves and fantasy and dragons and stuff, but spaceships are cooler."

"Ax is way bigger. The game world's like forty-seven times the size of RoI's. Plus, they don't have spaceships."

"Duh, it's fantasy," said Christina. "What would they do, player-character galleons or something? Space has a lot more possibilities than ocean."

"Stop a sec. I gotta piss," said Dakota.

"What?" asked Eric. "There's nothing out here."

She glanced around at the open nothingness they'd been driving past for almost an hour. "Yeah, exactly why I'm tired of waiting."

"You're just going to pee in the open?" Christina leaned into the gap between seats, her eyebrows up.

Dakota grasped the door handle. "I've been kidnapped, tied to a chair, shocked with a stun gun, slapped, punched, and shot at today. If someone rushing by at ninety catches a split second glimpse of my bare ass, I couldn't care less. It's either that or the seat's getting wet."

"Whoa. This is my mom's car." Eric swerved into the right lane, braked hard, and pulled to a stop on the shoulder.

Christina found that hilarious and cracked up laughing.

After all three of them watered the grass on the far side of the guardrail (Eric waited for the women to finish), they resumed driving. Dakota called William again to check up on him. She explained what happened at Christina's, and he confirmed that he remained alive and had not seen anyone suspicious. She relayed her plan to seek refuge with her brother and his friends. It took a bit of convincing, but William relented and agreed to at least give the idea two days. With Christina and Eric listening in on speakerphone, they decided to hide out with Nebraska and spend two days trying to come up with a better plan than going to the police and hoping not to get charged with cybercrimes.

At 9:31 p.m., Eric parked in front of a nice, but small house in the suburbs of Philadelphia. The neighborhood looked like something from a Spielberg movie, with neat lawns and evenly spaced neighbors—the kind of place where nothing bad ever happened, and sometimes kids had aliens living in their closet or built spaceships out of old amusement park rides.

Dakota's cell phone rang.

She pulled it out, but didn't recognize the caller ID. "Should I answer it?"

"Why not? If it's the people trying to kill us, answering it won't tell them where you are. Maybe you can cut a deal or something." Eric wagged his eyebrows.

"Right," she muttered, and answered. "Hello?"

"Fawkes?" asked William. "I'm looking at a car parked in front of my house. Please tell me that's you."

She froze. "Yeah. You, umm, aren't pointing a gun at us, are you?"

"It's not a gun. It's a rifle," said William. "Do me a favor, flick your lights?"

Eric obliged.

"I see the lights flashing," said William. "Be right out."

"Wow," muttered Christina as soon as the phone call dropped. "This guy one of those paranoid types?"

Eric chuckled. "After what happened so far, can you blame him?"

The front door opened a moment later as a man in a green Army coat and camo BDU pants stepped out carrying a full-size duffel bag, likely William. A tween with wild shoulder-length blond hair followed, lugging a fat backpack. The kid wore a smaller version of the same coat with jeans and sneakers. A thin face, delicate features, and frightened eyes made Dakota want to run over and hug her.

Christina seemed oddly nervous.

Dakota hopped out as William and the girl crossed the lawn past a dark blue pickup in the driveway and walked up to the car. William had the pale cheeks of a cubicle farm worker and the nascent wrinkles of a person creeping up on forty. The kid looked even paler, so white her skin practically glowed in the moonlight. She had the body language of boredom, but her hazel eyes couldn't open any wider.

"Hey," said Dakota to William, before smiling at the girl. "Hey kiddo. Sorry about this mess. Shit, you didn't tell me you had a daughter. Uhh, you know the place we're going isn't exactly the greatest spot to bring a kid."

The girl finally made eye contact, and sighed.

"This is my *son*, Shawn," said William. "He likes his hair long."

Dakota cringed.

"It's okay." Shawn shrugged. "I get that a lot from people who don't know me. No big deal. Besides, I thought you were a dude playing a chick character. You play kinda aggressive as DPS."

"Heh." Dakota examined her chest. "Last time I checked, all girl."

William nodded at the car. "Pop the trunk? And I'm not letting him stay here all by himself. Not with all this crap going on. There's no one to leave him with, and I'd rather not risk the chance our *friends* try to grab him."

"Nice," said Christina from inside the car, smiling at William. "Kavan uses his real voice too in the game. Wow, you don't look anything like I expected."

Eric hit the trunk release.

"What did you expect?" William lugged the duffel around and tossed it in the trunk.

"Sorry," muttered Dakota.

Shawn shook his head, cracking a grin at Dakota. "It's cool. If it bugged me, I'd have cut my hair a long time ago."

"He plays in a band already." William beamed with pride. "I guess the style of music requires long hair. But, it's his hair, so his choice."

Dakota fidgeted. *Great. Now there's a child involved. Shit. I should just end this now.* "Look, maybe I should forget this and go to the cops. I don't want to drag a kid into danger."

"He's already in it," said William. "Not taking the chance. If they found Christina, they're going to find me."

When he reached up to close the trunk lid, his jacket lifted enough to expose a huge handgun on his belt.

Dakota gasped. "Umm... is that legal?"

"Yeah." William patted it. "Got a permit."

"But we're going into Manhattan. Guns aren't legal there."

Eric laughed. "Tell that to your bro and his buds."

Her eyebrows knit together. "Yeah... Seems like the cops only care about guns if you use them on someone with too much money."

William climbed in back with Shawn sitting between him and Christina. The boy offered a weak smile, then focused his stare at the floor. Eric started the car and pulled around in a U-turn, heading back for the interstate. Mechanically, Dakota plugged an address into the GPS that would bring her close enough to Nebraska's hideaway beneath the bridge.

"You guys are sure you're all okay with this?" asked Dakota.

"Better than being shot at." Christina scratched at her head. "I'd rather be home, but... yeah, they literally tried to kill me. I'm okay with your idea."

"Whatever you want, babe," said Eric.

"Two days." William nodded. "If we don't get anywhere in two days, then we can talk about going to the police."

Dakota scooted around in the passenger seat to face everyone. "I'm not sure where this is coming from as I've never really been the 'jump on the grenade' type of person... usually when shit gets real, I find a hiding place, but—"

"Just like a rogue," said Shawn.

She laughed. "Yeah. Look. It was my idea to go after that back door in the first place. If we can't fix this in a couple days, I'll tell the police you guys had no idea what I was doing in there."

"Damn noble of you, but let's not scuttle the ship just yet." William patted the back of her seat.

Dakota shifted to face forward, letting her mind wander around theoretical possibilities. Would blasting the information about the election manipulation and mind-reading marketing scheme to major news outlets create so much of a shitstorm that it would become pointless to attack her and the others? Or, would going to the cops and keeping everything quiet work better? *Depends on how corrupt stuff is. If the NSA or CIA is involved in this, the cops are basically working for them...*

"Do you guys think this is like, big time badness? Like CIA/NSA level crap?" She rubbed her hands up and down her legs, wincing when she grazed the stun gun burn. "If they're involved, and they know about the brain hacking, going to the cops could be the exact *wrong* thing to do."

"Maybe the CIA's who tried to kidnap you," said Shawn.

Dakota shook her head. "No. If the CIA wanted to kidnap me, I'd be kidnapped. Those guys were definitely not professionals."

"Look," said Christina. "Stop worrying yourself to death. Let's take some time to collect ourselves. If this place we're going is as safe as you think it is, we can relax and plot out our next move."

"Oh crap." She spun to look at William. "We forgot Nighthawk."

"No, you didn't." Shawn lifted his gaze off the floor. "Hi, everyone."

Dakota stared at him. She thought of Nighthawk's bizarre reaction to that woman hitting on him—like he had no idea what to do. Or, how he always laughed whenever anyone cursed or said the word 'balls.' Or how he got bored so easily. Or any of a thousand different little idiosyncratic behaviors that didn't seem right for a grown man. She shifted her eyes to William. "No wonder you cringed whenever anyone swore... our pilot's a kid!"

"Wait, didn't you say you weren't twelve?" asked Eric.

Shawn flashed a cheesy smile. "I'm not twelve. I'm eleven... as of four months ago."

"Wow, so much makes sense now!" Christina giggled.

"Yeah," said Eric, "like how he's so damn good at twitch flying."

Dakota nodded. "He really is probably one of the twenty best pilots in the game."

Shawn grinned.

"Hey, did he name the ship?" asked Dakota. "*Stormbringer* sounds a little, uhh... like we're taking ourselves too seriously."

"Yeah." Shawn nodded. "You don't like it?"

"Better than his first choice." William rolled his eyes.

"*Dad!*" Shawn play-punched him on the arm.

"Oh, I gotta hear this," said Eric. "What was the first choice?"

The boy's face reddened.

William tried to keep a straight face. "Deathwing."

Shawn sighed at the roof. "Come on, Dad. I was only nine then! Even *I* think that's lame now."

"Oh, crap, he's a kid!" said Eric.

"You just realized that?" Shawn scratched his head. "You might need glasses."

"No, I mean... that creepiness with the little girl on that one quest." Eric peered at the rearview mirror. "Totally different feel to that now."

Shawn blushed. "She looked like this girl from school I kinda wanna go out with. And she seemed so scared and sad."

"Oh shit. I bet the game pulled her look straight out of your head," said Dakota.

Shawn went bug-eyed.

William put an arm around Shawn. "He took it kinda hard when he realized it wasn't his friend playing."

That explains the disappointment when he realized she was fifteen, not twelve. She exhaled in relief. *Not* a twentysomething man crushing on a child. No longer having to entertain that disgusting thought brought out the first genuine smile Dakota experienced since her chat with Blake.

"I'm hungry," said Shawn. "Can we get food?"

"Me too." Christina patted her stomach. "It's way past when I usually eat."

"I'm on it," said Eric.

He took an off-ramp and stopped at the first fast food place they found, a Chipotle Amazon.

"Good grief," said William. "Do they own *everything?*"

Dakota shrugged. "More or less. Either them, Disney, or Walmart. Disney glommed up all the burger chains and Walmart got the chicken ones."

The ride back to New York ate two and a half hours, including the twenty minutes it took to get food. Dakota took over for the GPS once they arrived in Manhattan, and a bit shy of midnight, they arrived in the shadow of the bridge.

"Umm. Is the car still going to be here if we get out?" asked Eric.

"It won't be if you leave it out here, but give me a sec." Dakota got out and ducked in to make eye contact with Eric again. "Be right back."

She shut the door and trotted across the street to the two guys in yellow wool caps guarding the gate. The one on the left, she vaguely recalled being named Manuel, but didn't want to risk pissing him off by calling him the wrong name. The other guy she recognized as Kyle by the silver eyebrow ring in an otherwise movie star perfect dark brown face. "Hey."

"Hey girl," said Manuel in Spanish. "You crazy bein' out here this late."

"Need a big favor." Dakota hurried an explanation of what happened. "You guys okay if my friends and I hang here for a day or two while we sort shit out?"

Kyle pulled the gate open. "Shit. You Brass' blood, yo. An' you done right by us with that pile o' bills."

"Awesome. Thanks guys." She waved at Eric to bring the car.

He pulled up to the gate, nodding a greeting at Manuel and Kyle, who peered in at everyone.

"Yo, that li'l Norwegian model you got's a little young, no?" asked Manuel in heavily-accented English. "You might wanna keep her away from Carlos."

Dakota forced herself to keep a straight face. "His name is Shawn."

Manuel cracked up laughing. "Yo, that might not matter to Carlos."

"Dude." Kyle shook his head. "Not right."

She swallowed the unease churning in her gut. "You serious about that?"

"Nah." Manuel waved dismissively. "Carlos' girl's like nineteen. He's forty-something. We just pick on him for chasin' them young."

"Ugh." Dakota cringed. "That's almost as bad."

"Come on, get in so we can close the fence," said Kyle.

Dakota walked inside, weaving around the concrete lane dividers set up as barricades. Eric navigated the Sentra through the maze at a walking pace until they reached a wider area with no way out. There, he parked, killed the engine, and got out.

Christina wobbled out of the car and stretched, pacing around in a stiff-legged circle. Her nose scrunched up at the reek of low tide, trash, and burning plastic in the air.

Shawn climbed to his feet and stared around at the underside of the bridge, the burn barrels, cargo-box 'rooms,' and armed gang punks. "Whoa, this is like... post nuclear." He pivoted in place, open-mouthed at the scenery until a gust of ocean breeze threw his hair in his face.

"Hmm." William pulled his bag out of the trunk. "I've heard of laying low, but this is beyond low. This is underground."

"Yeah..." Dakota offered a helpless shrug. "Only place I could think of. But... there's no way anyone will find us here. At least, not in two days."

William flashed an appraising frown. "If it *is* the CIA or the NSA, they're probably five minutes away, following our smartphones. But then again, if that's the case, it wouldn't matter where we tried to hide."

"Thank you for the confidence." Dakota kicked her sneaker at the ground.

"Does this place have a bathroom?" whispered Shawn.

Dakota pointed deeper into the compound, where higher fences covered with corrugated steel blocked out ambient light from the street. Scraps of unidentifiable material dangled from the cavernous bridge ceiling, swaying in the breeze. "There's a bathroom over that way by the blue tarps."

Shawn stared into the darkness and gulped. "Umm..."

"I'll go with ya." William walked up alongside him. "Yeah, this is not the kinda place I like havin' my son around."

The boy tried not to act as scared as he looked.

"These guys are okay. None of them will give you any trouble. I guess you could say if this was an army, my brother's like an officer."

"Fair enough. Normally, I'd say let's get started right away, but it's late, so I think sleep is in order first," said William.

Shawn yawned, which got Dakota yawning. Christina held up a middle finger as she yawned next.

William and Shawn walked off in the direction of the toilets.

"Kota!" shouted Nebraska. He jogged out of a shadow by a pylon, ran over, and threw his arms around her. "What's up? Kyle texted me something about you getting shot at?"

She found herself clinging to him, having to fight not to cry. Her crazy, stupid, living-on-the-street-like-an-idiot brother was still family. *If I don't wind up dead, I'm gonna visit Mom and Dad.* Thinking that she hadn't seen them in person since she'd been eighteen got her eyes misty.

"You okay?" asked Nebraska.

"Yeah... Just... Wow." She held on for a moment or two more, and blew up into a babbling mess about the kidnapping and guys trying to shoot Christina. She told him about hacking into CSI, and that she'd found some freaky-scary stuff about how they could use the gaming helmets to mine data straight out of people's brains or insert ideas.

"Holy fuck, Kota... that's... We gotta take this shit down. That's like every-thing we're fighting against."

"I know. I know." She paced, grabbing two fistfuls of her hair. "I'm too wound up, fried, tired, and pissed off right now to think clearly. Can you set us up with a place to sleep? I need a lot of coffee and a clear head."

"Yeah, sure." He took a step, waving for them to follow.

Eric and Christina followed them past a couple pylons to a 'village square' with a big fire in the middle, and out the other side to where a large group of oceanic shipping containers had been lined up and packed with improvised mattresses and hanging sheets or tarps to divide the spaces into rooms.

Nebraska stopped at the fifth metal box and banged on it twice. "Here, you guys can take this one. Only had two guys in it, and they're both away for a bit."

"Mission?" asked Eric.

"Nah. Jail." Nebraska sighed. "Got picked up for vandalizing an office tower downtown. I told them the project was too damn big, take too long."

"What'd they do?" asked Christina.

"Spray painted a three-story tall middle finger on the building." Nebraska grinned. "Covered wit' the names of some people the company killed over in Africa with that pipeline bullshit."

"Damn." Dakota stared down at the pavement. "That sucks."

Her brother held his hands up in a 'what can ya do?' gesture. "They won't be in long. Couple months at most. And they'd do it again to spread the word."

"Gonna go find that toilet," said Christina, eyeing the cargo box with a cringe of mild disdain.

"Sorry it's not exactly a Motel 6." Dakota pulled a drape of blue hair away from her eyes. "But we're safe here."

"I am going to take a nice long shower when I get home." Christina winked, set her bag down, and wandered off to explore the compound.

"Well, let me know if you need anything." Nebraska pointed at an orange cargo box about thirty yards away on the other side of the square with the big fire. "That's my spot."

"Okay." Dakota hugged him again.

"Now are you glad you didn't talk me into getting a real job and an apart-ment?" Nebraska playfully punched her shoulder.

She stared at him for a moment, and shook her head. "Honestly? No. I'd rather have you safe and healthy somewhere, even if it doesn't suit my imme-diate physical needs."

"Wow." He blew air past flapping lips. "Well, I'll try not to get myself killed doing the right thing." He winked, backed up a couple steps, then turned and walked off to his 'room.'

Dakota shuffled into the cargo box and flopped on a random mattress covered with an assortment of old sleeping bags. The place didn't smell *too* bad, but she already missed home. At least they'd run a cable through the wall to a Wi-Fi repeater.

William and Shawn arrived a short time later. The boy's persistent fear ebbed a bit at the sight of the cargo box, which he thought 'cool.' He darted in and claimed a sleeping spot all the way in the back while his father stood by the door, arms folded, surveying the camp.

"Well, I suppose this will do for the time being," said William, "but if we weren't getting shot at…"

Dakota smiled up at him. "Yeah. Sorry. I won't ask you guys to slum it with me long."

He walked in, dragging his duffel past her with Shawn following. "We got in this mess together. We'll work something out."

Eric jogged back from the bathroom and took a seat beside her. "You okay?"

"No. Not even close." She leaned against him. "But I could be worse."

He held her, making the rough accommodations somewhat bearable. Christina entered a while later and took a bed. Random snips of conversation in English and Spanish drifted in from the outside, along with the occasional hiss of a distant passing car. Shawn's soft whispery voice echoed from deeper in the cargo box, alternatively comparing this place to surviving the end of the world and asking if 'those people' are going to kill us. She about got up to reassure him her brother's associates were trustworthy, but realized he meant the people who'd kidnapped her and shot at Christina.

Eventually, he fell asleep, as did Eric. Dakota snuggled into him, her human blanket, and tried to get her mind to stop spinning in circles. Thoughts of her Niath alt flying over the beautiful landscape of their home world helped her relax somewhat, but it also got her angry.

She'd gone almost twenty-four hours without logging in to Axillon99.

30

NO RESPAWN

gentle nudge to the shoulder jostled Dakota awake. She peeled her eyes open and came nose-to-nose with a slender-faced young woman. She had dark brown skin, black-purple lipstick, and long, straight brown hair. Her tattered denim-leather ensemble made her affiliation with Nebraska's gang no secret. She could've been anywhere from sixteen to twenty-or-so.

"Hey," said the woman before asking, "you awake?" in Spanish.

"I am now." Dakota yawned.

"Hungry?" The woman held up a big white bag. "Randy and Tito made a food run."

"Food?" asked Shawn, emerging from behind a hanging sheet that walled off the back half of the cargo container.

"Oh, what are you doing bringing a little girl here?" asked the woman in Spanish.

"Not much choice." Dakota reached into the bag and grabbed a breakfast burrito. "We got in the crosshairs of a corporation... or a politician... or both. William can't leave his kid home alone."

"Bastards," said the woman in Spanish.

Dakota switched to Spanish. "By the way, he's a boy."

"Ay! Wow." The woman grinned at Shawn. "When he's older, he's goin' to be so damn hot." She bit her lip and shook her head. Dakota reached for her purse, but the woman shook her head. "Don't worry about it. You technically already gave us the cash."

"Heh. Or someone who looks a bit like me did." She winked.

The young woman laughed, then handed out food to everyone, enormous burritos stuffed with scrambled eggs and onions. A few smelled of bacon. Dakota munched, jealous she hadn't grabbed one with meat.

Despite feeling drained and exhausted, she couldn't fall back asleep after eating, even with a full stomach. She unpacked her PlayStation 7, hooked it up, and pulled out her laptop. Her brain hadn't quite gotten moving yet, so she sat there drumming her fingers on the Neurona 4 helmet beside her.

The same woman who brought breakfast came back with a box of coffee and a bag of paper cups.

"Oh, you are a goddess!" Dakota grabbed a cup and poured herself a black coffee. The smell reminded her of having to go to work, but at the moment, she didn't care. Coffee trumped everything.

Everyone except Shawn had some, despite his asking to try it. At least, until the woman mentioned they had a spigot for water nearby... at that point, William relented and let Shawn have coffee instead of trusting water from a pipe under a decommissioned bridge.

"Good call," muttered Christina, who lapsed into discussing her first coffee experience at the age of nine.

Eric sat cross-legged beside her as she racked her brain. Christina, Shawn, and William decided to log in to the game, since the 'net connection here worked and they had nothing better to do.

"Wait," said Dakota before they could finish setting up. "You just gave me an idea."

She opened the laptop and called up the program code for the anti-brain-reading mod. Over the next half hour or so, she used it as a framework to develop another mod that would cause their helmets to be invisible to any sort of back end process on the network. The Axillon99 client, or any other game software, could interact with the helmet, but no administrative user would see the helmets as connected. For example, if CSI had their network people scanning for these particular helmets' hardware ID, they'd appear to be offline.

"Gimme your mod fobs," said Dakota, hand out.

"What did you do?" William walked over, carrying his helmet.

"If CSI is looking for us, I don't want them to find us. I just threw together another helmet mod that'll keep us invisible. We can access the game, but CSI operators can't see us."

"Won't that make us obvious?" asked William? "Or set off the cheat detection?"

She grinned and shook her head, deliberately throwing her hair over her face. "Nope! The front-end client can still see us. It's like proving a negative. Their back end tools won't see us as online so they can't know we're missing."

He crouched and peered at the laptop screen, reading over the code. "Hmm. Looks solid. All right."

Everyone handed over the mini USB fobs with the previous mod software on it. She uploaded her new mod to each one. She did her helmet last, slotting the little black square in place, closing the hatch, and patting it twice.

"Okay, more safety." She sighed at the worried look in Shawn's eyes. "What am I doing? Dragging you all to this shithole..."

Shawn grinned.

"Oops." She grumbled.

"Dad gets upset about cuss words, as if I haven't already learned them all." Shawn folded his arms and puffed a lock of blond off his face.

"Kids at schools these days are kinda rough," said Eric.

"Nah." Shawn shook his head. "Dad thinks he's a mechanic. Every time he tries to work on the truck, I learn new cuss words."

William picked up a Neurona helmet and held it high like he intended to throw it at Shawn, but caught it with his other hand and laughed.

"So, yeah. I can't ask you guys to stay here. We should go public with the information and hope people are too freaked out by the implications of having their brains hacked that the company forgets to come after us." She ran her hands up over her head, clamping her hair against the back of her neck. "Ugh."

"I agree..." William raised an eyebrow with a sly grin. "But not right away. We found the teleport algorithm for the *Reckoning*, right? Let me take a crack at it. Maybe we can get the prize money before we torpedo the game."

"Aww." Shawn grumbled. "I don't wanna shut down the game. Can't we like make CSI get rid of the scummy crap but not shut down the whole game? Like tell 'em get rid of it or we go public?"

"We'd have a bullseye on our asses," said Christina. "I do like William's idea. Two mil is tempting."

"Like they'd actually pay out on it to us." Eric gestured at nothing in particular. "The very people they're trying to kill or kidnap."

"They'd have to. The game itself will announce the winner because of that damn leaderboard." William ran back to his bag and returned with a laptop. "Let's find that ship."

"Or they lure us into a trap." Eric raised an eyebrow. "You ever see *Running Man*? I don't want to wind up like that."

"No, but I read it." William logged into the laptop, then looked at Dakota. "You still got that algorithm code handy? If we win that money, we become celebrities at least for our fifteen minutes of fame. People will notice if anything happens to us. This prize would be like insurance."

Dakota opened a browser to her throwaway email account. "Okay. That's at least a good place to start."

While she and William began tossing around program code on their respective laptops, Eric sat protectively close and watched.

"So where'd you two meet?" asked Christina.

"Huh?" Dakota looked up, noticed Eric's hovering, and grinned. "Oh... in Axillon."

"She couldn't stand me at first." He put an arm around her.

She poked him in the side. "That's not entirely accurate. I just have this thing about mixing magic and technology. Magic belongs in fantasy games.

When I joined the crew, I pretended Rallek didn't exist because he's a Techno-mancer. That didn't have anything to do with Eric, just me not wanting to acknowledge magic existed in the game. Once I got to know him..."

Eric sat up straight, one hand to his chest. "My powers of charm over-whelmed her distaste for magic. I shall regard that as a compliment."

"Ahh. That's cute." Christina smiled, then noticed Shawn hiding in the back of the cargo box, his expression like some innocent suburban kid acci-dentally sent to an inner city 'scared straight' program. She pushed herself up off her mattress and crept over to sit beside him. "Hey. How are you holding up?"

He shrugged and mumbled, "Are we gonna have to stay here long?"

"Not that long." Christina shifted cross-legged and started asking him about the various fighter ships available in the game.

The boy answered her first few questions tentatively, but the more he talked about the game, the more at ease he became.

"She's good with that," said William in a near-whisper.

Dakota made a 'well duh' shrug. "She's a nurse. Probably has a lot of prac-tice distracting kids from bad shit."

"Yeah, but she can't have had that much practice at it, she's just outta school," muttered Eric.

"She's thirty-five," whispered Dakota. "Saw a birthday card."

William's eyebrows ticked up a notch.

"Daaaaamn," muttered Eric. "She don't look it."

"Why thank you," said Christina. "I may be an old maid, but my ears haven't gone yet."

Eric whistled innocently.

"Shawn's not used to such a rough area," said William. "No offense."

Dakota muffled a laugh. "Oh, it's cool. If I didn't know these guys, I'd be scared too. They look like a street gang, but they're really more a pack of anar-chists-slash-social-warriors."

"So, what, like Greenpeace without a leadership structure or day jobs?" William grinned.

Eric bowed his head and snickered.

"Something like that." She backed up a few keystrokes and retyped a line. "So basically, we build an engine around this algorithm and feed it the star map data, it should be able to tell us where the *Reckoning* will be at any given time."

"That is the plan." William nodded.

They wrangled code for an hour or so before William's ass demanded a break from sitting on the floor of a metal cargo box. He tried to convince Shawn to go get some air by walking around the compound, but the boy didn't seem thrilled about the idea. When Christina offered to go with them, he relented.

Once Eric and Dakota had the cargo box to themselves, she found herself increasingly distracted from programming. One well-placed hand on her back set off a most bizarre reaction in her mind, and got her all fired up on a mixture of adrenaline and the thrill of doing something dangerous.

Dakota leaned into a tongue kiss, her hands roaming his body as much as he caressed hers. When their lips parted, she hung for a moment in confused silence before staring into his eyes. "This is so messed up. Everything that happened yesterday, and I'm so damn turned on right now. It doesn't make sense."

"Some things aren't supposed to make sense, babe. I say roll with it if you want to."

She grinned and leapt into him again. Eric slid over to the side and wound up flat on his back with her on top of him. They writhed together, lips locked, fingers slipping under shirts. Dakota couldn't stop herself, grinding against him, almost ready to explode with her clothing still on. Hungry gasps and mewls leaked from her as she fought with his T-shirt and slid both hands up over his bare chest underneath.

"Someone's gonna walk in us," whispered Eric.

"So?" She peered back for a second before pushing her hands up higher, spreading them out to cradle his shoulders. "That's the best part. The risk."

The scrape of beard stubble across her neck made her eyes roll back. She let out a long, low moan and her hands slipped down.

"Gah!" Eric sat up fast, clutching his left arm where he'd been grazed by a bullet. "Ooh."

She hopped off him and sprawled nearby, both hands over her mouth. "I'm sorry! Is... is it bleeding?"

Eric pulled his sleeve up and looked. "No. Just... sore."

Dakota lowered her arms, her sexual fire gone as fast as it had come out of nowhere. Cold fear seeped into its place. "Fuck. This is for real, isn't it? You really got shot."

He reached over and grasped her hand. "Yeah. No health packs or respawn."

"I don't wanna go to jail." She scooted closer.

"You won't. You're way too good. You pulled off better shit than this and walked away clean."

She stared out the cargo box at the distant gang punks wandering around, some with visible guns, some not. "Yeah. I don't know what's happening to me. I used to be all like, 'fuck the man' and ready to literally like, go to war with corporations. Now, I just wanna go home. Be with you. Pour coffee..." Dakota sighed. "Play a game."

"Well, you know, my mother always says that there's nothing quite like being abducted and tortured to make you rearrange your priorities."

She squinted at him. "Your mother did not say that."

"All right." He held up his hands. "You caught me. All I'm saying is that anyone who went through that would get into a little knock-down-drag-out with self-doubt. You can do this thing, babe. I know you can."

"I'm not exactly about to lead the peasant revolt against the corporate oppressors. I'm writing a module to cheat at a video game."

He rubbed her back. "Yeah, but all revolutions start off with some ordinary person saying 'Aww, man, fuck this shit.'"

Dakota cracked up giggling. "I can totally picture John Adams saying that exact thing."

Still grinning, she scooted back over to the laptop and cracked her knuckles.

"Okay, CSI. Game on."

31

A FEW MOVES AHEAD

The others returned not long after. William sat down to continue programming, while Christina grabbed her bag with the medical supplies and headed out to take a look at a few minor injuries among Nebraska's gang buddies. Much to everyone's surprise, Shawn wanted to go with her.

While William developed the routines that aligned an image file of the game's star map to the proper coordinate matrix, Dakota built the engine around the algorithm that calculated where the game would put the *Reckoning*.

Since he had the beefier system, she sent him her portion of the code once she finished it so he could splice everything together and compile it.

"Good grief, woman. You call this commented code? #Main bit. #Clock thingee. #Mappy stuff here?"

She shrugged. "Usually, the stuff I write, no one else is gonna read."

"Except for you reading it years from now and getting lost in your own code."

"Purist," she muttered.

"Slacker," he muttered.

"Naw," said Eric. "She's just bucking convention. You know, that whole anarchist thing. I'm sure she'd comment code someone paid her to develop."

"Oh, and completely sell my soul to corporate America. Become a cube fungus." She shivered.

"For someone so averse to corporate America, you picked a really weird place to work. Amazon Café? Can you get any more mega?" William grinned.

"Ugh. Don't remind me. But hey, they didn't change it too much when they bought it. We still even have the mermaid logo on everything. The coffee is still good, so."

"Speak for thine own self," said William.

"Oh, you like Disney Donuts?" Dakota stuck out her tongue. "That stuff's like brown water. It's the rinse-water after we clean our brewer."

"DD coffee tastes like coffee. Not the burnt ashes of suffering."

Dakota gasped, open-mouthed. "Your coffee is weaker than a paraplegic grandmother with one eye."

William and Eric both stared at her.

"Uhh, what's having one eye gotta do with how strong the ol' lady is?" asked Eric.

"Argh!" She grabbed two fistfuls of her hair. "Forget it."

"Wow, she's passionate about coffee."

Dakota narrowed her eyes. "You have no idea."

"Okay." William held his finger over the keyboard like a spike. "Ready to compile."

"Wait! Jinx." Dakota shifted to kneel and held her hands over his laptop like a priestess blessing holy water and chanted, "*Pro omnibus et. Pro* I'm-on-da-bus. Shit, I missed da bus."

Again, the guys both stared at her.

"Sorry, habit. Every time I don't say that before compiling, there's a billion bugs."

"There are always bugs. No one writes code without bugs." William hit the button.

"Yeah, but I'm talking about a program code contaminated with a couple of bugs or bugs contaminated with a couple lines of functioning program code." She winked.

The compile finished in a few minutes. William ran the program, which displayed a star map with a blue icon flashing near the southern border, roughly in the middle.

Dakota pointed at the map, tracing an almost plus sign shape over it.

"The spawn algorithm is mostly random, but it has exceptions that I think translate to areas of high player density, the core systems. Also, that doohickey at the end is a population check. Basically, the *Reckoning* isn't going to teleport anywhere players are congregating. It'll pick a new location."

Christina and Shawn walked back in.

Dakota looked up at them. "Just in time."

"For?" asked Christina.

"Cool. Can we log in now?" asked Shawn.

"I think so." She gestured at the map. "We've got a way to tell where the *Reckoning* is. Since the last mission clue we got appears to be a really stupid way to try and follow this thing, I'm sure the next thing we need to do is find the ship. With this, we can. It predicts where the ship will appear using a random seed value based on the current time, with exceptions for high-population sectors."

"Great," said Eric, "but we'll still be racing all over the place to get to it before it moves. It'll probably jump before we reach it."

"We can sit in the middle of the map." Shawn tapped the core-most system. "Makes for the shortest possible trip to any point."

William rubbed the bridge of his nose. "It still takes over an hour and a half to fly to the edge, and this thing teleports every half hour."

"Wait." Dakota held up a finger. "We can go back to DB224. I'll dive into the network again, maybe I can modify the game files to give the *Stormbringer* the same teleportation drive?"

"No way." Eric shook his head. "They'll definitely know we cheated then and disqualify the prize for sure."

"Yeah." Shawn gestured at the map. "But didn't we already cheat with this thing?"

"Technically... yes." Eric nodded. "But, it's nothing they can prove. This doesn't modify the game files or even touch their network at all. Unless they read our minds, they won't have any way to know it existed."

"Reading our minds is evidently not off the table." Christina tapped a finger on her head.

"We're good. Fawkes gave us head condoms." Shawn patted the helmet.

William shifted awkwardly while everyone else laughed.

"Think of it like chess," said Eric. "We gotta be a couple moves ahead of the game."

"He's right." Dakota grabbed William's laptop and swapped to the compiler window. "Let me add a couple lines here... timer plus thirty minutes, timer plus one hour. I'll add two more ship icons, one green for where it'll be in a half hour, one red for where it'll be in an hour. Blue is now."

"That's a ship?" Shawn tilted his head, staring at the icon on the map display. "Looks like a turd in a circle."

Dakota cackled. "It's based on the in-game art for the *Reckoning*. It's kinda shaped like a giant icicle. Pointy at the nose, fat in the butt."

"Sounds like my ex mother-in-law," muttered William.

"Ouch." Dakota grinned. "Okay. Compiling."

"You forgot the chant," said William.

"Already chanted this app. Mods don't count. Just the first compile."

Nine minutes later, she ran the updated program and three ships appeared on the map.

"So, blue is where it is. Green's thirty minutes from now, and red's the one hour location," said William while pointing at the screen.

"Correct." Dakota nodded.

"Well..." William tapped the red icon. "We should just go there now and wait."

"Wouldn't that look a hair suspicious if we're sitting on top of it when it appears?" asked Eric.

Dakota rubbed her hands back and forth over her knees to burn off energy. "That's a possibility, and it might not go to a sector with any player ships in it."

"Best if we make it look coincidental," said Christina. "Even if we act like we're doing the quest right. Go to a spot it's been at so the game triggers a log update when our ship's sensors pick up the trail that prototype warp drive left. Then we grab a mission that will send us to a system near the ship so we can say we just stumbled onto it."

"That's going to take some coordination and planning." William rubbed his chin. "But it shouldn't be impossible. Let's do it."

Everyone scrambled to get their helmets on before attempting to position themselves comfortably on the cruddy mattresses and sleeping bags.

Dakota held her helmet to her face, breath from her nostrils forming two fog patches on the pink plastic. "You be good now. Don't go poking my brain where you're not supposed to."

As messed up as the past day and a half had been, being about to log back into the game felt *right*, like a little kid getting their lost security blanket back.

The blackout visor came down over her eyes as she settled the helmet in place. For a few seconds, the sound of her slow breathing drowned out the world before a pleasant female voice broke the quiet.

"Welcome to Axillon99," said a pleasant female voice via speakers. "Neurona 4 interface initializing. Security option has been set to cortical imprint."

"User DM01852 authenticated," said the voice. "Press start button to initialize."

She reached up, her hand shaking from excitement and nerves, and pushed the little rubber button.

"Synchronizing with game server. Welcome to Axillon99."

32

FIRELIGHT

Axillon99 had a built-in mini-game by virtue of an inventory item, the targeting drone. The baseball-sized bot would fly around at varying distances, playing target to whatever ranged weapon the character had equipped. In a fit of realism breaking, when the drone was active, the player's weapon didn't cause damage to anything else and didn't consume ammunition.

Consequently, players tended to use them only in safe places where no wandering creatures could start a real fight while the player's weapons behaved like toys.

To blow off steam at being kidnapped, Fawkes spent over an hour in the *Stormbringer's* engineering bay trying to shoot her target drone. She pictured it as Light Voice, a man whose face she had never seen, and he became an amalgamation of two boys from high school she'd hated plus a handful of movie villains. Over and over again, she shot the robotic orb as it zipped and glided about, or tried to 'take cover' behind objects. It had a mode that let it fire back, but she wanted to punish something, not have a contest.

During that time, Kavan flew them toward the blue icon's location, with no expectation that the *Reckoning* would still be there. He'd found a mission fairly close to that spot, and plotted a meandering course that would take them through the sector where the ship had been.

Sure enough, they did not encounter the giant, mysterious vessel—but the viewscreen displayed a ghostly blue apparition somewhat like the Aurora Borealis in appearance. A mission update announced that their ship's computer had detected a trace of the prototype drive, and a new map mode, 'tracking' became available. That would show all the locations where they found traces, as well as the times of when the computer estimated the *Reckoning* had been at each location.

"I don't know how they expect anyone to find this damn thing," said Angel813. "By looking at this, you would think the ship follows a predictable series of jumps."

"You would think." William nodded, making funny eyes at everyone as a reminder not to speak about their little helper. Anything they said as their characters inside the game might be recorded somewhere on a CSI server.

"Well," said Rallek, sounding mostly sincere. "I guess we just keep running around until we have enough traces to figure out where to go."

Fawkes glanced back over her shoulder at the voices echoing down the ship's main corridor. The targeting ball peeked up from behind a large metal component in the middle of the room, something supposedly vital to the engine, and emitted a raspberry noise, complete with holographic fluttering tongue. *Screw it. I need to unwind.* She decided to ignore the conversation on the bridge and shot the little orb, which careened into the back of the room while emitting an overacted wail of agony.

The mission Kavan picked didn't involve leaving the ship, and probably wouldn't have been appealing to a full crew, as it had been intended for a solo pilot. Fawkes mostly disregarded the space combat, though she did slot a couple ship buffs while they sparred with a pirate corvette. Winning involved simply blowing up the other ship, which Kavan and Nighthawk handled rather easily. Knowing the brain behind their ace fighter pilot belonged to an eleven-year-old made looking at the twenty-something Nighthawk a bit awkward, but it explained everything she'd ever thought weird about him.

After the pirate battle, Nighthawk walked around the ship saying dumb things with his natural childish voice emanating from the body of a muscular, handsome pilot. Once the amusement value of that fell to nil, he set it back to the 'character voice.'

Kavan threw the *Stormbringer* into warp, crossing the universe to a location nearer the system core. Hours melted away as they played cat and mouse with old spawn locations. Eventually, William suggested everyone else log out for some rest and he would keep checking the mission boards for something that lined up with the predicted location of the pirate battlecruiser.

Dakota ran off to use the bathroom, which occupied the innermost of a series of crumbling chambers under a section of bridge closer to the water. Whatever building it had once been probably belonged to the Transit Authority or something. It hadn't been a bathroom at the time, but after being abandoned, some of Nebraska's friends Frankensteined three functioning commodes with some creative use of garden hose, old toilets, and a cobbled-together series of pipes that went off to who-knows-where. The gang had been living here for two-ish years, and the toilets hadn't backed up or overflowed yet, so she trusted them enough to sit down.

Of course, no one had bothered with any sort of privacy barrier other than them being in a mid-sized room with cinder block walls and a tarp over the only way in. She tried to cover herself as much as possible while sitting on the bowl. The place didn't even have electricity, so she peed by the light of her smartphone.

Soon after she started, Shawn walked in and stopped dead in his tracks two paces away from the entrance, staring at her. For a few extremely awkward seconds, only the echoing drips of an interrupted stream broke the silence.

"Crap. Oops!" He whirled away, putting his back to her. "Sorry."

"Uhh, yeah. Wow, this is uncomfortable. Not your fault."

"I'll, umm, wait outside." He hurried out without looking back.

Whew. She finished up as fast as possible and used a dangling garden hose to 'flush.' On the way out, she tried not to make eye contact with him. Not that he could've possibly seen much given the dark and her defensive posture, but still.

He muttered, "Sorry," again and ducked past the tarp.

Dakota trudged across a chamber several times bigger than the bathroom littered with trash, while the wind whistled over the cracked remnants of the bridge superstructure overhead. A distant radio spat out the last few seconds of reggae before an old Carlos Santana song started. She slipped past another hanging plastic tarp serving as a door out to the area beneath the bridge that didn't have solid walls on the side. Thousands of tons of concrete and steel blocked out the stars overhead, but offered no protection from a stiff breeze blasting in from the side.

Arms folded, she hurried past burn barrels and gang members, most of whom gave her nods of acknowledgement, waves, or smiles. Being in this place felt far too much like being homeless. That worry got her maudlin over her inability to talk Nebraska into getting off the street, but it also reinforced her determination not to let CSI or some corrupt politician chase her away from her life—humble as it may be.

She stormed back over to the cargo container and flopped on the mattress by Eric. Only William remained logged into the game. Since the map positions had updated, she typed in the three sectors (now, now plus thirty minutes, and now plus one hour) on a note application in her smartphone, carried it over to where William lay, and sat beside him.

"Update," said Dakota. "Now: AE184.48 GD102.20."

While in the game, a player would hear sounds occurring in the real world as distant and ghostly. To be sure he got the coordinates, she waited a few seconds and repeated them before moving on to the 'in thirty minutes' set, and the hour away coordinates.

Christina yawned and rolled over.

"Hey Kota," said her brother by the open end of the cargo box.

"Brass..." She looked over at him. "What's up?"

"You eat anything yet?"

"Not since the burritos this morning."

Nebraska walked in with a paper bag full of hamburgers. "Here. Julio's kid sister works at the place a couple blocks over. Slips him a sack if she can get away with it."

"Cool." Dakota took a pair of basic cheeseburgers before holding the bag out to Christina.

"Ugh, do you know how bad those are for you?"

She shrugged. "Are they worse than starving?"

Christina sat up and took the bag. "Debatable, but thank you."

"Huh?" Eric woke up when poked in the side. "You have food?"

Christina tossed him the bag. "Again, debatable."

Her brother sank into a squat at her right, leaning his back against the wall. "Those dudes will regret it if they try any shit here."

"We're here because I'm hoping they can't find it. But... thank you." She patted his leg.

"So, when do you get to go back to your nice, clean apartment?" asked Nebraska.

"Clean is a matter of opinion, but it *is* nice." Eric grinned before taking a bite of his second burger.

"Yeah... I have like important stuff to do. Moving clean clothes from the floor to the dresser isn't one of them." Dakota munched on her cheeseburger. "Not sure. We agreed on two days, which is tomorrow... so, I'm probably going to wind up talking to the cops."

Nebraska gasped. "Shit, Kota, the cops? Seriously? You know they're just a corporation like everything else."

"Now you're starting to sound like Dad. The police aren't as bad as you think. I talk to them every damn day at work. They're just people with jobs."

"But—"

"There's shitheads in every group." She picked a bit of hardened cheese away from the paper the burger had been in and ate it. "Corporations manipulate the politicians who control the cops. I guess in a way, 'trickle-down' works."

"Only if you're talking about piss." Nebraska hung his head, chuckling. "Oy. What happened to this country?"

"I don't plan to be in this cargo box long enough to answer that." She snuggled against Eric.

"Oh, look at you." Nebraska waved his hand around randomly. "Next thing you know, you'll wanna spawn, and you'll have two, and a real job, and you'll fade into the indistinguishable mass."

Eric's eyebrows shot up. "Whoa hold on now. Who said anything about married with kids?"

"You did." Dakota turned her head to peer up at him. "Eric. I'm twenty-two. *If* that's in my future, it's not imminent."

He overacted wiping sweat from his brow.

"But..." Dakota glanced down at her phone. "I'm not sure how many days

I'll be able to 'call out sick' before Hal replaces me. He's cool and all, but it's not like I'm vital."

"Tell the dude someone kidnapped you," said Eric.

"Already did. I'm not sure if he believed me, though."

"But police?" asked Nebraska.

Eric shrugged. "I know, right."

"Maybe that's not such a bad idea," said Christina.

"Cops will leave me alone," said Shawn from the space between Christina and the wall, where he'd sacked out. "I'm only eleven, but you guys are pretty much screwed."

Dakota shook her head while holding her hands (and burger) up. "I'm not going to make these people upend their lives. I hacked into the CSI network. If I talk to the cops, there's a damn good chance I'm going to go to jail." She savaged a chunk of hamburger off and chewed it fast. "No, wait. I'm gonna send it out there anonymously. I'll set up an info packet ready to blast to the media with all the information about Steyr."

"Right on," said Nebraska, adding a slight nod.

She locked eyes with him. "I *will* take them down for that, but I don't want to light myself on fire doing it if I can help it."

"Sweet." Eric leaned close. "What are you gonna do?"

Dakota mumbled, "I'm still thinking," past a mouthful of food.

33

INCOMING

"It's here," said William.

Everyone froze.

Dakota leaned forward to peer around Eric at him. "What do you mean by 'it's here?'"

William offered a weary smile. "Found a mission that sent me one sector away from the now-plus-one-hour. So, I went 'afk' and waited. The *Reckoning* just appeared. He lifted his helmet up, about to put it back on. "You guys up for it?"

"It's go time!" yelled Shawn, while scrambling to crawl past the cloth partition to his PlayStation.

Eric grabbed his helmet. "Shit yeah, that's a hard ship to find!"

"Mmf!" Dakota inhaled the rest of her second burger and grabbed her Neurona 4. "Brass... keep an eye open, huh? We're gonna be out of it for a while."

"You got it." Nebraska sat by the cargo box entrance.

Dakota fired up her PS7, selected the Axillon99 client, and ran it before diving onto the mattress and jamming her helmet on. Heart racing, she lay flat and hit the button by her right temple.

"Synchronizing to game server. Welcome to Axillon99," said the placid female voice.

The fetid air and mildew smell of her temporary bedding faded to the clean, metallic scent of the *Stormbringer's* interior. With virtuality came a sense of confidence and immortality borne of respawns and impermanent death. Dakota Marx became Fawkes for the thousandth-some-odd-time. Her body appeared out of the darkness, warped bands of white gleaming across her almost-black chest armor. She stared down at her hands, the gadgets on her belt, the CL32 heavy laser pistol on her hip, and in that moment, she realized she belonged here.

This was reality. Not some helpless barista/hacker/wannabe-anarchist.

"I am Fawkes. I'm going to kick someone's ass." She struck a confident pose... for all of four seconds. "And I think I need some serious help."

She laughed at herself before running down the hall to the bridge, where everyone else gathered.

Angel813 gave Nighthawk a squeeze. "Hey kiddo. You doing okay?"

He yawned. "Yeah, and please don't call me kiddo in game."

"Why?" asked Rallek. "Afraid it'll hurt your chances with the ladies?"

Nighthawk looked over at him. "What?"

"Anyway!" yelled Kavan.

"Oh," muttered Nighthawk. "That must've had something to do with sex. Dad only gets that awkward when someone starts talking about sex."

"Anyway!" Kavan cleared his throat and pointed at the viewscreen. "Behold."

A cyan box highlighted a small turd-like shape on the screen. Its dull matte-grey color blended into the starscape so well it would've been almost impossible to see without the targeting aid.

"That teeny thing?" asked Angel813.

"It's a sector and a half away," said Nighthawk. "Holy crap."

"So?" asked Angel813.

Nighthawk spun to look at her. "It's far away and we can still see it. That means it's effing massive."

"We knew the *Reckoning* was a battlecruiser," said Rallek. "That's a capital ship."

"Yeah, but"—Nighthawk gestured at the screen—"you could stab a planet with that thing."

"Don't panic yet." Rallek edged up to the viewscreen. "Let's get closer and see what we're dealing with."

Kavan tapped the console, increasing thrust. A faint wave of inertia made everyone else lean back.

The *Reckoning* gradually became larger. After six minutes, it filled the viewscreen and they still hadn't gotten close enough to aggro it. What at first appeared to be a decorative pattern of 'technology bits' across the hull began to look like laser turrets as they neared—thousands of them.

"Damn..." whispered Rallek.

Fawkes clutched the back of the pilot's seat. Her heart sank, dragging hope with it into a spinning black abyss. This thing had to be designed for a group of forty separate crews to take on. The largest raid composition possible. Forty corvettes, two-hundred players. The *Stormbringer* all by its lonesome wouldn't even chip the paint on it.

"Sorry guys," muttered Fawkes. "This isn't happening."

"You know, for a chance at two million bucks, I wouldn't necessarily mind eating a one week lockout when we blow up." Angel813 laughed.

"Thank you for not saying *if* and making me correct you." Kavan exhaled hard. "What are the idiots at CSI thinking? How can anyone do this quest without a full raid group?"

"Maybe their plan all along was to give the ten million dollar prize to a raid group so like everyone gets fifty grand." Rallek set his hands on his hips. "Companies have done lamer things than that in the past. The whole thing is a marketing gimmick anyway, right?"

"So a bunch of random people chase this quest for months, realize they can't possibly kill the *Reckoning* without a full raid group... and all band together?" Fawkes scratched at her right eyebrow. "I can't see that happening."

Rallek patted her on the back, slid his hand down, and squeezed her ass. "People who spent months daydreaming about ten... or two million are gonna be pretty pissed off when all they get out of it is fifty grand."

"That doesn't make sense. Why the leaderboard then?" asked Nighthawk. "They showed individual ships there. That sounds like they're saying, hey, these guys are close to getting the money."

"Messing with us," said Kavan. "Create the appearance that a single player or crew can win, so it stretches out as long as possible before they have to pay anyone."

Fawkes pushed off the chair. "Well, so much for that. I'll set up an infobomb to go out to the media. It's late. Let's sleep and I'll go to the cops in the morning." She started to trudge down the hall to her engineering room, but stopped when Nighthawk shouted, "Wait."

"I got an idea." Nighthawk's head nearly blurred from looking back and forth between the viewscreen and Kavan so fast. "Let me fly the *Stormbringer*. That thing's billion guns are useless if we get close enough. Capital ships have battery turrets to handle fighters on 'trench runs,' and those little lasers won't do enough damage to a corvette's shields."

"That's because corvettes don't skim the hulls of capital ships," said Kavan.

Nighthawk clutched Kavan's shoulder. "I can do it. I can get us in there and stay away from the big guns."

"That thing couldn't even hit us with the *big* guns." Rallek chuckled. "Why do they put enormous cannons on capital ships? No player can control a cap ship."

"Yet," said Angel813. "They're talking about it in an expansion, once they figure out if they're going to require large player crews or just make it all automated."

"Trust me. I can pull it off," said Nighthawk, sounding an awful lot like a kid despite the adult tenor in his voice.

Kavan swiveled the pilot's chair to face everyone, mostly Nighthawk. "All right, let's say you get us in there. What then? If that thing sat dead still and didn't fight back, it would take us like twelve hours of continuous firing for our guns to put out enough damage to kill it."

"This encounter is a raid." Rallek shook his head. "It's not meant for one crew. Hell, it's not meant for twenty crews."

Nighthawk flailed. "Yeah, but the rules don't apply in space combat. It's a twitch game. If I can fly the ship so it stays out of laser beams, we stay alive."

"Okay, so what are we going to accomplish if you can even keep us alive?" asked Fawkes.

Rallek broke into pacing. Kavan pursed his lips.

Angel813 sat in the co-pilot's chair and whipped out a small army of vanity pets. Soon, purrs, trills, mews, and cute alien noises filled the silence.

Hmm. Fawkes edged closer to lean on the pilot's chair, and stared out at the menacing techno-icicle glimmering back at her. The hull had the color of dark silicon grey, flecked with a regular pattern of small luminous blue dots, perhaps windows or some unknown technology. More likely, the developers simply thought it looked cool. Awhile back, they'd even used images of the ship for promotional materials, but the planned storyline arc never materialized. In the whole span of the game, the crew of the *Stormbringer* were probably the only players to ever see the elusive battlecruiser 'for real.'

"Wait." Fawkes' eyebrows shot up as an idea hit her. "I just realized something."

"We're galactically fucked?" asked Rallek.

Angel813 coughed. Nighthawk giggled.

"Guys. Now that you know Shawn's only eleven, would you kinda try to ease back on the language?" asked Kavan.

"You sound like my boss." Fawkes grinned. "Look at the size of that thing. It's worth at least one f-bomb."

"Dad only curses when he tries to fix things." Nighthawk jumped back when Kavan tried to grab him. They had a brief staredown before both cracked up laughing.

"So you were saying?" asked Rallek.

Fawkes pointed at the *Reckoning.* "That ship was in the game from launch."

"So?" asked Angel813.

"They didn't create it for this prize. It's always been here. The same way they used that pirate starbase for this quest even though it's a raid. Maybe we don't have to kill this thing at all. What if we have to board it? That fits with Will—uhh, Kavan's theory that they're trying to make this take as long as possible or even be so difficult it's technically impossible. Who would ever think of boarding a world boss raid ship?"

"We got like six minutes until the thing warps out," said Angel813. "If we're going to do something, we should do it now."

Nighthawk patted Kavan's arm. "C'mon, Dad. Lemme take the stick. I can do this."

"Okay, fine. Screw it. If we're gonna eat a lockout, might as well." Kavan got up.

"Going in. Hopefully, it won't teleport out if we start the encounter."

"We're going to die," said Rallek.

"Probably." Nighthawk laughed. "But this is going to be epic."

Fawkes ran down the hall to the engineering station. "I'm gonna slot four shield boosters to keep us alive long enough to find something."

"What are we looking for?" shouted Rallek.

"Anything. Docking bay, a door, a hole, some way to get inside," shouted Fawkes while twisting a fictional screwdriver-like tool at the shield generator unit. One by one, the metal-plated icons for shield booster buffs appeared in the 'tray' on the screen.

Acceleration made her slide a few inches toward the back of the room.

"Uhh," yelled Nighthawk. "You guys might wanna hold on to something or grab a chair. This is going to get... spinny."

Fawkes scrambled into the seat she rarely used and put on the belt as the background music changed to the space combat track. Alarms rang out indicating an enemy vessel had targeted them. "Shit, I should've slotted at least one missile decoy."

She punched the fourth shield booster, using it up, and grabbed a different tool that resembled a soldering iron, which she manipulated at the sensor console. That combination of 'tool' with 'component' resulted in a short-lived defensive cooldown that neutralized the guidance systems of incoming missiles.

Hope it works on raid bosses.

The *Stormbringer* lurched into a hard spiraling maneuver that would've flung Fawkes out of her chair if not for the belt. She yelped and braced her boot on the console while grabbing the seat on either side of her ass. When she glanced left down the corridor to the bridge, a black blur flashed by from left to right. A heavy *whump* happened next, followed by Rallek moaning.

"Holy crap. That did health damage," said Rallek.

Nighthawk's voice strained as if he attempted to lift something too heavy. "That missile would've done a whole lot more."

The spiral came to an abrupt stop, tossing Fawkes against her seatbelt in the other direction. She gasped from the shock to her abdomen, but held on. Somewhere deep in the ship, a sound like boxes of metal fragments bouncing down stairs echoed.

"Wow," said Kavan from the bridge. "The physics engine is getting a workout."

Rallek chanted some of his made up nonsense and a pale shimmering light washed over the floor, walls, and ceiling, creeping from the bridge end to the rear. "Did that do anything?"

"Uhh," yelled Nighthawk.

The *Stormbringer* whipped back and forth, pitching and rolling. Every so often, the room shuddered with a minor impact and a loud digitized squelching noise—the sound effect for an energy weapon strike on shields. It alarmed her somewhat that she could tell from the briefness of the noise that the laser blasts skipped off the shield bubble in shallow angle grazes rather than direct hits.

I spend too much time in this game. She cringed as a loud *bang* came from behind, followed by a raining shower of sparks falling on her. *Heh. No such thing as too much. Reality sucks.*

"Yeah it did," shouted Nighthawk. "Controls are more responsive. The handling got better."

"Sweet," cheered Rallek. "Stat boosters work on ships."

"What the hell was that explosion?" shouted Kavan.

"Something back here blew up. There's like smoke and sparks now," said Fawkes.

Angel813 cackled. "Aren't you the engineer? Don't you know?"

"You realize this is a video game right? I'm not actually a starship mechanic. I see damage bars and poke things with tools." She twisted around in the seat to examine one of the boxy pods in the middle of the room that somewhat resembled a tiny version of the engine from a giant ocean liner. It had a generally 'engine' like shape, but instead of wheels, belts, and hydraulic stuff, panels of cool-looking glowy bits and circuitry covered it. "Umm. I think it's just cosmetic animation from the shield taking so much damage so fast. There's no health bar showing on it, so it's not actually damaged."

"That's good," yelled Nighthawk.

Fawkes shot forward, or perhaps she stayed still while the room whipped to the left, ramming the seat belt into her gut. For a few seconds, her only point of contact with the chair was the narrow strip of material across her stomach. She hung suspended like a meat flag, arms and legs touching as the *Stormbringer* rocketed around in a flat spin.

"Urk!" she yelled. "Stop!"

"Oh, this wall tastes lovely," said Rallek.

A stream of profanities came from Kavan.

The ship leveled off hard, slapping Fawkes into the seatback.

Boots clanked in the bridge, getting louder in the hallway. Rallek came running into the engineering room and leapt into the second chair. His health bar had dipped to ninety-one percent, but he didn't appear injured. After a few seconds of hard breathing, he reached forward and opened a 'net window.

"You okay?" asked Fawkes.

"Yeah. Took me a minute to get my feet under me. I feel like a shoe in a clothes dryer." He chuckled. "That kid can fly, but damn... Good thing this is a video game or he would've snapped this ship straight in half."

"Huh?"

"Physics... The length, shape, and size of this ship shouldn't be able to tolerate such hard, rapid maneuvers. They didn't program material stress into the game, or we'd have broken apart already."

"Maybe it's because it's space and there's no air friction?" asked Fawkes.

Rallek typed on a floating holographic keyboard. "That probably helps, but I still think we're twisting in ways that should've crumpled us up like an empty beer can."

She groaned from the seat belt biting into her gut. "What are you looking for?"

The *Stormbringer* shuddered with another pelting of near misses. Gravity quadrupled in seconds.

"Ugh," yelled Fawkes, struggling against the forces crushing her into the seat. She glanced up at the chase view, where the ship careened out a dive, amid a hail of red and orange streaks of light. The hard pull-up left them skimming the hull of the *Reckoning* with probably only ten to fifteen feet of separation. She looked away. "Holy shit... I can't watch."

"It's a game, hon."

"Yeah, that would be a lot easier to handle if we weren't shaking, smelling smoke, and basically experiencing everything for real." She peered through a curtain of pink hair at him. "Guess I'm getting too into it."

"A little." He leaned forward to read something on the panel.

"What are you looking for?"

"Info on the *Reckoning*. If anyone has ever posted about boarding it or anything."

Kavan tromped down the hall and went up the ladder to the roof turret while Angel813 jumped down the opposite ladder to the underside turret.

"We got fighters coming after us now," yelled Kavan. "Rallek, do some of that magic crap!"

Fawkes grabbed the floating window and pulled it over. "Go. Keep us alive. Do magic or whatever. I got this."

"Right..." He put his hand on the console and invoked a spell.

"Nice. Handling just got better," yelled Nighthawk.

"I re-cast the agility boost." Rallek chuckled.

While he kept tossing spells on the ship, the same ones he usually used to enhance summoned technological minions, Fawkes skimmed article after article about the *Reckoning*. About half of them claimed the ship didn't really exist as anything more than a bit of in-game folklore or a marketing gimmick. Nothing had useful information. Not one player had even encountered the ship before, much less a full raid group to evaluate or comment on potential strategies to beat it. Usually, the world bosses had simpler strategies than the ones inside instanced content, since encountering them depended on randomness. Especially in the case of the *Reckoning*. A player would have to be incredibly lucky to find it at all, and if a raid group wiped, by the time the lockout let them use their ships again, the battlecruiser would be long gone. Practicing a strategy for it would be a colossal pain in the ass, since a guild might never find it twice.

The *Stormbringer* shifted side to side, slaloming giant towers springing up from the hull of the battlecruiser. In the absence of the capital ship laser barrage, everything had fallen to an eerie calm, though the constant 'pew-pew' noise from Kavan and Angel813 picking off enemy fighters kept her on edge.

There's got to be a way for one crew to deal with this mission. It's the pirate space station all over again. They just used this ship for the money quest because it's such a bitch to find. She tossed the internet window aside and accessed the in-game scanning console. Usually, that would give her specs on a ship like its armor values, targetable sub-locations, internal system status, and so on. She'd gotten high enough with the engineer sub-class to read shield points, recharge rate, and identify weapons or critical weak points. Every ship in the game thus far possessed at least one critical spot that, if an attack hit it, would do severe damage. In the case of fighters, it often wound up being the size of a dinner plate. Not an easy shot.

The *Reckoning* didn't show any critical vulnerabilities (nothing turned yellow), but she did notice an odd purple spot a bit forward of the midpoint along the underside. She zoomed in on it, never having seen a ship system appear in that color before. The spot expanded into a rectangle with rounded corners, vertical compared to the hull around it on the side of a raised box. She rotated the image to put the battlecruiser on the bottom of the screen, and the area she'd zoomed in on resembled a bad computer graphics rendering of a simple house with one way in.

It's a door!

She mashed her finger into the screen, tagging that location in the *Stormbringer's* computer so it lit up for Nighthawk in the bridge. "I found a way in!"

"Uhh, that door is way too small for the ship," said Nighthawk.

"No kidding." Fawkes tapped her finger on the console, staring at the purple rectangle. "It's for people."

"Damn..." Rallek glanced over at her. "You think?"

"No clue, but it's something to try."

Kavan muttered a few more profanities over the comm before raising his voice back to a normal level. "The fighters are so damn thick behind us, it's impossible to fire and not hit something."

"You think the raid fight expects people to go inside the ship?" asked Angel813 between laser blasts.

Distant explosions outside made Fawkes grin at the old 'no sound in space' gripe.

"No way in hell," said Nighthawk. "How many pilots could've gotten in this close without being vaporized? And there's only a few corvettes that can maneuver like this. Most of them handle like garbage trucks. No way people are supposed to go inside just to beat the world boss."

"Can you get us to that door?" asked Fawkes.

The ship swerved hard left and right, dodging another tower of tech jutting out from the *Reckoning's* hull.

"Yeah. Hang on. The spot she tagged is like a mile away and on the other side. I gotta hug the ship all the way around or we'll get torn up by the lasers."

"Might as well do it," yelled Kavan. "We're already here."

Rallek cast another spell into the ship, skipping his usual made up chant.

"Incoming!" roared Nighthawk.

"Oh, shit." Fawkes stared at the chase screen.

The raid script caused the *Reckoning* to fire six giant torpedoes, each one twice the size of the Gremlin fighter. One of those would eat all the *Stormbringer's* shield points and erase probably half the hull points. Since the encounter had been triggered by only one ship, the game couldn't randomly target separate corvettes for torpedoes—so they all converged on one. Six energy trails wrapped around the hull of the giant battlecruiser as the torpedoes came together in formation a few hundred yards behind them, gaining fast.

"Umm, torpedoes," said Fawkes.

"Yeah," muttered Angel813. "Wow I've never seen ones that big before."

Kavan sputtered; Fawkes laughed.

"Why is that funny?" asked Nighthawk. "Those torpedoes are huge."

"We are galactically fucked," muttered Rallek.

34

THE RECKONING

Fawkes stared at the chase screen, transfixed by the six massive torpedoes creeping closer and closer to the *Stormbringer*. Flashes of green laser continued streaming from the top and bottom turrets, setting off explosions and chain reactions within the dense cloud of tiny fighter ships chasing them.

"Shoot the torpedoes!" shouted Fawkes.

Both turrets focused on the torpedoes, but the shots appeared to glance off shields inches from the nose cones.

"It'll take too long!" roared Angel813. "The torps have shields!"

"Focus on the middle one," yelled Kavan. "We set one off, it'll destroy the others."

The turrets converged on the same torpedo, but it didn't look likely they'd destroy it before the warheads caught up to the ship.

"Hang on!" yelled Nighthawk.

The *Stormbringer* leapt up and away from the *Reckoning's* hull, so vast it appeared to be a land mass of metal instead of a ship. In seconds, the blinding barrage of the large laser batteries filled the blackness of space. Nighthawk dove as soon as they started taking fire again. The bunny hop maneuver pulled the torpedoes into the path of the far more powerful beams from the *Reckoning's* primary turrets.

A brilliant explosion filled the monitor a split second before a concussive wave hit the *Stormbringer* hard. The expanding blue plasma ball from the multiple torpedo detonation incinerated most of the pursuing fighters, setting off a rain of ash particles that blackened the battlecruiser behind them. Two-thirds of the *Stormbringer's* shield collapsed, and the ship went spinning forward like a model airplane kicked into the air. Screaming, Nighthawk managed to get it under control before it flew like a Frisbee into another giant tower of antennas and blinking lights. He flipped the ship over another blast of large lasers and dove back down to skim the hull.

Grunting against inertia, Fawkes reached forward and set off one of the shield boosts, surging it back up to eighty-two percent.

"Okay, we're clear. How long before it launches torpedoes again?" yelled Angel813.

"I'm going to hope it won't if we stay close to it. It fired those before we got under the lasers," said Nighthawk.

One of Angel813's vanity pets, a bright violet and pink foxlike creature with wings, raced by on the wall, shrieking and chittering.

"Door!" yelled Fawkes.

"On it, we're—gah!" Nighthawk yelled in surprise, and the ship shuddered with a heavy *clank*. "Oops."

The shield dropped by eighteen percent.

Fragments of a fighter craft dribbled around the blue bubble surrounding the *Stormbringer* on the chase screen.

Three more fighters popped up in front of them. Searing blue beams from the primary laser cannons lanced through the pack, barely slowing down.

"You shot a fighter with the main guns," said Kavan in a deadpan tone. "That's unsportsmanlike conduct."

"Usually, it's impossible to even hit a fighter with them." Rallek laughed. "He just killed a fly with a hand grenade."

"I'm that good." Nighthawk laughed. "But they were still coming out of a docking port. Sitting ducks. Hey, the agility boost wore off. Rebuff!"

Rallek cast another spell into the floor.

"Okay..." Fawkes tried to tune out worrying about the real likelihood of the ship exploding at any given moment. "Set down near the door, let me out, and I'll go inside."

"Not alone," said Kavan.

"None of you can sneak." She gnawed on her finger.

Kavan's face on the little comm panel displayed a frown. "We have no idea what's in there. Rallek can take the turret over. I'll go in with you."

"I should go, too," said Angel813. "In case you need healing."

"We need you on the turret more. If the *Stormbringer* gets destroyed while we're inside, we're screwed." Kavan fired a sweep of lasers, sending two more fighters spiraling to flaming deaths against the battlecruiser's hull. "Hah. This is pretty damn fun. Rallek, get up here."

"On the way." Rallek pulled off his seatbelt and stood. "You be careful in there, okay?"

She grinned. "Not trying to talk me out of it?"

He leaned in and kissed her. "It's only a game. Death isn't permanent. I promise to talk you out of stupid crap in the real world though."

"Hah."

Nighthawk banked the ship in a series of zigzag turns around columns and superstructures protruding from the cruiser's hull. The roundabout path kept the ship close enough to avoid taking fire from the big guns. A steady pelting of anti-fighter lasers kept the shields bouncing between ninety-six percent and ninety-nine percent, unable to do damage fast enough to overpower the shield's normal recharge rate.

Ugh. I already forgot what quiet is like. Fawkes re-slotted shield boosters and threw in one anti-missile buff before leaving her seat and running down the hall. The ship's maneuvering to avoid incoming lasers kept tossing her side to side, but she bounced off the walls and kept her footing. Kavan met her in the central hallway, and they hurried down the stairs to the cargo bay. When they reached the wall at the rear end, standing on the ramp door that would lower them out into space, she glanced over at him.

"Ready?"

"I guess. But we're not there yet."

"I mean, mentally ready."

Kavan activated the shield on his left forearm, examined it, and turned it off. "Yeah. If there's raid mobs in there, let me die. You stay hidden. We won't be able to fight our way through them."

"I don't think they put raid mobs inside. They designed this fight for ships only."

"Well, I got some good news," said Nighthawk. "We're well past the teleport time and it's still here. Guess it won't go away until combat ends."

"Here come more fighters," said Angel813.

With no chase screen to watch, Fawkes listened to the rapid firing of lasers and grumbles of the shield taking small hits, hoping that her imagination interpreted the sounds worse than they were. Gazing at the plain grey steel in front of her didn't instill any more confidence.

"Coming 'round the side." Nighthawk's voice emanated from a speaker overhead. "I'm gonna set it down by the door, count to four, and take back off. We can't sit still or the fighters will chew us up. Even four seconds is really dangerous."

"Okay," said Fawkes.

Kavan hit the button to open the ramp and the floor beneath them lowered. Fawkes went wide-eyed and wrapped her arms around the hydraulic strut at her right. A landscape of metal raced by below, bursting with orange flames wherever fighter parts collided with the *Reckoning's* hull. Twenty feet of ship extended out above, the end lit by the glow from the main engines, which emitted a constant, loud roar. She glanced left at Kavan, at all the little blue light spots reflecting on his visor from the fighter craft coming after them.

"We're standing on an open door while flying hundreds of miles per hour, thirty feet away from an enemy capital ship," she yelled over the engines.

"Yep," shouted Kavan. "But it's only a game."

"Right. Tell that to my brain." She laughed nervously. "I think I'm gonna pass out."

"Amazing what they can do these days, isn't it? Used to be, video games were limited to a screen. Then they made this little box that gave off smells. Then the sensory hat."

She shivered. "I remember having one of those hats when I was like ten. Some game had spiders in it and the thing made me feel like I had bugs crawling over me. I had nightmares for weeks."

Kavan laughed. "Yeah, and now they put us right inside the damn game."

Another small fighter ship burst into flames and went spinning to the 'ground.' She watched it until the tumbling bits of metal disappeared among the general chaos. "William, do you ever wonder about weird stuff? Like what if *this* is real and the life we think is boring and mundane is actually the simulation?"

"Nope." His helmet turned toward her, revealing a big grin. "Life doesn't have background music."

"I... maybe I just want that to be true. Maybe I'm tired of being a nobody." A near miss with a tower structure caused an audible *whuff* despite there being no air in space. She clamped onto the strut tighter, staring at another crashing fighter rolling by sideways like a flaming metal tumbleweed. "When I was like twelve, I got it in my head that I could change the world, do something about all those greedy corporations always getting away with whatever they wanted while the little people suffer... but I'm just some coffee girl with a whole apartment full of deflated dreams."

"Why haven't you chased a career?" asked Kavan, confident in his one-handed grip on the other ramp strut.

Fawkes shrugged. "I dunno. I have a hat full of reasons; pick one. Lazy. Didn't want to 'become part of the machine.' The café is comfortable. Maybe I hate change."

"So the girl who wants to change the world hates change in her own life?" Kavan poked her in the side. "Gotta start somewhere. Where better than from the inside of one of those 'evil corporations.' Get in the door, climb the ladder, make changes from within. Companies aren't inherently bad, it's usually one jackass at the top. It doesn't have to be a 'war,' you know." He pointed out the ramp at the swerving metal terrain. "Look what we're doing here. Big ass ship. We can't possibly take it on in an up-front fight, but we're going to infiltrate."

She laughed. "Ha. Ha. Are you working up to a joke about a reckoning?"

He tapped his chin. "No, but now that you mention it..."

Fawkes sighed. "Well, maybe if we don't wind up dead or in jail, I'll send you a resume. It's not too impressive though. I look like I just got out of college. All my achievements are, uhh, not exactly legal."

"You *do* look like you just got out of college. I'm not saying you'll get in the door high up the totem pole, but you gotta start somewhere. And tell me you're making 120 grand a year slinging coffee."

"Nah, just thirty-eight bucks an hour. Barely enough to keep my apartment."

"That's about what, eighty grand a year? Not bad for a barista. A couple years down the road, you'll be over 200 at my place. 120's a starting salary for a coder."

"Where are your horns, o dark tempter?" She laughed.

"Door coming up!" shouted Nighthawk. "Get ready."

The ship decelerated hard, pulling Fawkes back into the cargo bay. Blurry dark metal terrain sharpened into millions of sections covered in circuit pattern, small openings, panels, and glowing lights. They slowed to a jogging pace and overflew a large, plain cube of silicon grey with no textures on it except for a generic armored door on the side facing the back of the *Storm-bringer*. As soon as the ship cleared the box, it dropped the last fifteen feet and made contact with the hull on its landing skids.

Fawkes leapt off the ramp without thinking too much about it. Red laser shots from the swarming cloud of fighters struck the metal all around them; any one of those beams would mean instant death for a player character outside a ship.

Jaw clenched in determination, she ran like hell to the cover of the 'build-ing' in front of her. The fighters shot overhead, chasing the *Stormbringer,* which had taken off, leaving them behind. She spun around, back flat against the metal, staring down the artificial landscape.

"Holy shit. This ship is so big it feels like we're on a planet."

Kavan slid to a stop beside her, shoulder against the wall. "Yeah. Well, we're not dead, so maybe there's something to your idea after all."

She slapped the panel for the door, but it wouldn't open. "Of course." After connecting her override kit, she stared in disbelief at an enormous hacking mini-game node map. "God damn... they really don't want anyone getting inside."

"Can you do it?"

Fawkes looked up at him. "Hey, who are you talking to?" She winked. "It's not *difficult*... just huge. A time sink."

"Well get going. My kid isn't going to be able to fly forever."

She nodded and focused on capturing nodes. Against her nature to hoard the one-shot software buffs, she burned through them in an effort to save time, specif-ically using the 'instant capture' ones to take nodes in one second rather than eigh-teen to twenty-five, and *Freeze* softs to stall the red security lines chasing her.

For several minutes, she worked while Nighthawk and the others cheered, screamed, and swore over the comm link. The 'sky' overhead flickered with a constant storm of red and blue lasers. Eventually, she took control of the CPU node and unlocked the door.

Kavan pulled it open and stepped in, raising his transparent force shield like a techno gladiator. She followed, entering a featureless corridor shiny and silvery like an ingot of raw silicon. It had no doors, decorations, or even any light fixtures despite it being bright enough to see clearly.

"Whoa. This is like base models. They didn't bother to add any texture maps." Fawkes hurried forward at a brisk walk. "No mobs at all in here."

Kavan followed, his boots striking the metal underfoot with a sharp *thunk-thunk-thunk* cadence. "If this is part of the quest, they should've given it interior."

"Maybe they planned on us getting a raid group and blowing it up after all… and finding whatever the quest objective is in the debris cloud."

He whistled. "Whatever object we're supposed to find in here might not even exist until the ship is destroyed. It could spawn only after the *Reckoning* blows up."

"Do you think CSI would force people to form a raid group for the prize quest and then think to go hunting the debris field for some random drop?" Fawkes didn't slow down. "I dunno. If they're shitty enough to kidnap me, maybe they did. But we're already in here. Might as well see where this goes. Even if your kid can keep the ship alive, it would take hours flying around shooting it before we destroyed it. The *Reckoning* has forty-two million structure points in the hull."

"Oh," said Kavan, "I'm sure the kidnapping was more about the other stuff than the prize money."

The featureless hallway hit a T branch after a few minutes. Both sides went a short distance to corners going the same way they had been going already, a giant tuning fork shape. The game provided no mini-map for the interior here.

"Ugh."

She randomly decided to go left. They walked down more unremarkable corridor. Soon, they found branching hallways that led to open chambers full of nothing. From room to room, she jogged, hunting around for anything more useful than areas of an incomplete map.

"Damn. It's like the designers made a basic level layout, but never populated it with objects." She darted across a hall and peered into a huge room that could've been intended as a cafeteria or barracks. "It's so weird that our voices aren't echoing in here."

"Weirder than going out into space with only a little force field over our faces?"

"You've got a full helmet." She tapped him on the visor.

"Heavy armor. Most heavy armors do. Doesn't matter though."

Fawkes laughed. "Yeah, we can go out in space and the armor stops us from suffocating, but poison gas somehow still does damage to us."

"Oy. Reality taking a back seat to 'game mechanics.'" He stuck his head down another offshoot passage. "Empty."

"Hey guys," said Rallek over the comm, a steady barrage of laser blasts in the background. "I noticed you were roaming around, and there doesn't seem to be a minimap available, so I started tracing your route manually."

"Awesome. Guide us toward the nose end?" asked Fawkes.

"Sure. As soon as you start moving. I can't tell which way you're facing."

She jogged onward. "How's this?"

"You wanna turn left ninety degrees whenever you can. You're heading to the right side of the ship."

She doubled back to where she'd seen a turn, and took it.

"There. Now you're heading for the nose," said Rallek.

Kavan looked around. "Nose?"

"Well, if there's a bridge," said Rallek, "it's probably closer to the front end, right? This thing doesn't have a big superstructure type deal. It's kinda turd-shaped with one really skinny end and one fat end. I guess that's more of an icicle."

Kavan laughed.

"Space turd," said Nightwing. "That's the name of our next ship."

"No," said everyone else at once.

Fawkes jogged down the hall, taking directions from Rallek whenever the layout forced her to make a turn. Endless hallways the same size, shape, and color gnawed on her brain and made her feel hopelessly lost. Though the game sent no temperature feelings to her head, the stark metal made her shiver with imagined chill.

Eight minutes after entering the maze of corridors, a violet glow reflecting on a distant wall got her attention.

"There." She pointed, and ran for it.

Kavan trucked along behind her. She rushed down a hundred yard section of corridor before rounding a rightward corner where the light gleamed on the semi-reflective wall. At the end of a much shorter section, perhaps twenty feet in length, the corridor expanded into a big, round chamber with a metal obelisk at its center. The light emanated from a bowling-ball sized orb of violet energy hovering above the pedestal.

"Well, that's something," muttered Fawkes.

She crept up to it while eyeing the featureless chamber. No seams, turrets, cameras, or anything stood in the way. Upon reaching the middle of the room, she basked in a pleasant warmth radiating from the orb, like a campfire. That she noticed it despite her armor lent an air of supernatural eeriness.

Kavan sidled up next to her. "Well, that's something. What is it?"

"Well, if you want my technical opinion..." Fawkes folded her arms. "It's a 'quest objective.'"

"What do we do with it?"

She shrugged one shoulder. "Take it and bring it somewhere probably."

Fawkes started to reach for it, but wound up flailing her arms to keep balance when the room shuddered and rocked. "Nighthawk, what did you do?"

"Umm, nothing. Just trying not to die. Why?"

"Did something hit the *Reckoning*? Everything just shook."

"Fawkes..." said Kavan in a wavering tone. "You might want to hide."

She turned on her heel to look at him, and almost passed out.

A giant wide-bodied alien being had appeared in the formerly empty space between them and the only hallway out of the round chamber. Easily twelve feet tall and as wide as four humans, with a blobby, pudgy body of purple spotted skin that swelled out between armored panels, it clutched two rifles big enough for her to stick her entire head in the barrel, and missile launchers sprouted from each shoulder. The creature's head resembled the elongated body of a squid without tentacles. Six yellow eyes as big as tennis balls arranged in two vertical rows of three fixated on them.

"Oh, he doesn't look happy to see us," said Fawkes.

"Feeling's mutual." Kavan activated his shield.

Fawkes *Flickered* into stealth before creeping off to the left. After using that ability to hide instantly in plain sight, she had four seconds to get away from its vision cone or it would see her. Kavan raised his shield to absorb a pair of particle beam shots from its ridiculous rifles, but decided at the last minute to dive to the ground. Two rays of blinding orange light as thick as telephone poles flew across the room.

The alien trundled forward, chasing Kavan, who backed around the pedestal.

She stepped in behind it, raising her CL32 for an ambush... but froze when she looked at the health bar. It had 2.8 million hit points.

A raid boss meant to face off against twenty people or so.

"Shit. We can't fight this thing."

Kavan, being a party member, could still see her. He gave her a 'well duh!' stare. In that second of distraction, the alien lunged in and walloped him with one of its rifles (which also had a bunch of blades sticking out of the front end). He flew into the wall so hard he skimmed around the curve and fell to the floor twenty yards away.

"Ouch," said Kavan. "Well, that's my shield gone."

The alien emitted a series of burbling grumble noises somewhere between annoyance and indigestion.

She again raised her weapon, pondering an ambush to draw its attention off Kavan, but chickened out. While he could take a hit or two from this thing, it would paste her in one shot. He leapt to his feet and dove into a somersault to avoid another blast from the particle beam rifles. When he scrambled upright again and ran in circles, he flailed at her.

"Grab the damn orb!" yelled Kavan.

"But..." Guilt came and went. *Video game. He'll get back up.* "Okay."

While the alien boss smacked Kavan around the chamber like a kid with a shiny new ball, she approached the energy orb on the pedestal, holstering her CL32. A tingle spread across her fingers when she grasped it in both hands, like picking up a huge wad of warm cotton. The standard gesture to take an item, trying to stuff it into an inside jacket pocket, worked.

As soon as the orb disappeared into her inventory, and its purple light no longer flooded the chamber, the giant alien boss spun around to look straight at her. A faint *whoosh* sound accompanied Fawkes' body solidifying from semi-transparency, as if she needed the subtle clue to tell her she'd been spotted.

She locked stares with its eyestalks. "Well... shit."

35

EXPECTATIONS

Fawkes backed up a few steps.

The boss trained its gargantuan particle rifles at her.

Before it could fire, she activated her *Evasion* cooldown. The extra +90% to dodge caused the beams to miss her by inches on either side. Kavan had pulled it away from the entrance, so she did the only logical thing possible: ran like hell.

"We need a ride!" shouted Fawkes. "We got a big ass problem in here."

"Oh, wow. That's Glomulus," said Angel813, no doubt watching her via a 'spectator' window. "He's the second boss in the Stars of Eternity instance. Ugh, I remember wiping over and over to him for like three weeks. What's he doing in there?"

"Programmers are lazy," said Kavan. "For something like this that they thought only a handful of people would ever see *if* anyone ever saw it, they wouldn't develop a whole new boss fight."

"Why that one though?" asked Nighthawk.

"He's considered overly difficult." Angel813 grumbled. "The Halls of Infinitum, the next raid instance after SoE, is rated one tier harder, but Glomulus is still a rougher fight than everything in there except Hadrian... the last boss."

"So," asked Fawkes while sprinting down a plain grey tunnel, "what you're saying is, we're probably not going to kill this guy?"

"Two of you, not even sixty yet without even one purple item? No way, girl." Angel813 laughed. "Forty of us in full tier 1 gear took three weeks to learn that fight."

"I think Fawkes was being sarcastic," said Nighthawk.

Laser blasts, growling, and heavy slamming footsteps chased Fawkes down the hall.

"Oh, duh, right." Angel813 laughed.

"You got the magic pill," yelled Kavan. "I'm pounding this guy as hard as I can and he's not even noticing."

Rallek laughed. "I'm not going to make a joke out of that since we have a kid on channel."

"Hah!" Fawkes giggled. "Don't make me laugh now or I'm gonna die."

As if on cue, a particle beam missed her head by inches. She screamed and dove to the side, darting behind a corner to block line of sight. Without the *Evasion* cooldown protecting her, a raid boss would not miss a character twenty levels too low to be in the same room with it. A level forty had no business being here. Fortunately, this game didn't cheat by allowing a boss' shots to pass through walls. She hated ROI for that bullshit.

"You're going the wrong way," yelled Rallek. "Back toward the nose on the other side."

"Shit." Fawkes scrambled up to a right turn and darted around it.

"Good thing this guy is slow. But he's too damn fat for me to get past," said Kavan. "He fills the whole damn corridor."

"Sounds like Mrs. Reinhold," said Nighthawk amid laughter.

Kavan yelled, "As long as you've got that orb, I can't get aggro off you." His voice dropped to normal speech. "And don't talk about your teachers like that."

"We're circling close." Nighthawk let out a '*woo hoo!*' "I found a canyon in the hull that's like a big racetrack loop. Forces the fighters to get really close behind us so Angel and Rallek are mowing them down."

"They're endless," said Rallek, sounding exasperated.

"No kidding. They just respawn." Angel813 faked a yawn. "This is a video game people. It's not like this ship has a limited reserve of fighters and it'll run out."

Fawkes skidded around another corner two seconds before a missile exploded behind her, flinging her off her feet. She slid a few yards on her chest, bounced off the wall, and rolled to all fours amid a haze of smoke that reeked of rotten eggs. Glomulus thundered into view behind her, swinging his giant rifles up.

She couldn't help it and screamed; the scent of metal, the chill of the air, the stink of alien body odor far too real. For that instant, she feared the alien monster more than the men who tied her to a chair.

Kavan pointed his rifle at her between Glomulus' legs and fired.

A *pthoonk* noise preceded a sharp *bang.* His knockback grenade launched her out of the corridor into an offshoot less than second before the huge particle beams gouged melt marks on the floor.

The jolt of getting hurled around by friendly fire snapped her out of the paralytic fear of death. Fortunately, the punt grenade didn't do damage, only pushed players or creatures around. She clambered upright and sprinted.

"Left as soon as you can turn ninety degrees," yelled Rallek.

"The hallways are all the same!" she shouted, but managed to reach the closest place to turn before Glomulus came into view.

One corridor blurred to the next. Despite her stealthy character, the strike of her boots on the floor seemed deafening. The corridor started to shrink around her, and her breathing grew difficult. Nighthawk's cheering reminded her that these people would try to kill an eleven-year-old for something she did.

Fawkes closed her eyes for a second, swallowed, and got her panic under control. A new determination set in. They'd already pulled off something the developers never anticipated. Or, maybe they did, considering the boss appearing here. Had the developers expected a player to grab the orb and run, or try to take the boss on in a raid fight?

"Bah!" she yelled, skidding around another corner seconds before a pair of missiles careened past and exploded against the far wall.

The blast wave bumped her forward but didn't knock her down. She ran only thirty yards to the nearest turn despite the corridor going much farther. Any longer and the boss would have a clear line of sight on her. One hit and she'd be gone.

*Shit. The entry hall is really long with no turns. I'm screwed. I—*she glanced down at her forearm guard. *Evasion* had reset. If she timed it just right, she could possibly make it.

Fawkes pushed herself up to a hard sprint, trying to buy an extra few seconds of distance ahead of the plodding Glomulus. "Anyone know if hit resolution is determined before or after the attack animation?"

"Uhh, dude," said Nighthawk. "This isn't 2018. There's no behind the scenes 'rolling' anymore in MMOs. Shots go where shots go. If you can avoid the beam, you don't get hit. Real physics."

She grinned. "Awesome."

"You're getting close to the door," said Rallek.

Fawkes kept sprinting hard, but risked a quick peek over her shoulder. Glomulus' purple flesh reflected in blur on the walls, but he hadn't come around the corner yet. She hauled ass, taking the rapid left then right around the tuning-fork-shaped area and entered the final straightaway, some hundred yards to the exit with nowhere to hide.

Particle beams, unlike lasers, traveled slow enough to perceive, even slower than bullets. An agile, aware player could, in some cases, dodge them. She kept glancing back over her shoulder, waiting for the fat alien boss to show itself. In seconds, she got her wish.

Glomulus' six eyes seemed to bulge with glee at catching her in a long, confined place where she had no corners to hide behind. He lifted his rifles like a twelve-hundred-pound squid-headed redneck one-handing a pair of shotguns.

Two plasma beams blasted forth.

Fawkes waited the fraction of a second it took them to make it halfway to her and activated *Evasion*. The instant the cooldown went off, she stopped caring about looking behind her or even if those two beams hit. Only speed mattered.

Energy buzzed past her on either side, scorching the walls and covering her with tiny blue sparks of ionization. Fawkes leaned into her stride, running like the three men who'd abducted her were right behind her for real. She ran like the time she'd first shoplifted a candy bar at nine, and thought she'd go to jail for the rest of her life.

She ran like failure would get all four of her friends killed.

Particle beam after particle beam whizzed by. Missiles detonated on the ceiling inches behind her, others overshot and blew up well in front of her, leaving a haze of smoke she sprinted blindly into. Splash damage from the explosions whittled her health down bit by bit. Thirteen seconds later (with two seconds left of *Evasion*) the door came into view. Her health had gone down to thirty-one percent from nearby detonations. Nothing had actually hit her dead on yet.

"Shawn! Land now!" she screamed.

The last second of *Evasion* protected her from another double-blast of particle beam. Fawkes hurled herself at the door, bursting out into the open. She almost tripped over her own feet in an effort to make a sharp left turn and break line-of-sight. Her whole body trembled with adrenaline. Despite all that running, she shivered with excess energy, wired up and jacked to keep going, not even breathing hard.

If nothing else, I can run around this building.

Five seconds later, the *Stormbringer* shot out from behind a distant outcropping of tech and glided toward her. Both turrets fired so fast at the gnat swarm of fighters that the green pulse laser bolts sprayed like water from hoses.

She started running toward the ship, but stalled when Nighthawk erupted in cackling laughter.

Glomulus, a twelve-foot-tall, nine-foot-wide blob of alien flesh, squeezed itself out through a door the size of a submarine hatch, and snapped free with enough force to wind up falling flat on its front. She gawked, stunned at the cartoonish ridiculousness of the way the game animated that.

"Crap! Too many fighters. Be right back," yelled Nighthawk.

Kavan emerged from the doorway, firing his rifle into the big alien's back, not that it noticed.

Fawkes snapped out of her mind fog and ran for cover behind a large component sticking up from the hull. Glomulus rose to his feet and fired, scorching holes in the high-tech forest around her. She leapt over a gap in the armor plating, only a short distance across but easily thirty feet deep. Chased by particle beams, she darted from cover to cover, hiding among the boxy protrusions and towers littering the skin of the *Reckoning*. Glomulus thundered after her, taking a shot whenever even one pixel of Fawkes' character came into his view.

"Over here, ya big fat slug," shouted Kavan, but despite his best efforts, the alien ignored him.

"Coming back around now," said Nighthawk.

Fawkes made her way in a circle, heading back to the clearing by the doorway. An explosion overhead sent a huge antenna collapsing toward her like a felled tree. She leapt back in time to let it crash to the ground in front of her, but the attack forced her to divert to the left and shimmy through a canyon between two long, boxy structures. She squeezed out the far end not a second after Glomulus lined up a shot down the gap. Fawkes dove to the ground out of the way of the particle beam, which hit an anti-fighter turret as big as her brother's van, destroying it in a shower of sparks and metal fragments. Two seconds after she stood back up, a burning fighter craft came hurtling straight at her.

Screaming, Fawkes dove into a hole that turned out to be a cylindrical recess with no exits. She curled up in a ball on the bottom, guarding her face with both arms for all the good that would do against an exploding starfighter. Everything shook with the explosion of the ship tumbling over the hull above. Metal bits and smoke poured in on her head.

Whoa. She simultaneously felt awe at the programmers for making such a realistic game, and nearly shit her pants at almost being pasted by a crashing space ship. Numb to it all, she leapt on a small ladder and pulled herself back out of the pit before Glomulus could catch up and trap her in a little hole where she'd have zero chance to survive.

He barely managed to point his rifles at her again before she leapt out of sight behind a huge, boxy component. With the tromp of the alien boss shaking the ground behind her, she ran to another fighter turret, which pivoted to the right in anticipation of something approaching. Glomulus fired a bolt that barely missed her face. With a squeak, she skidded to a stop and darted left, behind the turret.

The *Stormbringer* slid sideways out from behind a huge superstructure studded with smallish antennas. The turret she hid behind began firing tiny (by comparison) laser blasts into the corvette's shields, each dissipating in a beautiful ripple effect. Glomulus' gurgling rambles drifted closer. She started to run for the next place to hide, but four blue laser blasts from the *Stormbringer* converged on the giant alien. The main guns knocked him flat on his back, charred, with a little more than half health remaining.

"Whoa," said Nighthawk. "Tubby's got some hit points."

Glomulus let out an angry groan and wobbled upright.

Nighthawk fired the ship's lasers again and launched a torpedo for good measure.

The energy blast left Glomulus with a scrap of health. A conflict in the aggro mechanics must've occurred, as the boss couldn't seem to decide between firing at Fawkes or the *Stormbringer*. In the two seconds between laser strike and the slower torpedo arriving, he did nothing but shift facing back and forth between them.

With a fleshy *splut*, the torpedo stuck in Glomulus' blobby chest, knocking him back one step. All six eyes on little stalks bent down to look at it, but whatever code forced him to attack the character with the quest orb kicked in, and he raised his rifles at Fawkes. Before he could fire, the torpedo detonated, showering the area with purple slime.

"Come on!" shouted Nighthawk.

He wheeled the *Stormbringer* around to put its rear end toward them and opened the cargo ramp, which reached full extension the same time the ship touched down on its landing pads. Fawkes ran through a hail of laser bolts coming down from the fighter ships trying to hit the ship. Fortunately, even a player character in a fighter would have a hard time seeing, much less hitting, someone on foot, and NPC pilots had no programming to do such a scummy thing—at least on purpose. She jumped onto the ramp right as the ship started to lift off.

Kavan's leap fell short; he landed with a grip on the ramp, legs dangling.

"Don't close it!" yelled Fawkes. "Your dad's not all the way in."

"Sorry. Gotta move. Fighters," yelled Nighthawk.

"I'm slipping," said Kavan. "Screw it. I'll meet you after respawn."

The *Stormbringer* executed a sudden vertical dip and deceleration. Kavan floated up and shot into the cargo hold like a human missile, crashing into the far wall and losing another twenty-two percent health.

"Oof!" he rolled flat on his back and lay still.

"You okay? That didn't actually hurt, did it?" asked Fawkes.

The *whirr* of the cargo ramp closing almost overpowered the endless laser barrage from the turrets.

"It looked like it should've hurt, so I said ouch. Psychosomatic." Kavan grabbed her arm and let her help him up. "We should get to the bridge and strap in. This is going to be rough."

"Yeah."

They raced up the stairs and down the main hall to the bridge, leaping into the two seats on either side of Nighthawk. Fawkes squealed at the viewscreen showing a trench in the *Reckoning's* hull, narrow to the point the *Stormbringer* couldn't fit in it level. Nighthawk had tilted the ship diagonal, leaving mere inches of clearance on either side.

"Why are we playing chicken?" asked Fawkes.

"Uhh, too many fighters," said Nighthawk. "The encounter's tuned for forty ships, all constantly killing the fighters. The respawn is timed for that...

so since we're only one ship, we can't kill them fast enough. There's over 1,500 of them out there."

"It's a goddamned piranha swarm," said Angel813.

Nighthawk grinned. "We're flying toward the back end now. I'm gonna do the pop up thing again. The *Reckoning* will try to shoot us with everything it's got, and I'm hoping it'll take out a bunch of fighters in the crossfire."

Fawkes nodded.

"Ballsy," said Kavan.

Nighthawk laughed.

Fawkes clung to the armrests of her chair for thirteen seconds, vibrating with unfocused emotion. So many fighters chased them that red lasers fell like a rainstorm on the artificial terrain scrolling by on the viewscreen. Elation and dread merged into a single, irresistible need to scream—a raw outburst to release tension.

Nighthawk jerked back on the stick, and the hull of the *Reckoning* fell away to reveal the starry expanse of outer space. A soft, roaring explosion rumbled in the distance behind them, probably hundreds of small fighters blowing up as the capital ship's large laser batteries unleashed their fury.

Angle813 whooped. "We made—"

Fawkes' vision filled with fire. The burn intensified until the entire world became silent whiteness. Only the sound of her hard breathing existed for a few seconds, echoing over deep silence.

Shit. Did they melt our brains?

The blinding glare faded to black.

"You know, I really should've tried doing something reckless, like engaging the warp drive too close to another ship instead of trying to climb out." Nighthawk's voice came from everywhere at once.

"What happened?" asked Fawkes.

"Ship blew up," said Kavan. "We're dead."

"What's with the blackout?" asked Fawkes.

"Never died in a ship before?" Nighthawk chuckled. "The game is trying to figure out where to respawn us. Give it a moment."

"We died?" asked Rallek.

Fawkes cracked up laughing. "We tried to take on a forty-crew raid boss with one ship. What did you expect would happen?"

36

QUEST TURN-IN

Fawkes floated for a while in blackness before a sense of gravity returned. Floor manifested under her boots. Background music of the cantina persuasion started, and scenery filled in.

Silver-accented round booths with black cushions lined the walls of a modest-sized bar. Stairs off to the left led up to a second floor with more of the same over-stylized tables. Rallek, Nighthawk, Kavan, and Angel813 had all appeared standing near her under the flickering glow of multicolored light beams that reacted to the music.

The soft *ping* of an incoming message chimed from everyone at once.

She opened a display window to check. An email with the title 'Ship Destroyed' appeared as new.

Your spacecraft was destroyed during a raid event, and is inaccessible until the next reset day. The ship will be available at the starport facility on Malinoa IV, the nearest settled planet.

Considering they'd pulled this on a Sunday, they only had to wait a few days for the reset.

Kavan growled. "Dammit. We're stuck on this planet."

"Not necessarily." Rallek smiled. "We could use a portal."

"Oh, Mr. Moneybags," muttered Kavan.

"Says the guy who bought his ship with real cash." Angel813 grinned and leaned a little closer to him.

Fawkes glanced at Rallek with a 'you see that?' expression. Rallek remained oblivious. When Kavan returned her smile and took her hand, Fawkes almost gasped.

The crew migrated to a seat at one of the tables, filing one by one past the narrow gap to the ring-shaped bench.

An NPC woman with hot pink skin and green hair approached. "Hi, can I get you guys anything?"

Nighthawk ordered chicken nuggets and fries.

After he finished laughing, Rallek got the same. Plus a beer.

"You have steak?" asked Fawkes.

"I'm sorry, this is mostly a bar. We have pizza, hot pretzels, wings, nuggets, fries, onion rings, and glorblatt."

Everyone cringed at the same time.

"Uhh, wings," said Fawkes. "And a beer."

Kavan got a basket of onion rings and a beer.

The woman smiled, thanked them, and walked off.

"Woo!" Nighthawk raised his hands, clapped, and pounded a little drumbeat on the table. "That was awesome!"

"You're not at all upset we got shot down?" asked Kavan, still sounding miffed.

"Nah." Nighthawk shook his head. "That was super fun."

"It's damn amazing we stayed alive that long." Rallek reached across the table and clapped Nighthawk on the shoulder. "Nice work."

"Ehh. Thanks. I knew we were gonna die on the way out. As soon as I got under the laser's arc, I figured it would be impossible for us to escape, but hey, you got the thing right?"

Fawkes nodded. "Yeah." She sent out party invites to re-establish the group. Once the line of portraits appeared off to her right, she accessed her inventory and pulled out the purple orb. "I have no idea what this thing does."

"I just got a quest update for *The Lost Dreadnought*." Rallek gazed into space as if reading. "Says we've discovered the 'quantum core' that Dr. Prakash sent us to retrieve. Oops. Did we skip a step?"

Fawkes shrugged, examining the orb in her hands. "It's usable... I wonder what it does."

"Where do we turn it in?" asked Nighthawk.

"There's nothing in the mission log about that." Rallek glanced over at her.

Kavan scratched his head. "We never actually got a quest from a Dr. Prakash."

"Maybe we have to use the item for the update?" asked Rallek

"Okay." Fawkes 'invoked' the orb.

The cantina dissolved once more to black nothingness, except this time, all the characters remained visible.

"Well, that's different." Kavan gazed around. "I wonder what this is?"

"Holographic communication maybe?" Rallek shrugged.

Darkness gave way to subtle tones of blue-grey, and a large but austere office appeared around them, the sort of office that belonged more in the real world than a spacefaring video game universe. The characters slid around like chess pieces, going from sitting in a ring to a straight line upon a black sofa, facing a big silicon desk. Three men observed them from behind it.

Only one sat, a middle-aged man of Indian descent in an expensive-looking pale grey suit. Short hair slicked back over his head lent an air of menace to a smile that mixed predatory annoyance with admiration.

To his right stood another middle-aged man resembling an over-the-hill hippie forced into a shiny blue suit and tie. Though his beard had been trimmed neat (his hair less so), he had an air of not belonging in a place like this. He offered the most genuine smile of the three.

The third man, likely Japanese, appeared younger than the others, perhaps in his late thirties or early forties. His immaculate black suit didn't look as expensive as the others' outfits, though he clasped his hands in front of himself with an expression of stern propriety.

Behind the men, a window looked out over a modern real-world city. Amazon Secure police helicopters hovering around the Golden Gate Bridge in the distance suggested a view of San Francisco. Of course, that didn't mean much. Active-display windows could make any office appear to be anywhere. Plus, she felt pretty damn sure they remained in the game, considering everyone still appeared to be their characters.

She pulled a bit of her hair into view to check. *Yep. Still pink.*

"Welcome," said the Indian man. "I am Vinod Prakash, CEO of Cognition Systems International. With me are Gerald Barker, my co-founder, and Leonard Nakamura, senior vice president of our legal team."

"Congrats!" said Gerald, his smile widening. "I gotta say, you guys cleared that mission way faster than we ever expected."

Vinod's eyebrows flattened. His evident annoyance with Gerald didn't dent his false smile. "Yes, congratulations are indeed in order. I'm most curious how you found the *Reckoning* without meeting my alter ego in the game."

"Well," said Kavan, "We got the codes to let our ship's sensors pick up the warp trace it left behind, so we figured we'd have to run all over the star map to try and find a pattern to it. And, since we're running all over the place, might as well grab a mission. I picked one up to evacuate some settlers from a geologically unstable moon, and on the way there, we just tripped across the *Reckoning*."

Gerald's eyebrows inched up. "Wow. Luck. Guess it was a bad idea to build an instance for this quest inside a world boss that could be randomly tripped over." He nudged Vinod's chair. "Told you we should've put it on a planet somewhere behind a door that only appears to players on the right stage of the mission."

"Interesting." Vinod stared at Fawkes past steepled fingers. "Very interesting how you just happened to stumble across it like that. Almost as if you could read our minds."

Fawkes narrowed her eyes at him. "We're not the ones reading minds."

The predatory nature of Vinod's smile deepened. "I thought so."

Oops. Bastard baited me.

Kavan's smile went forced. Rallek put a hand on her leg.

"Okay, let's dispense with the bullshit then." Fawkes sat up straight. "Yeah, we found a back door into your network, but someone left the keys on the porch. It looked like a mission."

"It's still breaking and entering even if the homeowner left their key outside," said Vinod.

"Oh." Fawkes rolled her head around sarcastically. "If you're going to start splitting legal hairs, how about we discuss kidnapping, torture, and attempted murder?"

Nakamura glanced at Prakash, with one eyebrow up.

"Your associates weren't exactly subtle when they had me tied to a chair with a hammer ready to smash my toes flat until I told them what I did with CSI's information."

"And they tried to kill me," said Angel813. "Drove up to my apartment and started shooting."

Vinod narrowed his eyes. "You gained access to game data files, and then mysteriously located the *Reckoning* shortly afterward."

Rallek looked up from a holographic display panel. "Oh, if you guys are going to screw us out of the prize money, you might want to update your game before too many people notice the leaderboard page announcing that we won it."

Vinod's glare came close to glass-melting hot.

"What?" Gerald looked at him. "You think these guys cheated?"

Vinod tore his glare off Fawkes and peered up at Gerald. "How else do you explain them finding it so fast? Joe Nguyen assured me no one would be able to complete this mission for at least a year."

"Dumb luck would technically explain it," said Kavan. "The *Reckoning* warps around in a pattern, teleporting from sector to sector. At any given moment, it exists somewhere. I mean the odds are, pardon the pun, astronomical, but it *is* possible."

Fawkes shifted her gaze to him. *It's not a pattern. It's random.* She opened her mouth to correct him, but bit her tongue. *Duh. Calm down, Kota. You're too pissed off to think. We're not supposed to know it's random.*

Gerald chuckled, smiling so hard his eyes seemed to vanish. "The bread-crumbing from following the warp drive traces is supposed to lead to the wreckage of another corvette that tried to take it on, and it's got data logs of communication with the 'Doctor Prakash' character. He's developed a device that would allow a ship to predict where the *Reckoning* would be, and also a module that makes it impossible for the *Reckoning's* sensors to detect players' ship or the pulse laser batteries to target it."

"So you *don't* force a raid fight." Nighthawk grinned. "If we had that component, we could've flown right in and landed by that door."

"I'm still waiting to hear how you managed to do that without being vaporized." Vinod again glared at Fawkes.

Nighthawk tugged at the nonexistent lapels of his armor. "I'm just that good."

"Bullshit," said Vinod.

"Hey." Kavan raised a hand. "Easy. I know he doesn't look like it, but he's only eleven."

"Daaaaaad." Nighthawk sighed.

Gerald chuckled.

"Look." Nighthawk leaned forward. "I'm sure the game recorded that whole thing. Watch the replay. It's all legit. We didn't cheat."

"I was." Gerald grinned. "As soon as combat began between the *Reckoning* and a ship on the leaderboard, we all got a notification. I pulled up the spectator view expecting some hothead to be doing it wrong, but I went through two bowls of popcorn watching that epicness. What I'm curious about though, since you didn't have the quest update from the Dr. Prakash character, and you didn't use any information you found inside the network, how did you know to go inside the ship?"

Fawkes traced a box in midair. "You have heard of sensors right? I figured there was no way a single ship would be expected to take the *Reckoning* out, so I scanned it and spotted a purple component. Never saw purple before, so I zoomed in. Looked like a door. We were stuck in combat already, so... we decided to take a chance."

"Glomulus, really?" asked Angel813. "Everyone hates that piece of shit."

Kavan glanced at her. "Come on, guys..."

"Dad. Bad words aren't going to hurt me." Nighthawk overacted a sigh.

Gerald laughed. "Oh, yeah, we know. Used him because we hoped it would be a hint to run and not try to fight. You completely missed the reactor core the boss was supposed to fall into." He opened a display window already showing a map of the *Reckoning's* interior, and pointed out a huge room with a big pit in the middle, spanned by a narrow metal walkway. "He'd have chased you across this catwalk, but halfway across, would've crushed it and fallen to his death."

"Oh. Guess we went the wrong way." Fawkes shrugged.

"So you expect me to believe this is legitimate?" asked Vinod.

Gerald smiled. "Well, they clearly didn't know about the reactor room."

"Hold on there a sec dude." Fawkes raised a hand. "There's still the issue of CSI conducting an experiment on mental manipulation that resulted in that piece of shit Steyr winning an election he shouldn't have. Not to mention your plan to data mine brains and sell peoples wants and desires to the highest bidder."

Gerald blinked at her. "What?"

"You don't know?" asked Rallek.

Vinod fidgeted.

"Yeah, maybe this is one guy's pet project." Fawkes stood and leaned toward the desk. "I admit I followed Tom Urban's clues and found a backdoor into your real-world network through the game world... and I saw the files about the election and the data mining. The Neurona 4 helmets basically let your system index people's memories like a database. You can run a search on just about anything and extract snippets of memory, or even implant subliminal suggestions. That's why you tried to have us killed."

Gerald shook his head, chuckling. "Oh, come on... that stuff is part of a storyline we haven't implemented yet. The idea is to mix the game with a conspiracy angle in real life."

"Nice try." Fawkes held up her arm, but armor got in the way of showing off handcuff marks. Also, her character hadn't inherited them from Dakota. *Duh.* "If all that stuff is fictional, why did I get tasered and kidnapped? That was *not* fun."

Vinod flexed his steepled fingers back and forth for a moment in quiet. "You need to realize that Governor Steyr has some influential friends. Certain unfortunate events which may or may not have happened to you outside the game were beyond CSI's control or influence."

Gerald stared at Vinod in shock. "Seriously? That stuff is *real?*"

"It felt damn real to me. This one alley I guess was supposed to be foreboding or something looked an awful lot like a place where I had a real bad experience as a teen."

"Yeah, well..." Gerald grasped at the air as if trying to pluck words with his hands. "We know the game can prod the subconscious to invoke strong emotional memories. It's quite likely that the rendering engine picked up on nuances of that environment and incorporated them into the scenery to enhance the mood of the gameplay. It's all automatic in the engine. No one's actively viewing that or anything. Like, if someone's afraid of the color green, in a scene meant to be scary, it'll use a lot of green."

She clenched her hands into fists atop her knees. "Making me think about a guy assaulting me when I was sixteen is a little over the line."

"So is that why you broke into our network?" asked Vinod. "Some sort of revenge play for triggering you?"

She scowled.

"What is it you want?" asked Nakamura.

"Not to have to look over my goddamned shoulder for a black car," said Fawkes. "I wanna go home and not wonder if I'm going to wake up tied to a chair again."

"I just wanna play the game," said Nighthawk. "And going home would be cool."

"They're probably honing in on us now," said Kavan. "Fair bet they've disabled our logout so we're stuck here until their goons find us in the real world."

"Goons?" asked Gerald with a hint of a chuckle. "Who uses that word?"

"It wouldn't look good for CSI to back out of the prize after announcing we won it," said Angel813.

Vinod slid his index fingers up either side of his nose, rubbing, eyes closed. "How much damage is there? Who else knows about the information you found during the data breach?"

Her younger self, eager to exploit a chance to castrate an evil corporation got into a fight with the lazy, older Dakota who just wanted to go home and get back to her normal—if inglorious—existence. Pour coffee, play Axillon99, and maybe see where life with Eric would go. Mental gears ground together. If it affected only her, she'd have let out the defiant side.

Fawkes leaned forward and looked over at Nighthawk, seeing not the twentysomething, athletic pilot, but the terrified scrawny boy who lay unconscious not far from where her body ignored the real world. He didn't deserve to be caught up in a pissing contest with a company that had the clout to send killers after them.

"I've got a few remote clients set up to send out emails with all the data about Steyr's election and your plans to steal information from people's heads. So far, I haven't sent it anywhere as you're obviously aware of because there hasn't been a shitstorm. But I should probably hit the proverbial button soon to stop the script from automatically doing so. You know, a dead-woman switch."

Vinod's gaze felt like an x-ray beam.

"The gamer in us wanted to try and finish the prize mission first." Fawkes smiled, as innocent as she could pull off. "I figured if this leaked to the media, especially that CSI meddled with an election, Axillon99 would get shut down when the company imploded."

"Holy shit." Gerald ran his hands up over his wild mane. "You're really serious? We're doing this? We *did* that?"

Nighthawk's posture resembled that of an eleven-year-old about to be grounded. He frowned at the rug. "Don't shut down the game."

"Seems we've arrived at an impasse," said Vinod.

"Not completely. I have a suggestion." Fawkes pointed a finger gun at him. "I'll agree not to go public with any of the information we found in exchange for CSI giving all five of us the full ten million dollar prize for the contest instead of dividing it. We all stay quiet, you call off your dogs, and leave us alone."

"Whoa." Rallek looked at her. "You're gonna sell out?"

Angel813 bit her lip.

Kavan didn't look pleased, but also didn't voice an objection.

"Look. Nighthawk's only a kid. Yeah, maybe I'm offering to sell out, but I can't put his life at risk. Politicians and corporations are going to be scumbags no matter what I do. Sure, if we leak the info, CSI might go down in flames... and take our favorite game with it. I'm willing to stay quiet for the money, and so we're still able to play."

Vinod leaned back in his chair, again steepling his fingers in front of his face.

"I think they should stop reading minds, and making people do stuff." Nighthawk shook his head. "That's crappy. If people found out about that, no one would want to use a gaming helmet ever again—for any game, not just Ax. You guys make buttloads of money on subscriptions already. Bad guys *always* screw each other over. If someone pays you to read memories and gets mad enough, they go public and everything goes down."

"Kid's got a point," said Fawkes. "Everyone you do shade with becomes a potential blackmailer."

"Oh, no..." Gerald shook his head. "I'm not gonna be a party to this level of bullshit. This isn't what we built, Vinod. We're an entertainment company. We forge dreams, entire universes. Our legacy shouldn't go out like that."

Vinod sighed through his nose. "How can I be sure you will keep your word?"

"About as sure as I can be you won't send guys to kidnap me again." She smirked.

"Excuse us for a moment." Vinod looked up at Nakamura standing beside his chair.

Both men disappeared into thin air.

"Wow." Gerald paced around. "I'm really sorry about all this. I had no idea any of that nefarious crap was going on."

"Nefarious?" asked Kavan. "Who uses that word?"

Gerald laughed. "Touché."

"I still can't believe you're willing to sell out." Rallek's eyebrows tilted up in the middle. "It's like against everything you believe in."

"Not much choice here. Doesn't mean I'm going to stop resisting corporations that crap on the normal people. I just don't want a little kid's blood on my hands."

"I'm not a little kid. I'm eleven," muttered Nighthawk.

"This is a giant corporation with political connections. I'm a nobody barista. He's an eleven-year-old boy. I just want my life back. I want you guys to stop getting shot at."

"Getting shot at happens anyway. You saw where I live," said Angel813 with a faint grin.

"That can always change." Kavan glanced at her.

Nighthawk glanced between Angel813 and his father for a second, then grinned.

"It feels wrong to let them get away with it, especially that creep Steyr, but I see where you're coming from and I appreciate you thinking of Shawn." Kavan pulled off his armor helmet and scratched his sweat-dampened hair. "And the ten million is pretty tempting."

"More like six and change after taxes," said Rallek.

"Still." Kavan chuckled. "Nice little rainy day fund."

Vinod and Nakamura reappeared.

"I will agree to your terms on the condition that you sign non-disclosure agreements and a confession to illegally breaching our network. The confession will remain sealed as long as your lips do."

"No problem with the NDA, but if you want me to sign a confession, I want a video statement from you admitting that CSI hired mercenaries to kidnap and torture me and also conduct a drive-by shooting on Angel."

Vinod fidgeted, glancing at Nakamura who shook his head to the negative.

"Then you skip the confession and hang it all on the NDA. I'm guessing if we go public, we would have to pay back the prize money."

"That is correct," said Nakamura.

"Well, if we go public, there's a good chance our favorite game will die... so, we won't do that." She smiled.

"You're really that worried about losing access to Axillon99?" asked Gerald, eyebrows up.

Fawkes cackled. "Have you ever played it? To be transported bodily into a vast universe like that? It's amazing... I'm still pouring goddamned coffee for a living because I throw all my time at the game instead of hunting for a real job." She sighed. "What can I say... I'm an addict."

"I must say that I am surprised." Vinod gave her the 'up-and-down' look. "I'd expected a bit more rebellious idealism from you."

She rolled her eyes. "My idea of rebellious idealism is charging an asshole customer for an extra shot of espresso and not putting it in his coffee."

"How say the rest of you?" asked Vinod.

"I'm only eleven, so I can't sign anything. Up to my dad." Nighthawk smiled.

"Ten million ostensibly as winning the prize for *The Lost Dreadnought*, no one shoots at us, and we keep quiet? I can live with that." Kavan nodded.

"I want to get home to my cats," said Angel813. "I'm good with it."

Gerald kept staring at Vinod like the man had shot his dog.

"Very well. Mr. Nakamura will draw up the appropriate paperwork. You will, of course, all need to be present in person to sign the documents, the child notwithstanding. Our legal team will contact you via email in the real world and make arrangements to fly you to San Fran." Vinod's hostility melted off to the warm, if insincere, façade he'd likely have shown winners who hadn't discovered the brain wonkery. "In accordance with the contest terms, there's also some media appearances, and you agree that CSI can use your likenesses, your characters of course, in promotional materials. Insofar as the minor is concerned, we would include him only with his father's consent. Though..." He grinned. "A prodigy pilot like that could probably land some endorsement deals. Especially if he's photogenic."

"Great." Fawkes grinned. *The more famous we get, the safer I feel.*

"Very well then. If there's nothing else, we'll send you back to the game." Vinod smiled.

Gerald pulled open a terminal window. "Oh, may as well give you a little bonus." He poked a few buttons on the holographic panel, causing faint chirps. "There we are. As a token for how awesome that was, I've waived the lockout on your ship. It's waiting for you already."

"Awesome!" yelled Nighthawk. "Mission time!"

"Umm, not yet, kiddo." Kavan threw an arm around him. "We got a bit of a drive ahead of us."

Nighthawk's adult face somehow managed to convey the awed relief of a young boy. "Ooh, yeah. We don't have to hide anymore."

"Right." Fawkes leaned into Rallek and muttered, "And that's why I sold out."

37

NON-DISCLOSURE

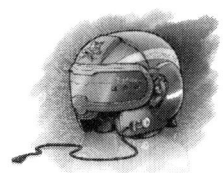

Dakota lay spread eagle in her own bed, one leg under the sheet, in her usual sleeping outfit: nothing. *Not* smelling stink or being in contact with fabric that hadn't seen detergent in time measurable in years left her content, with no desire to move.

William and Shawn had opted to take a train back to Philly, but not before exchanging contact information with Christina. Eric drove again, and they road-tripped her back to Hartford. Dakota had spent Monday in and out of sleep at Eric's place, wearing one of his shirts after running the clothing she'd been in for three days through the laundry twice.

She'd called Hal not really caring if she got fired, but she didn't *try* to get canned. He asked more questions about how she was doing and coping rather than when she'd be in again, but she asked about returning Tuesday, which he agreed to. Neither she nor Eric had touched Axillon99 at all Monday.

The alarm started beeping at 5:30 a.m., nine minutes after her eyes opened.

Dakota rolled over and silenced it, then crawled out of bed and headed to the shower. By 5:51, she'd exited her building and walked the few blocks to the Amazon Café. She went in, but left the doors locked since it didn't open until 6:00 a.m. Going about the normal routine of morning setup anchored her back to reality. Disappointingly enough, by the time she unlocked the front doors, the past few days no longer even seemed real, as though she'd never left work to live like a post-apocalyptic rebel.

Blake rushed in at 6:01 and grabbed her in a hug. "Oh my God, are you okay? What happened? Hal said you were abducted?"

"I was... it's dealt with." She thought over what to tell him, considering the NDA... but the company wasn't flying her out to San Fran until the end of the

week, and she hadn't signed anything yet. "I stumbled into a network by accident. They thought I saw some confidential stuff, but I didn't... just got into
the folder. As soon as I realized what happened, I backed out. They didn't
believe me about not seeing anything, hence the thugs grabbing me, but we
came to an arrangement."

He nodded. "Oh, good. When Hal said abducted, I thought..."

"No... thankfully." She sighed. "No bad touching... well, I mean not in a
sexual sense. They slapped me around a bit."

Hal arrived and rushed over. He began to reach for her, but froze.
"Hug okay?"

"Yeah." She accepted his embrace, which felt a bit like having a second
father.

"If there's anything you need to talk about, I'm here." Hal nodded once.

She gave him the same explanation as Blake about corporate espionage.
She still had a hint of red on her wrists, which she showed them, as well as the
photos she took of her earlier condition since some part of her still felt the
need to provide proof for calling out.

"Oh, Hal?" asked Dakota, as he wandered toward the office.

"Yes?" He turned around to smile at her.

"I hate to have to ask, but would it be okay if I took Friday and Monday? I
have to go to San Francisco."

"San Fran?" He blinked. "Seriously?"

"Yeah... you know that game I play? The contest they ran?"

He nodded. "Yeah."

"We won it." She grinned.

"No shit?" asked Hal.

Blake gasped.

She poked Hal in the stomach. "Language."

He leaned back with a deep, baritone laugh. "So, our girl is a millionaire
now?"

"Not technically yet. That's why I've gotta go to SF. Sign documents, pose
for some publicity stills, then lube up and bend over for the IRS."

Blake blushed.

"You plannin' on coming back?" asked Hal.

She folded her arms and looked around. "You know, most people probably
wouldn't, but I think I'm gonna stay, at least for a while. I love coffee and I
hate change. And... I'd miss you guys."

HER TRIP TO SAN FRANCISCO WENT BY IN A BLUR OF MEDIA ATTENTION,
limousines, and publicity photos. The whole crew got to meet some of the
voice actors for the NPCs, as well as a few of the programmers, digital artists,
and mission designers.

Vinod Prakash wound up being a bit shorter than she expected in real life. Their meeting, although pleasant, held an undertone of tension. Shawn became a minor celebrity within the CSI office, as most of the programming team gushed over the in-game recording of their run on the *Reckoning*. They'd posted the video on the company website, and it had clocked over eighteen million hits. As soon as their marketing people got a good look at him, they fawned. The kid might wind up making serious money if William let him do commercials.

Gerald Barker released a video congratulating them on the win and announcing that the quest remained active, but instead of a financial reward, any crew that completed it would win an exclusive corvette available only from that mission. They named it the *Stormbringer* class in honor of her crew, and also upgraded their ship to the new model. The overall shape remained the same, though slightly larger with more room for weapons and cargo, a sleeker design with silver edges and black interior, and increased stats that bumped it up two tiers. Other ships of similar tier were twice the size, but flew like bricks. The new design had hull and shield points to match its bigger tier-mates, but a narrower profile with almost fighter-like handling.

Shawn went over the moon.

Dakota felt a knot of shame at herself when she signed the forms agreeing not to disclose any proprietary information she may or may not have been exposed to during the course of the mission. The documents didn't outright state she'd invaded the network; everything had been phrased in maybes and conjecture.

Gerald pulled her aside and thanked her for not destroying the company he'd spent the past twenty years building. He assured her he would do every-thing in his power to shut that stuff down. She bristled at the voter manipula-tion most of all, but Eric seemed to think that with Steyr being an independent without the support of either major party, plus a known scum-bag, he wouldn't last long before some old scandal bit him in the ass and forced him out of office.

After enjoying the Hollywood treatment for a weekend, they returned home. Watching William and Christina get cute at the airport while Shawn grinned at them got her feeling all sorts of clingy with Eric. Eventually, they boarded a flight to New York, and a normal life.

A normal life plus a few million dollars.

Eric swooped into the Amazon Café on Wednesday. Dakota clocked off for her thirty minute break, snagged a turkey-gouda wrap from the cooler along with a sugar free iced tea, and joined him at the table.

"So how's it feel to be famous?" asked Eric.

She shrugged. "We're famous in a universe that doesn't really exist. Here, we're just some game nerds who got a prize."

"You didn't see that Japan thing did you?"

She tilted her head. "What Japan thing?"

"Our faces are everywhere over there. There's even Fawkes-themed tampons."

Dakota's cheeks flashed hot with blush. "You are making that up."

"'Fraid not. But they made you an anime girl."

"Ugh. At least tell me the character looks like an adult?"

"Yeah, but there's other sites—"

She put a finger over his mouth. "I'm going to stop you right there."

He took a box of chicken nuggets and fries out of a white paper bag.

Dakota chuckled. "Seriously?"

"What? I had an urge to eat like a kid." He winked. "I used to eat this stuff all the damn time at his age."

"But you're not his age anymore. That stuff'll kill ya."

"Old maid." He stuck out his tongue.

Lettuce bits sprayed from her mouth as she laughed.

They ate and chatted about whether or not they should log in tonight or do the date thing. Neither option gained ground, leading Eric to suggest flipping a coin. Dakota started to laugh, but froze at the sight of a familiar greasy-haired creep on the television over the counter. His eyes still had red around them from the Habanero Hammer spray. Text along the bottom read 'Man attacks Steyr campaign.'

"Blake," said Dakota, "turn that up a bit?"

"... has come forward claiming to have information that alleges Governor Steyr manipulated the election, and also that an as-yet-unnamed technology company has the ability to affect how people think."

Eric gawked at the TV before whipping around and whispering, "Holy shit! You broke the NDA?"

"Nope." She nibbled at her wrap.

"That's the dude you maced..."

"Yep." Dakota sipped her tea.

"But you gave him the info? Wow." He grinned. "I thought you really did sell out there for a while."

She offered a nonchalant shrug. "Who says I *gave* that creep anything? Johnathan Miles Parker, age twenty-nine. Employed at Amazon Whole Foods." Dakota rambled off his driver's license number, social security number, home address, parents' home address, bank account number, telephone number, and the names of his two dogs.

Eric stared at her.

She gave him a sly wink. "We promised none of *us* would go public or give the information to anyone. Nothing about anyone else oh, just happening to find Tom Urban's back door and going poking around in there on their own, into a specific set of folders that a particular company never managed to delete."

"You magnificent bastard," he whispered before chuckling.

She stole a French fry and pointed it at him. "I'm a girl. I can't be a bastard. Besides. Took him long enough to find it."

Eric stuffed a nugget and a mass of fries in his mouth at the same time, hurrying to chew it enough to speak, and wound up coughing on it.

"Don't kill yourself."

"Dayum girl. I bet them CSI mother—" He glanced at the small door to Hal's office. "Idiots from CSI are probably going to have a chat with him. Besides, you shot that Habanero crap straight up his nose. Dude probably *just* got out the hospital yesterday..."

Dakota shrugged and tossed the fry in her mouth. "Oops. He shouldn't have grabbed me."

He grasped her hand and squeezed. "Bad girl, I love it."

She leaned forward over the table, flashing Fawkes' grin. "I can be quite dangerous when provoked... now come here."

Dakota grasped a fistful of Eric's shirt, and pulled him over the table into a kiss.

fin

ACKNOWLEDGMENTS

Thank you for reading Axillon99!

Additional thanks to:

J.R. Rain for suggesting I write this book.
Alisha at www.damonza.com for the beautiful cover.
Merethe Najjar for a wonderful job proofreading.

ABOUT THE AUTHOR

Originally from South Amboy NJ, Matthew has been creating science fiction and fantasy worlds for most of his reasoning life. Since 1996, he has developed the "Divergent Fates" world, in which *Division Zero, Virtual Immortality, The Awakened Series, The Harmony Paradox, and the Daughter of Mars series* take place. Along with being an editor at Curiosity Quills press, he has worked in IT and technical support.

Matthew is an avid gamer, a recovered WoW addict, Gamemaster for two custom RPG systems, and a fan of anime, British humour, and intellectual science fiction that questions the nature of reality, life, and what happens after it.

He is also fond of cats.

Visit me online at:
  Facebook: https://www.facebook.com/MatthewSCoxAuthor
  Amazon: https://www.amazon.com/author/mscox
  Pinterest: https://www.pinterest.com/matthewcox10420/
  Goodreads: https://www.goodreads.com/author/show/7712730.Matthew_S_
Cox
  Email: mcox2112@gmail.com

OTHER BOOKS BY MATTHEW S. COX

Divergent Fates Universe Novels

Division Zero series

- Division Zero
- Lex De Mortuis
- Thrall
- Guardian

The Awakened series

- Prophet of the Badlands
- Archon's Queen
- Grey Ronin
- Daughter of Ash
- Zero Rogue
- Angel Descended

Daughter of Mars series

- The Hand of Raziel
- Araphel
- Ghost Black

Virtual Immortality series

- Virtual Immortality
- The Harmony Paradox

Divergent Fates Anthology

(Fiction Novels - Adult)

The Roadhouse Chronicles Series

- One More Run
- The Redeemed

- Dead Man's Number

- Heir Ascendant
- Ascendant Unrest
- Ascendant Revolution

- Nascent Shadow
- The Shadow Collector

- A Nighttime of Forever
- A Beginner's Guide to Fangs
- The Artist of Ruin
- The Last Family Road Trip

- Wayfarer: AV494
- Axillon99
- Chiaroscuro: The Mouse and the Candle
- The Far Side of Promise anthology
- Operation: Chimera (with Tony Healey)
- The Dysfunctional Conspiracy (with Christopher Veltmann)

- Convergence
- Containment

- Silver Light
- Deep Silver

- New Moon Rising
- Moon Mourning

Maddy Wimsey series (with J.R. Rain)

- The Devil's Eye
- The Drifting Gloom

Samantha Moon Case Files series (with J.R. Rain)

- Blood Moon
- Dead Moon

Young Adult Novels

- Caller 107
- The Summer the World Ended
- Nine Candles of Deepest Black
- The Eldritch Heart
- The Forest Beyond the Earth
- Out of Sight

Middle Grade Novels

Tales of Widowswood series

- Emma and the Banderwigh
- Emma and the Silk Thieves
- Emma and the Silverbell Faeries
- Emma and the Elixir of Madness
- Emma and the Weeping Spirit

Standalones

- Citadel: The Concordant Sequence
- The Cursed Codex
- The Menagerie of Jenkins Bailey
- Sophie's Light

Printed in Great Britain
by Amazon